ELEGY

VALE AIDA

BOOK ONE OF THE MAGPIE BALLADS

ISBN-13: 978-1723456350
ISBN-10: 1723456357

For everyone who's helped,
one way or another,
to unleash this book on the world:

Caitlin, Geraldine, Harold,
Mochi, & Zelda

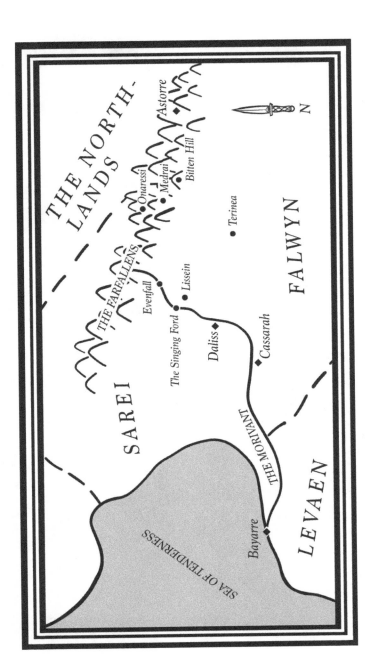

PRINCIPAL CHARACTERS

The Council of Cassarah & Their Households

- KEDRIS ANDALLE, Lord Governor and High Commander of Cassarah
    - His late wife DANEI CAYN of Terinea
    - His son SAVONN SILVERTONGUE, Captain of Betronett
- WILLON EFREN
    - His sons BONNER and VESMER
    - His captain of guards, CAHAL
- YANNICK EFREN, Willon's cousin, the Council's scribe and steward
- ORIANE SYDELL
    - Her nephew DARON
- LUCIEN SAFIN
    - His wife ARETEL DONNE
    - His son HIRAEN
    - His daughter IYONE
- JOSIT ANSA, Kedris's mistress, formerly a Saraian slave
    - Her captain of guards, ZARIN

The Soldiers of Betronett & Their Families

- SAVONN SILVERTONGUE, Captain of Betronett
- RENDELL, the Second Captain
    - His daughter SHANDEI
    - His son EMARIS, Savonn's squire
- HIRAEN SAFIN, a patrol leader
- DAINE, a patrol leader
    - His wife LINN

- NIKAS, Saraian defector and former assassin of the Sanctuary
- ANYAS, a patrol leader
- LOMAS, VION, ROUGEN, & KLEMENE, young recruits

Cassarah's Sometime Allies

- CELISSE, Lady of Astorre
- JEHAN CAYN, Lord of Terinea
- ROZANE CASSUS, niece to the Lord of Medrai

The Saraians

- MARGUERIT "the Magnificent", Queen of Sarei
- ISEMAIN DALISSOS, Marshal of Sarei
- "The Empath"

THE FIREBRAND

OVERTURE

My little songbird, my favourite game, my chiefest vice:

Is it strange to kill for an enemy? For you, I did it without question. At our final meeting three years ago you said, "There is something I must do," in that unsentimental way of yours. Joyless, fearless; just the razor-blade quality of your gaze, clean and cutting, and that cryptic twist of your mouth. You said, "After that we might not meet again."

I said, "Let me do it for you."

(It is true. I have killed for you and will again.)

I had no illusions about the battle lines between us. What I had was the scintillating mirth in your eyes, the softness of your curls, the steady companionship of your music. I knew that the name you gave me was as false as the one I gave you. You said, "Love is so terribly adolescent," and we laughed at the young couples kissing by the bonfires. What did I not tell you? Many things, and this: that I sacrificed often to Mother Alakyne, beseeching her to grant that we would never have to face each other across our swords.

If I had any premonition, I would have begged never to find out who you were. I would have prayed for you to be anyone else in the world, but it is too late. Now—sweetest of secrets, dirtiest of lies, son and henchman of that stumbling block on which my life was broken—now, I have your real name.

It is not strange to kill an enemy.

First I will find him. Then I will find you. (And here is another truth. I will kill you just as I killed for you.)

CHAPTER 1

"The Governor is dead."

Shandei clawed her way up the stairs, the refrain rustling like a mantra through the mourners around her. "Kedris Andalle is dead. *Murdered.*" With their own eyes they had seen the bier sweep into Cassarah through the Gate of Gold, trundling between the staid ranks of the honour guard on their caparisoned horses. Still their disbelief was palpable, and sharpened by fear. "Kedris Andalle, killed by *bandits!*"

On an ordinary day, Shandei—soldier's daughter, informed citizen, consummate loafer who for lack of more respectable occupation was all eyes and ears as far as gossip was concerned— would have had no shortage of opinions to air. But today she was preoccupied with a more pressing issue. Her father and brother were both in the honour guard, and would have a superb view of the funeral. She was not, and would not.

As she told all the neighbours (loudly), "Damned if I'll be left out!"

The presenting problem: the graveyard was full of important people. The councillors alone took up half the lawn with their entourages. There was no room on ground level for the likes of

Shandei. But she had gone to reconnoitre the terrain the night before, and found that the high sandstone wall around the yard made a decent alternative vantage point, if she could only find a spot there.

The further quandary: early as she had set out, the wallwalk was already crowded with other resourceful people three ranks deep. The only possible solution: gleeful, unfettered violence.

The funeral oration had begun by the time she summited the stairs and reached the parapet, her black gown and mourning veil thoroughly crumpled. The crowd on the balustrade shifted and murmured. "Kedris is *gone.*" Their incredulity was not without reason. Kedris Andalle was only forty-eight, after all: the force of nature that had united the fissile Council and kept their old enemy the Queen of Sarei in check, unbeaten in battle, with a fiendish charm that could talk the very swords out of his adversaries' hands. Short of a volcanic cataclysm, he should have been invincible.

Shandei's view was occluded by a solid palisade of heads. She considered the merits of fetching something—or someone—to stand on, abandoned the idea, and began, teeth gritted, to push her way to the front.

Applying her elbows liberally, she poured through a gaggle of plump matrons, rearranged one by one the limbs of a toothless old man so that he found himself behind rather than before her, and confronted by an auburn head and its accompanying pair of shoulders, she propelled their owner aside and wormed into his place at the balustrade. Then at last, she could see below.

It was festival weather: summer had arrived at last, tardy that year, but the northeast wind still brought sudden currents of crisp highland air that stole her breath away. Viewed from above, the graveyard was a sea of black hoods and veils. The bier stood near the front, white petals clinging to its wheels. The Betronett cavalry, who had brought Kedris home from his last battle in the Farfallens, flanked it in two neat lines, sitting their horses in flawless parade posture. Shandei picked out her father immediately, with her little brother Emaris next to him, their golden hair showing bright at the edges of their hoods. Under the rustle of half-shushed conversations, she caught snatches of the councillor Lucien Safin's voice, dignified and correct, reading the funeral oration from the rostrum. *Our High Commander... fearless in battle... adroit in strategy...*

The rostrum was an elaborate one, shaped like a giant falcon cast in bronze, with baleful eyes that stared across the graveyard and shining wings that rose ten feet into the sky. The thing was disturbing. Shandei turned to study the rest of the crowd instead. *Reformed our laws... freed the slaves, and made them our brothers and sisters in dignity...* On her father's other side was Hiraen, Lord Safin's handsome son, whose eye everyone was trying to catch. Beyond the honour guard stood the great families of Cassarah: the other Safins, the Sydells and the Efrens, whose representatives made up most of the Council, and who would soon be fighting among themselves for the governorship.

His compassion for the needy, his alms... sold his own house to provide...

"They make him sound half a god," murmured a voice in Shandei's ear. "Can a man be so many things and still remain mortal?"

It was the redhead she had pushed out of the way. She gazed at him with interest, eyeing the well-shaped cheekbones under the young gold-brown skin, the half-healed sword cut running along his jaw. A soldier, then. His hair was long and tousled; he had not even troubled to veil it for the funeral. "One would think," she whispered, offended, "the body was sufficient proof of that. Would you like them to open the coffin?"

The man wrinkled up his nose, childlike. "Please, no. It is, what, two weeks since he died? No wonder they are strewing flowers everywhere."

His speech, though fluent, was peppered with odd stresses and inflections that were distinctly foreign. If he was a stranger to these parts, that explained the lack of consideration for his hair. She allowed her expression to soften. "They can't help that. My father said so, when he wrote me from Medrai. He said it took them days just to get the bier out of the hills after the—the bandits attacked."

She had nearly said too much. His fine brows made a quizzical arch. "Bandits," he said. "Yes, that is what they say. But Father doesn't think so?"

Her father did not, but that was none of this fellow's business. It was evident that the oration did not interest her interlocutor at all: he kept looking at her, and his brows continued to be eloquent. "He wasn't there," said Shandei. She danced around the question, giving him only what was common knowledge. "They were supposed to escort the Governor and Lord Safin from Medrai to Astorre, the mountain city. But they were held up and Kedris didn't wait. A pity."

His brilliant victory at the River Morivant... smashed the Saraians... took back territory lost for five generations... By now, the news would have reached Queen Marguerit in Daliss. Her people would be feasting and dancing, and sacrificing to their strange gods. Shandei, who had been brought up with a wholesome distaste for all things Saraian, hoped they choked on their meat.

"Which one is he?" asked the man. "Your father?"

With relish, she leaned over the balustrade to point him out. He cut a splendid figure in his sombre black doublet, tall and broad-shouldered, his horse perfectly in hand. "Rendell, Second Captain of Betronett." And, unnecessarily—"Savonn Silvertongue's deputy."

The movement must have been visible from below. Emaris, a presentable if undersized lump on a pretty white mare, glanced up and spotted her on the wall. He broke into a sunny smile, then remembered himself and reorganised his face into stern solemnity. The man laughed. "Your brother. A fine little lion cub."

"Don't laugh," said Shandei, mortified. "We're at a funeral." Then, unable to resist: "He is Lord Silvertongue's squire."

The stranger's reaction was not the usual one. "Savonn Andalle," he said, pronouncing the name with exaggerated care. "The dead man's son, yes? He has been held up by bandits again? I see no kinsfolk in attendance."

"I never said they were held up by bandits," said Shandei, annoyed. The Betronett cavalry could have dealt with highway robbers in their sleep. "Their horses were hamstrung in the night. Nobody knows how or why. They had to go on foot to Medrai and—"

She shut her mouth so hard that her teeth clicked together. She had never met this man in her life, and already she had told him almost everything in her father's letter. "Oh, dear," he said. "Now I have succeeded at angering you, and henceforth it will be like standing next to a furnace. Come, gossip with me of harmless matters, daughter of Rendell. Where *is* Savonn Silvertongue? They say he will make a grand entrance."

The thought of Kedris's only son, the infamous actor-soldier whom everyone always seemed to be talking about for one reason or another, brought a reluctant smile to her lips. Last Midwinter the Safin manor had nearly burned down when, back on home leave, Savonn set off a firework in Lord Lucien's parlour over supper. The year before that, he had dressed up as a maidservant, seduced a smuggler and unearthed the hapless fellow's illicit cargo: a barrel of wild monkeys, which he promptly loosed on the streets, shrieking and chattering. "He might," she said. "He quit the theatre a long time ago, when he went to the Bitten Hill. But that's never stopped him."

She peered over the balustrade again. She was fond of her father's soldiers, and knew almost every face in the honour guard. It was simple, after all, to befriend a fighting man: you knocked him down with a good uppercut, and if he got back up and wasn't too proud to admit defeat to a woman, then you were friends for life. Savonn Andalle, who was impossible to miss, was not in the ranks. Nor was she the only one looking for him. The councillors had drawn together to mutter, and some were craning up at the parapet as if expecting to find him there. Keeping his head still and his countenance dignified, Emaris was watching them avidly.

"The great men and women are disturbed," the stranger observed. "Is Lord Silvertongue's absence a cause for concern?"

"Lord Silvertongue is always a cause for concern," said Shandei. "Now be quiet. We've missed half the oration."

We gather to send our lord on his last journey... never again another one like he...

"We've missed all of it," said the man. He propped his elbows on the balustrade. "Look, the pall-bearers are coming forward. In my country, the Priestesses of Strife and Sorrow would sing a hymn to sanctify the dead, which would be long and boring, and then the kinsfolk bring up the grave-gifts, and the pyre is lit."

"We don't burn our dead, but the rest is the same," said Shandei. Lord Safin had left the rostrum, but the temple singers were nowhere to be seen. She looked at the stranger's hands, the long and calloused fingers. "Where are you from? Astorre? Pieros? Bayarre?"

As a child she had visited Bayarre, the city at the mouth of the Morivant. The others were only names on maps to her. He shrugged. "I have lived in all those places. Came here to see an old friend, as it were."

Somewhere out of sight, a drum boomed.

Shandei fell silent, her question dying on her tongue. The man looked this way and that, and his gaze fell on the bronze falcon. "Hush," he said. "Something is happening."

"The priestesses haven't arrived," said Shandei. "What—"

She forgot what she meant to say. The falcon was speaking.

The voice was rich and deep and monstrous, like something excavated from an abyss and brought thrashing into daylight. It sank into her bones, rattling in the marrow. "Behold!" the falcon cried, its jasper eyes glinting. "Behold! The Lord Governor of Cassarah goes to his long sleep. Weep! Wail! Tear your clothes!"

Cymbals clashed. Shandei jumped, and felt foolish. Someone screamed. An infant began to cry. "The underworld opens," said the falcon with pulpiteering gusto. "His death is marked, and will be avenged."

A stream of guards issued through the graveyard with an urgency that drew the eye. Then they slowed, and began to vacillate in confusion several feet from the rostrum. "It's him," said Shandei to no one in particular, since the foreigner was no longer paying attention to her. "It's the Silvertongue. He's speaking through the falcon's beak."

The drum continued to pound. Several others joined in. Then a flurry of bright figures emerged from behind the falcon's outspread wings, lithe and quick-footed in tunics that shimmered grey and black in the morning light. Their faces were beastly, noses protruding like snouts, cheeks blanched white as bone, ears unfurling upward like miniature trumpets. Several rabbit-gaited heartbeats later, Shandei realised they were human. Costumed humans in masks.

"The Ceriyes," said the stranger. Inexplicably, he was smiling. "The demons of the underworld, attendants of a wrongful death."

Swanlike in grace, the flock of Ceriyes arrayed themselves around the open grave. "Behold!" cried the disembodied voice once more. The drumbeats quickened. A lute began to tinkle. Then, as one, the Ceriyes joined their voices to the music.

It was no song she had heard before. It began low and rhythmic, like a spellbinder's chant, forceful against the expert accompaniment of the lute. Then the sopranos came in, and the verse swelled strong and buoyant into the chorus.

The prince marshals his armies,
their thunder fills the sky;
The soldiers rush unto the breach,
blades gleaming in the dawn.
But now the flags are furled to sleep,
the battle-hymn forgone;
The lilies fall to kiss the ground,
the hoofbeats pass them by.

The pall-bearers, stiff with amazement, had to be prodded into shovelling the ceremonial handfuls of dirt over the grave. Emaris's mouth was hanging open in a soundless 'O'. But astride his sleek horse, Hiraen Safin was grinning.

The pall-bearers retreated. In well-timed harmony, the voices of the choir soared towards a fiery crescendo. The cymbals crashed. The drums boomed. The lute twanged. The singers gave a final shout, as if in triumph. Then, without warning, a profound silence fell.

Shandei cried, "Look!"

The man they had waited to see was standing behind the rostrum, lute in hand. Savonn Silvertongue did not glitter like his chorus singers. Instead he was dressed in a sober, high-collared doublet, a black hood drawn over his dark curls. Some way into his twenties, built light and whippet-small like the bull-leapers of old, he bore little resemblance to his magnificent father except in the smooth olive skin and the delicate angles of his face. Under the hood, a pair of bright eyes flicked to appraise the crowd, impersonal and calculating.

"The Master of the Revels," said the stranger in an odd voice, "come to receive his due..."

No one knew what to do. The councillors stood gaping and pointing, even as the choir melted away. The guards wavered in place. And then, amid the cavalrymen, Hiraen began to clap.

The sound echoed off the high walls and hung over the eerie stillness of the graveyard. Up on the wallwalk, someone else joined in. Then another, and another, splintering the awkward reticence, until at last Shandei said, "Damn it all," and clapped furiously.

It was not polite applause. What happened had not been in the least bit polite. In turn, the response was the sort of tumult that scared the horses, that could only arise from an overwrought crowd such as this: their emotions pent up for days, their minds worrying at the void where their leader and bulwark had been. But here was something certain, which they knew to be good—a fine piece of music and showmanship, crafted for their solace. The mourners clapped and stamped and cheered in relief, like the release of a long-held breath, and tears glistened on more than one face.

Savonn Andalle stood there only a moment longer. Then, without bowing, he slipped behind the falcon and vanished with his choir.

The girl next to Shandei said, "Is that all? Is it over? But what about the hymn?"

Shandei groped for her handkerchief and blew her nose. "I think," she said, "that was the hymn."

The crowd was still yelling. Judging by the wild gesticulation, the councillors were having an argument. Emaris had yet to close his mouth. "Well," said the stranger, "I did not know funerals in Cassarah were so hair-raising. The dead go unsanctified, the living try to arrest one another... I had best be gone, daughter of Rendell. The roads will be thronged as soon as people start to leave, and I do so hate crowds."

Shandei took a last look over the balustrade. "I'll go with you."

Getting out took nearly as much butchery as getting in. The man stayed close to her, letting her cleave a path for both of them. As she pulled open the stairwell door and he swung it shut behind

21

him, plunging them into sudden darkness, she realised he was whistling Savonn's song.

"What did he do that for?" she asked, pulling off her veil. Foreigner though he was, he appeared to know a thing or two. "The Council looked fit to tear him apart. If we hadn't started cheering they really would've arrested him."

The window on the half-landing was covered with a black mourning drape. Coming in from the sun, she could see nothing except the outline of his back retreating down the stairs. "Who can guess? Why do people like him do anything?"

A half-forged shred of intuition struck her. "Do you know him?"

He stopped. His answer was a beat too late, but it sounded cheerful enough. "We have met. That doesn't mean I know him. The soul is a shack built from oddments, my dear. Who really knows anyone?"

His abrupt halt had brought her up short next to him. She realised that they were quite alone, because no one else had left the wallwalk yet; and without the press of bodies around them, she had no reason to stand so close to him. She climbed back a step, reclaiming the higher ground. "Are you a diviner? You talk like one."

"No," said the man. "Just an observer who uses his senses. Lord Silvertongue seems to be promising vengeance, but your Council does not look interested. Soon they will be too busy squabbling over the governorship to concern themselves with anything else. Who does Savonn think killed his father, I wonder? Marguerit?"

She kept her face blank. At least the window had a low sill. There was always the option of shoving him out through the drape. "Marguerit?"

"—Ah," he said. "So you suspect she is involved."

She had not even said anything. But at the back of her mind was her father's letter from Medrai, heavily annotated in Emaris's

22

round scrawl. *Not bandits. Lord Safin thinks they were Saraians in Queen Marguerit's pay. Savonn is inclined to agree.*

She let out a breath. "You *are* a diviner."

"You think I read your mind?" asked the man. "Don't worry. It is nothing important. I would have found out anyway." He was smiling again, not unkindly. "If it pleases you, you may shove me out the window."

She managed, just barely, to conceal her shock. He laughed. "You keep looking behind me, you see. You give your tricks away like candy. How many years have you? Nineteen? Twenty?"

This time she made sure to keep her attention on his face, which was no great hardship. His eyes were long-lashed and deep-hollowed, hazel flecked with green and amber. "I'll tell you if you tell me your name."

He grimaced. "Names are just words. As a rule, I don't give out false ones. Is it a keepsake you want? You have my face, which seems to please you, and my hair, which offends you—"

She said, "It's a three-storey drop from here."

"Oh, dear," he said. "And you are not altogether joking, because you feel you have told me too much." He lifted his brows again, as if to say, *Am I right?* "Consider me nameless and faceless, but not godless, unlike the marvel we just watched. I mean you no harm, my bloodthirsty friend. Can you content yourself with that? I expect I could survive the fall, but really, I am no gambling man."

"I'm not bloodthirsty," she said.

"No? Good." And with that he darted around the newel-post and down the next flight of stairs, out of her reach. "A morning well spent. Thank you for the company, daughter of Rendell."

"You owe me!" she shouted. He bounded down the steps, humming as he went. His auburn head went round and round the stairwell, and Savonn's song wafted up to her in bars and snippets, until at last he pushed open the door at the bottom and disappeared into a flood of sunlight.

It was a long time before she saw him again, and under circumstances completely different.

CHAPTER 2

"These bloody roses," said the gardener, in a carping mutter that carried all the way across the lawn. "Dumb fuckin' roses, what do they need so many bloody thorns for?"

It was an apt summary of Cahal's morning, since—in what might have been mistaken for a morbid show of sentiment—Willon Efren had seen fit to convene the Council of Cassarah right over Kedris's grave. To be more precise, Lord Efren had elected to make his bid for the governorship in a pavilion surrounded by blooming hedges and noxious gardeners, so close to the graveyard that Cahal caught whiffs of fragrant incense when the wind was right. As far as gestures of sincerity went, this was not one of his lordship's subtler moves. But then, ten years as the Efrens' captain of guards had taught Cahal that none of them were particularly subtle.

The gardener continued to whine as Cahal passed him on his rounds. Lord Efren had made it clear that he meant to come away from this meeting as Governor of Cassarah or not at all, and would brook no ungodly interruptions like the one that had upset the funeral. "Gods take the morons who planted these things," said the gardener, with a piteous flail of his hands. "Look. Yon hedge's more prickly than a phalanx of spears. Ain't it?"

Cahal was surprised to be addressed. Like as not, this fellow was a freedman, and freedmen preferred to mind their own business. Most of the city's menial servants had once been slaves, taken in battle or sold in bankruptcy to their creditors, until Lord Kedris changed the laws, released them, and offered them work on his various gardening projects. If anyone was unhappy about it—and many had been—they had his Saraian mistress to blame, that woman Josit Ansa, who whispered things in his ears and put strange ideas in his mind. Or so Lord Efren said.

He stared at the gardener. A devastation of leaves and stems and scarlet petals lay strewn around their boots. "You're killing the hedge."

The gardener favoured him with a winsome grin. "The hedge is killing *me*." He was a young man, at least going by what Cahal could see of his face under his wide-brimmed straw hat. He had deep brown skin, and a smear of dirt under his left eye. The rest of him was swathed in the tattered folds of an immense cloak that might not have been washed since the Battle of the Morivant. "I've been pricked three times already. You a soldier? You ever had to fight for your life against a bloody plant?"

He must have been freed as a child, before servility was bred into him. "Can't say I have," said Cahal, drawn into conversation in spite of himself. He had nothing else to do, anyway. No rowdy chorus of Ceriyes had yet erupted to perturb Lord Efren's tender ambitions. "But I'd tackle a rose hedge over a charging cavalryman any day, if you take my meaning."

He resumed his progress down the garden path. Without asking permission, the gardener abandoned his ungentle ministrations and fell in step beside him. "Of course," he said. "But kill the cavalryman and you get gold and glory. Kill his lordship's hedge and you get flogged... What're they talking about in there that's taking so long?"

26

Cahal glanced over the top of the gardener's hat to the pavilion, visible through the spreading branches of a willow. He snorted. "This ain't nothing. I've known them to argue all day and most of the night after, when something's got them riled up."

"Well, something has, hasn't it?" said the gardener, polishing off the dirt under his eye with the hem of the frightful cloak. They rounded the willow, and one of Cahal's sentries dipped his head as they passed. "Else, what does he want with all you guards?"

Cahal eyed him. "What does who want?"

The man flung up his arms, necessitating a quick dodge on Cahal's part to avoid the shears. "Milord Willon. Who else? I may've been skewered by a hedge but I ain't stupid. You're in cream and bronze, the Efren colours. There's the eagle badge on your collar. And those are your men too, ain't they, bowing this way and that?"

They were within earshot of the pavilion now. Lord Efren was droning away, occasionally interrupted by one of the others. Cahal stopped dead, in part not to disturb the Council, in part because he was sorely tempted to remind the gardener what the lash of a whip felt like. "What his lordship wants is none of your business. Get back to your work."

The gardener was still walking, twirling the shears round and round with surprising dexterity. "The roses are too lethal. I shall try my hand at the tulips."

His trajectory, however desultory, put him dead on course for the pavilion. Suddenly alert, Cahal said, "You can't go in there."

He grabbed at the man's shoulder and came away with an odious fistful of wool. Pulled loose, the cloak puddled on the grass between them, tangling around Cahal's feet. He froze.

Beneath the cloak, the gardener wore a fine navy doublet, complete with embroidered sleeves and a high upturned collar filigreed with gold thread. His hose was dark silk, his calf-high riding boots good supple leather. He twirled the straw hat from his head and swept Cahal a deep showman's bow, black curls rippling. "My lord Cahal. How pleasant to make your acquaintance."

The last time Cahal had seen this face, it had been under the sweep of a bronze falcon's wings, surveying the mourners with a sardonic eye. The only coherent thought that surfaced was, *That explains the bad gardening.* "What in hell—?"

"Eloquent," remarked Savonn Silvertongue, son of Kedris. The country burr had sloughed off his voice like snakeskin. He spoke with the precision of a trained actor, each syllable crisp and lapidary. "Is your curiosity whetted, my lord? Shall we go see what Willon is talking about?"

Cahal felt for his sword. "He didn't invite you."

He confronted a perplexed smile. "Nor you, it seems. More's the pity. Don't draw your sword, good sir. Dear Willon can hardly afford to make a graveside scene... but, as we have all witnessed, I can."

The hat fell on the grass, tripping Cahal up as he lunged. By the time he recovered, Savonn had vanished behind the nearest hedge. He was right, damn him. One could not draw steel on the Governor's son while practically standing over his grave. The only course of action that remained to Cahal, however undignified, was to give chase.

He did.

* * *

As far as Willon Efren was concerned, everything was going according to plan.

Eminent patrician, upright taxpayer, a seasoned man in his sixties, he sat back at a predetermined pause in his speech and surveyed his four colleagues. Yannick, his cousin, whom he had convinced Kedris with such pains to appoint as the Council's scribe and steward. The man was feeble and jumped at his own shadow, but at least one could depend on him. Oriane Sydell, a

28

more vigorous if less helpful ally he did not like much. Lucien Safin, not yet cured of his wretchedly oppositional tendencies, but too spineless to be a serious threat. And Josit Ansa, Kedris's whore, who was of no account, and of whom the less said the better.

"So," said Willon with an expansive gesture, also rehearsed, "we have established that Kedris did not leave a will. One cannot fault our dear lord for this oversight: he was, after all, young and in the pink of health, and no one expected this tragic misfortune—"

"Misfortune!" said Lucien. It was not his first interruption; nor, Willon thought bitterly, would it be his last. He was slouched in his chair, rocking it back on two legs like a bored schoolboy, his arms folded behind his head. "Does anyone still believe that Kedris's death was an accident? After all I've done to convince this Council of the contrary?"

Willon glowered across the table. Every time the fool interrupted, he lost his place in his speech. "It's been three weeks since Medrai. You've certainly run your point into the ground."

Lucien drew breath to respond, but it was Josit who answered first. "What a pity that it was Lucien at Kedris's side that sad day. If it had been you," she said indulgently, gazing at Willon with her kohled eyes, "you would have beat them off, I am sure, and brought Kedris safe home."

Lucien gave a bark of laughter. Yannick released a loud, wheezing breath, and pressed his fingertips together in a gesture of forbearance. Willon stared at Josit with loathing. By no laws of genteel society should she have been there. Petite and pale as porcelain, with glossy ringlets of dark hair knotted above her shoulders, she had been related to the wrong people in Daliss, and so wound up in slavery when Marguerit took the throne. Somehow she had escaped across the Morivant and into the household of the Governor's late wife in Terinea, and soon after, Kedris had freed her and put an end to slavery. A lesser ruler would have been impeached for it. Or hanged. But Kedris was a law unto himself.

In a barbaric situation, Willon struggled for civility, and clung to it by his teeth. "My lady jests. Now, if you please—"

"Oh, get on with it," said Oriane. She was the oldest of the councillors, a broad, ebony-skinned woman with dark hair leaching to grey. "Or we'll be here all day. You were saying?"

Willon groped for the tail end of his sentence. The words emerged seething and stumbling, far too fast. "He was young and in the pink of health, and no one expected—no one expected his death. I am of the opinion, as are Lady Oriane and Lord Yannick, that we should proceed with all possible haste in choosing ourselves a new leader. The city cries out for a strong hand, a mighty hand, that will steer her through the course of this—"

"But your hand is trembling," said a new voice behind him, high and clear and unnerving with sweetness. "And you're reading off your sleeves. Don't worry, we understand. It's a very long speech."

Yannick knocked his cup over. Oriane sighed, rubbing her temples. Willon turned around so fast he cricked his neck, and all at once his temper became a good deal more slippery.

The owner of the voice was lounging in the pavilion entrance. Effete, insouciant and self-possessed, he stood over them, passing a pair of gardening shears—*why?*—from hand to hand. Clothed in sable and velvet, every line of his spare frame spoke of decadence, from the legs crossed lazily at the ankle to the elbow slung over the wooden rail. His eyes were an untrustworthy blue, or green, or grey, depending on the light, but the lurid gaiety that inhabited them was a constant. Willon curled his hands into fists. "What are you doing here?"

"Listening," said Savonn Andalle. Delicately, he tucked a runaway curl behind one small ear and turned on them all an ingenuous smile. Lucien—damn the man—was laughing again. "If you mean to do any steering, as you so pontifically put it, you should know the waters."

Willon's neck was sore from craning. "*What*?"

At that precise moment Cahal, his captain of guards, launched himself into the pavilion behind Savonn, carrying, inexplicably, a filthy cloak and a floppy sunhat. "You knave!" he shouted. His face was the shade of a grape. "You ain't supposed to be here!"

The situation, already out of hand, was fast taking on tragicomedic properties. "You, sir," said Willon, loosing a burst of spittle on the sibilant, "had orders to—"

"—keep me out?" asked Savonn. He had not moved. "Don't be angry, my lord. Cahal was good enough to escort me past all your fearsome guards. There are so many, one might think you meant to stage a coup."

"What, and they let you through?" Oriane asked. "Didn't they recognise you without the choir?"

"He was in disguise, ladyship," Cahal protested. "I thought he was a gardener."

Of its own accord, Willon's throat emitted a despairing honk. "Was it not enough to make a song and dance of your father's funeral? Must you turn up whenever anything of import is going on, like a—a wasp at a picnic?" The shreds of his patience slipped through his fingers at last. He crashed a fist onto the varnished tabletop with a meaty thump. "For heaven's sake, don't just stand there! I'm not going to twist my neck to look at you all day!"

"Shall I throw him out, milord?" Cahal asked.

"Yes, of cou—"

"But why?" said Lucien, who had regained enough sobriety to speak. His chair rocked on its back legs once more. "You are not, I presume, leading an armed coup? Why let the boy dismay you?"

Willon almost ricocheted to his feet. "You invited him? You planned this? *You* want to be Governor?"

With diabolic timing, Savonn had tiptoed round to the far side of the pavilion so Cahal could not extract him without climbing over Lucien. Josit's serene voice answered him again. The creature spoke Falwynian like a native. "I invited him, Willon. At a meeting where Kedris's successor is to be decided, it seems only natural to invite Kedris's son. His mode of entrance, I fear, was of his own devising." She smiled, flashing a row of white teeth. "Tell your man to stand down. It's rude to brawl in a graveyard."

"Mother Above," said Oriane, rolling her eyes skywards. "Now we'll really be here all day."

Willon, breathing hard, was beginning to regret convening the Council here. Since there was nothing he could do to dislodge the intruder short of unseemly violence, he dismissed Cahal with a withering look and reseated himself, clutching at his dignity. "Stay, if you insist. Though I would sooner welcome a kidney stone."

"I wish you good health, my lord." Savonn's smile was rapturous. "Now I will find myself a seat... Oh, no, Lord Safin, it is quite all right. Nobody get up. I shall bestow my person on the lip of this flower pot, while Lord Efren reconciles himself to my presence."

With a dancer's agility, he stepped around Josit and Lucien and arranged himself on the edge of a large ceramic planter filled with tulips. An elegant hand, sheathed in a fingerless glove, sallied forth like a cat's paw. It ensnared one orange blossom, plucked it, and stuck it in a coil of inky hair. Then, freshly adorned, Savonn beamed round at them once more. "There. Now, where were we? On the brink of electing Willon Efren, the loyal servant of two Governors before him, as our most puissant and majestic liege?"

Under that farcical gaze, all of Willon's steam had dissipated. He could not glance at his sleeves now without looking a fool. He said, "I served Kedris all through his reign, and Raedon Sydell before him."

32

"Unfortunately," said Savonn, wide-eyed, "it seems you were not privy to their innermost confidences. I don't suppose you know why the Lord Governor was at Medrai?"

He did not, Willon noted, refer to the dead man as his father. "A matter of trade," he snapped. Poor Kedris. His own sons were impeccably brought up. Two were helping their mother manage the country estate, and the youngest, Vesmer, was in the city guard. He would have died of shame if he caught any of them prancing around with flowers in their hair. "If you are otherwise informed, do enlighten us."

"Gladly," said Savonn. "Lord Lucien could have done the same, if you cared to listen. Lord Kedris suspected that the marauders in the Farfallens are no mere bandits. They are too many, and too organised. He's been concerned about the prospect of an invasion over the passes for years now. It's why he wanted an eye he could trust at Betronett."

"You?" asked Oriane, dubious.

"I am not quite certain," said Yannick, speaking up for the first time in his watery quaver, "why one would entrust a matter of military espionage to an actor."

"Me neither," said Savonn cheerfully. "But it pleased him to send me, and so, while my lord Willon polished his oratory skills and acquired baubles for his mansion, I spent the last six years defending our realm from brigands and thieves. When he was killed, Lord Kedris was on his way to Astorre to take counsel with Lady Celisse, whose forces guard the passes. He wanted evidence that the outlaws were in the pay of a higher authority. Conveniently, he died before he could find any."

He gazed around the table, one leg drawn up to his chin, the other dangling boyishly beneath him. "The fact is," he said, "Kedris Andalle was not killed by bandits. He was assassinated on the orders of Marguerit of Sarei."

A dull throb was insinuating into Willon's temples. The damned boy had muddied the waters beyond hope. Even if he was ejected from the pavilion now, there was no way Willon could get the Council, distracted as they were, to consent to his election today. His careful plans, the speech he had so lovingly crafted, were all gone to waste. "Where in hell do you get this nonsense from? We've been at peace with the bitch queen and her halfwit barbarians since you were a child piddling in your nursery. The last war cost her ten thousand men and her ugly palace's entire weight in gold. She isn't so foolish as to cross us again."

Josit's long-fringed eyes were on him. "She is a sore loser."

"Oh, for the Mother's sake," said Lucien. His chair slammed back to equilibrium with a thud. "Look, Willon. We were going up that goddamn mountain with enough silver and spices for Celisse to make even *you* look destitute. Our escort was over a hundred strong. No one in their right mind would have dared attack us. But these thugs, they knew their business. We were riding through a canyon, only about this wide"—he gestured to the breadth of the pavilion—"and then the rocks started falling, when we were strung out like prayer beads in single file and able to do damn all about it. And as soon as the rocks settled, they came."

Oriane arched her eyebrows. "I suppose you fought very bravely, Lucien?"

Unable to resist the opening, Willon chortled. "No," said Lucien. Spots of high colour appeared in his round face. "No, I hid under a wagon because I was afraid for my life, and I'm not ashamed to say it. They were vicious brutes, clad in mail and armed with good steel. They outnumbered us, and they struck to kill. And when they were gone, and I clambered out to find two-thirds of our men dead or dying—"

His eyes glazed over. "All the wagons were intact. None of the goods were stolen. The silver, the spices, all untouched. What imbecile robber launches an attack like that and leaves without taking anything? What imbecile," said Lucien, his voice rising, "could believe that is the work of *bandits*?"

34

"But," said Yannick, and flinched as Lucien made a noise of disgust and sagged back in his chair. "But if Kedris had so dire a hunch, why did he say nothing to us?"

"If I had to hazard a guess," said Josit, "he didn't want to alarm the people before he had gathered proof."

"You mean," said Willon, with undeserved gentleness, "he didn't want public opinion to turn against you, his Saraian councillor?"

Savonn made a near-imperceptible movement, then subsided into stillness. It was uncanny, really, how quiet he could be when he put his mind to it. "Yes," said Josit, unflustered. "Me, and all our Sarei-born freedmen. Kedris and I took great trouble to settle them into their new lives. An untimely rumour would have ruined all our work. But of course," she said, glancing at Lucien, "we now know this is no mere rumour."

"Do we?" said Willon. "You lack proof. Kedris learned nothing before he was attacked, and now we must take your word for it. I must say, Lucien, if you wished to put yourself forth as Governor instead of me, you could have done it in a less circuitous way."

"Gods!" said Lucien. His palm met his forehead with a smack. "Gods, no. I haven't the stomach for haranguing and dodging the point, as you do. And there's someone better qualified for it than either of us."

For one baffled moment, Willon stared at him. Then the ridiculous orange tulip drew his eye, and he turned to Savonn Andalle. His mouth fell open.

He said, "You jest."

Between lines and stage directions, the Silvertongue's face was inexpressive, a silent lute waiting with its strings in good order for the next song. It was impossible to tell what went on behind it. "A poor jest, if no one is laughing," said Savonn. "Perhaps you have forgotten that Lord Kedris was not only Governor of this city, but also High Commander of its army. Peacetime is over. If

35

you insist on burying your head in the sand, someone else will have to fight this war—someone," he added, "who knows one end of a sword from the other."

Flabbergasted, Willon chanced a look at his allies. Yannick looked terrified as usual, but Oriane appeared to be rigid with suppressed laughter. The sight prodded him into rage once more. "It has been a long time, perhaps, since I took the field," he conceded. He had seen one or two engagements in his distant youth, during which he vaguely remembered marching around holding flags and being very bored. "But you! A boy from the theatre, who grew up on stage with—with fire-jugglers and snake-swallowers and gods only know what else! You cocky, clueless, irreverent—"

His adjectives failed him. "Sword-swallowers," Savonn corrected. "They charm the snakes, my lord, they don't *eat* them."

"Have a care for what you say," added Josit. "Savonn has fought under the banner of Betronett since he was seventeen. He knows the Farfallens like the back of his hand."

"Then," Willon said, finding his tongue once more, "pray tell me how the Queen of Sarei is purported to have moved in and set up shop on his watch."

"Perhaps," said Oriane, backing him up for once, "Betronett is incompetently led? Kedris is dead, pardon me, because his escort failed to show up."

Savonn did not take the bait. If anything, his mincing smile broadened. "That's always a possibility."

Yannick mopped his brow with his sleeve. "But you see, my lord Silvertongue," he said, "however qualified you may be, it is, ah, *improper* to elect you after Lord Kedris. People will talk—they will accuse us of nepotism, and other unsavoury things—and besides, well, your family history on the point is, I should say, *delicate*—"

"He means," said Willon, "that Savonn Andalle is descended from a long line of violent lunatics who, having founded Cassarah, thought it was their divine right to rule in perpetuity and died

36

for it. Three generations ago, most of you were dead or howling mad in prison. Lord Raedon took a chance on your father and it paid off, but that was because Kedris was thrice the man most others are. The same, I'm afraid, does not apply to you."

"Oh," said Savonn. "Now we invoke my ancestors. Did you know one of them built a palace and made himself a king? It's a haunted ruin now." He grinned at Lucien. "Hiraen and I tried to find it the time we ran away from home, but we lost our way. Or rather, our nerve... but I digress." He swung himself off the pot, dislodging a few petals. "We have both made ourselves clear. If you do not relent, and neither will I, the Council stands divided. What shall we do?"

"The usual procedure," said Yannick, who could always be counted on to know such things, "is a public hearing. The—contenders—will make a speech before the people, and they will cast their vote." He dabbed his brow again. "But surely it is a waste of time. Lord Silvertongue, they will not vote for you."

Revolted, Willon remembered the applause at the funeral. A tasteless performance, yes, but the crowd had liked it all the same. Which was the whole point. The boy was more cunning than he had thought possible.

"No," he said. His knuckles had gone white. "Let him do what he wants. Let the people see how this scheming clownfish means to turn the office his father held with honour for sixteen years into a joke to amuse his charlatan friends. Let them be the judge."

The wide eyes gleamed. "Well said, my lord," said Savonn. "Now, if you will excuse me, I had better go see my charlatan friends. Else they won't vote for me."

He plucked the tulip from his hair and, with ostentatious courtesy, presented it to Josit. Then he went out the way he had come, humming as he went. They gazed after him in amazement. Lucien, Willon observed, looked like a man beginning to question the wisdom of his recent decisions.

"He has lost his mind," said Yannick, quivering. "I fear grief has turned him mad."

"Grief?" said Willon. He shook out his sleeves and gazed, sorrowing, at the half of the speech he would never deliver now. "*Grief*? I have never seen anyone so happy."

CHAPTER 3

The next day Rendell, Second Captain of Betronett, set out to dissuade Savonn Silvertongue from inflicting himself on the city of Cassarah.

It was a futile gesture, as the man in question seemed to have already done so. But Rendell supposed the least a friend could do—if they *were* friends, which changed from one day to the next—was try. Emaris had told him that Savonn could be found idling in the theatre. These days Emaris prided himself on being an expert in all matters pertaining to the Captain, which was useful in some ways and worrisome in others. Rendell no longer remembered why he had allowed his impressionable son to squire for Cassarah's greatest wastrel, except that Emaris had begged and Savonn had enumerated the prospects for promotion in his reasonable voice and, like so many other things, it seemed like a good idea at the time.

Mid-morning saw him in the Arena of White Sand, keeping an eye out for the social pyrotechnics that followed his commander wherever he went. The theatre was so named because duels and bullfights had been held there once, when Cassarah was young and her people more savage, and someone had decided that blood showed up better against white. But these were enlightened times, and not a grain of sand was to be found in the Arena now. The riggers and carpenters had begun hammering together the set for the Midsummer play, and the stage, built over the old duelling ring, was a confection of spires and cupolas and little spindly wooden balconies painted ivory and gold. Behind were the levers and pulleys that would make the gates open and shut on cue, and the doors slam, and the banners flutter as if in a wind. Tomorrow the speeches would be given here, the only place so many people could gather at once, and the citizens would choose their Governor.

The stage itself lay at the bottom of a colossal bowl of granite, surrounded by hundreds of rows of stone benches, enough to seat some sixty thousand. The theatre's faultless acoustics caught and amplified Rendell's footsteps as he descended, and a passing group of stagehands looked up. He beckoned to them. "Is the Silvertongue here?"

"Over there," said one of them, gesturing. Set below the lowest circle of benches was a heavy oak door carved with a grotesque unicorn head, scowling ferociously, its twelve-inch horn serving as a door-handle. "In the catacomb."

As Rendell well knew, having had to extricate Savonn from one too many raucous subterranean parties, the catacomb was a maze of tunnels and rooms that underlay the entire Arena. Twisting passages led to the curious chambers from which the machinery was operated, and a sprawling hive of dressing rooms, workshops, and prop stores nestled under the rings of seats. With trepidation, Rendell asked, "Who's with him?"

"Just the Safin boy. The others have left."

This was more luck than he had expected. He crossed to the unicorn door and pushed it open. It emitted a screech that must have announced his arrival to everyone in a one-mile radius, a failure of housekeeping which he guessed was deliberate: the theatre's denizens liked to have ample warning when their patrons

40

came seeking them. He was in a long, sepulchral tunnel, lit at intervals by wall cressets and interrupted by several unmarked doors on either side. Thirty yards down, the path curved and disappeared into shadow.

So early in the day, the place was quiet. The still air carried the faint smell of fresh paint and wood shavings, and under that, a lingering vestige of jasmine perfume. Rendell caterwauled the door shut and started down the tunnel. "Savonn?"

Silence. He crashed his fist on the nearest door. "Savonn!"

A voice drifted down the passage, hollow and echoing. "Pick a door, mortal. And 'ware the Sphinx, lest she devour you."

Once in a great long while, it was possible to get a sensible sentence out of Savonn. Today Rendell's stars were not aligned. Making up his mind to be stoic, he went down the passageway, counting the doors. Savonn's voice had not been far off. "I am not for eating," he called. He picked the sixth door to his left, and flung it open. "The Sphinx will have to go hungr—*Gods!*"

A head burst snarling out at him. He flinched back, colliding with the doorframe. Three rolling pupils stared from each white, insectile eye, like marbles in a bowl. Great wings protruded from the temples, hued in the blues and greens and golds of peacock feathers. Violet serpents dripped out of the cavernous ears, dangling like monstrous earrings over the shoulders. A fathomless mouth yawned open, and yellow fangs stretched towards his face, long and sharp as blades.

And then the Sphinx snorted, her serpents shivering as she suppressed a laugh.

"Fetching," said Rendell, shoving the head back through the door. His pulse was rattling in his throat. Savonn had been Captain of Betronett for three years now, having been promoted straight over Rendell's head on old Merrott's sudden death, but now and then he still behaved like a schoolboy. "Terribly grown-up."

Savonn pulled the mask off and let it clatter to the floor. Beneath was another sphinxlike smile, complacent and unknowable, all the more alarming for being human. "You made so much noise coming in."

"I didn't want to walk in on a tryst," said Rendell. Ever since the foreigner in Astorre, Savonn's private life had been attended only by prodigious rumour, never any physical entity one could observe, but his friends were not usually as chaste.

"Do you hear that, Hiraen?" said Savonn, glancing over his shoulder. "We must be on our best behaviour. Come in and help yourself to the floor. I'm sorry the mosaic is so ugly."

It was one of the small storerooms, with a low slanting roof and a vent high in the wall that let in some measure of fresh air. Here and there the floor was paved with colourful pebbles that must have once been part of said mosaic, but most of it had been chipped away by time and vandals. A rainbow of wigs hung on a rusty iron stand by the door, encompassing every shade from silver-blond to bright blue to pure black. Beyond that was a lute on a stand, and a number of music scores.

Hiraen Safin was reclining on a mattress at the back of the room, his bare feet propped against the wall. Savonn sat down by his head, jingling a palmful of knucklebones. Rendell settled opposite him and caught the piece skimmed at his head. "I don't suppose I can talk you out of this?"

"You can try," said Savonn. The coloured stones shimmered between his hands, fast as falling hail. "Just for fun."

A laugh bubbled from the mattress. Hiraen raised his arms over his head and stretched, biceps rippling, like a splendid hunting cat. "Don't bother. Father would be so disappointed. He's rather hung up on this idea of Savonn as Governor, gods save us all."

Rendell leaned back on his palms and gazed at his two protégés. Up to the day of his death, sculptors and painters had travelled across the realm to beg Kedris Andalle to pose for them.

Savonn had missed his father's head-turning looks, but retained a certain nondescript pleasantness about the face, an inoffensive symmetry that melded easily to any persona he chose to play. Hiraen, on the other hand, with his tousled chestnut hair and laughing green eyes, belonged to that blessed subset of mankind that was both obnoxiously handsome and filthily rich, and unaware of all the privileges this afforded them. Rendell seldom knew what to make of him.

Grimly, he set his mind to his self-appointed task. "Our men will vote for you. Those who are of age, at any rate." The soldiers of the Bitten Hill loved their enigma of a captain; or, at least, they hung around to see what he would do next, which passed for love when one was young enough. Emaris, several months short of the grand eighteen, had complained long and loud about his perceived disenfranchisement until Shandei threatened to cast her stone for Willon Efren just to shut him up. "That's about—"

"Two hundred, yes," said Savonn. "The rest will have to be persuaded."

"And you're certain you can persuade them?"

Savonn opened his hands, and a shower of stones skittered across the floor. "No."

He drew out the consonant, sounding very much like a petulant Emaris when Shandei was ragging on him about something or other. Rendell tried to imagine Savonn at a council table, quarrelling over policy with the likes of Willon Efren, and was beset by the hysterical urge to laugh. "Well—"

Hiraen heaved himself to a sitting position, hair sticking up at the back of his head. "No," he said. "I mean it. Don't bother. You don't understand why he's doing this."

Like a patron deity, Hiraen had to be propitiated before one could get through to Savonn. Judiciously, Rendell said, "Savonn would hate being Governor."

One had to admit there were few other choices. Willon, though experienced, was no battlefield commander. Neither was

Lucien Safin. But the idea of Savonn as overlord of a city was the stuff of nightmares and apocalyptic prophecies. Rendell did not say so; Hiraen was not a complete fool, and could see that for himself. "Maybe," said Savonn. "But someone has to prove that Marguerit is working some mischief, and stop her from doing whatever she's doing in the Farfallens. Besides..."

"Besides?"

"There is the niggling detail," said Savonn, "that by all the laws of gods and men, I am obliged to hunt down the Governor's killer and serve him justice in the most unsavoury way I can devise. Otherwise the deceased's vengeful spirit will roam the earth forever—a terrifying prospect for anyone who knew the good Lord Kedris—while the Ceriyes pursue and torment the unfilial kin for all eternity. Or something like that. As a godly man, no doubt you're better informed than I am."

Not even the sacred law of a blood feud was spared Savonn's flippant discourse. Unsmiling, Rendell said, "You have the gist of it."

"And this," said Savonn, as if he had not spoken, "is an excursion that will require more than two hundred men, doughty as they are." He looked peeved. "Where are my knucklebones?"

"Under the wig stand," said Rendell, his patience evaporating. The Farfallens campaign did not perturb him. Under Captain Merrott, both he and Savonn had spent plenty of time patrolling the passes, spying on Saraian merchants and trading news with Lady Celisse in Astorre. Between the two of them and Hiraen, they could easily lead an expedition there. It was the rest of it that baffled him. "Look, this thing tomorrow is hopeless. You'll make a good showing, I grant, but Willon will win. As he should. All you'll do is anger the Council."

"Alas!" said Savonn. He and Hiraen exchanged identical mournful looks. "Like Willon, you look but do not see. You assume that we abide by the same rules—indeed, that we play the same game—"

"What's that supposed to mean?"

Savonn gave a voluminous shrug. "Misdirection."

He opened his hands. The complete set of knucklebones lay in his cupped palms, not one of them missing. Rendell goggled at them. Then he looked down at the ruined mosaic. There was a ragged hole in the tiles near Savonn's foot, more recent than the rest of the damage. With typical sleight of hand, he must have wriggled loose a few tiles of about the right colour to use as decoys. "You haven't improved the mosaic," Rendell remarked.

"That's arguable," said Savonn. "When I was little, my chorus master told me that the mosaic used to be a picture of Ederen Andalle seated in state on his throne at Evenfall. After he died and his heirs were dispossessed, the people smashed all his images with clubs." He tossed the fistful of knucklebones at Hiraen, who caught them deftly. "You see, not all of us were born with fashionable surnames."

Hiraen produced a lavish grin. Rendell began to form an answer, something cutting about having come to make a point only to misplace it under the wigs with Savonn's mosaic stones. But just then the unicorn door gave its unmistakeable scroop, and they all fell silent. A heavy tread approached, then hesitated in the tunnel. "Lord Savonn? Captain, sir?" The door slammed again. "Lord Silvertongue?"

The speaker was unfamiliar. Rendell sighed, resigning himself to the end of their conversation. "Leave the Sphinx. Your face has the same effect."

Savonn looked affronted. "Stay here."

He stepped over Rendell and let himself out into the tunnel. Fortunately, it was his command voice that drifted back to them, brisk and exacting. "Are you invoking a pantheon? One name will do. What is it?"

After a fraught hesitation, the newcomer said, "I bring a message from my lord Willon Efren. He would be honoured if you would sup with him this evening."

45

Rendell's brows leapt upwards. Rumpled and scowling, Hiraen began to pull his shoes on. There was another screech, and the voices receded, but remained audible. Savonn had left the door ajar. "I tremble at the thought," he said. "Is the Council convening? Who else will be there?"

"It is only a dinner, sir," said the spokesman. "All the councillors have been invited."

"That's not true," said Hiraen. He was trying, without success, to tidy his creased shirtsleeves. "Father hasn't been invited. My sister would have mentioned it."

"So," said Rendell, "not Lady Josit either, I suppose."

"I will be otherwise occupied this evening," Savonn was saying. "A matter of much sadness and many regrets. Would you tell your master I said so?"

A pause. "Lord Efren will be very disappointed, sir."

"Not for long, I trust."

"But—"

A moment passed. Then, though Savonn had said nothing, they heard the spokesman retreat. Rendell could imagine the expression that had routed him. The rejection, he surmised, was unexpected. Willon wanted to meet Savonn before the assembly took place. But what for? And why, for the life of him, had Savonn passed up the opportunity to find out?

The immediate crisis having been resolved, Hiraen returned to his supine state on the mattress. Rendell said, "Wait here," and expelled himself from the room in a hurry.

After the torchlit catacomb, the unadulterated sunlight half blinded him. Dust motes rose and fell on invisible eddies of air, as if the light itself had solidified into little particles, settling on the bare skin of his forearms and the cotton of his sleeves. The stagehands were gone, the vast Arena empty save for Savonn, sitting alone on a bench in the lowest ring. Perhaps, divested of his toys and his conjoined best friend, he could be persuaded to listen for once.

Rendell shut the unicorn door and went to sit next to him. "Lord Safin hasn't been invited. I think Willon wants to talk to you alone."

"You think he's scared?"

"Perhaps. Might be he doesn't want to risk a vote. Might be he meant to try and pay you off some other way. You should have accepted."

"A bribe?" asked Savonn, his smile indolent. "For shame!"

Six years into their uneasy acquaintance, talking to Savonn could still put Rendell on edge. Few but him still remembered the Silvertongue at seventeen, the new boy in his patrol, trailing trinkets and frippery from the theatre. They had taken bets on how long he would last. Rendell also remembered, and tried to keep at arm's length, the various occult disasters that had befallen his tormentors. Flea-ridden bedrolls. Unexplained bouts of diarrhoea. Strange rumours about their virility or lack thereof. Somebody, he recalled with another burst of suppressed hysteria, had gone around hiccuping for three days straight.

"You could have bargained with him," said Rendell. "Willon as Governor, and you the High Commander of his army. Free rein to mount a campaign in the Farfallens. Men and gold to pursue your blood feud. He'd give you anything if he thought it would spare him the inconvenience of conducting a war himself."

"You underestimate his pride," said Savonn. "He'll offer me nothing but platitudes. Shall I submit my guesses? *You have no chance*, which is true. *It's a waste of time*, which is also true, but many necessary things are. *You just want to do right by your father*, which is not false, and *you'll feel different with time*, which is a matter for philosophers."

Stricken by a sudden, incoherent revelation, Rendell struggled for words. He heard again Emaris's outraged voice, yelling that their horses had been hamstrung; saw the walls and watchtowers of Medrai from afar, and Lord Safin white-faced and beside himself, hurrying out to them with the news. "Savonn," said Rendell. "What happened wasn't your fault."

"That," said Savonn, "is also a matter for philosophers."

"I know we haven't sent a patrol up there since Merrott died. We were at peace. If that was an oversight, the blame belongs to all of us."

Savonn's expression remained opaque. Aware how ridiculous he sounded, that he was all but asking to be humiliated, Rendell executed a rapid change of subject. "For heaven's sake. Put your philosophy away for a moment, will you? Willon will hold this against you when he's Governor. The Safins won't be able to protect you. He'll invent some excuse to put you in prison, or have you exiled, or *killed*. Would it hurt to go and make nice with him?"

With a sinking heart, he received the full brunt of Savonn's cold, luminous gaze. His lashes gave a grisly flutter. "What in the world," said the Captain of Betronett in his softest, deadliest voice, "gives you the idea that I require anybody's protection? Willon will rule this stinking quagmire if he wishes. With or without you, I can fend for myself."

"That's not what I—"

"But you doubt me. So," said Savonn Silvertongue, "I'll send another messenger ahead. *You'll* go to his dinner, and tell me if my predictions are right." As Rendell started to protest, he added with vast, savage satisfaction, "I hope you have a splendid time."

* * *

Full of misgivings, and wishing he had kept his mouth shut, Rendell braced himself for a thoroughly unpleasant evening with Willon Efren.

His own modest house near the Salt Gate—a neat, two-storey red brick affair with a white gable roof—had rung with the clack of wooden swords all afternoon. He watched from the stoop of the back porch as Shandei drove her brother across the yard with

48

swift, spare strokes, weaving between the beds of thyme and tarragon and the trellises where peas and tomatoes grew. Lord Kedris encouraged the cultivation of herb gardens with generous stipends, so that even if besieged, Cassarah could grow enough food within her own walls to feed herself for a year or more. The late Governor had been full of ideas, and more than that, he liked to care for things and watch them grow.

Quite, Rendell thought, unlike his son.

He coached the fighting until the shadows lengthened and both Shandei and Emaris disappeared on dinner appointments of their own, and then began to dress. It seemed absurd to go armed to Lord Efren's mansion. For all its shortcomings, the Council liked to maintain at least a veneer of civility. But Rendell had been a soldier all his life, and that wily fox Merrott had taught him never to let his guard down. He tucked his dagger into his right boot, reassured himself that his coat and doublet were suitably opulent for the likes of the Council, and set off into the warm night. He was, he decided, going to bring back the terms of some reasonable, adult agreement, and Savonn would abide by them whether he liked it or not.

The clouds looked ominous, and the air was tangy with petrichor. The Efrens lived on the far side of town, in the rich district by the Bronze Gate. He went on foot, since his route would take him across three of Josit Ansa's aerial gardens, through which it was forbidden to ride: the new covered bridges that spanned Cassarah's less traversable districts, their roofs and railings heavy with herb-beds and flowers. Crossing the first of these, the Hydrangea Bridge, his mind wandered. He thought of Shandei, who lacked the patience either to marry or learn a trade that did not involve knocking people down, and so passed her time with various odd jobs around the neighbourhood. He thought of Emaris, whose sweet, open nature was about as suited to dealing with Savonn as a paper kitten was for fighting off leopards. Most of all, he thought of Serenisa of Bayarre, their mother, a touring dancer he had met in Astorre long ago: the wild girl who had informed him in no uncertain terms that she would not give up her art to make a home with him, but who had borne him two children, and even visited them once or twice when her troupe took her upriver to Cassarah.

All things considered, it was unsurprising that he was on the other side of the bridge before he noticed that his footsteps had acquired an echo.

It did not bother him. The shops were closed for the night, and no one else was about, but this was not the sort of district where cutpurses and hooligans lurked in the alleys. Like as not, it was just someone who happened to be going the same way. For his peace of mind, he turned left into a side street, and then left again into a still narrower one, ducking for cover under the leaning eaves of a ropemaker's and a smithy.

The echo followed.

He wondered if this was another of Savonn's little amusements. Either way it was a nuisance: it was a bad night to get into a fight, with the assembly tomorrow, and he wanted to reach the Efrens' before the storm broke. He ducked into a dark archway at the back of the smithy and slid his dagger from his boot. He was late, and in half a mind to be ungentle.

His tail—whoever it was—hesitated at the end of the alleyway, then began to approach. Rendell pressed himself flat against the cool stone at his back. The follower was eight paces away, maybe seven. It was almost certainly not Savonn, whose tread was lighter. The dagger seemed to thrum in his hand, eager to fly. He pressed his fingers into its ivory hilt and inhaled noiselessly.

Four paces. Three. Two. He stood poised on the balls of his feet, blade firm and ready—and then a shadow slid across the lip of the archway, and a hand shot out lightning-quick to catch his wrist. "What are you doing here?"

Relief washed over him. He lowered the blade. "What are *you* doing here?"

CHAPTER 4

"What a lot of things," said Emaris, surveying the towers of crates that stood in the middle of the late Governor's apartments, and the denuded shelves that surrounded them. "Are you sure you don't want to keep any?"

They had spent the evening packing Lord Kedris's rooms in the citadel, the vast granite keep that rose from the heart of the city like a spur of bone. To put a finer point on it, the servants had packed, while Emaris got underfoot and Savonn did something he called *supervising*, which seemed to mainly involve reading on the window-seat and gesturing dismissively whenever someone tried to hand him something, be it a book or a map or other esoteric item. "Look," said Emaris, prodding at one of these: an odd contraption of coloured cylinders, rigged to dangle from a stick. It gave an obliging tinkle. "Where did he *get* all this?"

"You can have it if you like," said Savonn. "Are you coming? I, unlike you, have to be up at dawn."

They were alone. The servants had long gone, the relics itemised and crated up for sale. Nothing but furniture remained in the Governor's suite: the crimson velvet rugs on the marble tiles; the teak writing-desk swept clean of its papers; the empty bookcases, looking somehow bereft. Savonn tapped his foot at the window, gazing out across the roofs of the barracks and guardhouses to the great bowl of the Arena. Unlike Emaris, dusty and grubby-fingered, he was impeccable as always, dressed in a dark green vest and slashed leather jerkin that he wore cinched around the waist and open at the throat. There was no weapon on his belt. He seldom went about the city openly armed, which Emaris found bizarre in one of his standing. But then, his father had warned him often enough that Savonn Silvertongue was a bizarre man, and must be handled with caution.

"I can't believe you're going through with it," said Emaris, buckling on his own sword. "Have you written a speech?"

"On my shirtsleeves, like Willon Efren? Heaven forfend."

Emaris grinned. "Recite a bit for me."

Savonn arched a single brow. It was a trick Emaris frequently tried to approximate in the mirror, with little success. "Lightning in a bottle, my dear. If I let it out, you'll have to catch it and put it back."

Everyone said Emaris was insolent, the Captain most of all. But Savonn had gotten rid of two other squires before him, claiming they bored him to tears, so perhaps insolence was not a bad thing. Bearing in mind his father's admonishments, Emaris had outlasted his predecessors at the Bitten Hill, become the veteran of a hundred skirmishes (if one rounded up), and received a promise that he would be promoted to patrol leader as soon as he came of age. Born the year of the great victory at the Morivant, eighteen had always seemed a long way off to him, and longer than usual tonight.

He arranged his face into a sulk. "I'm not supposed to be there tomorrow. You might at least let me hear a little. Or I'll just assume Willon out-talked you."

"False assumptions," said Savonn, "are the most dangerous thing in the world. Also the most useful, but that's beside the point. Anyway, you're going to sneak in."

"How do you know?"

"Because that's what I'd do."

"I thought of disguising myself, like you," said Emaris, as they stepped out into the draughty hallway. "But Shandei said I could just get there early and hide in the catacomb before anyone else arrived. Like a stowaway."

Savonn considered him, his head cocked like a bird's. Laugh lines were mustering around the arches of his mouth. "Your whole family terrifies me," he said. "Escort me to the Safins'. Then you have my leave to make whatever dispositions you please."

The citadel was a hulk of thick stone walls and echoing hallways, reaching as far below ground as it did above. Built in Ederen's day to house the colonists who had come to Falwyn in their ships a thousand years ago, it could probably have sheltered the entire city's populace with room to spare. But these days it was uninhabited, though the Council still convened on the premises. The Governor had lived here, but he was dead; and it was well known that Savonn preferred to spend his nights at the Safins' rather than use his own apartments down the hall. They moved through the silent rooms without meeting anyone, ghosting past dark doorways that led into empty offices, archives full of forgotten books and solars dusty with disuse. A pair of sentries saluted Savonn as they crossed the drawbridge over the spiked moat, and passed beneath the portcullis into the square.

It was a starless night, cloudy and overcast. A sharp-edged wind was just beginning to pick up. The watchmen's lamps bobbed on the walls, tiny and indistinct, like ghost-lights on a marsh. Emaris drew his cloak more closely around him. "Do you believe in spirits, Savonn?"

The Captain glanced at him sideways. He hadn't far to look down now. By the end of the year, Emaris was sure to surpass him in height. "Scared?"

"Curious."

He had been thinking of the Ceriyes, and the bier he had escorted from Medrai with its grim burden. He had wept at the dead Governor's side. So had his father, and everybody else. Except Savonn, of course, who had merely been harder to read than usual, and displayed the annoying tendency to vanish whenever Emaris or anyone was looking for him.

"No," said Savonn, after a pause. "I don't."

The rain began to fall as they left the main street. Over the generations, as the people grew less reverent of their rulers, the shops and houses had crept closer and closer to the citadel. Savonn led them onto a knock-kneed alley that ran between jumbles of buildings, tailors and glaziers and fletchers piled almost on top of one another like the crates they had just seen packed. The upper stories leaned so close together that in some places they almost touched, keeping the street beneath dry. A boy pushed past them, carrying a long wooden plank on his shoulder; a woman with a wagon shooed them out of the way. They passed under the Lily Bridge, fragrant as perfume, and voices and laughter began to drift to them from the night bazaar.

They were on the Street of Figs. Most of the windows were dark, but here and there an eye of light looked out over the variegated outlines of roofs and chimneys where someone was sleepless in an upper room. Savonn had drawn ahead, his head bent against the drumming rain. Emaris kept his eyes on his feet, picking his way across the wet cobbles. If he fell on his face, Savonn was sure to laugh.

"Sir," said a voice several feet off, muffled by the downpour. "Spare a copper? Copper for my sick child?"

Emaris looked up, his wet hair dripping into his eyes. A hooded figure had detached from the shadows under the slanting roofs and approached Savonn with its palm out. In the dark, this was not the sort of place where one ought to fumble for one's purse, as Savonn well knew. "I haven't any," Emaris heard him say. The lines of his silhouette were pithy and taut. "Try the bazaar."

The panhandler caught at Savonn's arm. To Emaris's dismay, two more figures coalesced from the darkness farther down the street. "Just a copper, sir," said the first man. "Just the one. Have a heart."

"Unhand me," said Savonn pleasantly. "Or I will unhand you."

Emaris was running, skidding and sliding on the cobblestones even before the beggar's blade was out. Savonn sidestepped. The blow went wide. Emaris barrelled past them, yanking his sword from its sheath to meet the foremost of the other assailants. Under this man's hood were wide-set eyes and flaring nostrils, and in his hand was a long-handled knife that flashed up towards his face. Emaris ducked. "Get back from him!"

He brought his own sword down in a controlled arc, not meaning to hit anything vital, just to hurt and scare the ruffian off. The blade tore through the man's cloak and overshirt, and bit into mail.

Emaris recoiled as the knife descended again, nearly lancing his eye. Only this afternoon Shandei had knocked him into the dirt half a dozen times. "Help!" he shouted. "*Help*! Murder! Assassins!"

The yell gave his enemy pause. Emaris danced away from the blade, put his head down, and charged like a bull. He was not yet tall, but in the past year his shoulders had started to fill out. He smashed headlong into the man, knocking the breath from his own lungs, and allowed the momentum to carry them both into the wall of the nearest house. His sword clattered away somewhere. Savonn would give him hell for that. Shandei, too. His foe drew back his arm, so close Emaris could see the rust speckling the edge of his knife. As he prepared to stab, Emaris caught his wrist in both hands and forced it back, slamming it against the wall again and again in a grip slippery with sweat. The man grunted. A booted foot interposed itself between them, sharp against Emaris's shin, but he held on. Then at last the man opened his hand with a cry, and the knife fell twinkling to the road.

Thereafter Emaris fought like his sister: a hook to the jaw, a knee to the groin, an elbow to the back. The man dropped like a millstone. Emaris kicked the knife away, and turned back to Savonn.

Someone was hollering from a window, and people were running towards them. His shout must have brought them from the bazaar. The first man was on the ground, with a slim silver knife sticking out of his thigh. Savonn always kept a good number of sharp objects on his person. The other fellow was staggering to his feet several paces away, bleeding from the nose and favouring one ankle. Emaris came up behind him and kicked him in the bad leg. As he went down with a howl, Emaris kicked him again in the head, for luck.

Savonn came over, surveying the scene through half-lidded eyes. "You dropped your sword."

A throng of gawkers was gathering around them, and doors and windows were opening, tesselating the cobbles with squares of lamplight. "It's Savonn!" someone shouted from above. "Lord Silvertongue!"

Savonn's gaze strayed upward for a moment. Then it returned to settle on Emaris, unrelenting. "I let it fall," said Emaris. "Not enough room to swing."

"Good call."

The crowd was stirring, the bystanders jostled aside by an influx of new arrivals. These men were clad in steel cuirasses, swords gleaming at their sides. Emaris took an involuntary step towards Savonn. Then the ranks parted as their leader came forward into the light, and he saw that it was a woman.

In the first moment of recognition, he let out a sharp exhale, light-headed with relief. It was Iyone Safin, one of the pillars of Savonn's constantly changing group of friends. Under the canopy

56

two maids carried to shield her from the rain, she was tall and full-figured with fair, freckled skin, the brown Safin hair tossed in careless waves over one shoulder. She looked around, taking in the three prone forms, the open windows, the excited faces. "Your man Daine's just called at the manor, looking for you," she said. "What have you got up to now?"

"A little street brawl," said Savonn, with the air of a local guide pointing out the obvious. "Behold me in my hour of victory, sister, surrounded by the bodies of the slain."

They were not, in fact, brother and sister. It was an endearment the Captain afforded Iyone, and Iyone alone, sometimes with the gravity of an honorific, other times—as now—with the lilt of a shared jibe. "Slain?" she asked, brow lifted. "And then risen again, I suppose?"

One of the assassins was groaning. Savonn grinned, like a child caught in a lie. "No, they're not dead. My squire just got a little overzealous." He narrowed his eyes at Emaris. "You're not hurt?"

Emaris had gotten his breath back. "No," he said. He picked up his sword, and tried not to clutch it too hard.

At Iyone's command, someone brought a cresset. She held it high over their heads, illuminating the would-be assassins. "Who are they?"

The onlookers stirred and murmured, unsettled by the sight. "Let's ask them," said Savonn.

Emaris had knocked two of the men unconscious. The third, the one Savonn had knifed, lay in a puddle of rain and other things. Savonn held out his hand, and Emaris hurried to place his sword in it. He watched, uneasy, as Savonn spun the blade with a theatrical flourish and rested it point down on the man's exposed throat. "Do you try to knife everyone who doesn't give you money, or am I the exception?"

The man moaned. The knife was a wicked glitter against the fabric of his trousers. Again, Iyone said, "Daine is looking for you."

"Oh, come on, there's an audience," said Savonn. "Let me play. Go on, sir. I asked you a question."

He bore down on the sword-hilt, and a crimson bead appeared on the man's neck, growing lengthwise and spilling like a tear onto his shirt. The crowd oohed and sighed. The man gibbered a little, trying without success to wriggle away from the point of the blade. "Move, and I'll take off an arm," said Savonn. "Stay silent, and I'll take both. You will run out of limbs before I run out of patience."

The sweeter the voice, the greater the danger. Emaris stared, his heart in his teeth, as the man wheezed. "Gods have mercy. Never meant—never meant no offense—"

"Oh? I suppose you just drew your knife for a friendly little stab, then?"

"I think he means it wasn't personal," Emaris suggested. Savonn looked at him, and he clamped his mouth shut.

"Offered me money," the man rasped. "So much money—twelve drochii, and twelve more when the deed was done—"

"What deed?" asked Emaris.

The man swallowed hard. In the firelight, Emaris saw the lump in his throat bob up and down. Whatever he had been paid, it was insufficient to buy his silence when confronted by Savonn Silvertongue with death in his hand. "To see that you were dead by dawn tomorrow, milord. He said you went to the Safins' every night, and we were to waylay you in the street. This street, he said, before the bazaar."

A gusting wind had started up, blowing the rain sideways and making the shadows rear and dance in the struggling firelight. Emaris found he had stepped close to Savonn again. "Someone didn't want you to speak at the assembly," said Iyone, looking far more amused than the situation warranted. "The Council couldn't afford decent assassins?"

At this, the buzzing murmurs rose sharply to a drone. The Safin guards exchanged looks. Emaris shifted his weight from foot to foot. Since nobody seemed to be asking the obvious question, he said, "Who paid you?"

"I don't know, sir," the man sobbed. "Some man in a cloak and hood. Didn't give us a name, and I couldn't see his face. Only a go-between, I reckon. Rich folk don't talk to the likes of us."

"His voice?" asked Iyone. "Describe it."

A long, hiccoughing breath. "How do you describe a *voice*? It was a regular man's voice, milady—a bit soft, I'd say, because he didn't want to be overheard. I'd know it if I heard it again."

Iyone gave Savonn a satirical smile. "And if he can change his voice?"

The man wrung his hands. "Only d-demons can change their voices, milady. Please, please have mercy. I have children."

"I," said Savonn, after a long look at Iyone, "am worn to the bones from hearing about your children. Iyone, will you have your men bind these creatures and take them away? Not the citadel dungeon. Someplace secure."

"My house," said Iyone, sounding resigned. Someone had tossed down a length of rope from above. As the guards swung into action, she stepped out from under the canopy and put her head close to Savonn's, not quite touching him. Emaris was just close enough to catch her words. "Josit is there, and my father. They'll want to question this fellow."

"He's all theirs," said Savonn. His eyes were crinkled in bemusement. "I am offended, sister dear, that you think I would be so obvious."

"Just testing a conjecture," said Iyone. "It would be so handy for you if Willon Efren were accused of murder. We should always be thorough, shouldn't we? I will be at the house." And releasing him from her owlish, smiling gaze, she turned to go.

Emaris stayed where he was, confused, until Savonn stepped back and collided with him. The Captain frowned, though not in anger. "And you were so talkative just now. Scared?"

It was the second time that night the question had been asked. "No," said Emaris.

"Remind me one day," said Savonn, "to teach you how to lie."

The crowd had not dispersed with the Safins. On the contrary, more windows were coming open, and people in nightgowns had come out to watch from their doorways all along the street. There was a flurry of activity at the junction, and then someone pushed their way to the front. "Savonn? Savonn?"

"Over here," said Emaris.

It was Daine, one of Savonn's officers: a dark-skinned, thick-set man about Rendell's age, his bald pate gleaming in the rain. He shoved through a cluster of protesting silk merchants and made straight for them. At the first sound of his voice Savonn had begun to move towards him, Emaris's sword still in hand. "Iyone said you wanted me?"

Daine glanced at Emaris, and then took Savonn's arm as Iyone had not done, drawing him aside to whisper in his ear. Savonn went rigid, and Daine let go. Already chilled, Emaris felt another cold pincer wrap around his insides. This was not the Betronett way. Orders were shouted across the cookfires; gossip was shared liberally; even wounds were bound up under the open sky. He moved closer, needing to know. "—got to come," Daine was saying. "Hiraen took him to my house. It was the closest. My wife's with him now."

Savonn had gone very still. "Is it bad?"

"He hasn't much time," Daine said. "It might be over already."

Savonn turned, and saw Emaris listening. His eyes were unfocused. Emaris fell back a pace, but no admonishment came. He put his hands in his pockets to stop them from shaking.

"I'll run," said Savonn. "Stay with the boy."

He thrust the sword into Daine's hands and was gone without another word, stepping past Emaris and slipping silently through the mass of bystanders. Hands caught at his sleeves as he went, and someone called his name, but he paid them no heed. As he got free of the crowd, Emaris saw with inexplicable terror that he did, in fact, break into a run.

"Come on, boy," said Daine.

But Emaris was not listening. He had started to shiver. No one had called him *boy* since his first skirmish, no one but Shandei and their father. Something had happened.

"Excuse me," he said, and set off at a sprint.

Savonn had had a good head start, and some superstitious fear, cold and insidious, prevented Emaris from calling out. They had reached the junction. But instead of cutting through the bazaar towards the Safin manor, Savonn turned right, heading for the sleeping houses on the Street of Vines. Emaris pounded after him, vaulting a cart full of hay and nearly falling over a homeless vagrant and his mat as he rounded the corner at full tilt. Savonn was running lightly, his booted feet making no sound as he swung up onto a low brick wall and down the other side. If they were headed for Daine's house, it was not far. Why the hurry?

Savonn ducked into a narrow lane behind a row of big houses and swarmed over a fence into somebody's courtyard. Emaris followed, skidding on the wet grass. The air here smelled like moist earth and blooming rainflowers. Emaris tripped over a loose brick in the dark, flailed, and managed to catch himself against the wall of a shed. A dog barked at the racket; a guard burst out of the shed with a spear. Emaris swerved around him, narrowly missing the gaping mouth of a well, and threw himself up the opposite fence. He landed hard on a knee in the grass on the other side. Savonn was twenty paces away, maybe thirty—too far for Emaris to help if there were more assassins waiting in the shadows.

He staggered to his feet and pelted after him.

This street was narrower, the doorways low and dingy. All the buildings were dark save one, from which the faint sounds of laughter and music issued. The windows were rimed in red paint, and a lantern cast a gentle roseate glow over the courtyard. At seventeen, Emaris was worldly enough to know what the outside of a brothel looked like, though not the inside. A rickety switchback stair zigzagged up from street level to the roof of the building. Savonn must have known it was there. He made straight for it, with Emaris fast gaining on him.

It was excruciating. Their boots pounded like thunderclaps on every step, loud enough to wake the whole street. Someone giggled. Then a latticed window flew open, expelling a boy's primped head like a cuckoo from a clock, along with a cloud of strong floral perfume. The boy laughed, and made to catch Savonn's hand as he passed. "Hello, love! I knew it was you! Care to come in for—"

"I'm a little busy," said Savonn.

He had almost reached the roof. The boy turned his attentions on Emaris, still staggering up the final flight of stairs. "And you, sunflower? Also in a hurry?"

Emaris did not reply, but Savonn faltered for a moment at the top of the steps, and he knew his presence had been betrayed. Savonn did not wait for him. He picked his way across the mess of chimneys and skylights on the rooftops, found another wayward stair three houses down, and descended to the street with Emaris on his heels. Daine's house was at the end of the road.

When Emaris reached the gate, Savonn had already gone inside. He stopped in the yard for a moment, listening. His shirt was soaked through with rain and perspiration, and his breath seared his lungs in ragged, painful gasps. Savonn was saying something, and a woman was answering—Linn, Daine's wife, who had looked after Emaris and Shandei when they were small. Emaris recognised the voices, and the urgent prosody of the words, though not their meaning. Cold dread pooled in his stomach. He forced his leaden legs to carry him through the garden, and into the house.

The air was viscous in his nostrils, reluctant to be inhaled. He followed the voices to a back room, the door ajar, a thread of light filtering out through the crack. It swam towards him with dreamlike slowness. His feet barely seemed to touch the ground. Then the door swung all the way open, and the light pounced, flooding over his boots in a wash of yellow. The compact figure of his commander appeared in the doorway. "Emaris," said Savonn softly. "Come with me to the garden for a moment."

But Emaris, arrested by the smell of strong wine and blood, was looking past him into the room. The lamp was burning low, illuminating a basin of reddish water on the dresser and a pile of bandages on the floor. Hiraen was kneeling by the bed, Linn on a stool beside him. On the pillow was a gleam of honey-gold hair.

Emaris pushed past Savonn and went through the door.

He glimpsed Hiraen's eyes, hollow with shock; he saw the lifeless face on the bed, and the blood spilling through the shirt from the chest wound. Linn stood up abruptly, knocking the stool over. "Oh, gods," she said, and came towards Emaris with her arms held out.

"Don't," said Emaris, louder than he meant to. "*Don't—*"

She moved out of his way. His knees hit the floor.

He had been in a hundred skirmishes. He knew the look and smell of a mortal wound, but all the same he found himself scrabbling at the bandages on the dresser, searching for needle and thread, medicine, *anything*, until Linn's fleshy arms closed around him and made him stop. The room stank of ruin. Hiraen was crouched beside him, saying something incomprehensible; Savonn was looking on from the foot of the bed, silent for once; Linn was still holding Emaris by the shoulders; and his father, his father was dead.

CHAPTER 5

Returning to the manor with three criminals in varying degrees of consciousness, Iyone caused quite a stir. At her command, her guards bound the prisoners to stakes in the yard, within sight of the street. The ensuing interrogation was loud and shrill. By the time Josit arrived, a sizeable crowd of rubberneckers had gathered to watch the proceedings, peering like bright-eyed gnomes between the struts of the front gate.

"This is distasteful," said Iyone's mother, looking on from the shelter of the portico. Her father had no stomach for such things, and so had remained indoors. "You could at least have brought them inside."

"And ruin Father's rugs?" asked Iyone. The deluge was beginning to lessen. Beneath the captives' strenuous disavowals, they could hear the tenor of the crowd's eager speculation, and the names being bandied about. "Listen for yourself. This works in our favour. It doesn't even matter who did this. Everyone will go to the vote tomorrow thinking Willon Efren paid a rout of third-rate hitmen to murder his rival in the street."

"He'll deny it," said Aretel Safin. Tawny-haired and keen-eyed, she was not a woman to be crossed, though Iyone took inordinate relish from crossing her as often as possible. "And I for one will believe him. Willon isn't stupid enough to stoop to this. He would find it vulgar."

There were many things Willon Efren found vulgar, and very few that Savonn Silvertongue did. Iyone pursed her lips. "I know."

There were a few other things she could have added. But just then a ringing voice shouted a command, and the guards began to chivvy the spectators aside so they could open the gate. "Oh, look," said Iyone, as a knot of bedraggled figures struggled through the parting crowd. "The errant sons come in from the cold."

In came Savonn and Hiraen. Between them was a soggy blond boy Iyone recognised, swaddled in both their cloaks. Savonn looked across the yard to Josit and the assassins, and Iyone and her mother in the portico. He said, "Do something for him."

It was clear who he meant. Iyone gazed in fascination at the tearstreaked boy, who had been perfectly fine an hour ago. "He breaks all his toys."

"Don't be morbid," said her mother shortly. She swept over to the trio, took the boy under her arm, and started to lead him towards the house, talking the whole time. "Porridge? A bath?" Iyone heard her suggest. "Both sound good to me. And then, if you like, you can tell me what happened..."

Iyone was not so patient when it came to explanations. She turned an expectant eye on Hiraen. Her brother was so ashen as to be cadaverous, and moved like a sleepwalker in a nightmare; she doubted if she had ever seen him so pale. "Rendell is dead," he said. Then he drew her behind one of the tall gilded columns of the portico, well away from Josit and Savonn, and gave her a concentrated digest of what she had missed.

After that she was no longer amused. By the time she saw him off, still reeling, to break the news to his officers, the audience at the gate was beginning to disperse. She saw why: the guards were carrying away three limp forms, and Savonn was heading to the portico, wiping down a sword with a rag. Here and there, the wet grass was stained with patches of watery pink. Curtain call. The show was over.

It seemed this was to be a night of disasters. Irritated beyond belief, Iyone asked, "Why did you kill them?"

"It was kinder," he said. "The Council would have put them to any kind of torture to exonerate themselves."

"My concerns were more pragmatic," said Iyone. "They were evidence. Lord Efren and his lot would have wanted to question them... or perhaps there was something you didn't want them to know?"

She could almost see the cogs turning in his head. They understood each other perfectly. Born within days of each other, she and Savonn had practically been raised as siblings. His own mother, the sharp-tongued Danei Cayn, had had little love to spare for anyone in all her brief sickly life, least of all her son; and neither did Kedris have any patience for him. So he had gravitated to Iyone. Their childhood had been one long string of tricks, schemes and detonations, which Hiraen—a year older—occasionally extinguished, but mostly fuelled. Iyone had lost her taste for the more lavish displays, but Savonn, it appeared, had not.

He quirked a tired smile now, turning towards Josit, who had joined them in the portico. "Deliver me from her. They've already been questioned twice, loudly and conspicuously—"

"—like everything you do," said Iyone. With care, she added, "Did they kill your deputy?"

A pause. "No."

This would be vexing. "You believe them?"

"Yes."

He did not elaborate. "So do I," said Josit. Her gaze lingered on Iyone, narrow and thoughtful. "The man Rendell, however beloved, was of no import. Willon Efren did not need to kill him."

Before her rise to the Council, Josit had tutored them both. Hiraen, too, when he could be persuaded to sit still long enough.

Languages, lore, mathematics, music: she knew it all. If she was honest, Iyone had to admit that she had fashioned herself in the mould of Josit Ansa, whose eyes had beheld Marguerit of Sarei face to face, whose perpetually unimpressed expression declared that she had seen and survived horrors worse than these. "Willon didn't hire these men," said Iyone. She would wager her life on it. "But if you embroil him in scandal, I'd be astonished if he didn't encourage a second attempt. You should be careful."

To her consternation, faint triumph lit up Savonn's exhausted face. "Alas for Willon," he said. "This time tomorrow, I shall be long gone with my army. In another fortnight, I will be far in the mountains..." Josit had taken a sudden step forward. "What, my lady? Does this astonish you?"

Having lived in each other's pockets for so long, there was very little they could not say without words. With reluctant admiration, Iyone saw the pieces fall into place. "You never meant to be Governor," she said. Of course not. Over the years Savonn had cast himself in a series of increasingly absurd roles to please his father, but this was far-fetched even for him. "All that noise and nonsense—the stunt at the funeral, the business with the Council—that was just a diversion. You're mustering an army to take into the Farfallens."

"Warmongering," agreed Savonn, with profound satisfaction. "There is a killer to be caught, and I shall catch him."

Iyone gazed at their old tutor. From the first, she had known that this ludicrous challenge to Lord Efren had been devised by Josit, the freedwoman he so despised, and sponsored and nurtured by her own father Lord Lucien. But even Josit, it was clear, had not expected this. "What about the one loose in Cassarah now?" she asked. Her voice was less tranquil than usual. "The one who murdered your friend? Do you not care?"

"Josit, my dear," said Savonn. "You should know by now I only pretend not to care about things. Rendell had two children. This street thug is their jurisdiction. The one in the Farfallens is mine."

"But why defy the Council then?" asked Iyone. It was an academic question, but one ought never to leave a puzzle unsolved. "Why anger Lord Efren?"

Savonn regarded them both. He was about as tall as Iyone. Incongruously, Josit came just up to their chins, though Iyone felt she had been looking up to her all her life. "Because I needed to call an assembly of the citizens. Any other way, the Council would have found some pretext to arrest me before I could begin. I am, after all"—he smiled, cold-eyed—"something of a public menace."

That was an understatement. They all still remembered the incident with the monkeys. "So what now?" asked Josit. She never shouted, but Iyone had made a study of her long enough to know the signs of anger: the stiffness of her carriage, the tightening of the exquisite mouth. "Who else will be Governor but Willon Efren?"

Savonn's face was a peaceable mask. "Then I wish him the best of it. It was funny, but no longer." He inclined his head to Josit. "Excuse me, my lady. I have to see to my squire."

He headed into the house. Josit stared after him, her pale eyes wider than usual. Then she turned to Iyone. "I will not have that old fool as Governor of Cassarah."

History books thrived on moments like these, thought Iyone. People like Josit multiplied their chapters and fattened them on strife. "Why?" she asked. There was a strange thrill creeping down the rungs of her spine. "Because he looks down on you? Because he will afford you no power of your own? Or because he is not Kedris?"

Josit had loved the late Governor, she knew. Cassarah, with her graceful bridges and fragrant gardens, was the domain they had built together, side by side all these years. Iyone switched to Saraian, picked up in Josit's schoolroom long ago. "Just because you ruled through the father doesn't mean you can rule through the son," she said. "Find another avenue."

The anger was tidied away as fast as it had manifested, leaving Josit's expression as smooth and impeccable as ever. "And what avenue will you use?" she asked. "My restless hatchling?"

Here, in the lucid, canny eyes, was a puzzle Iyone had never been able to solve. "It has nothing to do with me. You want to rule."

"And do you not," said Josit, "when you were my pupil?"

She brushed some of Iyone's wet hair out of her face, tucking it behind her ear. "I think," she added, "between the two of us, we can deal with the Council."

Iyone said nothing. Without waiting for a response, Josit turned towards the gate. "By the way," she called, "someone should break the news to the dead man's daughter."

CHAPTER 6

Shandei had had the news already, from Linn. By daybreak she was in the back room of the couple's little cottage, gazing down at the man on the bed, while in another world the bells tolled to summon the city to the assembly. She barely heard them, nor could she have cared less. Her father was dead.

It had been the first truth of her life, held with iron-forged certainty, that he would be killed in battle someday. He was a soldier, and that was what soldiers did: they died. "And then, my pup," he used to say, he who had taught her to fight and—if need be—to kill, "you shall be mistress of the household, and watch over your little brother, and the two of you will be fiercer warriors than I ever was."

It was good and righteous to die in a fair fight. This, whatever it had been, was anything but fair.

"Hiraen found him," Linn said. "He sent for Daine, and they brought him here. We did what we could."

"Did he say anything?" Shandei asked. Her nose was blocked and swollen, and she sounded stupidly childish.

Linn shook her head. "He was beyond that, love. I'm sorry."

There was only one wound, a small, deep puncture near the midline of his chest, the sort made with a narrow blade at close quarters. "But he was stabbed from the front. He would have seen who it was."

"He didn't fight back," said Linn. She retrieved something from the dresser and showed it to Shandei—her father's dagger, the one with the long ivory handle, that he always kept in his boot. "It was in his hand, but not bloody."

"The rain would have washed it clean," said Shandei. They had found him in a side alley near the Hydrangea Bridge. He had had no reason to detour there on his way to the Efrens' unless he thought he was being followed, and tried to shake off his pursuit. There must have been many of them. Her father, who frequently sparred with both his children at once and came away victorious, could not have been felled by a single man. But in that case, why had they not stabbed him again? Why flee before he was dead, knowing he had seen them, and might live long enough to reveal their identities?

Gently, Linn said, "It could be the same lot that ambushed the Captain last night. Word is that the Council didn't want him to speak today."

Nobody with sense ever wanted Savonn to speak. Perhaps Willon Efren had been troubled by the rumours of Saraians in the Farfallens. Perhaps he wanted to silence the Silvertongue and his supporters once and for all. She heard again the diviner's voice, echoing silkily in the stairwell. *Who can guess? Why do people like him do anything?*

Her jaw set, she took the dagger from Linn and put it on her own belt. "In that case," she said, with a last look at her father, "we'd better go see what he has to say, hadn't we?"

* * *

Approaching the Arena, she heard the noise from three streets away. Every bench was packed full, and people were standing or sitting on the steps, getting in the way as she tried to descend. These were the citizens of Cassarah, born—like her—to at least one native parent, joined by the many denizens of the vassal towns and villages who had been granted citizenship for some contribution or other. The lowest rings, closest to the stage, were reserved for the councillors and their households. Next came the city guard, the mailed fist and shield of Cassarah, some ten thousand strong, spears and cuirasses flashing as the early sun kissed the lip of the Arena. With them were the men of Betronett, conspicuous in the black cloaks they had put on for their Second Captain, with their bows slung over their shoulders and their quivers at their sides. Civilians in silks and chiffon and cotton filled the rest of the theatre, every one gabbling to their neighbour. Their eyes followed Shandei as she went down the steps, drawn by the mourning veil she had donned once more. She heard what they were saying. *Killed by the Council, they say! And the Silvertongue assailed in the night!*

Not long ago they had been gossiping about another death. But there would be no splendid funeral for her father, who was neither a great lord nor a rich man, only a soldier who had done his best for his family. No grandiloquent oration, no chorus of Ceriyes, the attendants of a wrongful death...

Someone said, "Shandei!"

It was Emaris. Under the deep black of his hood, his eyes were red-rimmed, but the rest of his face was blanched of all colour. He came up the steps towards her, and to her own surprise, she flung out her arms and embraced him. "They told me I could come," he said into her hair, as if he thought she might turn him away. "We're sitting over there."

Unexpectedly, he led her not to his brothers-in-arms, but all the way down to the lowest bench, in the shadow of the wooden castle on the stage. Lord and Lady Safin were there with their daughter Iyone, but Hiraen was nowhere to be seen. With rising astonishment, Shandei realised that Emaris was showing her to a seat beside the councillor they called the Saraian, Josit Ansa. The Lady smiled up at her. "You must be Shandei."

Josit was past fifty, she guessed, a small, elegant woman with dark ringlets that fell around a fine-featured face in vivid counterpoint to the pale lustre of her cheeks. Shandei opened her mouth, at a loss for words, then closed it again. To her relief, Josit smoothed over the breach with easy courtesy. "I am sorry to hear about your loss. Believe me, we will get to the bottom of this."

Her hands found Shandei's and squeezed them tight. They were finely made, like the rest of her, but the fingertips were rough and calloused: the hands of a working woman. For some reason, that gave Shandei more comfort than anything she had said. "Thank you, milady."

"She asked to sit with you," Emaris whispered from her other side. The hem of his cloak was frayed where he had been fidgeting with it. "The Captain said I could leave his service if I wanted."

"Why?"

He looked miserable. "We have to find the killer and whoever hired him. It's our duty. And Savonn isn't staying here. He's going back to the Bitten Hill today."

"He *what*? What about the governorship?"

Emaris shrugged. "I don't think he cares."

"But he can't just allow that piece of—"

At that moment Josit, who seemed to have been listening, said, "Speak of the devil."

Shandei shut her mouth in time to see Willon Efren making his way to them along the bench, resplendent in a brocaded doublet and a cloth-of-gold overcoat. His carroty hair was peppered with grey, but his big frame was still tall and erect. His stride was vigorous, easily outpacing the young man who trailed after him, every bit as pompously dressed. "Lucien!" he called, waving to catch Lord Safin's attention. "Lucien! What the hell is going on?"

Shandei forced her fingers to straighten out of their fists and ordered a meticulously blank expression on her face. "Behold the Efrens," said Josit. "The one behind him is Vesmer of the city guard, the youngest of three sons. Willon believes that daughters are an aberration afflicted only on the feeble."

"Willon," Lord Safin was saying. "You've not heard the news? Peacefully abed all night, I suppose?"

Lord Efren scowled. "I heard about the assassins. You can be assured I had nothing to do with that. Does the fool boy think a bit of street gossip will turn the tide in his favour?"

Emaris was rigid with rage. Aware from long experience that he was only seconds away from leaping to the Captain's defence, Shandei trod hard on his boot. The movement was less discreet than she intended, and Lord Efren, his gaze arrested, looked down the bench towards them. But Josit spoke first. "Life is full of surprises, Lord Willon," she said, every word syrupy sweet. "I'm sure your speech will still be magnificently received. Have I introduced you to the Lady Shandei?"

"The who?"

"Shandei," said Josit, "is the daughter and heiress of the Second Captain of Betronett, who was murdered on his way to your dinner party last night. Her brother Emaris, as you surely know, is Savonn's squire."

The gauntlet had been thrown down. There was nothing for it now but to rise, and to sweep the man an exaggerated curtsey, with Emaris bowing at her side. "Milord Efren," she said. Unable to stop herself, she added, "I am so, *so* sorry that such matters have troubled your day."

This time it was Emaris who trod on her foot. Willon stared at her in dumbfoundment, as if one of his shoes had sprouted a mouth and started addressing his toes. "You have my condolences. Your father should have stayed home."

Her whole head pulsed with the force of her heartbeat. For a moment she thought she was looking at three of him, each ruddy, big-boned face running into the other, like a many-headed creature from myth. "Of course," she said. On its own volition, her face cracked into a hideous smile. "You didn't invite him. It was the Silvertongue you wanted. What a coincidence he was also attacked."

There was no telling what else she would have said, if Hiraen had not at that moment materialised at Willon's elbow, sleek and tanned and all in black. "My lord? Savonn sends to say that he defers to your seniority and invites you to address the assembly first, if you desire."

Willon rounded on him, Shandei all but forgotten. "Is this a joke?"

Hiraen's face betrayed the strain of a sleepless night, his green eyes shadowed by purplish-grey bruises, but the corners of his mouth twitched. "If you ask me, I believe he has a number of special effects that may unsettle your audience."

They gazed at each other for a moment, the young man and the old, the smiling face and the angry one. Then Willon said, "Your friend has made a farce of the assembly with his brawling and his calumny. If he wishes to further embarrass me, he will be sorely disappointed. I will not speak today."

"I'm grieved to hear it," said Hiraen, not troubling to look grieved. But Willon was already stalking off with his son in tow, and after nodding to them all, Hiraen vanished as well.

"The nerve of him," said Emaris under his breath, still glaring at the spot where Lord Efren had been. "The *nerve*... He killed Father, and nearly murdered me and Savonn too, and he dares to stand there and—"

"We haven't got proof," said Shandei dully.

"Proof, my girl," said Josit, "is a poor man's bribe. And the magistrates always rule in favour of the rich, don't you know? But never mind that. Here comes Savonn."

A gong sounded, calling the assembly to order. A pregnant silence fell over the lowest circles of the Arena and rippled up to the top. The Captain had emerged centrestage, with a wooden rampart over his head and a snarling clay griffin on either side of him, cunningly painted to look like stone. Perforce reminded of the Governor's funeral, Shandei checked each door and window of the castle for any sign of the choir. But the set was empty save for Savonn, and every eye was on him.

"Oh, gods," said Emaris. "He's going to sing, or make something explode, or…"

Savonn never rushed to speak. He studied his audience at leisure, secure in their attention. Today he was wearing a steel cuirass, vambraces and greaves, with a black half-cloak draped over one shoulder. A sword was belted at his hip, and his helm, with its tall silver plume, sat next ot him on a glowering griffin-head. "You all know," he said, "that this assembly was meant to be a public vote of the citizens."

He barely raised his voice, and yet it carried across the theatre like the cut of a knife. "The Council was undecided, and therefore you were invited to exercise your age-old right to choose your Governor. Last night, as you may have heard, someone tried to take that choice out of your hands."

No declaiming. No puffs of coloured smoke. Just this sober, plainspoken man, near unrecognisable as the one who had given them solace at their lord's funeral. Savonn had not appeared to them as Master of the Revels this time, but the Captain of Betronett, firm, ascetic, unyielding. No one made a sound. No matter the guise, the Silvertongue was always worth watching. "Don't fret," he said. "Today you will still get to cast a vote, albeit one of a different sort."

At the far side of the theatre, Lord Efren left his seat to confer with Oriane Sydell. They both looked anxious. Good, thought Shandei.

"Yesterday," said Savonn, "on his way to the Efren residence to answer a summons from the Council, my deputy Rendell was murdered in cold blood. I, too, was attacked in the same hour, and would have met the same fate if not for the valiant intervention of his son, my squire."

Heads were turning to follow his gaze. Emaris shuffled his feet until Shandei elbowed him in the ribs.

"When questioned, our assailants were not forthcoming, save to say that an unnamed person paid them generously to see that I did not live to address you this morning. I know you must be curious. Friends," said Savonn, with a sweeping gesture, "I present the severed fangs of the menace that stalks our streets, preying on those who seek to do right by this city."

Movement stirred at stage left. Shandei looked over to see half a dozen servants in the black and orange livery of the Safins approaching with a litter, heavily laden. Not even the witchcraft of Savonn's voice could keep the crowd quiet when they saw what was on it: three dead men, bound hand and foot and to each other with heavy steel manacles, their throats gaping where a sword had sliced them through. Their clothes were brown with dried blood. Shandei, who on any other day had the strongest stomach of anyone she knew, turned away feeling ill.

Savonn spoke over the outcry of dismay. "There is no shortage of people who would profit from such an arrangement. One need not look far to find them." A pause, so everyone had time to stare at Willon. "But alas, I do not refer only to matters of politics. I urge you all to remember the curious death of our Lord Governor, so lately slain."

Silence fell. Of course they remembered. The choir of Ceriyes had made sure of that. "I urge you to consider not only the jackals that squabble within our city, but the wolves that lurk without. For as long as Cassarah is leaderless, Marguerit of Sarei goes unchecked, and the question of Kedris Andalle's death remains unanswered. And while we sit around talking, some among us have already moved on to the knife in the dark.

"I," said Savonn Silvertongue, "am also done with talking. To-day I ride for the Farfallens to bring justice to our Governor's killer. Stay here if you will, and appoint as your ruler whomever you please, and pray to your gods that the Ceriyes do not find you next. Stay, and speculate, and quarrel, and fret. Or come.

"Come with me to the mountains. Let the babblers and the paper-pushers scheme among themselves. Come away with me to the wild country, where the arrow flies true and treachery has nowhere to lay its head, and let us make our own fortune where we find it. What do you say?"

An uneasy rustling. Then a clear voice answered from the middle of the theatre, behind Shandei. "We fight!"

She looked round. It was Hiraen, standing on his bench in the midst of his company, his bow lifted shining in the air. A moment later all his black-cloaked fellows were rising to join him, and the cry swelled from their ranks. "We fight! We fight! Savonn! Lord Silvertongue!"

Sound was strange in the Arena. There could not have been more than a couple hundred men cheering, but their voices seemed to rise and fill the theatre, coming from nowhere and eve-rywhere at once, building and rolling up and down the rings like spindrift. Shandei realised that the men of Betronett were not the only ones on their feet: that pockets of shouting had arisen as well from the Safin household and the city guard and even the civilians at the top of the theatre. Emaris was sitting bolt upright, fingers furled tight over the edge of the bench, tears glistening diamond-bright in his eyes. A muscle worked in Josit's jaw.

Savonn took a neat cat leap from the stage and came up the stairs. Those who had risen rushed to join him, clambering over the benches, swarming across the stage to take the steps three at a time. They swept up the stairs in a wash of shouting, Savonn's curly head nearly lost in their midst. The small host passed between the top benches, taking the loudest of the yelling with it, and vanished over the edge of the Arena into the rising sun. Those who still had their wits about them had stayed put. But many—about eight hundred, Shandei guessed, including the original Betronett company—had gone with the Captain. *Come away with me*, the Silvertongue had said, and people knew a good show when they saw one.

By now everyone was on their feet, peering at the top of the bowl to see where Savonn was going, or at the bottom, where Lord Willon seemed to be having a loud disagreement with Lady Oriane. Emaris's face was wet. He said, "Shandei."

He had not done this in a long time—come to her out of some trouble or other, a scraped knee or a broken toy or a scolding from their father, and looked at her as if she were Mother Alakyne made flesh, able to heal all hurts. Her chest ached. "Go with him, baby boy."

"But—"

"Father would want you to." She did not know if it was true, only that Emaris needed to believe it was. It would kill him to stay behind when all his friends were going. "We're a Betronett family, always have been. Leave the murderer to me."

He stared at her. Then he embraced her again, hard, and in the next moment vaulted the bench and took off running up the stairs. Shandei watched him until he was gone, her own eyes prickling. Lady Josit's slender arm came around her shoulders. "It's all right," she said. "Savonn will look after him. They have their work, and we have ours."

And so she did. She looked over at the Efrens again. Willon was shouting orders at his guards, somehow managing to look both confused and angry, as if in all this he was the one who had been wronged. *Your father should have stayed home*, he'd said.

Her hand clenched hard around the ivory dagger in her belt. *Hear me, Mother Above*, she prayed. *Hear me, Aebria and Casteia and all the Ceriyes. The law will not help me, but I will kill him. Even*

79

amidst his guards, his riches and his sons, I will find a way to strike him down. Be my witnesses. I will kill him.

* * *

Swept along with the crowd, Emaris followed the host down the street, past the forbidding walls of the citadel and the high-fenced courtyard of the Temple of the Sisters, and toward the Gate of Gold: the grandest of Cassarah's five gates, forty feet high, built from interwoven steel frets gilded with real gold. There was a great tiled courtyard near the entrance, surrounded by tall brick buildings, registrars and customs houses and the like. There, his brothers-in-arms were saddling their horses to leave.

It was clear that the exodus had been planned well before-hand. Ostlers led out horses with efficient calm; errand-boys came running with spare cloaks for those who had forgotten theirs; cooks and kitchen servants handed out parcels of food to last them until Terinea. Emaris, who had come just as he was from the Safin manor—sleepless and exhausted, without arms or armour—huddled by a pillar to keep out of the way. His father should have been here to tell him what to do. But he was alone, with no orders.

"Well?" said a matter-of-fact voice. Like an apple one kept trying to push underwater, Savonn had bobbed up at his side again. "How angry are the Council?"

"Lord Willon looked ready to bite off his own tongue," said Emaris flatly. "He'll never let you go."

"Won't he? It depends how much bloodshed he's willing to risk." Savonn studied him, eyes narrowed against the sun. He had sat up all night with Emaris in one of Lady Safin's spare bed-rooms, not talking, not coaxing, just sitting, only slipping away to the Arena just before cockcrow. "I already said you don't have to come. Did you sleep at all?"

Emaris ignored the question. One never looked for kindness from Savonn, but it came at the most inopportune moments. If he thought about it, his resolve would falter. "So try and make me go away."

"Sweetheart," said Savonn, "the gods themselves quake to contemplate it. You keep losing this, is all."

He was holding out Emaris's sword in its scabbard. Emaris searched his face for a hint of admonition, but found none. He took the sword and hung it on his belt, half wishing Savonn would say something rude so he would have no choice but to turn around and go back to Shandei. "I don't know what I'm doing."

"I seldom do. Turn around and start walking, I see the Council coming to accost me."

Standing on tiptoe, Emaris saw the councillors coming into the courtyard. Willon was in the lead, surrounded by his household guard. Lucien Safin had him by the arm, talking and gesturing and, by the looks of it, being determinedly ignored. At a word from Willon, the guards began to spread out around the edges of the courtyard.

"They're coming," Emaris observed. For lack of an alternative, he plunged with Savonn into the milling mass of man and horse. He had attained that special depth of fatigue that drowned all one's senses in an ambulatory coma, in which even the surreal and the lethal seemed pedestrian. At this rate they would find themselves in a stand-off with the Efren guards by noon, and have their heads on the block at nightfall. "He's giving orders to his men. Lord Lucien is yelling. Oh, now Lady Oriane's guards have joined them. They're looking for you. They're going to arrest you. Perhaps you ought to be arrested."

"Perhaps," Savonn agreed. "But it would rather ruin the scene. And Lord Lucien would call *his* guards, and there would be murder. Where's your horse?"

"I haven't a clue."

"Take Hiraen's, he's got at least twelve more."

Savonn was mounting his own black palfrey. After a moment, Emaris swung up onto the gelding beside it, and strung the bow that hung from its saddle. The men of Betronett were urging their horses into orderly ranks, and behind them Daine and Hiraen had managed to chivvy the rabble of new recruits into two long files on foot. At the end of the courtyard, the guards eyed them like a colony of plague-ridden rats.

"They're not barring the way yet," said Emaris, with only an academic interest in the proceedings. No doubt Savonn would do something awful to get rid of the guards, or they would all go to the headsman together. "I don't think the Council wants a blood-bath. We outnumber them, but if they couch their spears we can't charge. Are we charging them? Or are you just—damnit!"

A lieutenant had begun to shout. "Shut the gate! *Shut the gate!*"

A horseman in Efren cream and bronze exploded past them at a gallop, streaking towards the gate towers with the order. Hiraen stepped up on Savonn's other side, his bow already drawn. "Shall I stop him?"

"Yes," said Emaris.

"No," said Savonn. He rose in his stirrups, the wind stirring his hair. "Gentlemen! We make for the gate. Do you see this man with the bow? Fall out of line, and he'll shoot you."

Then he resumed his seat and spurred his horse, and they were moving.

The city wall loomed ahead, the gate standing open. Willon's rider had preceded them, and already the men at the winches were working the levers. Even as Emaris surged headlong down the road with the others in a cacophony of hoofbeats, the footsoldiers jogging behind them, the gate began to creak shut.

Savonn lifted his fist in the air. It was a signal they all knew, and had been watching for. Taking his hands off the reins, Emaris nocked and drew his bow, guiding his horse with his knees. He found a mark. He took aim. As usual, he considered missing on purpose.

"Stand down!" Savonn called.

The gatekeepers hesitated. In full stage voice, Savonn shouted, "*Stand down!*"

It worked like an enchantment. Faced with two hundred bows trained on them, they backed away from the winches and put their hands in the air. The gate stood open, with freedom beyond. "Brothers," Savonn called. "A salute for the Second Captain, if you please."

The bowstring twanged sweetly under Emaris's fingers. A flock of arrows rose shining with the sound of a great many birds taking off, and rattled against the steel struts of the gate. Someone whooped. A wordless cheer went up. Then they were clear of the walls, and on the road that would take them into the highlands.

They had come away without bloodshed. They had chosen to follow their Captain, this malicious, prancing popinjay who could spit in the Council's face and come away laughing, and henceforth were at no one's mercy but his. There were no banners, no heralds, no trumpets. Only their own cheers accompanied them as they streamed away from the city in a tidy column of horse and foot: the eight hundred who had chosen to follow Savonn Silvertongue, come what may, into the Farfallens.

ACT TWO

THE MAGPIE
AND THE
NIGHTINGALE

INTERLUDE

They say the Farfallens are a good place for falling in love.

I wouldn't know. I have had just the one love, after all—the statistics are hardly convincing. Still, I am inclined to agree. Do you remember that blustery autumn morning we ran into each other in the marketplace in Astorre? It had been months since we'd last met. I missed you, though I would not have admitted it even to myself. But I was with my brothers-in-arms, and you with yours—I recognised that tall fellow, blond as a crocus, who always seemed so vexed by you. (Most of your companions did. It was one of my favourite things about you.) We passed ten feet apart on opposite sides of a stall, and I could all but feel your heart beating, like the flutter of a hummingbird trapped in my hand. After so long apart, I could not bear to pass you by without speaking. I stopped to browse the wares, and so did you. It was wigs, or hats, or something like that. I held one up at random and said to my manservant, *It is so beautiful, but look at the cost!*

And you said to your blond friend, in your own tongue, which you knew I understood, *This is worth any cost.*

You believe yourself unreadable and unfathomable, but you see, my dear, I have perfect pitch for all the inflections of your voice. I knew, or thought I did, that you meant what you said. It salved the pain of separation, at any rate. And later that week you slipped in through my window, and we spent a joyous evening together, with neither your friends nor mine any the wiser.

I did not know, then, to whom you owed your loyalty. It was plain enough to me that you were not on your own side, so I thought you were on mine. It was an easy mistake to make.

CHAPTER 7

Unlike its recent predecessor, the funeral of Rendell of Betronett was small, tasteful, and decorous to a fault.

The only anomaly was the presence of Lady Josit, who arrived with her handmaids at the last minute. It was a matter of some chagrin for Shandei, who had not expected anyone besides Linn and her own handful of disreputable friends to turn up. The Lady was very kind, though, and made no comment on the humble proceedings. "Why this place?" she asked, when the burial was over and the mourners had begun to draw off in twos and threes. "Was it dear to him?"

Shandei had chosen a wooded grove two miles downriver from Cassarah. It stood on an escarpment where the Morivant had shifted its course westward sometime in its long, war-fraught history, leaving a low cliff and a sandy bay that sloped gently towards the lazy waters. "He used to take us here when we were small," she said. "We'd pick figs and catch fish with our spears, and he taught Emaris and me to swim. He used to say our mother was a mermaid from Bayarre."

Josit looked out over the water. It was almost dusk. The blood-red sun was plunging its rosy skirts over the river, gilding with fire the roofs and ridgepoles of the villages on the Saraian side. "You should know this," she said. "I moved to open an investigation into his death, and the attack on Savonn, but Lord Willon shut it down. I gather he thinks the whole affair an embarrassment to him."

"And Captain Savonn?" asked Shandei, thinking of her brother. "What does his lordship mean to do about him?"

"Nothing," said Josit. "The Council toyed with the idea of sending the city guard after him, but Lucien and I put a stop to that. Having our armies slaughter each other on the eve of war is exactly what Marguerit would like us to do. Now Willon is acting as if it was his idea to send Savonn to the mountains all along."

Shandei held her tongue. None of this was surprising. Besides, she had plans of her own. "I suppose he would," she said. "Ladyship, I'd better go. I have errands to run. Thank you for your kindness."

"Justice is not kindness," said Josit. "You are going back without an escort?"

Shandei smiled despite herself. "I should be all right."

On her hired pony, she was through the Fire Gate and back in the city in almost no time. She changed out of her mourning garb, put on a billowy dress that amply concealed the ivory dagger in her garter, and set out on foot again.

She had not spent the last few days idle. From a friend who had a friend who knew a cook at the Efrens', and from covert surveillance of her own, she had learnt that Lord Willon was unassailable. His household guard numbered some two hundred, commanded by a man called Cahal, and his residence—a veritable palace among the other mansions on the Street of Silver—was impregnable. The man himself was unlikely to tolerate an interrogation on his doings and whereabouts on the night her father died, and his wife and two older sons were far away running the country estate. Her investigation had but one hope: the youngest son, Vesmer, whom she had seen at the assembly.

From her various conquests in the city guard, she had no difficulty learning his patrol route. It was a long one, crossing a number of secluded areas that seemed like promising ambush spots. The one she picked was the Rose Bridge, which extended from the roof of the clockmaker's shop to the printing press two streets away, so decent folk did not have to traverse the unsavoury neighbourhood in between. Even to herself, her objectives were unclear. It was unthinkable that Vesmer Efren would be cooperative. But one had to try.

It was almost midnight when she got there. Swaying lanterns lit the length of the bridge and its rose hedges. A narrow alley wriggled below, its slovenly buildings quiet and secretive in their shadows. She had explored the district once, without permission: a hodgepodge of pleasure houses and usurers and underground taverns that served illicit concoctions more potent than any ale. She swung over the low rail to sit on the baluster, her crumpled skirts catching in the thorns and brambles beneath, and waited.

A couple of pedestrians passed her perch. The first gave her a wide berth; the second tried to proposition her. Then, when both her patience and her nerve were wearing thin, she heard the chink of mail, and knew her quarry had arrived.

She did not turn around. Every sense was informative, hearing more than most. His tread was leisurely and even, each step punctuated by a metallic clink. He wore a scabbard at his side—his left hip, which meant he must be right-handed. A tinny, rhythmic tapping made itself known, *ding-ding-ding-da-ding*, as he came closer and his footsteps slowed. He was drumming his fingers on something sonorous. A helm. "What are you doing, woman?"

The voice was bluff and bearish, like Lord Willon's. She stayed where she was, her hands folded in her lap. "Sitting."

"*Here*?"

"Is it unlawful, sir?"

Her tone offended him, as she had intended. "You state your business when an officer of the city guard asks for it. Why are you sitting here?"

"I'm not sure," she said. "Am I disturbing the peace? I would hate that. It's been disturbed so often lately."

He seized her arm and pulled her from the baluster. In a flurry of silk and cotton, she untangled her skirts and unfolded her legs and swung down beside him. The picture she had formed was accurate to the point of hilarity. He stood over her, a tall, sallow man with gingery hair, bushy caterpillar eyebrows and a boat-bottom jaw. Over his mail shirt he wore a studded leather vest, emblazoned with the silver badge of his rank. His sword was at his left hip; his helm was in his hand, which was still drumming away. *Ding-ding-ding-da-ding.* There was no sign that he recognised her from the assembly. He said, "I could fine you for back-talking."

He had yet to release her arm. As she gazed up at him, the restlessness that had plagued her since that bleak morning in Linn's house solidified and, like lead in an alchemist's furnace, transmuted into a boundless, throbbing rage. Now she saw why she had come. Such a sickness had to be exorcised in confrontation, leeched off like bad blood. "What about murder?" she asked. "What is the penalty for that? Or haven't you caught the fellow who killed my father and set the hitmen on the Captain?"

She thought the shock might make him recoil. Instead he came closer, his beady eyes roving her face with fresh interest. She could smell his breath, sour with garlic from his supper. "I've seen you before. Your father was the Captain's man." A faint line bisected the space between his brows, and his clam-like grip tightened on her elbow. "*He* sent you to harass me? The Silver-tongue?"

The arrogance of it rendered her mute for a moment. It meant nothing to him that a man had died. All these rich people were the same, blind to everything but each other's machinations. "I came of my own accord," she said. "Imagine that. Are you alarmed? Perhaps you and the good Lord Efren know something we don't?"

His jaw slackened with the same bewildered offense she had seen on Willon's face. Any moment now he would try to hit her. She was not afraid. She could see the end of him, clear as a divine revelation. It was as if a film over her eyes had dissolved, leaving the night bathed in a lucent, enchanted clarity. Never had she seen the world like this, the delicate arch of the bridge, the blooming roses, the gentle glow of the lanterns all sparkling with new beauty. The low railing was just a foot away. There would be no witnesses. Only a thirty-foot drop; maybe a scream, a crunch of bone. And tomorrow Lord Willon would be in mourning, like she was, the windows of the mansion on the Street of Silver curtained in black.

And her father would still be dead, her house cold and empty.

"Your insinuations," Vesmer was saying, "are slander, and you will answer for them. My father will be apprised of this. If I were you I would stop talking and start running."

He was not, it seemed, going to arrest her tonight. He would probably find it awkward if she slandered him some more in the hearing of his colleagues. Tomorrow, more likely than not, she would just wake to a rap on her door and a ring of Efren retainers around her house. It was too late to take anything back. "Where should I run, milord? This is my city."

He gave an expansive shrug. "Out of my sight."

He released her arm and flung her away, so hard she nearly hit herself in the face with the back of her own hand. She looked once more at the bridge railing. *Aebria, Casteia, avenge me,* she thought. But the moment had come and gone. She had lost the element of surprise. Already someone else was coming up on the bridge, a distant figure behind Vesmer. The night had lost its crystalline purity, and the cleansing fire of the gods had gone.

"Well?" said Vesmer. "What are you waiting for?"

She turned her back and walked away, her arms folded tight across her chest. His fingers were drumming again, *ding-ding-ding-dong*. She made her way to the clockmaker's at the end of the bridge and descended the stairs to the snarl of thready lanes and dingy shops below, her head pounding with the swift percussion of her heartbeat. She had accomplished nothing. Perhaps she ought to run, like he said. Perhaps she ought to pack her bags and flee to Terinea, to the Bitten Hill, to her brother in the mountains. But her father always said that once you started running, you never stopped.

She went home, bolted all the doors, dragged a bedroll into the cellar, and fell into a dead sleep clutching her knife.

* * *

She woke the next morning to a pounding on the back door. It was accompanied not by Vesmer's gruff voice, as she might have expected, but Linn's brisk, cheery one. "Shandei! Are you alive? I baked bread. Got news, too. Don't make me break down your door."

A glance out the window confirmed that Linn was alone, carrying an enormous bread-basket and a sack of herbs. "What news?" asked Shandei as she let her in, drowsy and dazed. She had a headache, and the back of her mouth tasted like something dead.

"Oh," said Linn, bustling in and setting the basket on the kitchen table. "Lord Efren's son is dead. The youngest. Vesmer, I think he was called."

It was a few moments before Shandei was aware of speaking. "What?"

If she sounded strained, Linn was too busy poking around the larder to notice. "They're saying he never came off his guard shift last night. His men went looking for him. Found him under the Rose Bridge, head bashed in and everything. Must have been pushed. I hear there were rose petals everywhere, like there'd been a hell of a fight. Where on earth do you keep your butter?"

Moving like a sleepwalker, Shandei retrieved the butter-plate and handed it over. It was exactly as she had envisioned, praying to the gods with her arm caught in Vesmer's grip. A sharp push, a quick fall, a long silence. "Who did it?"

"No one knows," said Linn. "A pity, I suppose. So close to Midsummer, too."

She set about buttering a chunk of bread. Shandei watched, unseeing. She had glimpsed someone behind Vesmer the night before, just as she turned to go—the indistinct figure at the end of the bridge. Had he been the killer? Who was that man, if indeed he was a man at all, and not something crawled out of the recesses of her mind? If anyone got word that she had been on the bridge with him—

They could not prove she had pushed him, but as Josit had said, that would hardly matter. It would be good enough for his father, who would condemn her for a murderer. And who was to say she was not? She had prayed Vesmer dead. For all she knew, the Ceriyes had heard her.

She went out to the garden, and tried not to be sick.

CHAPTER 8

Marching at a blistering pace, the army of Savonn Silver-tongue arrived at the fort called Onaressi on Midsummer's Eve.

This seemed like unfortunate timing to Emaris, but Savonn was preoccupied with other matters. The mountains that bordered Falwyn, Sarei and the Northlands were peppered with ancient fastnesses, built by settlers from one side or another and abandoned to ruin when the inhabitants found the lowland air more salubrious. In Merrott's day, the Betronett patrols had used them as waystations on their trips to and from Astorre. Now they should have been deserted. But the scouts of Medrai told them otherwise: Onaressi and the other forts had been overrun by squatters.

"Bandits, or so they claim," Savonn told the gaggle of young recruits that had taken to dogging his steps wherever he went. "As far as the good people of Medrai are concerned, any stone they trip over on the road is a bandit. They may be right. That, however, doesn't rule out the possibility that these particular brigands are in Marguerit's hire."

Unasked, but drawn by a pungent mix of irritation and jealousy, Emaris came closer to listen. Their numbers had grown since Cassarah. Savonn had called at most of the settlements they passed on their way, and the townsfolk streamed after him in droves to swell their host. Unfortunately, most of these happened to be peasant boys who barely knew how to hold a sword. "We should storm it," said one of these, now: the tallest of the lot, with deep umber skin, close-cropped hair, and—as Emaris had already noted in many others—a deplorable tendency to gaze at Savonn as if he were the moon. "I could lead your van, Captain."

They all looked up at Onaressi. The fort was built on a towering spur of rock at the point where the road split in half and became Forech's and Ilsa's Passes, the two main routes across the mountains. They were encamped at the foot of the cliff, where the overhang offered some shelter from watchful eyes and the nosewatering wind. "You may," said Savonn, spinning his sunhat on one tapered finger. "If you tell me how you propose to storm it."

"Through a postern," said another boy. He had positioned himself at the Captain's side, in the place where a squire might stand. Emaris frowned at him with unconcealed hauteur. "That's what they do in books."

As if reading his mind, Savonn said, "Master Emaris? Might we attack through a postern?"

Emaris unlocked his jaw. His father would have chided him for being rude. "No. The postern's round the back, facing away from the road. Nikas showed us on his maps." Nikas was a Saraian defector, the offspring of Terinean slaves, who had attached himself to their host at Medrai. He drew maps, and sometimes portraits, if they asked nicely enough. "We'd have to march round to the far side of the fort. They'd hear us before we got halfway there."

"Then we could climb the wall," said the tall black boy. He gave Emaris a hopeful look. "I climbed over the wall of my uncle's farm once. It wasn't hard."

"You're all out of your minds," said a third boy. This one came no higher than Emaris's chin. He had light yellow-brown hair, like a fawn, and a dusting of freckles on windburnt cheeks. "Didn't you look at Nikas's map? The fort's got a main keep, two other wings, and two gate towers. They could have a thousand men in there for all we know."

To Emaris's annoyance, Savonn looked at him once more. "Do they?"

"No," said Emaris, scowling. "Look how dark the ringwall is. If they were at full strength, they'd have sentries posted all along the perimeter, with lanterns and watchfires and all. We probably outnumber them."

"Which won't do us any good when they're behind that wall," said the small boy, peering up at Emaris with unbearable earnestness. "A couple of crossbows and well-placed boulders could take us all out. We'd have to get inside for numbers to tell."

"How perturbing," said Savonn, looking not at all perturbed. "Oh, well. Maybe we'll just walk through the front gate. Hold my hat, Vion."

He plunked the sunhat over the small boy's head, so the brim flopped over his eyes like a visor, and started towards his tent. There was a minor stampede to get there before him: Vion held the tent flap open, and the others ushered Savonn over the threshold with all the pomp and ceremony of a royal investiture. Emaris stared, incredulous. He was seventeen, and above such petty jockeying. He *knew* Savonn, after all. He had served him for years. Surely there was no need to fall all over oneself for his attention.

Emaris stuck his chin in the air, bustled officiously to the tent, paused in the entrance to savour the envious eyes on him, and ducked in after Savonn.

Hiraen and Daine were waiting inside with Nikas. The latter was ostensibly their guide, though why Savonn needed one when he knew the Farfallens better than any of them was beyond Emaris. Nikas, at least, was no peasant boy. He was about Savonn's age, if a lot taller and broader in the shoulders, with choppy black hair that looked as if it had recently been savaged

98

with a rusty knife. They said he had been a slave in some kind of assassin cult in Sarei before he escaped. "Well?" he asked. "Have your unweaned boys been persuaded to walk headlong into the jaws of death?"

Savonn did not join them on the camp stools, but stood over them with an air of mild reproof. With a pang, Emaris saw that they had left a place empty in their circle, a gesture so subtle it could have been an accident. "You tell me."

Hiraen glanced up from the blueprint they were studying. Since Cassarah, he had been keeping an eye on Emaris with a concern that bordered on the absurd. Tempted as he was to desert out of sheer pique, Emaris had done nothing more drastic than write letter after long letter to Shandei, none of which he sent. The fact was that he had always looked up to Savonn as an example, and if the Captain could bear his bereavement with a smile and a sharp-edged quip, so could he. "It's Midsummer," said Hiraen. "Your eager children will fling themselves off a cliff if you so much as gesture with your pinkie toe, but the others won't."

"It's bad luck," Daine agreed, "shedding blood on a sacred night."

Nikas smiled placidly. He was always smiling, just as his big callused fingers were always smeared with charcoal. "We could promise them a belated celebration in Astorre. The city of mischief, license, and artifice. Milord Silvertongue knows it well, I believe." He reached up to put a scrap of parchment in Savonn's hand. "I was watching you from the tent flap."

Savonn's face was unrevealing. Burning with an impatient curiosity he would not admit, Emaris peered over his shoulder.

It was another of Nikas's portraits. The sight struck him dumb for a few breathless moments. This one was of Savonn's head in profile, startlingly lifelike in detail for all that it must have been drawn in haste. The acute contour of the cheekbones, adroitly shaded. The flounce of the large, liquid curls. The knowing gloss to the sylphlike eyes, bright with silent laughter. It was a hugely flattering likeness. But to Emaris's disappointment, Savonn only glanced at the picture, then folded it up and gave it to him to hold. "Didn't I mention," he said, "that we aren't passing through Astorre?"

There was a new-honed crispness to his voice. "What?" said Emaris, distracted. He had never been to Astorre. It was the one thing he had been looking forward to. "Why not?"

"He doesn't want us to be led astray into vice and lechery," said Hiraen. "Like he was."

It was the same desultory tone Hiraen used for talking about everything, from the weather to the Queen of Sarei, but for some reason Savonn's stare took on a narrow, dangerous cast. Hiraen met it levelly. "What?" said Emaris again, looking back and forth between them.

Nikas made his eyes big and round. Daine cleared his throat. "You've seen the gate, Savonn," he said, bringing the discussion back on track. "Five thousand men couldn't breach it without cannon."

"And we have no cannon," said Savonn. "Pity we didn't think to carry off the Council's on our way out. Nikas, show them the matter we discussed."

"Oh," said Nikas, snapping back to attention. For one who had spent all his life in Sarei, he spoke excellent Falwynian. "Onaressi was built around a natural spring. It bubbles into the courtyard year-round and never freezes over, as far as anyone knows. Bad news for besiegers, good news for spies."

He tapped a finger on the blueprint he had drawn. Along the ringwall, just north of the gate, a spot had been circled twice in a light hand. "There's a muddy channel under the wall here, where the springwater flows out. It's just a glorified rabbit's burrow. Theoretically, you could get in that way if you don't mind some oozing. Like an earthworm."

Hiraen laughed. "Fighting on Midsummer, and no jaunt to Astorre? This lot'll mutiny."

In the light from the brazier, Savonn's eyes were pigeon-blue and perfectly dispassionate. "Might I remind you that we are not the only people in the realm to celebrate Midsummer? If you will all leave off being pessimistic, surely a solution now presents itself. Master Emaris?"

Emaris jumped. He was still thinking of Astorre, the portrait clutched in his hand. "Me?" Then his mind caught up with his tongue. "If it's Midsummer's Eve…"

"Yes?"

"The bandits—Saraians—whatever they are—will be celebrating. There'll be a feast. That's why the ringwall is dark. Most of them are probably indoors, roaring drunk."

Savonn twirled a finger in a *carry on, carry on* gesture, as if he were conducting an orchestra. Suddenly alert, Hiraen sat back on his heels. "We could take an advance force in, surprise the guards and open the gate."

"It's not so simple," said Nikas. He pointed to the two gate towers on the map. "The gate is worked by a special winch mechanism. To open it—"

"We have to turn the winch in each tower at the same time," said Savonn. "I know. I've been here. So we have to assail both towers, and hope for a miracle of timing." He turned to Emaris, a smile glimmering on his lips. "I don't suppose you'll let Vion and his friends lead the van?"

Dumbfounded silence. Then, with the air of one acquiescing to the inevitable, Hiraen said, "How lucky they have us to do it for them."

He grinned at Savonn, the hostility of a moment before quite forgotten. "I know what you're thinking. Five thousand men couldn't force that gate. Five could."

Emaris gazed at him, bug-eyed. Daine said, "Mother Above."

"Well done, Lord Safin," said Savonn. "This must be why I keep you around. I count five of us. Shall we go?"

* * *

An hour later, cursing himself and Savonn and all the capricious forces of fate and destiny that had conspired to bring him to this place and time, Emaris found himself creeping under the ringwall with four other madmen.

Savonn had put an officer called Anyas in command of the troops they left behind, with long and explicit instructions delivered in the siege-breaking voice no one dared contradict. They climbed a winding track, overgrown with weeds and mangy grass, to the top of the cliff. The ringwall was eighteen feet of old stone and crumbling mortar. Beneath, the wind buffeted them like a boxer's blows, and even in full armour Emaris found himself shivering. They could see nothing of the camp below. The top of the wall was dark, but faint voices drifted to them from the gate towers, and somewhere a brook was babbling to itself.

They halted. Nikas, who was in front, motioned to a spot just ahead.

Emaris saw with a sinking heart the hole in the wall they meant to infiltrate. The brook had carved for itself a flute-thin conduit under the ringwall, from which it splashed down the mountainside in a series of tiny falls and rapids. The passage was as narrow as Nikas had warned. They would have to go on hands and knees, in utter silence, and pray the guards at the towers did not hear them. "Best Midsummer of my life," Hiraen murmured, hand cupped over his mouth so the sound would not carry. "Shall I go first?"

"Nikas first," said Savonn. "Then you."

Nikas's dimples winked. For the first time, Emaris wondered if Savonn did not trust him. "I live to serve."

He waded into the middle of the stream, water swirling around his calves. A moment later he crouched down and disappeared into the hole. Hiraen cocked a brow at Savonn. "Cheers," he said, and vanished after.

After him went Daine. Then it was Emaris's turn. He stepped with trepidation into the stream, expecting the worst, but the water was warmer than he expected. Savonn, who did not even seem to be armed, waded in behind him. "The ringwall is only twelve feet thick," he whispered.

Emaris held on to that knowledge all the way through the tunnel, scrabbling along in a darkness so complete he could not even see where he was putting his hands. The air was alive with reek and rot. Twice he cracked his head on a jutting stone, and once something slimy eeled past him in the water. His bow and quiver kept scraping the roof of the tunnel with a thin rattling noise he was sure would rouse every bandit in the fort, but to keep them dry, he could not hunker all the way down. Twelve feet felt like a mile.

Just as his legs were beginning to seize up, a hand closed over the scruff of his neck, making him jump. Daine hauled him to his feet. "We're in."

Emaris staggered out of the stream, dripping, and put his back against the wall. The upper windows of the main keep were lit, and snatches of music drifted to them across the yard. Closer at hand was the idle chatter of restless men on watch in the towers, interrupted now and then by bursts of laughter. Savonn emerged noiselessly behind him. Hiraen, now in the lead, asked a question with his eyes, and Savonn gestured back. Then they were moving along the wall towards the closer of the towers, a hulking monolith rising black against the sky. A single window glimmered near its base, also lit.

Dear Casteia, Emaris prayed, *please let them all be drunk.*

Daine caught his arm, and they came to a sudden stop. Hiraen had drawn an arrow from his quiver. The ringwall cast a solid rectangular shadow across the grass near their feet, and along its rim, several yards from where they were huddled, a man-shaped figure was moving. "Sentry above," Hiraen whispered.

"Can you hit him?" asked Savonn.

"If I can see it, I can hit it."

He fitted the arrow to his bow. Emaris gripped the pommel of his sword with sweaty fingers, pulse hammering a furious paean. Watching the moving figure, his hands on the bowstring, Hiraen was so still he could have been cast from stone. Then, in a single swift motion, he launched himself out from the wall and drew.

He loosed so fast Emaris almost missed the flight of the arrow. The twang of the string was echoed by a second from above. At the same time, there was a gurgle like a cut-off shout. Another shaft struck the ground inches from where Hiraen stood. With a series of muffled thumps, a sentry toppled over the parapet and landed at their feet, still clutching a bow. An arrow, feathered with orange fletching, protruded from his windpipe.

The laughing voices did not cease. After a breathless moment Daine and Emaris each grabbed one of the fallen man's arms and propped him up against the wall, where—if luck permitted—he might go undiscovered for quite some time. Hiraen retrieved the other arrow and stuck it in his quiver. "He was the only one. Probably came out for a breath of air. A second later and he would've brought all the others running." He glanced towards the towers. "We'll need to split up. I can do the first tower, and Savonn—"

They looked to where Savonn had been standing. They looked around them, at the dark courtyard and the bright windows of the keep. Then they looked at one another. "Oh," said Nikas with interest. "Has our valiant leader deserted?"

Emaris stared. "He was there a moment ago!"

Under his breath, Hiraen pronounced a curt, precise curse. "He does that sometimes. Leave him. Let's go."

"But—"

"He's right," said Daine. "Savonn knows what he's doing. The job won't wait."

Still looking around wildly, Emaris made himself listen. "The towers are identical," Nikas was saying. "The guards will be in the common room on the first floor. Second floor's where the winch for the gate is. Remember, both sides have to be cranked together or it'll jam."

"Understood," said Hiraen. "Emaris, with me. Daine, go with Nikas."

They split up. Treading silently, Hiraen led the way to the closer of the towers, until he and Emaris could see through the ground-floor window. It looked into a small round room, where four or five men sat dicing at a table. They were clearly supposed to be on duty—each wore a mail shirt, and several spears leaned on the wall by the table. But Savonn had been right. The fort was not at full strength, or there would have been more of them. "Listen," said Hiraen. "Some of them are Falwynians."

The men spoke a rough pidgin that sounded like a melting-pot of Falwynian and Saraian, of which Emaris could understand maybe two in three words. "So, a mixed force," he said. "Bandits from either side of the border. How do we get in?"

"Front door," said Hiraen. "Do you see any other way?"

The tower walls were too smooth to climb, and in any case they could not get closer without being seen from the window. "No," said Emaris. "But I haven't got a death wish."

Hiraen grinned. "I'll distract them, you'll work the winch."

"*How*?"

"We'll see," Hiraen said, and set off at a saunter for the tower.

The door stood ajar, the edges limned in faint warm light. Not long ago, Emaris had crossed a threshold like this in Daine's house. The crippling horror lasted only a moment, after which he managed to move his feet. He could hardly be afraid to walk through open doors for the rest of his life. Hiraen knocked cursorily and pushed it open, and Emaris, preventing his hand from straying to his sword by sheer force of will, nearly ran into him as he paused in the entryway to survey the common room.

The five guards at the table barely looked up from their game. One of them, an older man with a broad barrel chest and a wrinkled face like tanned oxhide, hawked and spat on the rushes. "Did them feasting numbnuts up at the keep send you here with more beer? If not, ye can get lost."

"No," said Hiraen, matching to perfection their tone of sullen discontentment, if not the rough pidgin. "Thrice-damned misers, the lot of them."

Oaths and insults were universally understood. A chorus of curses arose, and the men settled into a half-hearted army grouse. "Hoarding all the best food for himself," someone said. Another added, "And our pay's late!"

"Got thrown out of the feast hall, didya?" said a big pasty fellow with a hairy mole on his nose, looking Hiraen up and down. "Didn't like you talking all posh up there?"

"Eh," said the man with the barrel chest, who did not seem inclined to chase them out after all. "The Empath's gone and showed up at last?"

Hiraen's hesitation was brief. "Think so. Milord said something about opening the gate." He pulled up one of the empty chairs at the foot of the table and slid into it, stretching out his long legs. His boots were still dripping muddy water from the stream. So were Emaris's. "Mother Above, what wouldn't I do for some beer now."

Barrelchest huffed something incomprehensible. "Brought an army with him, has he? All them high lords and generals, marching to and fro like they own the world." He made no move to get up and signal the other tower to open the gate. "Might be if we make him wait, he'll have Mordel's head on a pike. You stop eyeing my drink, boy, we ain't got enough as it is."

"I'll dice you for it," said Hiraen. "Winner takes all."

This spurred a round of general laughter. "What d'ye got to bet, posh-talker?" said Mole. His gaze slid sideways to Emaris, hovering at Hiraen's elbow like a cupbearer without a cup. "This little dandelion of yours?"

A pallid hand snaked out. Even through his cuirass Emaris felt it embark, rough and heavy, on the small of his back, and quest down to the vicinity of his rear.

Action came before thought, but revulsion preceded either. He caught the man's wrist and forced the clammy flesh back in one of the brutal grips Shandei had shown him, stopping just short of breaking the arm. A bone popped. Mole shrieked, tried to wrench his hand free, and shrieked some more, prompting another wave of guffaws.

"Oh, you don't want him," said Hiraen. His voice barely changed, but his eyes had taken on a flinty quality. "Pretty but savage, and mute as a brick. What about this?"

Nauseated, Emaris released the man with a jerk that sent him sprawling half off his chair. No one paid any attention, because Hiraen was holding up his bow. It was an excellent one: a double recurve designed to be shot from horseback, made from goldenwood and inlaid with silver, with a glossy ebony grip. Barrelchest's eyes were showing the whites. "That's one of them Betronett bows," he said. "Where'd you get it?"

Hiraen grinned, and made an expressive gesture with thumb and forefinger. The man howled a laugh, smacking his meaty palms together. "You're on."

It was a complicated game that involved eight dice and a lot of yelling, mostly numbers and profanities. Hiraen got the hang of it at once. Emaris left them to it and wandered to the window, gazing across at the far tower. No signal from Daine and Nikas. Mole was watching him again, his gaze hungry and unwholesome, the sort that felt like insect legs crawling on skin. But just then, Hiraen upended the cup of dice all over the floor and gave a triumphant shout—"Three sixes! *Three sixes!*"—and in the grumbling that ensued, Mole's attention snapped back to the game.

It was now or never. An archway behind the table opened onto the stairwell, which was unguarded. Emaris took a last look at Hiraen, still whooping over a fistful of dice, and started up the steps.

The stairs were dark and steep. The winch was on the second floor, Nikas had said. Here a door led into another room smaller than the one below, and quite deserted. A brazier stood by the wall, next to a pile of moth-eaten blankets. The glowing coals illuminated a jigsaw of cogs and gears that spanned one wall from floor to ceiling, shining like great brass teeth. A great wooden lever protruded from the maw. There was one just like it backstage at the Arena, which Savonn had once let him turn. With a despairing glance out the small window, Emaris laid both hands on the lever and tried to budge it.

"What the hell are ye doing?"

He spun round. The pile of blankets moved. It sprouted an arm, brown and gangling, and a matching leg. A tuft of sandy hair emerged. Then the pile opened to eject a boy much younger than himself, with big, baneful eyes and a fresh crop of pimples dotting his cheeks. The winch was guarded after all.

Emaris offered a wavery smile. "Opening the gate. Uh, Mordel's orders. The Empath and his army are here."

The boy glared daggers. "You talk funny. I ain't heard no orders."

Something moved in the window. A light was flickering in the second-floor room of the opposite tower, like a lantern being covered and uncovered. "Look," Emaris said, pointing. "They're signalling us. Give me a hand?"

The boy reached out, but it was to grab Emaris by the shoulder and heave him away from the lever. "That ain't how they do it. If they be wanting the gate opened, they sound a horn from the keep. You tryna get me in trouble?"

Boots were clumping up the stairs, a dull tread, approaching steadily from the common room. Fear thrilled down Emaris's spine, along with something very much like excitement. They were at close quarters. The boy's spear was leaning on the wall behind the door, but it would be cumbersome here. And his mail only covered him to the thigh. "Is that so?" asked Emaris, his eyes wide, his voice level. "Gods, I hate my bloody commander. No one tells me these things. We'd best report that light, then."

As he intended, the boy ambled forward to peer out at the other tower. Emaris could just make out the shapes of two faces in the opposite window, one fair and one dark. His sword hissed out of its sheath. The boy's head came around sharply, but it was too late. Emaris slashed down, and the blade bit deep into the meat of his leg.

The boy screamed. In the same heartbeat the door flew open to reveal Mole on the landing, large and grotesquely pale, already drawing his own blade. Emaris caught the boy's flailing arm, pivoted on his heel, and swung his foe's whole stumbling weight at the man in the doorway. Mole grunted. For a moment they seemed to hang suspended, the two bodies tottering on the landing. Then gravity triumphed, and they fell out of view, thumping all the way to the bottom of the stairs.

The common room exploded into shouts. Emaris slammed the door shut, groped for the bolts, and rammed them home. The lantern was still flickering. He flung himself on the lever and pulled for his life.

The mechanism was ponderous, but well-oiled. The cogs clanked into motion. The winch shuddered, like a great cat straining to burst free of a cage. Then, as his arms shook with the effort, the gate began to groan open. More feet were coming up the stairs—at least two pairs, he thought, and the door wouldn't hold for long. Hiraen was yelling. Unmistakeably, his bowstring sang.

The lever came to an abrupt halt, nearly pitching Emaris into the wall of cogs. The light had stopped flashing, and the gate stood wide open. Now for the signal. He cast around the room till his gaze alighted on the pile of blankets. He seized one and, holding it on the end of his sword, stuck a corner of the mouldy fabric into the brazier until it curled, blackened, and started smoking. Then he ran to the window.

The feet had reached the landing. The knob squeaked, and the door rattled in its frame. Once more the goldenwood bow hummed. Someone hit the floor. Emaris thrust the smouldering blanket out the window, ignoring the sting of heat on his hands, letting the wind feed the fire. When the cloth was burning merrily, he drew back his arm and threw it as far as he could.

There was no room for error. He held his breath, hands slippery on the cold sill. Perhaps the flame had guttered out. Perhaps the rest of the company, drawn up in their lines far below the ringwall, had missed the signal. Perhaps they had all deserted. But just as he was going for another blanket, he saw it: an answering flare of light from the pass, swinging back and forth in regular arcs.

His knees went weak with relief. It had worked. Anyas was coming.

The door rattled again. Hiraen shouted, "Emaris!"

"I'm all right!" Emaris yelled. "I did it!"

He retrieved his sword and ran to unbolt the door. Hiraen tumbled through, his bow in one hand, an arrow in the other. Emaris had a brief glimpse of Mole and Barrelchest lying prone on the stairs, their throats feathered with orange. The three other men and the boy were trying to clamber around them. As he watched, Hiraen fitted the arrow to the string and shot again, and another guard went down.

"They're going to rush the door," said Hiraen, out of breath but otherwise quite calm. Fine droplets of blood speckled his gloves. "You've got your sword?"

"Yes," said Emaris, squaring his shoulders. "For once."

But before anyone could move, there was a resounding crash of wood on stone. The front door had flown open. Nikas and Daine appeared at the bottom of the stairwell, their own bows trained on the guards wavering on the steps. "Take cover!" Daine shouted.

Hiraen caught Emaris round the shoulders and thrust him bodily into the winch room. Staggering, Emaris saw him nock and draw again. Three bows hissed in unison. Nikas giggled. Then silence.

Emaris peeked onto the landing. All the guards were dead, the stairs a grisly landslide of bodies. The sudden quiet was deafening. From start to finish, the whole business must have taken less than twenty minutes. "All right?" said Daine.

Hiraen frowned, mostly at Nikas. He was looking at the corpse of the boy, the one Emaris had thrown down the stairs. There was an arrow through his heart. Sprawled among the bigger forms of the men, he looked terribly fragile, little more than a child, with features that could just as easily have belonged to any Cassaran. "I wish," he said, "you had let that one live."

Nikas was bent over Barrelchest, relieving him of a pair of ornate daggers. He shrugged. "Why? He would have thanked you for your mercy and then, if he had any honour, turned around and stabbed you in the back. You didn't start soldiering yesterday."

Emaris opened his mouth to say something, then shut it again. After a moment Hiraen said, "You and I have very different ideas about honour."

Times like these, he reminded Emaris very much of his own father. "But of course," said Nikas, owl-eyed. He flipped one of the daggers to Daine, who caught it in mid-air. "You've never been a slave. Or a thief. Or hungry."

"That's got nothing to do with anything," said Daine, but all the same he slipped the dagger onto his belt. To Hiraen he added, not ungently, "You're going soft."

"I'm really not," said Hiraen. He picked his way over the bodies without looking at any of them, leading the way downstairs. "Any sign of that bloody fucker?"

"Lord Silvertongue?" asked Nikas, as they all trailed after him. "No. They probably haven't caught him yet."

They were back in the common room. The table had been flipped upside down, the dice scattered on the rushes. "I'll look for him," said Hiraen. When Emaris moved automatically to follow, he added, "Alone."

"Can't I come?" asked Emaris, dismayed. "Savonn—"

"—wants you to look after Vion and those mad children," said Hiraen, grimacing. He nodded in the direction of the gate. By the sounds of it, Anyas had arrived. "Stay here."

Forestalling all protests, he stepped out the door and set off at a jog for the keep. Emaris could not help but think that Hiraen had just wanted to keep him out of further danger. At a loss, he gazed around at his companions: Daine, busy salvaging arrows, and Nikas, whose hands were full of rings and necklaces and other trinkets the guards would never need again. He had forgotten all about the new boys. He had also remembered something far more urgent.

"Nikas," he said. They only had the vaguest idea of what the man used to do in Sarei, but this sounded like something he would know. "They're expecting someone called the Empath. Have you heard anything about that?"

A gold chain slipped between Nikas's fingers to pool on the ground. He looked up, his loot clutched absently in both hands. "Who said so?"

"One of the dead guards," said Emaris. "Do you know the name?"

Nikas gave a slow, mordant smile. His face had lost some of its clownish aspect. "Yes," he said. "Yes. By the gods, everyone does."

CHAPTER 9

Light and noise spilled from the feast hall on the keep's second floor. Slurred voices were chanting a drinking song, though Savonn was not certain which one, as nobody seemed to know the lyrics; and someone was keeping time, very badly indeed, by crashing a goblet on a table. On the ground floor, a window near the back of the keep opened on a cavernous kitchen bustling with activity. Stoves lined one side of the room, smoking prolifically, while a woman in a greasy apron strode from one to another, stirring and prodding and turning over whatever was in each pan. Several children sat at a long wooden table behind her, chopping carrots and dicing potatoes. The air was redolent of delicacies: roast goose and gravy, chicken broth and buttered bread, cinnamon and nutmeg heated in wine.

Savonn was still standing there, computing portions and costs in his head, when loud singsong voices drifted round the corner from the inner courtyard. He deliberated, then hoisted himself onto the sill of the kitchen window and swung over.

Nursing a vat of soup, the cook did not notice him immediately. A boy looked up as he slouched past, took in his dirty shirt and patched trousers, and returned to his chopping. Savonn filched a handful of chickpeas from a bowl and started down the room, weaving around pots and crates and barrels. He had just passed the line of stoves when a door crashed open, and a round, frazzled man strode in.

"Ey!" The massive haunches moved, trundling the man down the length of the kitchen. "Ey! Cook! Is the goose done?"

Savonn got out of the way, removing himself to a niche between a basket of unpeeled onions and a cask of wine. He took in the man's yellowing cambric shirt with the sweat stains at the armpits; he savoured the bow-legged stride of the meaty calves, the curious mingling odours of good food and stale sweat, the thick syllables of the highlander patois, and filed these away for future use. An actor could never have too broad a repertoire. The incoming tornado bowled his way to the stoves and planted himself at the cook's elbow. "His lordship's wanting it at table now. Says there's no point saving it if the Empath's not coming tonight."

The Empath. A funny thing, to name oneself after a myth.

"It's not ready," said the cook. "Give it a moment, Shit-for-brains Mordel can wait."

The resulting outburst was quite colourful, and contained some swears that were new even to Savonn. "Easy for ye to say, dandyhead, when ye ain't the one he'll be raving at. How much longer?"

"A moment," the woman repeated stubbornly. "Take him some wine, that'll keep him happy."

Muttering, the man turned himself around thrice before he saw the cask next to Savonn, who was trying to chew and be invisible at the same time. Two big ringed hands appeared, tipped the cask on its side and began to roll it away. Then two eyes, cat-like and hysterical, landed on the bedraggled figure next to it. "Ey!" the man shouted, brandishing a fat index finger. "You! Take this up to his lordship Mordel. Must I do everything myself?"

The cook had already turned back to her stoves. Savonn dismissed the first five answers that came to mind, produced instead a mollifying stream of *yes, milords* and *no, milords*, and took over the rolling of the cask. It was heavy. He eased it out through the kitchen door, got it twelve feet down the hallway, and abandoned it in the first suitably dark corner he came across. Then he found a stairwell and began to climb.

He had stayed at Onaressi several times with Rendell, back when Betronett kept a garrison here. The feast hall on the second floor was exactly as he remembered it from three or four years ago, the long echoing room with the twelve fireplaces and their belching chimneys, the brass candelabra and the stout arched windows that looked down on the bubbling spring in the yard. The men ate, drank, and sang at trestle tables that filled the room from wall to wall, while the officers sat at a board on a low wooden dais, a good deal more sedate, though they seemed to have had their fill of the Midsummer feast as well. The one in the carved stone chair in the middle, with the stick-out ears and the alarming jowls, must have been Mordel. Savonn counted about three hundred in all, though there had been enough food in the kitchens to feed plenty more. They were awaiting someone who had failed to show. This Empath.

He left the hall and continued to the third floor. The hallway here was dark and draughty, with many doors that led into solars and officers' quarters. Nothing stirred: everyone had gone to the feast, leaving their rooms unguarded. At the end of the hall was the door that gave onto the biggest and most finely furnished chamber, which Captain Merrott had used once or twice. Now, Savonn guessed, this fellow Mordel had claimed it for his own.

The door was locked. He slid a pin from his sleeve and plied the lock until it gave. Then he went in and shut the door behind him.

The window admitted some measure of starlight, silvering the furniture with a ghostly hue: the desk strewn with papers, the chests of personal belongings, the old hunting tapestry conceal-ing a four-poster bed and a tall pine wardrobe. There was a small trapdoor in the ceiling above the bed, and a ladder tucked behind the wardrobe for access to the hidden loft. The gate towers, visi-ble from the window, displayed no symptom of the violent coup that must have been taking place right about then. His men were doing their jobs.

He had a few minutes to do his. No point worrying about his doe-eyed squire. The papers, first.

It was necessary to light a lamp, a risk he did not relish. The first few documents he went through were inventories, penned in a scribe's neat hand; he doubted Mordel himself could read or write. The tallies from the armoury and the kitchens were enough to make anyone go green. If all the other forts were similarly pro-visioned, he would have no need to worry about supplies all through this damnable campaign.

Every document was written in Saraian, but that in itself was not telling. Neither were the maps. Then at last he got to the bot-tom of the stack, and found the dispatch addressed to Mordel.

His orders were brief and cryptic. *Do nothing to arouse suspi-cion. No action is required on your part except to hold Onaressi and avoid angering Astorre. The Empath will come to relieve you by Mid-summer. From him you will receive the other half of your wages, with further instructions.* It was signed *Isemain Dalissos, Marshal of Sarei.*

Savonn knew the name. It was a grand one, belonging to the supreme commander of Marguerit's armies, by whom the Queen had begotten one of her four heirs. Lord Kedris had smashed him at the Morivant eighteen years ago, but both Isemain and his ca-reer had survived the defeat. In that case, who was the Empath, and what had delayed him?

The door gave a creak. Someone must have glimpsed the light from the window. Swiftly, Savonn tucked the letter into his tunic and extinguished the lamp.

"Ho!" said the tornado from the kitchen, filling the doorway with his bulk. His sweet-sour smell preceded him into the room. "Ho! Snooping around in his lordship's chambers, are we? What are ye after? Gold?"

Savonn was, indeed, after gold: the first half of Mordel's wages, likely still unspent, since there was nothing here to spend it on. While the man fulminated, he moved round the desk and glanced behind the tapestry. The gold would be in the loft, of course. He would need the ladder, and his pin again.

"Oh, no," said the man. "Oh, no, no running away for you, my little one. You got a lesson coming. You know what we do to thieves here?"

A dull thud. He must have stumbled over a chair in the dark. Savonn glanced back. The man had produced a switch of some smooth, whippy wood that he held like a flail, waving it back and forth as he advanced. "Are you deaf, boy? I said, do you know what we do to thieves here?"

"I heard you," said Savonn. He twitched the tapestry aside and began to drag the ladder out from behind the wardrobe. Any moment now someone would raise the alarm. "I shouldn't like to deny you the pleasure of showing me. Where *is* the gold? I'm a terrible thief."

The man's face twisted. A fist the size of a mace shot out and caught Savonn by the hair, forcing his head back. The switch descended on his cheek like a thunderclap. Not even pride could prevent him from flinching. "Insolent boy," said the man. His chest heaved with stertorious breaths. "We'll take ye to his lordship, for starters. He'll have ye whipped, that's for sure. Or worse. What do ye say to a night in the stocks, eh? What do ye say?"

In the kitchen, the man had seemed like a compelling character: the Bad-Tempered Steward on a Feast Night, for whom the Scared Scullion Boy might adopt large eyes and a stutter to weasel out of trouble. But now that he had laid hands on Savonn, the man was no longer interesting, only a tedious mishmash of unexciting features and reused mannerisms, the latest in a long succession of looming adversaries. In the household of Kedris Andalle touch meant anger, and anger meant violence. Savonn could not remember a time when he had not held this to be true. There was nothing to do now but get rid of this latest threat as efficiently as possible.

He switched to Saraian, and made his voice low and harsh. "He says nothing." If he kept his lips from moving, like a ventriloquist, the words seemed to come from everywhere in the dark room at once. "But *I* say, you shall not touch him. And if you do…"

Something crashed in the feast hall, saving him from having to invent a threat. The man startled back, letting go of both Savonn and the switch. His eyes bulged. It was then a simple matter of speed and dexterity to slide a knife from one's sleeve and plunge it into his chest.

The man gave a choked grunt. Savonn pulled the knife free. "Touch me again," he said, resuming his normal voice, "and I will strip the skin from your living fingertips."

A wordless gurgle. He was not Kedris, just an angry little man with a stick. Savonn wished, now, that he had not resorted to lethal measures. "You might also want to stop looking flabbergasted," he advised. "Quite unseemly, you see, once the rigors set in."

By the time he wiped the knife and put it away, the quality of the noise had changed. The music had stopped. People were shouting, and more crashes resounded as tables and benches were shoved out of the way. A solid mass of men was advancing across the lawn towards the keep, smooth as an oiled wagon. The bows of Betronett bristled on every shoulder. And to his irritation, someone else was approaching the room.

There was no time to get the trapdoor open. Taking a quick look around the room, he drew the curtain over the window and availed himself of the ladder. Then he began to climb.

A moment later Lord Mordel burst into the room, and an unsurprising sequence of events began to unfold. Emitting a stream of orders to the two servants with him, his lordship cut himself off to swear at how dark it was. One of the servants fumbled towards the lamp, tripped over something on the floor, and began to swear, too. Further inspection identified the object in question as the Bad-Tempered Steward, having recently suffered an acute case of knife-in-heart, and being quite dead.

"Milord!" the servant squawked. "It's Emmin, sir! He's murdered!"

But Mordel was not listening. He reached for his ladder, which was still leaning against the wardrobe, and made to pull it under the trapdoor. It did not budge. His eyes followed its length up and up, and widened.

"Hey!" he shouted. "Who the hell are you?"

Sitting cross-legged on top of the wardrobe, Savonn waited until all three pairs of eyes were on him. Falling into schoolroom Saraian again, he said, "You are awaiting a guest."

This was a situation that might go any number of ways, depending on Mordel's wits and temper, and whose reinforcements arrived first. Mordel's mouth opened and shut and opened again. He said, "The hell do you know about that? Is he—"

Savonn said nothing. A sneaking suspicion exerted itself in the lines of Mordel's face. "It's you? *You're* the—the Empath?"

The servant had finally reached the lamp. "What a state I find you in," said Savonn, as the wick kindled. "Feasting and drinking with your gate wide open, and strange men overrunning your lawn. Dearest Mordel. You have disposed of your command with such care."

Mordel's jowls unhinged. Of course he had never met this Empath any more than Savonn had. The world was full of stories of gods and demons and dragons, but one only had to go to a temple and ask any worshipper if they had ever met Aebria or Casteia to know if they were true. "I—"

119

"Let me guess," said Savonn. "You were just about to fetch your arms and armour to repulse the intruders?" By now swords were ringing in the courtyard. A horn was blowing, wild and desperate, calling the revellers to arms. "No, of course not. You were going to get your gold out of the loft and escape through the postern. Half your wages, yes?"

"Milord," said Mordel. He had switched from the mountain patois to something that approximated formal court speech. "No—that's not—"

"Such a pity," said Savonn amiably, "that you will never receive the rest of it now."

The door flew open a third time.

He was beset by a rib-racking urge to laugh. It was not Hiraen, as he had hoped. The newcomers were three men in mail, whose faces he recognised from the dais in the feast hall. The officers, here for their orders. Distracted, Mordel and the servants stared at them, and Savonn saw his chance.

He put his weight on the ladder and swung it off balance. It swayed and crashed down into the middle of his audience, taking him with it. A rung cracked Mordel on the forehead. Savonn's weight, arriving in the next moment, rammed him flat to the floor. The knife from his sleeve dispatched one of the servants; a well-placed foot took care of the other. The three officers yelled, and advanced on him.

"Impostor!" Mordel gasped, crushed beneath two inert bodies and the ladder. "Impostor! Seize him!"

Cornered, outnumbered, and rudely upstaged, Savonn did begin to laugh, and set himself to doing as much damage as possible. He ripped another knife from his sleeve and sent it flying into the first man's neck. The second he tripped. The third grabbed his arm and tried to pin him, and he careened backwards, slamming his shoulder into the man's body. The grip did not loosen. He trod hard on his captor's foot, annoyed. The fellow swore, hopping, and shoved him face-first onto the flagstones.

Then the second man, who had recovered, delivered a shattering kick to his side.

The sounds of fighting had reached the keep, echoing in the hallways below. "All right," said Savonn. "All right. I yield."

They wrestled him to his knees. It was going to be a long evening. "Check him for more knives," said the one who had kicked him. "He's stabbed three people already."

They patted his sleeves down, unearthing the pin, several matches, a vial of noisome green liquid he had won in a bet with an apothecary, and two more knives. "There's another in my shoe," said Savonn helpfully. "Left or right, I can't remember. And one strapped behind each shoulder."

They searched all the places he recommended, and found he was not exaggerating. "This little bastard's got more knives than surface area," said one man. An educated sort; his least favourite type of captor. "How's that possible?"

The noise was coming closer, surging up the stairs. Behind them, Mordel was moaning and making ineffectual attempts at getting up. "We ain't got time," said the other man, who still had Savonn's arm caught in a socket-jarring grip. "Just knock him out and—"

"What? And miss my pouch of diamonds?" asked Savonn. Out in the hall, someone was approaching at a run. "It's in one of my sleeves. They're a special kind, made from the tears of a phoenix and—"

"Savonn?"

It was the voice he had awaited; a good thing, because he did not, in fact, possess any diamonds. The men froze. "Oh, dear," he said. "Quite the after-dinner party, isn't this?"

"Savonn! Where in blazes are you?"

If he called back, they really would knock him out. "That's me," he said. "My friend's a stupidly good shot. You'd better tie me up and get behind me. I don't suppose you have any rope?"

They did not. They conferred briefly, and one of them went to unfasten the curtain cord. As soon as the fellow was out of reach, Savonn twisted around and bit the arm holding him down.

Hot blood filled his mouth. The man screeched. He tried to draw his sword, found he did not have enough hands, and released his grip on his prisoner. In an eyeblink Savonn had flung himself away, tittering with disapproval. Hiraen shouted, "Get down!"

He was already down. A bowstring hissed, and the man behind him hit the ground. "I yield, sir," said the other, waving the curtain cord like a banner of surrender. The bow twanged again, and there were no further sounds, save that of Mordel gasping.

Savonn got up carefully. "There is," he said, "always a certain relief in watching you walk into a room."

His cheek was smarting, and his side felt as if it had been staved in with a hot rod. "You missed the fun at the gate," said Hiraen. "Been busy?"

He had found Mordel, spitting half-conscious imprecations from where he lay. "That's the leader," said Savonn. "Don't kill him yet, I haven't questioned him."

"*That* one's no soldier," said Hiraen.

He was looking at the prone form of the Bad-Tempered Steward. The statement carried just the lightest hint of censure; or perhaps it was just that Savonn cared too much about what Hiraen thought, and always would. He said, "He touched my face."

A pause. In a much different voice, Hiraen said, "Oh."

Savonn turned away. None of his ribs appeared to be broken, so he retrieved his various implements and dragged the ladder over to the trapdoor. It was not hard to jimmy the lock. The way open, he climbed into the loft and found himself on a cramped platform under a slanting roof, too low for him to stand upright. He was surrounded by steel coffers that had clearly come a long way, dented and tarnished, but the locks still intact. He pulled the nearest box to him and picked that open, too.

"What's up there?" Hiraen called.

Savonn was silent at first, looking at the contents. He had known, and Kedris had guessed, but it was different seeing it for himself. The game had begun in earnest.

"Not much," he said. He picked up a handful of the stuff and tossed it down the ladder. "Just this."

Hiraen did not answer. All he heard from below was the clatter of coins against the flagstones, each one of new-minted gold, with the square-jawed profile of Marguerit of Sarei embossed front and back.

* * *

After a brief charge into tepid resistance, during which Emaris discovered to his astonishment that Vion and the other boys were not half bad with their swords, Onaressi fell once more into Betronett hands.

Sentries had been posted on the walls, and the dead piled in cairns—ten bandits for every one of theirs, Casteia be praised. Tired, bloody and ravenous, the men barged singing into the feast hall and sat down to the Midsummer banquet their enemies had abandoned. The servants lost no time making themselves pleasant to the conquerors, and neither did the cooks. None of the boys would shut up while they waited for the food to be served. "Did you see?" asked the tall one, who seemed to have imprinted on Emaris and taken to following him around like a duckling. "Did you see how I dislocated that fellow's jaw with the hilt of my sword? Broke it, perhaps." Then, perfunctorily, "My name's Lomas."

"I'm Vion," said the small one, as Lomas passed around the plates and cutlery. "You all know that. Where's the Captain, Emaris? I've still got his sunhat."

"I've no idea—"

"That's Emaris," interrupted Lomas for the benefit of the others. He jabbed a finger into Emaris's chest with the air of a dealer showing off a racehorse. "Savonn's told us all about you. He said you saved his life and your father was a great general and your sister showed you how to break a man's rib with a fork. Here's a fork. You can demonstrate on Vion."

Vion threw a goblet at his head. It hit him between the eyes with terrifying accuracy and clattered to the floor. "Give that back. Emaris, where are you going? Aren't you hungry?"

He was, but the thought of Savonn on the loose did not help his appetite. "I'm going to look for the Captain," he said. "Save something for me."

He found Savonn outside Mordel's quarters, leaning against the wall in the third-floor hallway. "There you are," said Savonn. Not one of his curls was out of place; and Emaris wondered, resentfully, if he had even done any fighting. "I was just beginning to wonder if you'd got yourself killed."

Having been abandoned by his commander mid-battle, Emaris was in a vindictive mood. "You shouldn't get your hopes up like that."

"It's my nature," said Savonn. "Why aren't you with Vion and his lot?"

Hiraen said something inside the room, and Daine laughed. There was a clang, and a jingle of coins spilling across the floor. A wave of familiar anger washed over Emaris. He felt rootless and displaced, and worse still, unwanted. "I helped you take the fort. Are you now telling me to go play with the little boys who sauntered in, sword in hand, when the hard part was done?"

He loathed the words as soon as he had spoken them. Savonn's eyes widened in mock concern. "Dear me. Were they so craven?"

It was too late to back down. From long practice, Emaris did not avoid the Captain's gaze. As with encountering a mountain lion, there were principles one followed when dealing with

124

Savonn Silvertongue: stand your ground, maintain eye contact, don't present your back. "No. They fought very bravely, insofar as there was anyone to fight. Since you don't seem to need me any more, perhaps I should squire for Hiraen instead."

He prepared to be flayed alive. But Savonn only squinted at him with his head canted, as if reading a page of extremely small print. "Perhaps you should. Hiraen will be flattered. But the candidates I handpicked for your patrol will be terribly disappointed."

Presently Emaris realised that his mouth had fallen open in unflattering stupefaction. He shut it, conscious of the needling eyes on him. "I haven't turned eighteen."

"I'm feeling fickle," said Savonn. "And I have a surfeit of small boys to dispose of. Is there a problem?"

Emaris said nothing. He had always imagined receiving the news of his promotion from his father. He gazed at the ajar door, the familiar sense of dread stealing over him again. Savonn gave him one of his unsettling, appraising stares, as if he knew what Emaris was thinking; then, with sudden briskness, pulled the door open and held it for him. "If not," he said, "I should like to introduce you to Mordel, erstwhile commander of Onaressi. He was just telling us how he has never met the Empath and hasn't the faintest clue who he, she, or they are. You haven't missed much."

"Nikas said—"

"I know what Nikas said."

Emaris walked in. The room was cluttered with heavy steel coffers. Nikas was sitting on one, sketching, with Daine clinking a handful of coins beside him. Hiraen had another open, making tally marks on a sheet of paper. Behind them was a middle-aged man with large ears, trussed up on the floor in a heap of ropes. Forcibly reminded of the questioning of the panhandlers, Emaris was in a mind to walk back out, but Savonn was getting in the way with all the skill of a lifetime's practice. "Go on, sir," he said. "Tell my squire what you told me."

The prisoner made angry noises of protest. "I'm not your squire," Emaris said, sitting on one of the coffers. "You dismissed me."

Savonn eased himself into the chair behind the desk, a trifle stiffly. "I promoted you."

"If you don't mind," said Daine, sending a coin spinning across the floor, "what *is* an empath?"

He was looking at Nikas, but Savonn answered. "A mythical being who senses feelings, and possibly has twelve eyes and a serpent for a tongue. They exist only in fairytales. So you see, I am very entertained, but not at all convinced."

"Then—"

"It's true," Mordel spat. He sported an enormous bruise on his forehead, but no other injuries as far as Emaris could see. "He never writes directly. Sometimes his lieutenants come and inspect the garrison, but they never speak of him. Not so much as a name. Trust me, I've asked. Methinks they're scared stiff."

He met a formidable silence. "I swear, I never killed your Governor," said Mordel, his voice splitting. "We even had orders to leave him alone. The Empath's courier told us that he'd been seen on the road to Medrai, but we weren't to lay hands on him, only make sure them horsemen from Betronett never joined him—"

"That was you!" cried Emaris. "You lamed our horses!"

Mordel shrank back from him. "Beg pardons, sir, but I'd lame them a hundred times over if it'd keep the Empath off my back. Men have disappeared, nay, whole *squadrons* have disappeared when he's mad. And he was very plain, see—his lordship's son wasn't to be there or else..."

Hiraen, who had been silent so far, looked at Savonn. Savonn returned the look with a belligerent arch of an eyebrow. Without glancing up from his drawing, Nikas said, "You are now addressing that son, who has an interesting temper. Tread carefully."

Mordel swallowed hard. "How did the Empath know we were coming?" asked Daine. "Word couldn't have gotten to Daliss and back so quickly."

"Not Daliss," said Mordel. "Astorre. He's Queen Marguerit's man, methinks, but he's based there. Or at least that's where his couriers come from." His face glistened with sweat. "I'm just a nomad tryna earn my keep, milord. I don't belong to no lord and no lord tells me nothing. I swear that's all I know."

"Really?" said Savonn. At the mention of Astorre, something had sharpened in his expression. "I see. We'd best not keep you any longer."

Mordel brightened. Frowning, Daine said, "The Council needs to see this fellow. And the gold, too—"

One never saw where the knives came from. One saw only a quick movement of the hand, a flash like a comet; and then one cried out and slumped dead, as Mordel now did. Daine's coins scattered, chiming across the floor. Emaris jolted bolt upright. "What was that for? Isn't this the proof the Council wanted?"

Hiraen scowled. "Did this one touch your face too?"

"He's too much trouble," said Savonn shortly. "The Council can have these dispatches instead, and a Saraian coin or two as a keepsake. I will require half the gold for supplies. The remainder we shall distribute to the men, to spend on food, drink, and attractive persons of extortionate tastes in Astorre. For," he said, "it seems we now have no choice but to go there." His eyes were like the points of his knives. "Why the dour faces? Where is the rejoicing?"

Nikas opened his mouth, received a loaded stare from Daine, and swallowed whatever he had been about to say. "Hurrah," said Hiraen. "I'm going down to the feast."

The door closed in his wake. They looked at one another. Then Daine shrugged and shuffled out after him. Nikas watched him go, his brows raised in a comic parody of fascination. "Well?"

said Savonn. Alarmingly, his gaze had come to rest on Emaris. "Aren't you joining them?"

Emaris was in no mood for feasting. Something potent had shivered through the room, something threatening, which he could not quite name. He could no longer remember why he had wanted to go to Astorre. But Savonn in such a mood was not to be gainsaid. Resigned, he got up and moved towards the door.

"Not you," said Savonn, as Nikas made to follow. "I want a word."

Emaris slammed the door between them, angry all over again. He was tired of being shut out. It was childish, he knew. But Savonn was being unjust, which was worse. So what if Nikas smiled a lot, and drew nice portraits, and did not mind killing people? Emaris had been with Savonn from the beginning, had left everything behind to follow him. One could at least do him the favour of telling him what was going on. No doubt his father would have done so.

He had begun to walk away, thinking that Vion and his friends might be better company, when Savonn's lackadaisical voice drifted through the door. "A night well spent. If this clown was telling the truth, we will soon have to fight your countrymen. I hope you are not prone to attacks of compunction?"

Glasses clinked. One of them must have been pouring drinks. "I thought I told you," said Nikas. "I was raised in Daliss, but my parents were Terinean slaves. Or my mother was, at least, Aebria rest her thrice-damned soul. The Saraians are not my country-men. I look forward to fighting them."

"I wonder why."

Curiosity having long since triumphed over anger, Emaris stopped in his tracks. Silence from within. Then—"I see," said Nikas. "I thought you wanted to ask about the Empath in private. Instead you are asking about me. I would have thought tonight's fight had proven me honest."

"It has," said Savonn peaceably. "Which alarms me. I distrust the honest."

"A common symptom among liars," said Nikas. The last word was gilt with mirth. "Why don't you like having your portrait drawn?"

"An excess of conceit. Why did you want me to go to Astorre?"

"I enjoy seeing a jewel in its natural setting. Why did you take me on if you don't trust me?"

"Because," said Savonn, in the honeyed timbres Emaris disliked, "I relish a good game. Because I am bored, and you are reasonably nice to look at. Because I wish to teach my squire a thing or two. By the way, I never suffer from the illusion of privacy. He is at the door now. Don't say anything scandalous."

Emaris flinched. His boot squeaked on the flagstones, more than loud enough to prove his presence. To his outrage, Nikas began to laugh. "Fair enough. You are a hard man to follow, milord... but of course you ought to know where I came from. I have told you a little of why I defected."

"Tell me more."

There was no point retreating now. Decency gave way to spite, and Emaris put his ear back to the door. "I have spent my whole life in the Sanctuary," Nikas was saying. "An odd name for an assassin cult, I realise. The god of death has a sense of irony. You *do* know him? The consort of Mother Alakyne, a deity so terrible no one has dared give him a name. Oh, I forgot. You are not religious."

"No," Savonn agreed. "And you have abandoned your god. Peas in a pod, aren't we?"

"I wouldn't say so," said Nikas. "By the time we are four or five, we know more ways to kill a man than numbers to count them with. When we are six, we are given a kitten to care for. When we are eight, we are made to slaughter it with our bare hands. Those who balk have the job done for them by the priests, over a number of days..."

A deadly quiet. Bile rose to the back of Emaris's throat. He was no longer hungry. "When we are ten, we duel a playmate to the death with all the skills we have acquired. Those who survive these trials receive their initiation into the cult, and are made full priests and priestesses of the Nameless Father. I," said Nikas, with audible loathing, "have received my initiation."

"I see," said Savonn. Even when one could see his face, it was difficult to tell what he was thinking. Now, with no cues except his modulated stage voice, it was impossible. "You ran away in search of a better life. I wonder if you have found it."

"Shall we put a finer point on it?" asked Nikas. "I ran away in search of my mother. I have not found her."

"Mothers," said Savonn crisply, "are a luxury, and fathers an affliction. It is best not to be sentimental about them. Tell me about the Empath."

Emaris had pressed himself nearly flat to the door. After what felt like a long time, Nikas said, "I thought you weren't interested in fairytales."

"I am not."

"Good," said Nikas. He had recovered his usual airiness. "Because this is not one. All Daliss has heard of him. The diviner who knows, unfailingly, what you are going to do before you do it. Who has saved the Queen's life over and over, sniffing out assassins by their fear and hatred long before they ever got close to her. They give him many names. The Empath. The Red Death. The King of Slaves. But all agree he is a man of surpassing wit, as beautiful as he is cunning, as brilliant as he is cruel. Very much," he added, "like yourself."

The pause this time was very long. Savonn said, "You know him?"

Nikas laughed. "You find it hard to believe that such a man exists, don't you? I heard about your choir of Ceriyes. You worship nothing and hold nothing sacred, not even the gods..."

Again, louder. "You know him?"

Emaris sucked in a breath and held it. "Yes," said Nikas. "Very well. He, too, is a servant of the Father. We trained together in the Sanctuary."

Glass chinked on wood, a loud, dissonant noise. Nikas was not laughing now. "He is real, my lord Captain. Though most people who meet him find themselves wishing he wasn't. Perhaps you will prove an exception."

A chair scraped back with brusque finality. The discussion was over. Savonn said, "We shall see."

CHAPTER 10

The death of a son was far from the only disaster that had befallen the Efrens in the last fortnight. Other strange things had happened, or so Linn said when she came round to the house with a pot of hot broth and a leg of ham for Shandei. One of their servants had been knifed in the marketplace. A shed had collapsed, near killing a groom. A basket full of writhing grass snakes had been upended on a maid's head as she passed under the window of an untenanted house. "And can you guess what else was in the basket?" Linn asked, spooning the broth into a bowl.

"What?"

"Roses." Linn dropped her voice conspiratorially. "There were roses on the scene of every accident. *Accidents*, I say, but we all know they aren't. The culprit left his signature, plain as day. The Rose Killer, people are calling him. Or the Thorn."

The broth curdled in Shandei's mouth. They said Vesmer's body had been scattered with roses dislodged by his fall, scarlet petals strewn beneath the bridge like a morbid benediction. "Do they think that—all these things—they were done by the same person?"

Linn shrugged, bustling off to cluck at the contents of the pantry. "Could be more. The Efrens have plenty of enemies. All rich people do. But if you ask me, with the luck he's having, Willon would be lucky to pluck off just one Thorn."

Willon did not need luck, Shandei thought. Not even brains. What one needed to catch a killer was money and power and a certain degree of bone-headedness, all of which the Efrens had in abundance. They had put the city under curfew for three days after Vesmer's death, arrested several people, interrogated them, and—at Lord Lucien's insistence—released them again. And she had noticed a great many unfamiliar people crossing and recrossing her street, staring for just a little too long at her house. *The killer is at large*, their faces seemed to say. *The killer is here.*

"Well, no one's surprised," Linn was saying. "The old man still means to be Governor, and not everyone's happy about that. I for one am not. You wouldn't happen to have the stink of roses about you, my dear?"

Shandei spat out her broth and looked up sharply. Linn was smiling. It was just a joke. But surely her blood feud with the Efrens was common knowledge; surely everyone knew the Ceriyes must be with her. If she had prayed Vesmer dead—if she was responsible for his death—did it mean she was responsible for all the rest?

Willon might think so. And sooner or later, he would be upon her.

* * *

It was in this state of mind that she went to the Temple of the Sisters to be purified for Midsummer.

The Temple was a tall, narrow building behind a once-white fence swarming with creeping vines. One could judge the piety of the present rulers from the décor. Raedon Sydell, a devout man, had furnished the High Priestess with a sizeable income, only for

Kedris to divert it all to his gardens as soon as he came to office. This left the Temple appointed in a style fashionable two generations ago, with arched bay windows that always seemed dark no matter how many candelabra were lit, and ornate stone balconies ponderous as battlements. The walls were painted a garish gold, the windows and doors offset in crimson. The courtyard was tiled with slate, spotted with small patches of yellowing grass. It was as if nature itself feared the goddesses, and dared grow nothing here.

Today the grounds were thronged with people. Devotees queued all the way out through the temple doors, across the courtyard and beyond the gate, waiting to be purified lest they carry their guilts and misfortunes with them into the new year. Shandei had to wait over an hour before she reached the front of the line, where an acolyte in pure white robes ushered her through the doors. She was led up a sweeping marble stair and down a gallery overlooking a gloomy terrace, and thence into the hall where the goddesses dispensed their blessing on—or withheld it from—their supplicants.

Coming in, the altar always struck one into an awed stillness. The Sisters were never depicted separately, for the daughters of Mother Alakyne manifested hand in hand. Their stone likenesses towered over the hall, twelve feet tall and terrible in majesty: Aebria the younger, Goddess of Sorrow, in a mourning robe and veil; Casteia the elder, Goddess of Strife, armed in mail and carrying a spear. Their carnelian eyes shone red in the light from the altar candles. In silence, Shandei crossed the hall, stopped the proper number of paces from the altar, and knelt on the cool flagstones.

She was alone. That was odd. On festive days like this, the priestesses were known to bless five or six supplicants at once. The hall smelled of incense, of the myrrh and sandalwood and other precious things that smouldered on the altar. There were no windows. It was quiet here, far from the crowd that thronged

134

the lawn, and the heavy air cloyed in the passages of Shandei's nose and throat.

Then a creak fractured the strange, perfumed hush, and she lifted her bowed head half an inch to peek.

A door had opened behind the altar. For a moment it looked onto an abysmal darkness. Then a gargoyle head protruded from the crack, wizened and prune-like, topped with stringy tufts of white cottony hair. It jerked this way and that as if worked by ill-maintained machinery, filmy black eyes staring out of the withered face. Then the waxen stalk-neck retracted, taking the head with it. As Shandei stared, decorum quite forgotten, the door came open all the way and a small stooped figure tottered out.

She stood about four feet tall, maybe five if one straightened out her back with a bonesetter's hammer. Her robes were a motley of colours, tassels and frills, as if some deranged tailor had tried to sew a rainbow into a mockery of a wedding dress. They hung from her scarecrow frame like a curtain on a fence-post, fabrics rustling and hissing as they slithered across the floor in her wake. A necklace of enormous pearls dangled almost to her waist. She paused within arm's reach of Shandei, and the viperine eyes drank her in with unwholesome thirst.

"Daughter," she said. The rasp was like the scrape of a sword on a whetstone, with an odd singsong quality. "Come ye to be purified?"

Belated recognition came to Shandei, rapidly followed by amazement. This must be the High Priestess herself. Shandei had glimpsed her once, presiding at a Midsummer play from her palanquin many years ago—one that she remembered with pristine clarity, because her mother Serenisa had been there on a rare visit, so her father's smile shone like the sun. But she had been very small then, and Emaris only a toddler, and since then the High Priestess had grown older than she thought possible. The woman must have been at least a hundred. Perhaps a hundred and ten.

"Yes," she managed. "Your Holiness."

A desiccated hand, like a winter branch, emerged from one capacious sleeve and stretched its long fingers towards Shandei's face. She felt the curious urge to jump back and climb on a chair, like the neighbour's children did when there was a spider in the house and she was called in to remove it. She forced herself to hold still, even as the dry fingertips with their yellowing nails brushed against her cheek. "Oh!" cried the crone, withdrawing her hand as if scalded. "This one! The righteous fire, the unrighteous vessel!"

Her heart sank. "My name is Shandei," she said. "Daughter of Rendell."

"I know your name," sang the Priestess. "I have seen you in my visions. My pious, violent daughter. Even now your father's dagger is in your sleeve."

This time she had not given herself away with her eyes. How on earth could the old woman have known that? But of course, she was a servant of the goddesses, and was privy to more than earthly knowledge. Shandei said, "Vengeance is my right."

"Vengeance!" The shriek was piercing. "The Ceriyes are thirsty. But they will not drink blood from your idler's hands."

She had given them blood. She had delivered Vesmer Efren into their hands, or they into hers. Or had she? Who had been that spectre on the bridge? A drunken passer-by who would pick a fight with a guardsman and send him plummeting to his death, or a spirit of vengeance she had called down on an innocent youth only to hurt his father? If the latter, what did that make her?

"From whose hands will they drink, then?" she asked. Her voice was shaking again. All these disasters, and still her father's shade wandered unavenged. "My brother's? Holiness, where shall we find the killer?"

A choking noise emanated from the mummified throat, like a saw on wood. This time she could not arrest her physical recoil. It was a moment before she realised that the crone was laughing,

136

but not in mirth. "Emaris?" the old woman asked, the syllables of the name made hoarse and grating. "He has absconded with that devil child of a devil father, on whom the gods do not smile. Idler's hands! Is that why you are here? To seek absolution for him?"

Shandei drew a long, shaking breath. "No. I have come to be purified for Midsummer. That is all."

The Priestess distended her lips into a smile, revealing a mouth full of small brown teeth, crooked and overcrowded. "Yes. Why not? A little incantation, a little sprinkling of water. Then blood shall be washed away and your wrongdoings made clean. Or so one supposes."

She regarded Shandei with her cold black eyes, and slithered back into the dark room from whence she had come.

It was another priestess, this one much younger, who came to purify her. After all that, the ceremony was over almost at once: the priestess laid a hand on her head, and murmured the invocation that would cleanse her of Aebria's grief and Casteia's rage and enfold her once more to the Mother's bosom. Water from the altar, warm and sweet-smelling, was sprinkled in her hair. The deities having been propitiated, the priestess kissed her brow and bade her go.

It was like climbing out of a mine. After the drenching of incense, the fresh air was shocking as a cold bath. The noonday sun was so brilliant that Shandei, walking down the gallery outside the hall towards the distant rumble of human voices, flung up a hand to shield her watering eyes. Down the marble stair, across the landing, through the front hall. A passing acolyte stared at her, then hurried away with her head down. Shandei had just reached the temple doors when they swung open, and a group of women came in.

In later days, out of the jumble of memories that constituted that year's Midsummer Eve, that moment would take on disproportionate significance to her mind, acquiring a vivid, underwater quality like something out of a fever dream. It took her several flustered heartbeats to recognise Iyone Safin, who was taller up close, and younger than Shandei had thought. She stood among her attendants, statuesque in shades of amber and bronze, hair coming loose from its bun to frame her face in artless chestnut waves. "Lady Shandei?" she said.

A pair of acolytes ran up to them, looking displeased, but at Iyone's sharp look they fell back again. Her sleeves were rolled up nearly to the elbow, as if for work, though the hands were smooth and unblemished. Shandei felt weak and heavy-headed. Her tongue tied itself into knots, then unravelled altogether. "That's me. What—if I might—milady has need of me?"

Flint-grey eyes regarded Shandei's face, dipped to her feet, and rose again. Distantly, Shandei was aware that the chatter drifting in from the courtyard was no longer desultory. The supplicants had drawn together in twos and threes, muttering. Some stared openly at Shandei; others had left the line altogether to peer out towards the street. "Oh, nothing of import," said Iyone. "I've just witnessed an accident involving a bridge and two unpleasant men, and I thought it my pious duty to inform the priestesses that some of their devotees may be a little... delayed." Her eyes glinted. "What a pleasure to meet you. I was sorry to hear about your father."

Shandei glanced at the throng of people in the yard. Her palms were beginning to perspire. "If I may ask—what accident, your ladyship?"

"Iyone. Please." She turned around and walked back through the doors, and without thinking, Shandei fell in step next to her. Heavy stares followed them across the courtyard, the thought behind them nearly audible. *There she goes, that idler with no schooling and no money, taking up with a councillor's daughter. Whatever next?* "The Carnation Bridge performed an admirable curtsey while Lord Willon and Lord Yannick were passing beneath it on their way here. Judging by the yelling I heard, Lord Willon at least suffered no hurt to his lungs and vocal apparatus, but one never knows. The Efrens have had such execrable luck this week."

Under Iyone's purposeful look, Shandei's mouth went dry. *Oh, Mother. I was nowhere near him.* They had reached the street, full of people talking at the top of their lungs, though no one seemed to know what had happened. The bridge in question was out of sight behind the citadel, a couple of streets away. Shandei started towards it, but Iyone's hand closed around her wrist, surprisingly strong, and drew her to the side of the road. "Elysa. Take the others and find out what happened."

The tone of command was undeniable. One of the maids, a stout older woman with flyaway grey hair, nodded and hurried off with the other attendants. Iyone turned back to Shandei, who was conscious of nothing but the man's life on her conscience and the woman's hand on her arm. "Go home," said Iyone, in the same peremptory voice. "Go around the temple and use the back way. Don't pass the bridge, don't stop to talk to anyone."

Shandei might have swallowed sawdust. "I don't understand."

Iyone's eyes were no longer laughing, though they retained their jewel-like crispness. "Really? Have you heard nothing about Lord Willon's mysterious ill-wisher? The Thorn?"

"I didn't—" She tripped over the half-truth. Iyone had yet to release her. "I don't know anything about that bridge. Or the servant who got stabbed, or—or any of the other things."

"What you know is irrelevant," said Iyone. "As a matter of fact, *I* know you did nothing to the bridge, because I have had you followed since the rumours began. Yes," she added, seeing Shandei's expression. "High-handedness is a bad habit of mine. Anger is perfectly within your rights. However, consider this: yours is the first name people will attach to these *accidents* once they start thinking hard enough. Regardless of your guilt or innocence, you are in spectacular danger."

Shandei had begun to realise that this run-in with Iyone was no coincidence. Suddenly dizzy, she said, "Maybe I *am* the Thorn. You wouldn't know."

"It doesn't matter one whit to me," said Iyone. Her grip was patient and steady. "The Efrens are nothing. I don't know you. I am trying to help you because my brother feels responsible for your family. You may take or leave my advice. That advice is to go home now, quickly, and stay there until I call on you again."

Shandei released a shaky breath. "Are you a friend?"

"As someone I know would say," said Iyone, with a double-edged smile, "that is a matter for philosophers. I am going to see if Lord Willon needs rescuing. Do what you will."

With a finality just short of bereavement, Shandei felt the hand withdraw from her arm. The crowd swallowed Iyone in its midst, and she was alone again.

She gathered her nerves, and did exactly as Iyone suggested.

CHAPTER 11

To Iyone's disappointment, Willon Efren was alive, unhurt, and in a towering rage.

The bridge had not fallen in. A strut had merely come loose from where it had been abutted on the roof of a tavern, crushing two servants in the Efrens' train. Willon and Yannick were unhurt. Nobody had been killed, though one would not know it from the impressive bluster to which Willon treated the entire street, and the swoon into which Yannick fell. It took Iyone a quarter of an hour to disperse the crowd and convince the injured parties to take their histrionics indoors. She did not miss, and did not comment on, the rose petals drifting among the fallen carnations on the road.

Afterwards she collected her father and mother at the manor, and went with them to pay the Efrens a visit. Yannick had his own house and lands, but at present he was propped up on a daybed in Willon's sitting room, palpitating under three blankets. "We could have been *killed*!" he said, over and over again. "Willon, for heaven's sake, must they kill us all before you give up?"

"Ask her," said Willon, scowling across the daybed at Josit, who had just arrived. "Your bridge almost killed us, your ladyship. We could take this to the magistrates."

Josit glanced up, and caught Iyone watching her. Her voice was debonair with boredom. "I have already filed a civil suit with the magistrates. The tavern roof was ill-maintained, and my freedmen would have been in grave danger when they went up to tend the carnations. I have hopes," she added, "of an exorbitant compensation."

As Willon started to argue, Iyone removed herself to join her mother at the window, so recently curtained in mourning black. Lady Aretel narrowed her eyes, keen as a panther. "Josit tells me you ran into this girl Shandei at the temple today."

Iyone's brows shot up. "Did she? How did she know?"

Aretel ignored the question. "Why the sudden interest in this young lady?"

As far as Aretel knew, her daughter only ever paid attention to comely blonde women for one reason, and it was not the goodness of her heart. It was best not to disabuse her of her theory. The truth, or what Iyone knew of it, was far less palatable. She still dreamt too often of Hiraen's exhausted, pleading face from the rainy night in the colonnade. "I don't prey on mourning orphans, Mother. Where's Oriane?"

Aretel never missed a change of subject, but this time she let it slip. "At home. She sent her sympathies and a bottle of wine. They say she's been afraid to go near the Efrens since Vesmer's funeral."

It was difficult to imagine Oriane being afraid of anything. "What happened?"

"Nothing, except she got home after the burial and found a white rose on her pillow. The long-stemmed sort, the kind you lay at gravestones. No doubt it was meant as a threat."

"Oh, dear," said Iyone absently. Her thoughts were already elsewhere, trying to make sense of this new riddle. "Lord Willon's supporters are melting away one by one. How unfortunate."

Her mother frowned. Yannick chose that moment to start wheezing above Willon's querulous voice, and Iyone turned back to the group sitting around his sickbed. "I told you a hundred times it's the girl," he was saying. "The one who fancies you murdered her father. I *told* you to have her put away."

"That rude little thing?" asked Willon, screwing up his face in distaste. "What was her name again? Shiera? Shayna?"

"Shandei," said Iyone, though no one had asked her. Willon's head snapped up, as if he had just remembered that she was there. "I was with her at the temple today. If she induced any bridges to fall on you, I didn't notice."

Aretel had interposed her restraining presence at Iyone's side. Yannick frowned. "Her brother took up with the Silver-tongue. And *he*, we know beyond doubt, has a vendetta against us."

"I thought we were done with Savonn and his imaginary plots," Lord Lucien grumbled. "By now the boy will be deep in the Farfallens with all his supporters. How, precisely, is he supposed to have done this?"

"Voodoo?" Iyone suggested, favouring Willon with an icy smile. "Sorcery? When one discards logic, after all, the possibilities are endless."

Willon stared at her with a mixture of consternation and disgust, as if a brightly coloured snake had crawled over his foot. "Perhaps," he said, looking back at her father, "not all the Silver-tongue's followers were brave enough to follow him into the mountains. Some few—the weak, perhaps, or the battle-shy—must have stayed behind."

The unspoken insult was plain. Her father's voice swelled by several magnitudes. "Look here—"

Josit said, "The girl Shandei does have a blood feud. She takes it seriously."

Several beats of silence met this pronouncement. Yannick gave Willon a meaningful look. Lucien glanced at Iyone, then at her mother. Josit took a sip from her glass and settled back in her chair, placid and disinterested.

And she could afford to be. As plots went, this one was masterful. Foolproof, even. Shandei was the perfect scapegoat for anyone working to further Savonn's interests. One only need suggest her name, and let the Efrens' paranoia do the rest. It was, like everything else about Josit, terribly elegant.

"She does," said Iyone, after a brief moment's thought. This did not have to be painful. She had always wanted an excuse to match wits with her tutor head on—even if the circumstances were, thanks to Hiraen, a shade less than ideal. "But these disasters have befallen everyone in Lord Willon's periphery except Lord Willon himself. My lord has been frightened but not hurt. If filial revenge is the Thorn's goal, she is failing hilariously."

Yannick frowned. "Also true."

Iyone turned her smile on Josit, who returned it like the Sphinx, small and unfathomable. "Observe, however," she went on, "that she has done a marvellous job preventing poor Lord Willon from becoming Governor. It appears there are many people who share this motive."

"Lucien," said Willon, ignoring her, "I wish you would prevent your ill-mannered dependents from barging into Council meetings. It's extremely rude."

Lucien shrugged, pouring Yannick a fresh glass of hot brandy. "This isn't a meeting. Iyone just wanted to reassure herself that you and your good cousin were uninjured."

"Did she?" asked Willon, aggrieved. "Then why was she…"

He stopped. Then he jerked his chair round to look at Iyone properly. "Why were *you* with Shiera? Shayna? Why were you there when the bridge collapsed?"

Aretel stepped forward. On the verge of laughter, Iyone shut her mouth before her mother could tell her to do so. Her father, less amused, put down the brandy bottle with a loud chink. "Willon," he said, "are you quite sure you wish to make that implication in front of me?"

"Well, it's hardly far-fetched!" Willon exploded. "Yannick and I are being terrorised. Even Oriane's been threatened. Only your family seems to be safe from this Thorn. Doesn't it strike you as the least bit suspicious?"

Into the deafening quiet, Iyone said, "There's also Josit." She produced a virtuous curtsey. "I'm leaving now."

* * *

The Council took a long time dispersing, held back as always by parting gripes and insincere niceties. Iyone wandered out onto the lawn to wait. Rearing above the sculpted hedges out here was a sleek alabaster centaur, larger than life, familiar from her childhood. She and Hiraen and Savonn had often trailed their parents to some interminable function at the Efrens', and been shooed out by the adults to play in the garden. She was tall enough now to reach up and brush her fingers over the uneven place where once—during a particularly endless supper—they had taken turns to climb the plinth and scratch their initials into the centaur's flank. Hiraen, the oldest and boldest of them all, had gone first, clutching the sharp pebble Savonn had produced from somewhere about his person. Then, while Savonn stood a giggling watch below, he pulled Iyone up beside him and kept a steadying hand on her shoulder as she carved her name with her tongue between her teeth.

That was just like Hiraen, she thought. Protector, defender, leader of the van, loyal to a fault even if it cost him the seams of his own soul. She would have to find a way to untangle this calamity he had wrought.

145

A foot scraped on the grass behind her. She turned and saw, without surprise, that Josit had followed her from the house.

They gazed at each other, alone with Willon's leafy potted plants and the centaur's disapproving stare. "So," said Josit presently, "you have appointed yourself Shandei's advocate. I take it you enjoyed her company today?"

She moved round to the centaur's far side, where they were less likely to be overheard from the porch. Iyone followed her. "Very much," she said. "As you already know, since you are spying on me. Which of my servants is in your pay? Elysa?"

Josit laughed, fluid and melodious. The mirth was genuine. "I wouldn't ruin your sport by telling you."

It was inconvenient that Josit knew Iyone so much better than she knew Josit. She said, "Shandei is determined to find her father's killer."

"And," said Josit, "we both know it wasn't Willon."

Popular opinion held that Iyone Safin had never in her life been afraid. Even Savonn half subscribed to this belief. That it was patently untrue was known only to herself and Josit. She forced a steadying breath into her lungs. "She thinks you're being kind."

"I have told her," said Josit, "that justice is not kindness. And you know, better than most, that kindness is not necessarily just." Whatever betrayed itself on Iyone's face made her smile. "Don't grow attached to your pawns, Iyone dear. It makes for bad chess."

Adrenaline made Iyone vicious. "Are we talking about chess? You think you're playing against those old men. But if you use this frivolous, defenceless girl in your schemes, you are playing against me. And I tend to win."

Behind them, Willon and her parents had emerged on the porch, trying to smooth over their argument with small talk. "She is hardly defenceless," said Josit. "Though, admittedly, rather unwilling to kill... A good thing I had her followed the night she confronted Vesmer."

"And he had to die," said Iyone, "just so you could strike a blow against his father?"

Josit made a helpless gesture. "There is nothing to twist a parent's heart like the death of a child."

Willon and the others were drawing closer. Without lowering her voice, Iyone said, "I didn't know you'd had children."

She watched Josit's eyes. They flicked to the side, judging the distance between them and the approaching group. Willon was discoursing loudly, frequently interrupted by both her father and mother, and it was not likely they had been overheard. But the damage was done. Weakness had been revealed. And weakness, deftly handled, offered leverage.

Josit recovered quickly. "One can't know everything," she said. "Will you take some advice from your old tutor? Have a care for yourself, and stay away from the girl. It will be terribly sad if you end up on the gallows together."

"I take advice from no one," said Iyone.

Fear was impermissible. She stalked over the lawn to join the others, and did not turn around, though the quizzical, laughing gaze burned between her shoulderblades for a long time.

CHAPTER 12

A few days away from Astorre, it became evident that the Betronett force was not alone.

Their course from Onaressi had been rambling and oblique. They left Anyas to hold the fort with a hundred men, which was as much as Savonn would spare him, and struck off into the wilderness west of Forech's Pass, where half a dozen smaller forts stood. Most, like Onaressi, had been occupied by squatters claiming to be anything but Saraians. These they drove off. It was simple if tedious work, and Savonn took his time, making each skirmish a game and a lesson for the recruits. Their numbers were down to three hundred by the time they garrisoned each fort and returned to the Pass, and between fighting and training, Astorre had begun to take on a mirage-like sheen in Emaris's mind.

He had gone to scout ahead one afternoon with some of the boys Savonn had foisted on him. The Pass wound through a treeless ravine scoured by little streams, the short grass speckled with patches of slippery ice that glistened in the shadows under the overhangs. They trudged along the dense undergrowth on the overlooking bluff, all on foot, since they had left their horses and wagons with Anyas. Emaris rubbed his chin absently. None of them had been near a razor since Onaressi, and his scratchy stubble was fast developing into an even scratchier beard. "Does anyone think," he said, "that the grass down there looks a little flattened?"

"Can't tell," said Lomas. He had blown his nose eight times in the last hour, and it was turning an interesting carmine. "All I see is frost. It's devilry, it is, to see frost in summer. It better be warm in Astorre."

"It is," Vion piped up. "They channel hot geyser water under their streets and through the walls of their houses, so it's warm all year round. And everybody is rich, and the theatres are roofed with gold, and all the playwrights are drunk on absinthe."

A disbelieving chorus of challenges arose. Usually the boys accepted whatever Vion said as fact, because he had been to school, and his parents were much-travelled cartographers. That he had been raised a girl called Evione was also well-known, but no one's business. "In the choir," said another boy, Klemene, who had been one of Savonn's singing Ceriyes, "they say the Captain had a lover in Astorre. A foreigner. But either he died, or Savonn left him."

Rougen tugged at Emaris's sleeve. He never spoke, though word was that he could hear an acorn fall on the other side of a wood. No one took notice. "That's just hearsay," said Lomas dismissively. "He's made of ice, the Captain. He probably eats men alive."

Rougen prodded Emaris in the side. "It's true," Klemene insisted. "Isn't it, Emaris?"

"No," said Emaris tartly. In fact he had no idea and did not care. "What is it, Rougen?"

But there was no need for an answer. In a moment, as they fell silent, they all heard it themselves: the unmistakeable sound of laughter, floating up to them from the ravine.

No one spoke. They knew better than that by now. Emaris took a quick look around, and motioned them to follow him.

149

He picked his way across a crag of glistening basalt rocks, avoiding the grass, which might rustle and give them away. Below, several voices bantered in playful argument, and something—a harp? a lute? Savonn would know—tinkled a lively song. Whoever it was, they were making no effort to be quiet. Emaris stopped several paces from the overhang, dropped onto his stomach, and wriggled towards the edge.

Here the cliff was less steep, and a goat path wound across the rocks down to the ravine, where a company of about twenty— both men and women—had stopped for a meal by a stony brook. He had hoped they were merchants. But they were plainly soldiers, and no meanly paid ones at that. Each of them had a tall cornelwood spear, and their cuirasses were polished and well-fitting. One of the men was perched on a boulder in the middle of the group, playing a lute. Several knobbly ponies grazed around them, their saddlebags heavily laden.

The words that drifted up to Emaris were Saraian. Even in the cold air, beads of perspiration broke out on his forehead.

The others had joined him on the ground. Silently, Lomas nudged him and motioned to the lute player, his eyes wide. Emaris saw why. Next to the man leaned a longsword in a scabbard richly worked with gold and amber, encrusted with enough rubies to ransom a prince. He must have been the leader. His hair, long and auburn, was bundled back from his tanned brown face in a careless knot, and from his shoulders fell a cloak that was sable on the outside, scarlet on the inside. Emaris did not know the song he was playing, but he recognised skill when he heard it.

Twenty soldiers. The bandits at Onaressi had seemed to think an army was coming. Where was the rest of it? Lurking in the barren wilds above the Pass, probably. Or lying in wait to bar the route to Astorre. His heart stuttered at the thought. Savonn had to be told. Even now, they could be blundering into a trap.

The music stopped. The leader got up and laid the lute aside, moving to the edge of the group. The others were still eating, laughing and swearing at one another over heels of bread and skins of wine. The lute player paused by one of the donkeys to rub its nose, then cupped his eyes with a hand and gazed up and down the ravine, his burnished hair shining red-gold in the afternoon light.

Emaris flattened himself to the ground. The others imitated him. The angle of the overhang would hide them from below, as would the glare of the westering sun. The lute player said something; a command, by the sounds of it. For no reason that Emaris could discern, the laughter ceased.

Cautiously, he peered into the ravine again. The redhead had resumed his seat. Five of the soldiers, grumbling, put their food aside and fetched their spears. Then, to his horror, they started up the goat track towards the overhang.

On his right Vion, ash-pale, mouthed, *What now?*

Emaris scrambled to his feet. "Run!"

Klemene was off like a sprinter from the starting post, dragging Rougen behind him. Vion and Lomas scuttled after them. Emaris brought up the rear, yanking an arrow from his quiver as he picked his way across the crag. The lute was tinkling again. A jagged column of rock stood out on the overhang like a leaning pillar. He ducked behind it, nocking his bow. As soon as the foremost of their pursuers came into view—a big, grizzled man with a javelin—he drew and released the bowstring.

The javelin struck the rock an inch from Emaris' temple. His arrow hit the man in the thigh, and he went down, roaring. Two others came up behind him. Emaris nocked again, saw in his mind the perfect arc of Hiraen's orange-plumed arrow under the ringwall of Onaressi, and loosed. Another soldier went down. But the last two had gained the overhang, and now they were three against one.

"Out of the way!" someone yelled.

Emaris ducked. Vion had appeared with the fallen javelin, which overtopped him by about three feet. Before Emaris could ask what he thought he was doing, he wound back his arm and threw.

His technique left him flailing on one foot with the force of the throw, but his aim was true. The javelin plunged squarely into the neck of the closest pursuer. Then there was a yowling cry, and Lomas burst out from the other side of the rock column and bowled over the remaining two, slamming their heads against the ground. He had not, Emaris noted with vague disbelief, even drawn his sword.

No one else came after them. Impossibly, the lute was still playing.

Shaken, they dispatched the soldiers—three men and two women—with their daggers. Klemene and Rougen were waiting at the edge of the basalt outcropping, looking astonished to see them alive. Klemene yelled, "I thought we were done for!"

"I think that redhead let us escape," said Vion, still panting. He glanced over his shoulder, as if he thought to find the Saraians hot on their tail. "He just wanted to frighten us. Right, Emaris?"

The Red Death, Nikas had said. Emaris could not answer. His stomach was churning. "We were quiet," said Lomas, rubbing a bruised jaw. "I'd swear we never made a sound. How the hell did they hear us?"

"Maybe," said Emaris slowly, "they didn't."

With a sinking heart, he realised this was not an explanation Savonn would accept.

* * *

"I told you," he was saying two hours later, when they got back to camp. "We were careful. You taught me how to scout properly. You could at least believe me when I say we didn't pick a fight on purpose."

Savonn had been in a queer temper since Onaressi. His voice was the lethal, silky one they all dreaded, and his smile was edged like a diamond. "So careful," he said, "that you brought five Saraians down on your heads and left behind fifteen others who now know we are here."

"We took care of it," snapped Emaris. He was standing before Savonn in the Captain's tent, while Hiraen and Nikas gave him commiserating looks over the map they were studying. "I shot two myself and my patrol did for the rest. What were we supposed to do, kill the lot of them?"

"To get away unseen would have sufficed," said Savonn. "Courage, as a rule, does not make up for incompetence. On the contrary, it tends to exacerbate it."

"All right," said Emaris, nearly beside himself. "Henceforth I shall be both cowardly and incompetent. Whatever will you do next time you're attacked in a deserted street?"

He fancied, for a moment, that Savonn's eyes widened fractionally. "This man with the lute," said Nikas, with a sidelong glance at the Captain. "He glimpsed you? Heard a footfall, perhaps?"

"No," said Emaris hotly. "They made enough noise to cover a riot. The fellow never even looked up. He was still playing his bloody lute when we ran off." He drew a deep breath. "We think he's the Empath."

"Oh," said Savonn. "I suppose he heard the clarion-call of your righteous rage? Now, of course, we have to break camp and march to Astorre another way, in case your mythical siren has followed you back here. It will be cold and dangerous and if anyone complains I shall point them to you."

He was already at the tent flap. Seething, Emaris swung round to follow him. Mortification made him bold. "Nikas told you he was real. And now I've seen him. Why won't you believe it?"

"Because," said Savonn, "superstition is for children. As are angry outbursts. Control yourself."

153

He stalked out. Presently Nikas got up, bright-eyed and thoughtful, and went after him. "It's not fair," said Emaris to their receding backs, aware that he sounded as juvenile as Savonn claimed.

"If it matters," said Hiraen, stirring from his seat near the brazier, "I believe you."

Emaris looked at him. One could tell things to Hiraen. He would listen, and if he laughed, it would not be in scorn. "We were afraid," he said. The words tumbled out in a rush. "I was sweating, and imagining all the places his army could be lying in wait, and that's when he gave the order to go after us. As if he sensed it. Our... our fear."

Outside, Daine was yelling orders to break camp. Hiraen shrugged. It was a careless gesture, but his eyes were searching, as they so often were when he looked at Emaris these days. "The world is full of oddities. Being one himself, Savonn knows this. You mustn't take it personally. He's been in quite the mood these last weeks." He rose, rolling up the map. "If you will believe it..."

"What?"

"He's upset," said Hiraen, "because he doesn't want to go to Astorre. He made a mistake there once." He smiled ruefully. "And I keep reminding him about it."

* * *

They turned away from Forech's Pass that evening and began their ascent into the steep peaks that lay between them and Astorre. The threadlike track they followed was serpentine and precipitous, passing over sheer drops into shadowed valleys and disappearing here and there under slick patches of hoarfrost. The wind howled like a pack of hungry wolves, and not long after dark, a dusting of soft white fluff began to swirl around them. Snow, in high summer.

They snatched a few hours' rest under a rocky outcrop on the summit of Lady Fidelity; which, as Nikas explained, was the guardian mountain of Astorre. No one slept well. Already a feared name when they broke camp, the rumour of the Empath hounded them all the way up the mountain, and by nightfall had taken on fangs and fire-breathing properties. Emaris laughed at the speculation in the hearing of his patrol, but tossed and turned and mouthed prayers when no one was looking, so cold he was afraid to close his eyes in case they froze shut for good.

But the night was uneventful, as was the next day. By the second evening they were shuffling down Fidelity's bosom towards the city in her lap. They came on Astorre at sundown—the perfect time, Nikas assured them, for viewing the polis as it was seen by painters and poets. It was an abrupt manifestation. One moment they were trudging down a mud-slick track, still looking over their shoulders for the Empath; and the next thing they knew, they had rounded a bend in the path and were looking out on a tableau of green and gold.

Below them was a rocky chasm spanned by a tremendous drawbridge with balusters of gold, wide enough for eight horses to gallop abreast. On the other side lay Astorre on her grassy plateau. The fields sprawled in languid serenity, verdant as emeralds; and behind the triple walls, each higher than the one that surrounded it, a hundred towers and minarets spired into the sky. The glazed roofs, the stained-glass windows and the gleaming steeples drank the last light of the sun and threw it back, multiplied hundredfold, to dazzle the eye. "It looks like a brooch," Emaris murmured, awestruck.

"Like a carving on a wine goblet," said a voice at his side, startling him. "The more you drink, the thirstier you get."

Emaris had thought it was Vion beside him. He turned, apprehensive. But Savonn's level stare gave no inkling of what had transpired the day before. "Astorre, as the poets say, is a wild maenad who has supped full of the fortunes of Falwyn and Sarei and the Northlands. Placed as she is, trade is her only way to survive. Merchants and artisans from three nations and more have settled here under truce, and anyone who lifts a hand against an enemy is put to death."

He smiled, though not quite at Emaris. "But of course, there's a perennial rivalry between her three theatres—Akiron, Aereas, and Charissos, which are Saraian, Pierosi, and Falwynian respectively. During every festival they compete to outdo one another in acting, singing and dancing, all of which the Astorrians do very well, and to excess. I saw fourteen plays the first week I was there, and thought I could die happy."

Emaris gazed at him, surprised. He detected, for the first time, a strain of nostalgia in Savonn's voice, never present when the men settled round their cookfires at night and spoke of home. On impulse, he said, "They say you had someone there once."

Astonishingly, Savonn did not say anything sarcastic. Perhaps this exceeding civility was his way of making up for his outburst the day before. "Do they?" he asked. "It's a good place for meeting people. I wonder who we'll encounter this time."

It turned out that, as was to be expected from a city under a strict and fragile truce, Astorre did not take kindly to strange armies showing up on its doorstep. The men were made to wait on the far side of the drawbridge, while Savonn went across with Hiraen and—after suffering a protracted, beseeching gaze—Emaris to speak with the chief guardsman. The gates were ebony and jet reinforced with steel, ornamented with intricate carvings of the sun and moon, and the pink-faced young man who met them there introduced himself as Gelmir. He addressed them in Bayarric at first, until he learned they were from Cassarah, upon which he switched to serviceable Falwynian. Here, it seemed, everyone was a polyglot. "You come with hundreds of armed men, Captain," he said, looking with distaste at the waiting column behind them. "Have you not heard that there is also a sizeable troop of

156

Saraians lodged with us at present? Some of them, in fact, have just preceded you here."

Emaris glanced at Savonn, failed to meet his eye, and caught Hiraen's instead. "We thought so," said Savonn. "They evaded us, and we evaded them. A complicated situation, I grant."

"Everything you lowlanders do is complicated," said Gelmir. "What do you want here? You are not traders."

"No," said Savonn. Emaris could tell by the crispness of his enunciation that he was growing impatient. "We are three hundred very cold, very hungry people who came headlong across the Farfallens in a hurry to spend all our money here, and leave again before snow closes the passes. Is that so much to ask?"

"We're not here to fight," added Hiraen. "We've had more than enough of that."

Gelmir snorted. "Like hell you're not. Every meeting of Falwynians and Saraians has ended in violence ever since your Governor died."

"If you recall," said Savonn unexpectedly, "I do have a certain propensity for averting bloodshed."

Emaris had to blink several times to be sure of what he was seeing. It was as if Savonn had put on a mask, or perhaps taken one off. His shoulders relaxed, his stance loosening to let Gelmir make the most of the two-inch advantage he had in height. His smile was sly, his heavy-lidded gaze alight with obscure mirth. The disconcerting thought struck Emaris that this was Savonn as he must have been at seventeen or eighteen, far away from home for the first time, running Merrott's errands and getting into trouble on the side.

Hiraen seemed mildly entertained, if unsurprised. But Gelmir's mouth had fallen open, revealing a couple of gold-plated incisors. Then he closed it and began to grin. "Savonn! You rascal, is it really you?"

Looking severe, Savonn said, "I feared I had aged badly."

Gelmir guffawed. "Can you blame me? Up you come tramping with yon lot of muddy men, with a full face of stubble and not a bit of kohl round your eyes, talking to me all stern like one of them lowlander princelings! Who the hell would recognise you?"

"For sure, I don't even recognise myself," said Savonn. "Well? Are you going to leave an old friend out in the cold?"

"Why, you know you're always welcome here," said Gelmir. "But your men—"

"I go where they go."

Gelmir hesitated, glancing over the drawbridge again. "Perhaps," he said, "you would like to speak with the Lady? Last I heard she was giving an audience to the Saraians, but they must be nearly finished by now. Your men could wait in the guardhouse in the meantime."

"Excellent," said Savonn. "Must we disarm? I can give you one of my six knives."

They disarmed, not without reluctance. Savonn, having with great generosity surrendered four knives and his vial of poison, was for a moment swallowed up by a crowd of acquaintances on the steps of the guardhouse. Listening to the ensuing flurry of *how long it's beens* and *do you remember whens*, Emaris learned that Savonn had once been responsible for, among other escapades, an infestation of moulting ducks in the barracks and the sudden manifestation of a screeching cuckoo-clock in the common room chimney-shaft. Gelmir was still chortling when at last he dispatched a boy to take them to the Dome of Stars, where Lady Celisse lived, and Savonn swept away again with Hiraen and Emaris in tow.

"How'd you acquire this one?" Hiraen asked, once they were out of earshot.

"Tavern brawl," said Savonn.

Unable to stop himself, Emaris asked, "Did you fight him?"

"Rather," said Savonn, "I broke it up."

There was no mistaking Astorre for Cassarah. There were no stately bridges, no aerial gardens. While the buildings at home were solid and ponderous, like castle bulwarks, Astorre's were sleekly sinuous, roofs and balconies and curving window-frames flashing like brass jewellery in the sun. The roads were not paved with stone, but a strange amber-brown brick. Stained-glass lamps swung on every street corner, already lit against the encroaching dark. They passed one shaped like a shark's maw, and another like a lion's head. It was as warm as Vion had foretold, which—as far as Emaris was concerned—made this the only place to be for the next year or so.

The great serrated dome that gave Celisse's home its name was painted, white on bronze, with intricate star-maps of the constellations and planets in orbit. Beneath, the palace was full of fluted marble columns and slender archways under elaborate rosewood friezes. Windchimes sang in echoing stairways; golden carp swam in deep murmuring pools. They were received by a clucking chamberlain and made to comb their hair and wash their feet in a powder room. Then, newly presentable, they were taken to the Lady's solar.

It was on the second floor, with casement windows overlooking a garden where children were playing ball among the rhododendrons. There were no tables or chairs. Instead a number of colourful rugs were laid out on the painted tiles, strewn all over with cushions. A low stool in the midst held three glasses of some pale orange liquid. Sitting cross-legged on one of the rugs, sipping from a fourth glass, was Lady Celisse.

She was not yet forty, with long gold-bronze hair and skin like polished mahogany. Her blue chiffon gown had moonstones sewn into the collar and hems, and a silver shawl twined around her shoulders. Rings glittered on all her fingers. "Did you bring your choir, Lord Silvertongue?" she asked, smiling. Like Gelmir's, her front teeth were gold. "The Saraians had a lutenist. I could put you together and make you sing for your supper."

Once more, Emaris failed to catch Savonn's eye. "I didn't bring my lute," said Savonn. "I suppose I could always juggle knives and conjure fire." He approached her rug and, kneeling, bent to kiss her hand. "Allow me to present my friends. This is Hiraen Safin, who fetches things from high shelves for me; and Emaris, who laces me into my corsets. You knew his father."

"Your deputy and your squire, I take it," said Celisse. "Come, sit and drink. I was very sorry to hear about Lord Kedris. We used to keep up a most salacious correspondence."

Emaris managed, in time, to straighten out his face. They sat down on the rugs. "And yet," said Savonn, handing out the glasses without taking his eyes from her, "you admitted the Saraians?"

"Your feuds are none of my business," said Celisse. "Marguerit is a dear friend. With this fellow Isemain around, the roads have been remarkably clear of bandits. *He's* been here for a few weeks, you know," she added. "The Marshal of Sarei himself, with a force of two hundred. A decent if unimaginative fellow. The lutenist was more interesting."

They must have split their forces. The Marshal had gone ahead to Astorre, while the Empath tarried on his errand to Onaressi, stalking the Betronett company across the Pass. "Perhaps so," said Hiraen. "But the bandits are in their pay."

"Which keeps them from waylaying merchants for *their* gold," said Celisse. "So all parties are pleased except, sadly, you. I'm surprised you didn't come to clear out the forts sooner. The bandits have occupied some of the smaller ones for two or three years now."

"They moved in around the same time as Merrott died?" asked Hiraen.

"Thereabouts."

Hiraen glanced at Savonn, who seemed oblivious. Emaris did not understand. He was sampling the drink, which tasted like honey but burned like brandy going down his gullet, and had started up a steady smoulder in his stomach. His head felt light, and in danger of detaching from his neck. "I see," said Savonn. "So, if—hypothetically—we were hoping you would throw the Saraians out of the Farfallens, we would be disappointed?"

Celisse's smile was small but tolerant. "Hypothetically, yes. I would be breaking my own truce, and Marguerit would be very cross with me. If it helps, the weather will close the passes soon enough. The Saraians will have to go home soon or risk being stuck here till spring. The same goes for you, of course... Oh, by the way, that's Astorrian summerwine."

Emaris, who had been frowning with concentration into his glass, looked up with a start. The Lady winked at him. "It's something of a legend. The ingredients are a secret the brewers will keep with their lives."

Without comment, Savonn returned to the discussion at hand. "There are several more forts along Ilsa's Pass to be cleared of bandits before autumn sets in. We hoped you might help us. Your traders would be glad of it."

"What?" said Celisse, looking amused. "Send your friend Gelmir to garrison a few frosty rocks? The poor man. I may think about it for the sake of our friendship. Give me some time to decide."

She rose from the carpet with easy grace, and so did they. "I don't like lodging opposing armies under my eaves, but I'll make an exception for you. You may stay as long as you like, provided you keep out of trouble. In a few days we are throwing a masquerade to honour Amitei, our deity of love. The Saraians are invited. So are you."

"It is an honour," said Savonn. There was no trace of the grinning youngster who had so charmed Gelmir. His handclasp was formal, his expression bland. "But as you say, we ought to hurry home."

Hiraen led the way out, followed by Emaris, dazed from the summerwine and rather disappointed to hear they were not staying long. Celisse called after them as they reached the hallway.

161

"The Savonn Silvertongue I knew would not have passed up the chance to attend a masked ball for love or money."

"That," said Savonn, "was years ago, my lady."

The chamberlain escorted them downstairs, and invited them to take their ease in the garden while suitable lodgings were found for them. The sun had set while they were talking. A rainbow of lamps glowed among the fragrant hedgerows, and fireflies flitted in the dark that lingered in between. But far beyond the city wall, there loomed another, more sinister light.

"Look!" said Emaris. "The mountain is bleeding!"

In the daytime he would have laughed at himself. But now, rearing her white-capped pate above the twilit city, Lady Fidelity glowed brilliant red, her slopes stained like an altar after sacrifice, and he could think of no other way to put it. The lesser peaks in the distance were tinted the same hue, as if every stone in the Farfallens had been lit from within by some great conflagration. Even Hiraen was wide-eyed. But Savonn's countenance did not change. "Alpenglow," he said. "The air captures the light and clings to it after the sun has set. When it happens, the Astorrians say the Lady is in red."

Emaris had never seen anything so beautiful, or so disturbing. The chamberlain hurried up, beaming, to explain. "Milord Captain knows the local lore? Alpenglow is a sign of Amitei's blessing, and the most auspicious of omens for lovers. It is said that if a couple takes their vows on an evening like this, their passion will endure forever."

"Gods deliver them," said Savonn dryly.

Hiraen grinned. "He isn't superstitious."

But Emaris was no longer paying attention. The children had left with their ball, and in their place half a dozen newcomers in leather and mail were strolling among the rhododendrons. Sluggish with wine, he had not noticed that they were speaking Saraian. One of them stopped under a lamp to examine a carved fresco. It was hard not to stare at him: he had the shoulders and legs of a marble king on a plinth, and twice the poise; and his hair was the same auburn as the mountain.

Emaris hissed, "Savonn!"

Unthinking, he seized Savonn's arm. Savonn, who had been having what sounded like a philosophical dispute with the chamberlain, jerked as if he had been shot, and Emaris released him at once. "It's him! It's the Empath!"

Here, at last, was corporeal proof that he had not hallucinated the man. The redhead had given up his sword like the rest of them, but he still had his black and red cloak and his lute slung over his shoulder in its leather case. He was too far off to have caught Emaris's whisper, but all the same, just as Savonn was looking around, he turned.

They stared at each other across the garden. In the first shock of the impact, both faces were inexpressive. Emaris shivered, beset by the absurd urge to duck behind Hiraen. But the Empath did not so much as glance at him. His features were straight and chiselled and haughty, his brow creased as if in thought, and his gaze was for Savonn alone.

Behind them, the chamberlain chattered on unheard. The mountain glowed. Red, and red, and red.

After what felt like a long time, the Empath dipped his head in greeting. Savonn exhaled, a breath Emaris realised he had been holding for a while. His eyes were large and ruinously bright between their long lashes, and his lips were parted as if to speak.

Slowly, fastidiously, he returned the nod of acknowledgement. Then he turned around and cut the chamberlain off mid-sentence.

"Sir," he said. "Will you take a message to Lady Celisse? Tell her we shall be pleased to attend her masquerade after all."

CHAPTER 13

In the morning Savonn was chiefly preoccupied with preparations for the ball, and could not be made to discourse intelligibly on any matter besides heeled shoes and fancy hats. Emaris, approaching with a question, was offered an unsolicited and highly critical opinion on the state of his hair, and dispatched to a barber so he would "stop looking like a very blond bear," as Savonn put it. And then: "Take Nikas with you. His mop will benefit from the experience. You may repeat that to him, if you wish."

This proved more diverting than he expected. Brought out shopping for evening wear after they had been washed and shaved and barbered, Nikas dispensed a constant stream of commentary on the sights and history of Astorre, only interrupting himself at one point to haul Emaris to a booth of animal masks. "Put on that mask and look behind us," he said, holding up a hand mirror. "That man at the opposite stall is our unwitting sponsor. Isemain Dalissos, Marshal of Sarei."

Just this morning Daine and Hiraen had parcelled up the loot from Onaressi and handed it out to the men. Breakfast had been a jovial affair, and already Emaris had glimpsed Vion and Lomas spilling out of a tavern, shrieking with laughter and bedecked in new clothes from head to foot. He put on the long-horned gazelle mask he was holding and pretended to appraise his reflection in the mirror. There was a man in his fifties at the stall across the street, so tall his forehead threatened to bump the scaffolding, the muscles of his back more than evident even through his long-sleeved white brigandine. His skin was tanned brown as a nut, his wiry greying hair cropped unfashionably short and combed in a no-nonsense part. One or two of the faces around him were familiar: Emaris thought he recognised them from his disastrous scouting trip. "Is he the Empath's commander?"

Nikas laughed, setting the mirror down. "Only in name. No one commands the Empath. He comes and goes as he pleases, just like our own Lord Silvertongue. Tell me, why do you think Savonn decided to attend the masquerade?"

Emaris frowned. "I suppose he wanted to meet the fellow."

"Did he really?" asked Nikas. "The Empath spends a great deal of time in Astorre. So did Savonn once. I would be astonished to learn that their paths had never crossed."

He grinned like a dolphin. Emaris had seen those in Bayarre a long time ago, when he and Shandei and their father spent a summer there: strange grey creatures that spun and danced and wove through the sea-foam, smiling as though they knew all the world's secrets. He pulled the mask off. "*Have* they?"

"That," said Nikas, "is something you ought to ask Savonn yourself. The gazelle suits you. You should buy it."

* * *

On the third evening, a gong sounded at sundown, and they streamed to the Dome with the other partygoers to attend the ball thrown in Amitei's honour.

The Astorrian deity of love was never depicted in sculpture or painting, for they were legion, and could take many forms: young or old, fair or dark, man or woman or both or neither. There were no altars or incense-burners in Celisse's banquet hall, only music and food and people, all of them in masks. The walls were bedecked with gold and silver streamers, the painted windows flung open to let air into the crowded room. Tables groaned under the weight of luxuries—poached eggs, honeyed oats, veal, venison and so on, and a veritable river of that blessed summerwine. But there were no chairs, except for the elderly. Astorrians did not believe in sitting down when they could be dancing. Accompanied by spinet, lyre and drums, a quartet of singers was belting its way through its repertoire, and people were already getting up to twirl each other across the hall.

Emaris was in his gazelle mask. He had grown another inch over the summer, and his antlers necessitated caution when passing through low doorways. Nikas had settled on a feathery cockatiel for himself, which he kept switching for Lomas's wolfhound and Daine's white-maned horse, causing a great deal of confusion. Hiraen, a lion, surfaced now and then from the hordes who wanted to dance with him in order to offer Emaris some pastry or other. By far the most daunting was a fruit tart the size of a small tortoise, covered in peach slices and raisins and leaking strawberry jam thick as mulch. He leaned in to whisper as he handed it over, nearly impaling his ear on Emaris's antlers. "Try not to get too drunk. The mammoth, the pony, and the—what the hell is that, some kind of sentient plant?—are Saraians. I haven't seen the Empath."

Their masks only covered them to the nose, so as to make eating possible. Altogether *too* possible. Unarmed and stuffed full of food, Emaris was aware that if their redhead friend tried anything clever, he had no weapon except his dinner knife with which to fend him off. "Where's Savonn?"

They had glimpsed him once, gliding into the hall behind Celisse at the start of the banquet. The Lady of Astorre turned all heads in her snow leopard mask and sleeveless silver gown; and Savonn was a magpie, with a rhinestone-encrusted beak and

166

elaborate black and white plumage that belled around his face like a fan. Like Emaris, he had spent a productive half-hour with the barber the day before. His curls tumbled past his ears and over the high embroidered collar of his doublet, so deep a black they shone, and beneath the mask his smile was smug and sharp-tipped. "I've no idea," said Hiraen. "Dancing, probably. I'll keep a lookout. You enjoy yourself."

An octopus had flung its tentacles around him, and was trying to lead him onto the dance floor. "All right," said Emaris, backing out of their way. "Have fun."

He ate the tart, which was as alarming as it looked. Then he found himself drawn into a circle of dancers and flirted with in four languages simultaneously, none of which he understood. People kept pressing drinks into his hands. After the fourth or fifth he learned to say *No, thank you*, in Bayarric; and then, *But you too are beautiful*, in Pierosi. A new song had started, much louder and faster than the ones before. Couples and trios and quartets flitted round him against a wild pulsing of drums. One of his companions, an unfortunately short giraffe, called to him over the music. "The new spinet player is very good."

Emaris glanced at the dais at the end of the hall, where the musicians were playing. A moment ago the person at the spinet had been a wolverine in a spangled dress. Now, he saw, it was a magpie.

He plastered a smile on his face, already weaving away from his protesting partner. "Let me fetch you another drink."

The dance floor was overflowing with people. Three collisions and half the song later, he had gotten close enough to ascertain that the spinet player was, in fact, Savonn. When he had replaced the wolverine was a mystery. The party was spilling out onto the garden, where several naked acrobats were piling themselves into a pyramid to raucous cheers. Vion and the others were nowhere to be seen. Hiraen was dancing with Celisse, surrounded by their combined flock of admirers. Two of the Saraians were helping themselves to more dessert, and the third was dancing with the octopus. No one was paying attention to the musicians, save Emaris himself.

And another. At the very edge of the floor, near the banquet tables, a nightingale stood sipping from a goblet. Tawny feathers plumed from the rim of his cedar mask. His pourpoint shimmered gold, his belt was studded with topaz and sunstone, and his hair, falling to his elbows in a thick careless braid, was a deep auburn.

Emaris's full stomach gave a half-hearted lurch. The nightingale glanced in his direction, then back at the spinet. Savonn, too, had noticed his audience. Beneath the rim of his jewelled mask, the corners of his mouth lifted.

A pause like a held breath. The singers wailed in seamless harmony, drawing the song into its final chorus. Across the hall, the lion dipped the snow leopard, who was laughing. The lion was not. The music leapt from summit to summit beneath Savonn's fingers, fierce, irresistible, so joyous as to be a mockery; and at last the Empath lifted his goblet in a silent toast and returned the smile.

People had begun to yell for an encore before the last notes of the song quite faded away. But Savonn had already risen from the bench to sidle round the spinet. And in the next moment, as if by accident, the magpie and the nightingale met on the dance floor, among the swaying couples and the lingering backbeat of the drums.

"I thought," said Savonn, "some good music ought to lure you out of hiding."

Emaris crept closer under the pretext of fetching himself another tart. Neither of them took any notice. The drums died away. Someone started a new song on the spinet—this one was slow and soft, and Emaris had no trouble making out the nightingale's response. "Not hiding," he said. Unlike Nikas, he spoke Falwynian with the slightest of accents, a minute elongation of the vowels and a softening of the fricatives. "I have been in the garden, seeking fresh air. The crowd is excitable, and my senses are... delicate. Have you a thirst?"

"Yes," said Savonn, "but not for water."

The Empath glanced into his goblet and made a wry face. A serving-girl passed them with a crystal tumbler of wine. He beckoned for a new cup, and held it out to Savonn. Pulse throbbing unheeded in his throat, Emaris watched the Empath brush the cup's bronze rim against Savonn's lip, watched Savonn tip his head back to drain it dry. Something of his furious song seemed to have diffused into his eyes; it burned there, bright and dangerous, like a poisonous flower. "So the rumours are true," he said. "An empath *and* a priest of the Sanctuary. You grow more fascinating every day."

"Some are born with fewer than five senses, others with more," said the nightingale, dismissive. He sounded like a buttered biscuit, Emaris thought: light and smooth and full of air. "Mine is a priceless curse. Marguerit has never had a spy like me, nor will she ever again. It is, I fear, quite a headache."

"Literally?" said Savonn. "Or ethically?"

They were moving gently to the music, not quite touching, but otherwise as close as the couples around them. "Do not be alarmed," said the nightingale. "Your heart shames you no more than your haircut—"

"Thank you."

"—and in any case, the human senses will suffice for you. On the lute or on the spinet, your arrogance is unmistakable."

"You have heard me on the lute?" asked Savonn. "Oh, yes. Recently. How did it go? *The prince marshals his armies, their thunder fills the sky...*"

"*The lilies fall to kiss the ground, the hoofbeats pass them by.* Clever," said the nightingale, as Emaris caught his breath. "Yes. I was there. I plunged my spear into that man's black heart and watched the black blood gush out, and then I thought to myself, I must see what his son makes of this. I was not disappointed."

He had not troubled to lower his voice. A few heads turned. Then, because he was smiling, they turned away again. After a moment Emaris realised that the pounding in his ears was no drumbeat, but the bellows of his own heart. Savonn's face did not alter. He had let the Empath lead the dance. They were so close that the feathers of the magpie mask stirred the nightingale's plumage; a guttering lamp flickered in the hair's breadth between their bodies. "I hoped the killer, whoever he was, would have style enough to come to the funeral," said Savonn. "The elegy was a promise. I pay my debts, and forgive none owed to me."

The man's laugh was sweet as birdsong. "As do I. You are not the only one with a blood feud, my dear. Perhaps, one of these days, I shall tell you about mine. About what your father did to me and my people."

In the eyeholes of his mask, Savonn's stare was feverish. "You could have fought me at Onaressi."

"And by now you would be dead," said the nightingale. "How dull. How banal. One should conduct such affairs with a little more panache."

"I see," said Savonn, "that we agree on most things." His voice was half an octave lower than usual. "Whatever shall we do? You wish to kill me, and I return your ardour most fervently. Yet here we are, dancing together in a city under truce."

"Have patience," said the nightingale. "Your mind is made for games. So is mine, and there are many we can play without swords. Have I told you that your mask is beautiful? In my country, we have a folktale about a magpie. I would like to tell it to you."

"Go on. Or perhaps, let me guess. Once upon a time, when the world was young—"

"—and the earth clean and untrodden under the new-made sun, the magpie was a shapeshifter."

"The cleverest of all beasts, and the most cunning, and the most guileful."

Savonn had matched his voice to the Empath's, or perhaps the other way around, so it was hard to tell who was speaking. Emaris edged closer still. "He made himself into a squirrel, and fleeced the nuts from the trees. He made himself into a sheep, and lured the flock into the wolves' jaws. He made himself into an elephant, and tied all the other elephants' trunks into knots. When the humans tried to catch him, he simply melted away, and thus he reigned a thousand years, a disembodied demon of the wood."

"And one day?"

"One day," said the Empath, "a travelling minstrel passed through on his way from the city. He had grown very rich, playing for the Queen in her palace all summer. And the magpie peered down from the treetops, and glimpsed the sparkle of treasure in his pockets, and greed touched his heart, the hungry heart that longed to be all beings and possess all possessions."

"So," said Savonn, "he changed into his bird form, feathers aflutter, to pinch a coin or two."

"Yes. But just then, the minstrel sat down on a rock by the wayside to play his lute. And—"

"That isn't how it goes."

"I have changed the ending," said the Empath. "Now it goes like this. At the first note, the song struck deep into the magpie's heart and quivered there like a spear. He fell in love with the music, as all birds must, and never again did he want to be a squirrel, or a sheep, or an elephant. His powers fled from him, and henceforth he could change no more, nor fool no one. And all the beasts of the wood knew him for a trickster, and drove him from their midst."

There was a long pause. The spinet fell silent. They had stopped dancing, and Emaris's hand had grown cold around a plate he did not remember picking up.

Softly, Savonn said, "I do not fear you, whatever you are."

171

"No," said the Empath. He took hold of the magpie mask between thumb and forefinger and tugged it loose, letting it fall to the floor. "It is not me that you fear."

Under the mask, the rich brown of Savonn's cheeks was highlighted with a faint, warm pink; and a curl of hair, loosened by the heat of the overcrowded room, was slipping down over his forehead. The Empath held his gaze, but neither of them spoke. Then a trio of laughing dancers in butterfly masks jostled past Emaris, blocking his view, and when they had passed, the nightingale was gone.

Emaris took a hesitant step forward. But before he had made up his mind whether to approach, Hiraen emerged from the crowd, pulling off his lion mask. He was perspiring, and someone had stuck a battered corsage of wildflowers to his collar. "Are you all right?"

Savonn's eyes refocused on Hiraen. Then the heavy, penetrating gaze fell on Emaris, and swept across the rest of the hall, as if he was only then remembering where he was.

"Yes," he said. "Why would I not be?"

"Is he..." The muscles moved in Hiraen's throat. "Not like what you remember?"

Emaris stared. Savonn retrieved his mask from the floor and tied it jauntily over the crown of his head, like a hat. "On the contrary," he said, "he is exactly as I remember."

CHAPTER 14

The rest of the night was a confusion of over-loud music and too-bright lights. Emaris remembered trying to ask an ill-phrased question, only to have Hiraen send him headlong into the many arms of the octopus, who transpired to be an excellent dancer. By the time he untangled himself three songs later, Savonn had downed an entire tankard of summerwine and was cheerful again, if stricken by the tendency to cantillate—loudly, mournfully, and perfectly on key—a variety of gazelle-related verses every time Emaris opened his mouth to speak.

Soon after, Hiraen retrieved Nikas and bundled them all into a carriage bound for their lodging. Emaris dozed and woke and dozed again, voices flowing over him and melding into the fabric of his muddled dreams. "I will reiterate," said Nikas, "that the prospect of fighting my former brother-in-arms does not trouble me. If you ordered me to kill him, I would."

"Your conscience or lack thereof is not my affair," said Savonn, each syllable loose and lazy. There was no other sound save the regular clip-clop of the horses' hooves. Hiraen must have gone back for Daine and the others. "Did you think I hired you to do my killing? How... pedestrian."

"Didn't you?" asked Nikas. "No, I suppose not. You had other things in mind."

It occurred to Emaris that Nikas was dead sober, and disquietingly, Savonn was not. "And you have performed impeccably in all regards," said Savonn. "Like the eager hound, leading its hunter to the boar... You may stay to watch the kill, though I cannot promise you a share of the meat."

* * *

Emaris awoke in bed sometime in the late morning, with a blinding headache and an empty bucket on the floor beside him.

As soon as the world was navigable, he padded out in search of Savonn. They were lodged in a whale of an old warehouse long since converted into a manor, as far from the Saraians as Celisse's stewards could wrangle. He shared a long, dormitory-like chamber with the boys of his patrol, all still asleep, while upstairs Savonn and Hiraen had a room of their own. In a stroke of luck, Savonn was alone, reading on the windowsill. As soon as Emaris came in, he laid his book aside and intoned, "O gazelle!"

The sun in the broad window made it impossible to look directly at him. Head pounding, Emaris sat on the foot of Savonn's bed and addressed the washstand instead. "What was that last night? Why didn't you tell me you knew the Empath?"

The keen gaze, not welcoming, played on the side of his face. "I didn't think it worth mentioning."

"You *didn't*—? After he nearly killed us on the Pass?"

"As I recall, you dealt with that admirably," said Savonn. "We have met. You may be assured he didn't call himself the Empath when I knew him. Can you guess what we're doing tonight?"

Not to be thwarted by this change of subject, Emaris asked, "How did you meet?" And then, in desperation latching onto the one thing Savonn could not in all decency ignore: "Did my father know him too?"

174

Against the light, Savonn's face was lost in shadow, but Emaris fancied his voice softened a little. "The Empath did not kill your father. Of that I am certain. He seems to have killed mine, a definite complication, but not a fatal one... You haven't answered my question."

"What?" said Emaris, squinting at him. "What are we doing? Fire-setting? Choir-mustering? Tightrope-walking?"

"We," said Savonn, sliding off the windowsill, "are going to see a play. Namely because Nikas has it on good authority that his lordship Isemain, Marshal of Sarei, is going to see a play. How odd. He doesn't strike me as much of a thespian." He paused, studying Emaris. "But if that is too tame, I could always teach you to swallow a sword."

"No, thank you," said Emaris, easing himself back to his feet. He needed to take something for his head. "I have no wish to swallow your sword."

Savonn's eyes grew round with mockery. "Why, perverse child, did I say it had to be mine?"

Emaris flushed hot to the bone. "Shut up," he said, and fled from the room.

* * *

Sundown found him squashed between Savonn and Hiraen in the House of Charissos, Astorre's Falwynian-speaking theatre. His headache was gone: a small mercy, considering how crowded and noisy the place was. The theatre was much smaller than the Arena of White Sand back in Cassarah, but grander—roofed in gold like Vion had promised, the walls stuccoed, the floor carpeted in plush red, the benches strewn with silver cushions. Technically, it was a full house, but Savonn knew someone who knew someone who knew someone else, and by some miracle they had been offered three seats in one of the topmost circles. Far below, the heads in the front rows were like little coloured dots.

"Where are the Saraians?" asked Emaris. "And why are they attending a Falwynian play?"

"I think that's them," said Hiraen. "Five rows down, a bit to the left."

Emaris saw the Marshal at once. Tall as he was, with his short dark hair and wolfish eyes, he was hard to miss. With him were two women and a man, all of whom treated him with obvious deference. Emaris scanned the benches for a glint of auburn, but saw none. Hiraen seemed to be thinking the same thing. He glanced at Savonn. "Where's your friend?"

Savonn shrugged, in one of his uncommunicative moods. "Define your terms. Or just be quiet. It's starting."

The black curtain was rising over the stage, sending the audience into a deep hush. The set was made up like the deck of an ancient trireme, complete with mast, sails, stern and bow, with a chorus of sailors arrayed on deck. A harp chinkled, and they began to sing.

"Oh, gods," said Emaris with faint alarm, halfway through the first verse.

"*The Lay of Evenfall*," said Savonn, recognising the song at the same time Emaris did. He gave Hiraen a cold look. It was like being wedged between a hammer and an anvil. "You said it was *The Foamriders*."

"Nikas said it was *The Foamriders*," Hiraen corrected. "It's not too late to walk out."

But Savonn did not move. The chorus sang of the twelve ships that had arrived in the Bay of Diamonds a thousand years ago, masts streaming, pennants shining, the only remnant of the great colonist fleet that had set out from the ancient Kerani empire. The curtain fell, and rose again on a backdrop of hedges and trees, and two men came on from opposite sides of the stage: one with a circlet and flowing golden hair, the other dark-haired and sombre and dressed in mail. "Ederen, brother of my soul," said the

176

blond one. "How good it is to see you without the deck pitching beneath our feet. How fares Cassarah, your city by the river?"

("Vayan Herrines," Hiraen explained. "Leader of the exiles and the first King of Falwyn.")

This high up, they could barely make out the actors' faces. "Well indeed, Your Grace," said the man playing Ederen Andalle, Savonn's distant and much-disliked ancestor. "I have been warring and slaughtering and amassing great numbers of slaves. They are building me a palace as we speak, a palace on an isle in the Morivant that will dwarf all the world."

"A palace!" Vayan exclaimed. "So the drifter has found a home at last. And what of marriage? You know my daughter Cleole has long had her eyes on you."

Cleole came onstage and danced, trailing an impressive dress train of white silk. Predictably, Ederen was stricken at first sight. There were dramatic proclamations, and a kiss, and the curtain fell and rose again on a wedding banquet. More dancing. Then, as the stage lights were trimmed and the happy couple prepared to retire, a cymbal smashed, and all the lights came on again. The King was going to die.

In Cassarah they still did plays the old way. No one ever died on stage, lest the audience's sensibilities were offended. The Astorrians had no such qualms. King Vayan fell down dead at the banquet table with a great crash of dishes, hands clutching his throat, painted apples jouncing across the stage to roll under the benches of the front row. The wine had been poisoned. A herald ran up, prostrated himself centrestage before the startled guests, and announced, huffing, that the Crown Prince Ismil had been caught trying to flee.

The chorus singers tore their robes and fell on their faces. Cleole and Ederen wept, putting on a convincing show of heartfelt grief. Ismil Herrines—as blond as his father—stormed on stage to plead his innocence, to no avail. The Queen, unable to face the prospect of executing her own son, sent him into exile instead, and more wailing and hand-wringing ensued. Prince Ismil lamented extravagantly on a harp. The actor's voice was sweet and smoky, his skill considerable. Emaris turned to tell Savonn so, and found with a shock that the seat to his left was empty.

He whispered, "Hiraen!"

Hiraen looked over, and rolled his eyes. "Again? Let him be."

The trireme made another appearance. Ismil was on a ship on the storm-tossed sea, working his passage as a deckhand with his shining hair tucked beneath a hood. The Queen died of a sudden illness, and against the backdrop of a great golden palace ("Evenfall," Hiraen explained) Cleole wept. Servants crooned as they fanned her, and Ederen stared broodingly into the distance. "Alas for my dearest friends!" he cried. "With your mother and father dead, and your brother in exile, the throne passes now to you, my love."

"Woe!" cried Cleole, beating her breast. "To think that such a burden should come to me!"

The lights dimmed, the servants departed, and she and Ederen exchanged secret smiles.

Up and down went the curtain. Ederen and Cleole ruled from twin thrones in Evenfall. Ismil wandered through village after village, rallying the people to depose their false rulers with hymns to Casteia, the goddess of war. A battle was fought, mostly offstage. Emaris's father had once brought him and Shandei backstage during a play, so they could see how the sound effects were made and reassure themselves that no one had actually died. Finally a flute began to whistle, accompanied by an ominous drumbeat, and Ismil barged fully armed into the throne room at Evenfall for the final confrontation.

His hair gleamed. His voice vibrated with righteous anger. "Begone, faithless king! Begone, trickster and liesmith, transmuter of truth into falsehood!"

("Oh," said Hiraen. "They changed the script.")

Cleole had long fled with her infant children, a historical fact for which Emaris supposed Savonn was grateful. Ederen remained alone on his throne, sword laid bare over his knees. "I have won my crown with steel and blood, and I will never yield it to such as you."

"But I have come," said Ismil, "with steel and blood of my own."

They came together in a whirl of blades. Even from this distance it was plain from the footwork that both actors were trained swordsmen. The one playing Ismil was particularly good, leaping with catlike grace around the bejewelled throne, knocking down hangings and ornaments on his foe's head with deft slashes of his prop sword. It was a short fight, but expertly choreographed. With a feint and lunge, Ismil drew his blade in a flashing arc across Ederen's throat, and the king toppled at his vanquisher's feet with a spray of fake blood from some mechanism Emaris could not see. The audience cheered.

But it was not over. Ismil stepped over his adversary's body, climbed onto the throne, and held his sword up to the audience. "By the sun and moon and stars," he declared, "by my mother and father and all the gods, I call down unending wrath on the line of Ederen Andalle and my treacherous sister Cleole. May they be dispossessed, driven as leaves before the wind; may swords hunt them from every point of the compass; may Casteia attend them, and Aebria hound them all their lives. May they be fugitives, homeless and hungry, destitute and desperate, from this day till the sun goes out."

The curtain descended. Stagehands ran to uncover the lamps. And in the ensuing applause, Emaris saw, it was Marshal Isemain and his friends who clapped the hardest.

One by one, the actors came out to take their bows. Vayan and Ederen had been played by older, good-looking gentlemen, who seemed to be well known among the Astorrians. The people screamed and stamped for them. The lead actress curtseyed, pelted with flowers, and flung Cleole's crown into the audience. Then the last actor came up to join them, pulled off Ismil's golden wig, and swept them a deep bow.

His hair flamed red in the lamplight. Even without that, the set of his shoulders would have been undeniable, and the genuine soldier's strength in his muscled frame. Emaris flew to his feet. "How can he—?"

Fortunately, the entire theatre was standing by then, and his shout was lost in the general applause. Hiraen, too, was rising amid an impressive stream of profanity that culminated in, "—for each other, these bastards, I swear to all the nineteen hells—"

Smiling, the Marshal caught Hiraen's eye and gestured. Hiraen and Emaris turned. Savonn had come back, and was perched on the bench between them, the better to see over everyone's heads. "Did you know it was him?" Hiraen demanded.

Savonn did not answer at once. He was almost incandescent: his cheeks glowed, and his eyes had taken on the lucent sheen of a lantern set ablaze at nightfall. In the harsh light of the theatre, every plane and contour of his profile looked harder and clearer than usual, a jewel scintillating under glass. "Traditionally," he said, without looking away from the stage, "this play is performed by three actors, one of them playing both Vayan and Ismil. I asked around backstage. The man playing Vayan is getting too old for swordfighting, so they hired a fourth to take Ismil's parts." Then he added, "I would have known him from his voice, in any case."

The actors had disappeared backstage. Behind Savonn a young man was calling his name, trying to get his attention. No one looked at him. "Can they do that?" Emaris asked. The question strained towards a shout. "Don't they know who he is?"

"He threatened you in front of everyone," said Hiraen. "Celisse could have him thrown out."

"No, he didn't," said Savonn. He hopped down from the bench, nearly crushing the man behind him. "He was just reading his lines. How perplexing. Yes, Gelmir? It doesn't look like it, but I am paying you the fullest attention."

Belatedly, Emaris recognised the man as the guard from the gate. "Look, I'm sorry," said Gelmir. "It's terribly awkward, but Celisse wants you to call on her at the Dome at once. It's just—there's been some altercation, a street scuffle involving some of your men and the Marshal's—"

They all looked at one another. "Nothing serious," Gelmir assured them. "No one was hurt. But a couple of punches were thrown, and some bystanders joined in, and it might've gotten ugly if my guards hadn't stopped it. Those involved are in my custody. If you will come with me..."

Savonn glanced back to the stage, now empty. The crowd was beginning to file towards the doors. Another guard had approached the Marshal and his companions, and was whispering urgently to him. "How perplexing," said Savonn again, to no one in particular. "How ingenious. Yes, we're coming. Lead the way."

* * *

This time they were taken not to the cosy solar, but a long hall that served as an audience chamber, with a carved ivory chair on a dais at one end. Celisse was not there yet, but the brawlers were. There were a couple of Saraians Emaris did not recognise; and, separated from them by a scrupulous line of spearmen, were Nikas, Vion and Lomas.

Emaris stopped in the doorway. "What the hell is wrong with you?"

It came out in the same hoarse half-yell he had been using in the theatre. Nikas, who was sitting on the marble floor, glanced at him and then away. Emaris rounded on Vion. "I thought you knew better. What have you done?"

Vion looked utterly unrepentant. "Oh," he said. "We ran into *them*"—he waved at the Saraians, who glared back—"outside a

181

tavern. One of them recognised Nikas and called his mother a—a rude name. So he threatened to kill them, and that one—"

"You never even knew your mother!" Emaris exploded.

"—the big ugly one, he threatened him back, and I told him to go away, and he called me a girl and said I should take my dick out to prove I wasn't. So," said Vion gaily, "I punched him. And he tried to hit me back, but Lomas did that thing he does—you know the one—where he just walks at someone till they fall down—"

Emaris groaned. "I walked at him till he fell down," Lomas added, "and Nikas did something to the other one that made him fly six feet in the air. I asked him to teach me but he wouldn't."

"Only," Vion went on, "there was some kind of scaffolding on poles in front of the tavern, because they were repairing the roof, and the flying one hit the poles and brought it down on everyone's heads. Then the guards came and arrested us all." He gazed at Savonn. "I threw the first punch, sir. You can tell them to let the others go."

If Savonn was listening, he gave no sign of it. "Flawless," he said, mostly to Hiraen. "Don't you see? He devises a way to threaten and insult me without breaking the truce. Then his men orchestrate a fight in which one of us lands the first blow, so that Celisse throws us out. And once we're beyond the city limits, they can kill us with impunity."

"It's hard to miss the kinship between his mind and yours," said Hiraen, with no trace of amusement. "Why do you look so happy?"

"Do I?" asked Savonn. "I admire artistry. I thought you did too. Any moment now, he or the Marshal will come in all smiles and apologies, and they'll be in Celisse's good books all over again."

But Celisse arrived before anyone else did. Today she was wearing a plain white dress with rectangular sleeves that covered her to the wrist, belted at the waist with a black sash. Her hair was tucked under a brown cap, and behind her, a page carried her sceptre of office on a cushion. One had to remember she was not only the snow leopard of the revelries; she was the richest woman in the world, the protector of the Farfallens, and she had not come to power only through masquerades and dances. Seating herself on the ivory chair, she said, "I thought I made clear the terms of your stay. What happened?"

Swiftly, Savonn came forward. He retold Vion's story, using so few verbs that it sounded as if the scaffolding had collapsed all by itself, and the whole incident like some unavoidable misfortune, a rotten tooth or a broken sandal-strap. Once or twice the Saraians tried to interrupt, only to be silenced by a look from Celisse. "We believe that these men started the fight on purpose," he finished. "But we would be glad to make you any form of recompense you desire. We have, for instance, a good deal of gold."

"Gold?" said a voice from the door. "We can do better."

At once, the Saraians prostrated themselves on the floor as if in the presence of an emperor. The Empath had arrived. He must have come straight from the dressing room: he was clad only in shirt and hose, and his wavy hair was dark with moisture from a wash, falling unbound over his shoulders. In shoes of soft black kidskin, his tread was silent, the prowl of a hunting cat. "Did these gorillas of mine breach your truce, ladyship?" he asked. His voice was the voice of Ismil, rich, mellow, tuneful. "If Lord Silvertongue will lend me a knife, I shall relieve you of their presence."

Celisse looked from him to Savonn, eyebrows raised as if in curiosity. Then she gave a minute nod.

They had last met as actor and spectator. Now they stood side by side, a matched set: thunder and lightning, wildfire and mercury, twin kings across a chessboard. And the Empath was still performing, though in a play of another sort. With deliberate care, Savonn drew from his sleeve two of the silver knives he had not surrendered to Gelmir and held them out hilt first. The Empath stepped forward to take them. Their fingers did not touch, but their eyes held. Then, with a knife in each hand, he turned to the two men at his feet.

It was fast, brutal, and elegant. "Noiseless and painless," said the Empath. His hands were clean, as was the floor. He stepped over the bodies, stopped before the dais, and sank into an exquisite bow, the obeisance of a skilled courtier used to royalty. "An upward thrust between—"

"—the fourth and fifth ribs, straight into the heart," said Savonn. "And not a drop of blood spilled. Astounding knifework."

The Empath's bowlike lips curved into a smile as they brushed the back of Celisse's hand. "Rise," said the Lady. "And what of you, Silvertongue? What recompense can you offer me that compares with this?"

Savonn's gaze travelled over his men, less blithe than usual. Vion and Lomas had their mouths hanging open. Nikas had gotten back to his feet. *He would not*, Emaris thought. *He would never.* All the same, some visceral instinct drove him forward, pushing past Hiraen to plant himself in front of his boys. *He can try, and I shall fight him.*

He held Savonn's trenchant stare for the span of a prolonged breath. Savonn looked away first. "None," he said to Celisse, "save the loan of my unlawful knives. And the gift of this man's name, if you would ask it."

"But she has it already," said the Empath. "My true name, and not the one you know. After you, I stopped giving out false ones." He rose in a fluid movement. "Your ladyship, I plead for leniency for the Falwynians. We can expect no better from men who are led by a charlatan. Tolerance is for their betters, and clemency."

Next to Emaris, Hiraen sucked in a loud breath and clamped his jaw shut. Celisse looked tickled. "How can I say no to such gallantry? I am terribly fond of you both. See how he intercedes for you, Savonn."

Savonn did not reply. He was looking not at her, but the Empath.

"Here is what we shall do," said Celisse presently. "I cannot house trucebreakers in my city. You, Silvertongue, must be gone with all your men by daybreak. As for the Saraians, they have been punished enough. I shall host the Marshal Isemain and his companions for a fortnight longer, to ensure you do not encounter each other and come to blows at my gates. Thereafter," she said, turning to the Empath, "you, too, must depart."

"We shall do so with sorrow," he said. "Milady is wise."

"Then, my lord Empath," said Celisse, "will you be so good as to summon my chamberlain and have these men removed? I tend not to enjoy corpses as a decoration in my home, however skillfully slain. Savonn, stay a moment. The rest of you may go."

The Empath made the obeisance again, a showman's curtain bow. He glanced at Nikas on his way out, and Nikas returned the look with an equally indecipherable one. Then the door shut between them. Hiraen put a hand on Emaris's arm and murmured, "Come on."

* * *

After they were gone, Savonn remembered his manners, and detached his gaze from the place where the Empath had been standing. He inclined his head to Celisse. "My lady?"

Celisse was smiling. Savonn had had enough dealings with her to know that she enjoyed a spectacle. He was not in the mood to produce any. His head felt light and rarefied, as it did after a couple of absinthe shots. The Lady said, "Gelmir tells me you and the Empath met at a tavern brawl back in the day."

Memory did not bear remembering. During the long years apart he had often fantasised about encountering the Empath again, but he had not imagined it would be like this. He said, "We did."

Celisse's eyes were piercing. "There is nothing sadder than friends becoming enemies," she said. "And I need not tell you that you have been matched above your weight class. You are out of your tessitura, so to speak."

He said, "I know."

She looked disappointed when he failed to elaborate. Like Iyone, she had an affinity for puzzles; unlike Iyone, she was not averse to scandal and furore. "We were not friends," he added, for her sake. "The fault, then as now, was mine. Either he will kill me or I will kill him. There is nothing new in such an arrangement."

"You were not friends," she agreed. "You were much more. If you survive it..." She leaned forward. "Listen, Savonn. You are not banished. If you decide you are tired of masquerading as a soldier, there will always be a place in Astorre for you. The trouble is that you are too convincing an actor."

He said again, "I know."

In the wake of the elation that had come over him at the theatre, he was supremely tired. He wanted to be dismissed. He longed to be alone, to curl around the memory of the evening's events like a dragon on its hoard and study them at length. But he had not been truly alone for a long time. He was beleaguered by little boys who thought the world of him; and one who was not so little, whose good opinion was beginning to carry a frightening importance. He should never have let Emaris come along.

Celisse was frowning. "I am going to ask you a question," she said. "I hope that, inasmuch as you are capable of such a thing, you will answer honestly."

The prospect brought a bubble of joyless laughter to his lips. "Can a peacock fly? I may produce a few compelling flutters, for a price."

Her business was trade. She was used to barter. "What do you ask?"

"His true name."

"All right," said Celisse. "Then tell me: why are you doing this? You are not godly enough to concern yourself with a blood

186

feud, nor will I believe that you are afflicted by filial grief in any shape or form. You did not love your father."

He dredged up the most hideous smile from his repertoire, and displayed it, hyena-like, for her benefit. "Well, I did give up the theatre and become a good little soldier boy at his behest."

She was too shrewd to be thwarted by chicanery. "Did you really?"

"No," said Savonn after a brief lapse. If he did not answer, she would never let him go. "No, that wasn't for him. It was to protect Hiraen, if you must know. My brother in all but blood. Otherwise Kedris would have—"

He abandoned that thread of thought. "That isn't the question you asked. This answer is less sentimental. I believe in cleaning up after myself, is all."

"Oh?" said Celisse. "You blame yourself? Why, for not getting to Medrai in time?"

"The rot runs deeper than that," said Savonn. "But this peacock, as always, fails to take flight. Will that be all, my lady?"

Celisse raised her brows. "I thought you might like to know why I asked. Shortly before he died, your father wrote to me asking for the names of all the foreigners you had had dealings with here. I had only just composed a reply, saying he should ask your old patrol leader Rendell, when I heard he had been killed."

One could only breathe, and hope one's stagecraft masked what one felt. "So has Rendell."

"Is that so?" asked Celisse. The merriment had returned to her eyes. "Step carefully, old friend. There are those who will notice how very convenient that must have been for you."

His training nearly failed him. If not for the other half of the bargain, he would have turned around and walked straight out. "And the name, ladyship?"

She told him. The unfamiliar syllables settled into his consciousness with dreadful finality, like the toll of a death knell. What was learned could not again be unlearned. The game had changed. They were dealing no longer with falsehoods, but in truth.

And there, he knew, he was standing on slippery ground.

* * *

Hiraen escorted them only partway back to the lodging, and returned to the Dome to wait for Savonn. The unpleasant duty of rounding up the men and breaking the news of their imminent exile thus fell to Emaris, who did so less gently than he could have. By the time they had all gone to bed grumbling, it was past midnight, just a few hours before they would be ejected into the freezing wilds again.

Emaris's own eyelids were drooping, but he lingered in the common room long after the others had turned in, determined to stay up till Savonn and Hiraen got back. Nikas was there, too. He pottered around the shelves and side-tables, picking up ornaments and putting them down again, seemingly unaware of what his hands were doing. Emaris watched him, hesitant. Now that he had had space to think, he was beginning to remember his outburst in Celisse's audience chamber with something like shame, and it seemed imperative to apologise.

He was alone with Nikas in an eerie, sullen silence. If he was going to say something, it might as well be now. "Nikas," he began. "What I said just now, about your mother—"

It was uncalled for, he could say; or, *I barely remember my mother, and wouldn't lift more than an eyebrow if anyone insulted her, but of course, one ought never assume...* But Nikas cut him off before he could choose the right words. "Forget it." In the glow of the sole lamp burning on the mantel, his expression had lost some of its customary nonchalance. "You were quite right. It was foolish to start a fight."

Emaris fidgeted in his overstuffed armchair. He could not help but feel he was being let off easy; that if it was Savonn he had

188

offended, he would have been reduced to bone and sinew by now. "You said she—she was a slave in Terinea?"

Nikas nodded. "Hearsay."

"Is she—"

Emaris swallowed back the question. He seldom missed his own mother, nor had he taken much interest in his father's stories about her. For as long as he could remember, Shandei had been the one he went to when he was sick or hurt or in trouble, and she had always put things right again. "Have you tried looking for her?"

"I found her," said Nikas.

In the half-darkness of the room, Emaris could see only a sliver of Nikas's face. "Then—she must have been freed years ago. Have you written, or visited, or—"

Nikas turned around, a crystal inkpot lying forgotten in the palm of his hand. "Both of those," he said. "The trouble, you see, is not that she is dead or enslaved. The trouble is that she will not acknowledge me as her son."

A few moments slipped by. Emaris said, "I see."

"So," said Nikas, "there is no need to concern ourselves with her." He set the inkpot down. "I despise her, and yet..."

He left the room, and went upstairs to his own quarters.

* * *

It was another hour before Hiraen returned with Savonn. Emaris, who was drowsing in his chair, came awake at the sound of their voices. By all appearances, they had been fighting the whole way. "Oh, I don't know," Hiraen said in a loud whisper, as the door banged shut behind them. "You still seem remarkably fond of him. What if I hadn't been waiting for you? Would you be with him now, sharing a wineskin and some supper and making fun of us all?"

189

Emaris's eyes came wide open. His armchair faced away from the door, and they had not noticed him curled up in the seat. They headed for the stairs, still arguing. "If that's what you think," said Savonn, "perhaps I should've gone."

They reached the upper floor. A door slammed. Since Onaressi, Emaris had done his best not to listen in on any more private discussions. But if Savonn insisted on disappearing into rooms and having loud conversations, then, he reasoned, no observant passer-by could be faulted for overhearing a thing or two. With all the stealth developed in a long career of eavesdropping, he crept up the stairs and stationed himself in the hallway outside their room. "—no point seeing him again," Hiraen was saying. "You burned that bridge long ago. So did he."

Every syllable of Savonn's reply was like the snap of icicles. "I burned it to keep you safe. From beginning to end, everything was for you."

"Do you think I've ever let myself forget it?" asked Hiraen. Like normal people, unlike Savonn, he allowed heat into his voice when he was angry. "I do know one thing. He is you. Whatever foul primeval ooze your soul is made of, his is the same."

"Well," said Savonn, "that explains a great deal, doesn't it? For instance, why he killed for me when you wouldn't?"

After a long silence, Emaris remembered the need to breathe.

"Oh, put that look away," said Savonn, the words light and flaking. "If I can be accused of conspiring to murder the Lord Governor, and Rendell as well, and possibly anyone else who has ever stubbed a toe within five feet of my ill-starred presence, then you can hardly escape contempt just because you kept your hands clean."

There was another aching pause. "That," said Hiraen, barely louder than the hiss of a blade, "is a lie."

Feet paced, crossing each other in the confines of the small room. Then Hiraen added, "Don't act as if you despise me. You envy me, and you always have, because I had the courage to stand

190

up to your father. If you had any shred of honour, you would have killed him before he made you do what you did."

The pacing stopped. Savonn said, very quietly, "Get out."

Before Emaris could move, the door flew open, and Hiraen stood framed on the threshold.

They stared at each other. The room was dark; no one had bothered to light a lamp. Savonn was invisible. As the shock began to recede, Emaris got himself out of the way. "I didn't hear anything."

Hiraen's face was drained of all colour. He pushed past Emaris and disappeared down the stairs. The front door slammed again.

There was no sound from within the room. An apology seemed futile, a retreat cowardly. If he was to be eviscerated, it was better to get it over now. Straining against the self-preservatory instincts of every muscle in his body, he made himself step inside.

He could just see the outline of Savonn's head and shoulders against the starlit window, still as a stone bust. "I didn't mean to eavesdrop," he said. "I was asleep in the front room and couldn't help..."

It sounded feeble to his own ears. "O gazelle," said Savonn. "What is it like to be you? Sensitive to every change of wind, always listening for the wolves and the hunters..."

His voice sounded broken. He stopped. As no evisceration seemed on its way, Emaris drew a steadying breath and said, "You can tell me if you like. I won't tell anyone."

There was a hesitation. In the dark, he could not ascertain its cause. Earlier he had placed himself between his commander and his patrol, ready to fight with his bare hands to save them from certain death. It was beginning to occur to him, with shameful tardiness, that the look he had seen in Savonn's eyes then was hurt.

All traces of it had since been tucked away, like a room made neat for guests. "I wish," said Savonn, "you wouldn't be so noble all the time. It's bad for the health."

Emaris was tired of being mocked. "The Empath—"

"—is a man with a name, who can be killed like any other," said Savonn. "There is no need to fear him."

"And will you kill him?"

He knew that he had outstayed his reprieve. "If you present an opportunity, I will," said Savonn, brisk and cold once more. "Since none are available right now, I shall turn in for the night. Must I beg your leave to do so?"

Emaris backed away. He locked the door from the inside, so that no one else would stumble in on Savonn's wrath, and fled to his own room.

* * *

As agreed, they were gone before daybreak. By the time Emaris woke, Savonn and Hiraen had come to some sort of un-spoken rapprochement, and their combined charisma got the griping company out of the house and marching to the gate. Celisse did not send them out empty-handed. They had fresh ponies and a fortnight's worth of rations in their packs, enough to see them to the forts in Ilsa's Pass, the second of the major highways between Astorre and the Bitten Hill. The men complained, but Vion and Lomas were silent, and even Nikas was subdued.

The Saraians were nowhere to be seen. Only the Empath was watching from the top of the city wall as they filed through the gate and over the drawbridge in their neat ranks, his hair a striking banner against the pre-dawn sky. Savonn did not glance his way, and following his example, neither did Emaris.

CHAPTER 15

The message from Iyone came the day after Midsummer.

It had been a long wait. Heeding advice, Shandei pleaded an alarum of the womb and missed most of the festivities; which, according to her friends, was no great loss, since the Midsummer play was puerile, the actors distracted and the chorus out of tune. A stable on the Efren property caught fire. Lord Willon's housekeeper quit, convinced that the family was cursed. The hours dragged on, sluggish as frozen butter, and by the time Linn called, Shandei had decided in a pique that Iyone had probably forgotten all about her.

The note, delivered by Linn with a piercing look, was brief, terse, and nearly incomprehensible. *Not yet able to come in person. Because we were seen together the day the bridge fell, W. has convinced himself that I am abetting you in your Thorny activities. The real Thorn is also spying on me. A ticklish mess. Continue to lie low until I make some headway in pruning them both. Linn is a friend in the most unphilosophical sense, and can take me a message if you need me.*

It was not signed. Shandei supposed that someone with a presence like Iyone would not see the need for such trifles as signatures. She sat clutching the scrap of vellum long after Linn had gone, studying the brisk, firm hand, the fine letters marching across the page without loop or flourish. If she ran her fingers under the writing, she could feel the deep indentations the quill had left on the page. *The real Thorn.* So Iyone knew who was behind the Efren disasters. Had she found out, too, who had killed Vesmer?

Shandei had no answers. What she had was the start of a lurking fear, that Iyone—the one person who had tried to help her—was in danger, falling under suspicion herself. And following hard on its heels, blossoming in her fingertips as if transmitted through the ghost of Iyone's firm hand on the page, was a hardening resolve. She could not stop the Thorn from hounding her footsteps, bringing calamity wherever she went. She could not bring Vesmer back to life. But about this, at least, she could do something.

Continue to lie low. Her father had always said she would make a terrible soldier, because she never followed orders. As in all things, he was right.

She knew how to help Iyone.

* * *

The weeks went by. Amid a storm of half-formed plans, Iyone received a letter from Hiraen, delivered from the mountains through a circuitous relay of couriers. It was full of trivialities but purposefully vague about the company's movements and whereabouts, and ended with, *I have tried to make this letter as long as possible, because I don't know when the next one will be. If you still pray, pray for us. And thank you for what you promised me.*

Iyone did, in fact, pray: to the only goddess she believed in, her mother. Informed of her recalcitrant daughter's quest for blackmail material, Aretel Safin was predictably unhelpful. "Josit? *Children?* Not that I've heard, and we've known her for years."

"Since she came to Cassarah with Savonn's mother," Iyone agreed, keen to keep the conversation moving at the same break-neck pace at which she did most things these days. Their privacy was circumscribed. They were in the parlour, drinking tea, and any moment Elysa would come in proffering biscuits or something. "What about before that? She could have had children in slavery."

"Well, of course," said Aretel. "But they would be hard to trace. They would be free now, like her."

"Yes," said Iyone. That had already occurred to her. "So the better question is: if she's had children, where are they now? And why didn't she acknowledge them as soon as she was freed?"

One can't know everything, Josit had said. Aretel shrugged. "Perhaps they're dead. Perhaps she couldn't find them, or didn't want to." She frowned at Iyone across her teacup. "Does this have anything to do with that girl Shandei?"

"Oh, no," said Iyone. "Just a hypothesis I was testing." There was a tap on the door then, and Elysa came in smiling, with a platter of scones.

From the highlands also arrived, without explanation, a couple of Dalissan coins and a bundle of dispatches written in Sara-ian. Savonn had sent an accompanying note, signed in his official capacity as Captain of Betronett. *The spoils of war are shared among the victors, proportionate to the part they played in the victory.* Iyone was there when, tight-lipped, Josit translated the dispatches for the Council.

"Well?" said her former tutor, when it was over. Lacking her usual sweetness, she sounded older, hoarser. "By the looks of it, Marguerit has had her hirelings ensconced in the Farfallens for years. Now we have proof. What do you mean to do about it?"

But it was clear that Marguerit was the furthest thing from Willon's mind. Since the collapse of the Carnation Bridge, nearly all his hair had gone grey. He had grown a beard, straggly and unkempt, beneath which his jowls sagged like the sail of some becalmed ship. He frowned at Josit, the loathing palpable. "I thought the Silvertongue was fighting them," he said. "I thought that was the *point* of him. May we discuss more pressing issues in the meantime? Such as the killer in our midst?"

It was impossible to forget said issues. For one thing, the Council now convened only in a fortified tower in the citadel, armed with a full complement of guards and food tasters. For another, Josit was seated right across from Iyone at the meeting table, unassailable as a wolf in sheep's wool. The only good thing was that Yannick Efren had fled to his country estate after the Midsummer scare, and grudgingly, Willon had permitted Iyone to fill the scribe's seat at the table. This was probably just because he wanted her where he could see her, but even small victories counted for something.

Her father was speaking. "This missive was written weeks ago," he said, pointing to the date on Savonn's letter. "But we have a corroborating report, more recent and more troubling. The Lord of Medrai writes that a large Saraian host is stirring in the Farfallens. Rumour has it that the Marshal is leading it in person with a"—he shrugged, part chagrined, part resigned—"a redhaired sorcerer called the Empath. The villagers are abandoning their homes and harvests and streaming to the lowlands in droves."

Iyone felt her brows rising. "Peasants are prone to superstition, Lucien," said Oriane. "I didn't think you were."

"I repeat," said Willon, cutting across whatever retort Lucien might have mustered, "I thought Lord Silvertongue was dealing with this. He ran off with eight hundred men and more horses than I care to count, promising to do exactly that. Why hasn't he stopped this host?"

Of late, Iyone's temper had been braced on eggshells. The worst thing was that Willon had a point. "Against a foe who has the unqualified support of Queen and government behind him, your lordship," she said, "you'd be astonished how few eight hundred really is."

Her father shot her a cautionary look. It was less effective than one of her mother's, but given how much there was at stake, Iyone subsided. "He needs reinforcements," said Lucien. "If Marguerit means to invade this fall, Savonn can't hold her off alone. Look, if we each send just a hundred men from our own households—"

"Marguerit won't come now," said Willon, annoyed. "The passes will snow over. She'd get stuck there all winter. Now, if you please—"

"If you please," said Lucien icily, "some of us have sons in the Farfallens we haven't seen in months."

Quite by accident, Iyone caught Josit's sardonic eye across the table. With a shared sense of inevitability, they watched as Willon's chest swelled with a preparatory inhale. "Some of us," roared his lordship of Efren, "have sons who are *dead*!"

Oriane gazed towards the high rafters of the meeting room, as if in silent prayer for temperance. Into the tense silence, Josit said, "I doubt the fact has slipped from any of our minds. I agree with Lord Lucien. If you are so doubtful of Savonn's capabilities, surely we ought not let him face Marguerit alone."

Silence, as Willon tripped over this stumbling-block of hard logic, flailed, and regained his balance. Changing tack, he said, "Who'll lead the force? You?"

"I could send my captain of guards," said Josit. "A doughty, reliable freedman, with much experience of war."

"With respect," said Oriane, "a Saraian can hardly lead the charge against Saraians. No one would ask that of you."

Josit smiled tolerantly. Apprehension prickled down Iyone's spine, only half understood, like the first rumblings of a thunderstorm still far off. She said, "Send Cahal."

"Are you crazy?" snapped Willon. "I need him. Oriane—"

Oriane was frowning at Lucien, her teacup half raised to her lips. "I can spare a hundred men, but someone's got to lead them. Josit's right. Lucien, you've seen the roads and trails above Medrai, and the Silvertongue's more likely to heed you than anyone else. But of course..."

Her father's jaw was pulled taut, his face less round than usual. "*What*?"

But it was Josit who answered, leaning forward solicitously. "Of course, you don't want to go. Not after Kedris, and the things you saw."

Seized by belated, horrified understanding, Iyone half rose. First Hiraen, and now this. "Send one of your other sons, Lord Willon. Send the city guard. Send—"

Lucien cut her off. "No," he said. His eyes glinted from under their wrinkled lids, cold and unamused. She found she could not remember the last time he had lost his temper with her. "Be quiet, Iyone. Don't you see what they're saying? Josit is a Saraian and Oriane is afraid for her life and Willon is beleaguered by Thorns. And you, I suppose, think me too craven to go myself."

"*Father—*"

"Well," said Lucien Safin, getting up to loom his full height over the Council table, "I will be most delighted to prove you wrong. I'll go."

* * *

The discussion that ensued was circular as ever, revolving around tedious matters of logistics and strategy. Losing both nerve and interest, Iyone excused herself—no doubt to everyone's relief—and walked out.

Josit had won another round. Naturally, she was worried for Savonn, her protégé. She wanted to send him help. And the manner of the sending was a blow struck against Iyone as much as

Marguerit. *Look what I can do*, it said. *Look how easily I can ruin you, just as I am ruining the Efrens. So sit tight and do not interfere.*

Check, and check, and checkmate.

It was a pity Iyone was only human, born to a mortal family she loved, with all the frailties and pressure points this entailed. Playing alone, she might have enjoyed the game with Josit. But as it was, her father was going to war. Her brothers were already embroiled. Hiraen had entrusted her with something that was proving even more of an inconvenience than she had expected. And Josit was still on the move. Yesterday there had been a second fire in the Efrens' kitchens, and another bouquet of roses had found its way into Oriane's residence. Once the muster of reinforcements had been seen to, Willon's attention would no doubt return to Shandei. Who was far too stubborn to stay in hiding for long.

Josit had found her leverage. Iyone was still looking for hers.

It was later than she thought. The sun had set, leaving the streets shrouded in that penumbral stillness peculiar to twilight. She had left Elysa and her other maids at home, and managed to give her father's guards the slip at the portcullis. These days she was never quite sure who was reporting to whom.

She passed under the Marigold Bridge on her way home, taking a side alley that curved between rows of boarded-up shopfronts. Overhead, several freedmen were packing up their shovels and manure bags for the night. The street was deserted; no one liked to be out after dark with an assassin prowling the city. Already people were muttering that in the days of good Lord Kedris, no innocent soul had ever been afraid to walk abroad at night, and that perhaps they should all have gone on campaign with the Silvertongue—a slippery little bastard with a heart like the bottom of a moat, to be sure, but a real circus-master. At least one would not die bored.

A stone rattled along the road. Iyone had thought herself alone. She turned, seeking the source of the sound.

There was no one in sight. Then a foot scraped on the cobbles behind her, far closer than she would have thought possible for someone to approach unseen, and a pair of hands closed around her throat.

She screamed. Immediately this struck her as an egregious failure of planning, because she was now out of breath, and the hands prevented her from drawing any more. She clawed at her attacker's wrists, trying to prise them off. The bones were small and slim, though their strength was vicelike. An irrelevant detail; surely there were petite assassins just as there were giant hulking ones; gods, what was the matter with her? She could not focus, could not reason a way out. Her lungs burned. Black spots danced before her eyes. It was beginning to occur to her that she—Iyone Safin, who prided herself on living life as a purely intellectual pursuit—did not want to die, bored or otherwise. It seemed a bad time for a philosophical epiphany.

Blindly, she kicked out behind her like a donkey. The heel of her boot made glancing contact with her attacker's shins. To her surprise, the hands loosened their grip. She sucked in a dizzying lungful of cold, sweet air. "Murder!" she shouted. "Murder! Help!"

From far off came an answering shout. The hands were still around her neck. She flung them away and whirled around; and there she stood, her Thorn.

A drab grey hood covered the straight golden hair, and a cloth had been wound around the face from the eyes down, but Iyone would have known her attacker anywhere. She stood clutching her throat, half stunned, unable to think. Not far off, a great many people—armed, by the sounds of it—were pounding up the street towards them.

"Scream," Shandei advised.

Reason returned. With a sudden, immeasurable delight, Iyone understood. She drew a great sobbing breath and yelled, "Over here! Hurry!"

The Thorn shoved her, not ungently, so that she cut herself off in mid-shout and stumbled to the cobbles. Before she had quite recovered her breath, the cloaked figure was gone.

Still dazed, she did not notice the livery of the approaching guards until they had spread out to search the street, and their leader was kneeling beside her, calling her name urgently. "Lady Iyone? You ain't hurt?"

It was Cahal, clad in cream and bronze. Efren guards. The irony did not evade her, nor did the unlikelihood of a coincidence. She laughed shrilly, and Cahal's brows knitted in concern. "Milady? Did he give you that?"

She looked down. On the ground by her hand was a single red rose, a little crushed, thorns bristling along its stem. The whole thing had been perfect, down to the smallest detail. Nothing had been forgotten.

"Yes," she said. "How romantic. Why were you following me?"

A shifty look crossed Cahal's face. "Lord Efren's orders. He was worried for your safety. Milady, did you see who it was?"

"Of course," said Iyone. "A jowly fellow with a big black moustache and lips like caterpillars. And a unibrow." She dropped her head into her skirts and, with effort, turned another laugh into a sob. "No, by gods, don't listen to me. I'm hysterical."

If Cahal was sceptical, he was too polite to show it. He offered his arm and helped her to her feet, while his men clattered around with shields and spears. "I hope," he said, "your ladyship is not offended that we followed you?"

She had recovered enough composure to smile. "On the contrary," she said, "I am very offended. But also very grateful. You may tell Lord Efren I said so."

* * *

She allowed Cahal to escort her home, and suffered the over-wrought embrace of her father and the baffled concern of her mother. Elysa fluttered around with warm towels and steaming milk and other useless paraphernalia; and Willon Efren, who seemed to be under the impression that he had saved her life, called on her with a flood of questions. With vindictive pleasure, she refused to say a word to him until he had apologised, thrice, for casting aspersions on her integrity, and then told him as little as she had given Cahal. He left soon after, manfully promising her father that he would "get to the bottom of this".

Despite her protests, her mother swept her upstairs. Elysa, thankfully, had been sent on some other errand. "How lucky," said Aretel, ushering Iyone into her bedchamber, "that there were guards within earshot."

"I don't believe in luck."

"Neither do I." Aretel shut the door with a decisive clap, not quite a bang. This must have been the second shock of the evening. She would have heard by now that Lucien was going to war, and why. "You know who the Thorn is, don't you. That's why you've been shielding Shandei. Why haven't you told Willon?"

Fired point blank, the questions could not be dodged. Aretel had the sort of motherly omniscience that made it futile, when one had broken a window or eaten all the dessert, to try and feign ignorance. "Why should I?" asked Iyone. "There are three different people responsible for this mischief, and Willon is so far from the truth he might as well not even have started looking. Who is that at the door?"

"The physician," said Aretel. "I have sent for her."

Iyone fought down a fresh wave of inopportune hilarity. "I don't need a doctor, Mother. What I need is a vase."

She was still holding the battered rose. The servants had tried, exclaiming, to take it from her, but she hadn't let them. Aretel looked pained. "Trust me. If you know what you're doing for that girl, you'll want to see this doctor."

202

There was something meaningful in the severe gaze that, as usual, made Iyone shut up and acquiesce.

It was the physician who had tended her childhood ailments, a plump older woman called Poire, with a hearty laugh and broad eyes skirted by laughter lines. "Iyone!" she crowed, bustling in with her bowls and phials of noxious unguents. "Fighting off assassins all by yourself, I hear? You're more trouble than five of your brother. Let me feel your pulse."

Her pulse was fine. Iyone made herself smile, and stuck out her wrist. "Look at you," said Poire. She had always been a talker. "So tall and strong, when you used to be such a scrappy little thing. I attended your mother at your birth, you know. You were terrifying. Dawdled on your way for two full days, and a fortnight premature at that. The High Priestess herself showed up in case Aretel needed her last rites done. Here, wipe your face."

Wearily, Iyone took the warm towel and daubed her face with it. It smelled of peppermint. "She's always told me I was going to be the death of her."

Poire chuckled. "Now Hiraen, that was a different tale altogether. Popped out in a matter of hours, glowing like the dawn and yowling to bring the house down. It's rare a first birth is so much easier than a second."

For some reason, none of this surprised Iyone. "What about Savonn? Did you attend his birth too?"

"Oh, no," said Poire. "His mother Danei was an odd one. Daughter to Jehan Cayn, the Lord of Terinea. It's always in the great houses that you see this sort of madness."

"Madness?"

Poire looked disapproving. "Poor fierce thing, she was half crazed all through her pregnancy. Sequestered herself in a convent of Mother Alakyne in her fourth month, refused to speak to any doctors, wouldn't even see her family. I was in Terinea near the expected time, and went to offer my services, but she screamed at me and flung me out."

Iyone allowed the towel to fall from her face. Aretel, subtle as ever, had brought in this woman for a reason. "What? But I heard she was frail. Surely someone had to look after her."

"She had the women of her household with her," said Poire, retrieving the towel. "A couple of handmaids, and that slave of hers." She cupped her hands over her mouth, her eyes going wide. "Oh, that's terribly impolitic. She's all high and mighty now."

It was difficult to look disinterested. "No one's listening but me," said Iyone. "You're speaking, of course, of Lady Josit?"

Poire grinned, her elderly face full of youthful mischief. "The very same. They were good friends, you know. Insofar as a free woman can be friends with a slave." She lowered her voice. "It's no wonder they didn't mind sharing Kedris."

Iyone managed a giggle. "So," she said, "when Danei sequestered herself in the convent, Josit went with her? You didn't happen to see her there, by any chance?"

Eagerness made her blunt. But Poire was not Aretel, and enjoyed the gossip too much to be suspicious. "No. Only Danei, big as a balloon and twice as fragile, the darling. Truth be told, I was astonished she survived the birth."

She mixed a hot posset for Iyone and departed not long after, in a flurry of exhortations to stay warm and drink echinacea tea and not to quarrel with any more assassins. Iyone drank the posset, but did not go to sleep. She found a vase for the rose, filled it with water, and placed it at her bedside. Then she sat down to think.

Danei had been sequestered from her fourth month to the birth of her child. That was half a year in which Josit was unaccounted for. If they had conceived around the same time, then neither pregnancy would have been visible before they entered the convent. Josit could have given birth there in secret. Only Danei would have known, and she was eight years in her grave.

But this meant that Josit's child must have been born the same time as Savonn, or not long before. July 1512. His birthday had just passed unremarked, as had Iyone's own. As children they had celebrated with joint parties, much to Hiraen's jealousy. They had been inseparable, after all, and their birthdays were in the same week—

She sprang to her feet.

No. That was not possible. Poire had attested to Iyone's own birth, not in some Terinean convent, but in this very house in Cassarah. And Aretel, for all her subtleties, was not a liar. Josit was not Iyone's mother. It could not be.

It was, she had to admit, something of a disappointment.

CHAPTER 16

Iyone would have liked nothing better than to call on Shandei the next morning. But Aretel, looking dubiously at the rose blooming by her bedside, said it was still a bad idea to be seen together, so she had to satisfy herself with word from Linn that the girl was safe.

The rumours permeated the city by dawn. Lucien's brave daughter, she of the lofty stare and the insalubrious humour, had fought the Thorn all by herself and sent him running. She received visits from several old admirers, their interest rekindled; and even from Oriane Sydell, who seemed to prefer Aretel's company to Lord Willon's these days. But Iyone knew that their esteem was misplaced. If anyone had been courageous last night, it was Shandei—Shandei, who had planned the feint, and risked capture and death to divert suspicion from Iyone.

Now it was Iyone's turn to do something for her. She pondered all day, and then at suppertime paid a visit to Josit Ansa.

Kedris's mistress had never lived with him. She had her own manor on the Street of Canaries, as small and graceful as its occupant, with a few apple trees in the garden and an elaborate marble fountain fashioned like a leaping trout. The steward, a freedman with impeccable manners, ushered Iyone into a solar, and soon afterwards Josit arrived. "Why," she said, seating herself on a low rosewood settee. "I thought you would have lost your taste for walking about after nightfall."

Iyone was at the harpsichord, playing an elaborate waltz Josit had once taught her. "I brought all my guards today," she said. "And Elysa. How awkward for her if she *is* spying for you."

Josit gave an obscure smile. Kohl and powder made her look ten years younger than she was, slender and fragile, but Iyone knew she was far from decorative. She had survived years of slavery, had swum the Morivant to escape Sarei and, twenty-three years ago, had borne and hidden a child. "You do know, my dear, that I would never lay a hand on you? Yesterday's attack had nothing to do with me."

"I know perfectly well who it was," said Iyone. "So do you."

Her patience for equivocation was wearing thin. The topic of Shandei was raw and sore, an open wound she had to cover. It was stupid not to have considered that the girl might make a move of her own, which would put Iyone in her debt. Another unforgivable oversight. No wonder she was losing.

"Then," said Josit, "why are you here?"

"To play your harpsichord," said Iyone. Her hands danced across the keys, guided more by instinct than conscious thought. "To let you know that you have made your move, and it is now my turn. You put Shandei in danger. If you do not desist, I have one or two very damning plays of my own to make."

Josit raised her brows, as if Iyone were a toddler throwing a tantrum. "The matter of the children? Really, just because I made one trifling remark?"

"As I recall," said Iyone, "I was the one who made the remark. I know that your child was born in July 1512, in the same convent where Danei Cayn gave birth. I know that you want this to remain a secret. And I can reveal it, if and when I choose."

She turned back to the harpsichord, ignoring the rapidly changing meteorology of Josit's face. "I wonder," she mused, "why you went to so much trouble to hide the child? I could ask Danei's old handmaids. They may still live in Terinea."

An uninterpretable pause. She did not look up. There was a sharp movement at the corner of her eye, and then Josit came up beside her on silent feet and crashed both palms on the keys. A thunderous cacophony rang out, interrupting the waltz. Iyone's fingers stilled.

"I," said Josit, "would like to hear your guesses."

Because Iyone was seated, Josit had the advantage of height. "Was it the father?" Iyone asked. "Were you afraid of him?" As soon as she said the words, she knew they tasted wrong. Josit had never been afraid of anyone. "Was it whoever enslaved you in Daliss?"

Josit's lip twisted. "The father is dead. His identity will not astonish you. The woman who sold me into slavery, however, is very much alive."

Iyone got up, rocking the bench. Everyone knew Josit's story. King Romett of Sarei, an imprudent man who believed in nothing but self-indulgence, had died leaving at least a dozen putative heirs. Of these, it was Marguerit who butchered her way to the throne. The Court had been all but decimated in the wake of her accession, entire families wiped out for having picked the wrong side. Josit must have sprung from one of these extinguished houses. There was no Dalissan family called Ansa, but this was no doubt an assumed name.

"You mean Marguerit," said Iyone slowly. "But it's been so long. Why would she care?"

"Because, my poor, slow novice," said Josit, "there is no one she fears more than me. I brought all her secrets to Cassarah. I taught Kedris how to defeat her at the Morivant. And worst of all, I was her sister, and very nearly her queen."

Iyone's hand fell onto the keyboard, and created a plash of sound.

"Right father, wrong mother," said Josit. She had recovered her composure. "The rest is easy to figure out. The child I bore, bastard son of a bastard daughter, could have threatened her legitimate heirs. But she no longer needs to worry. And neither do you. The child was stillborn."

Iyone was silent. "So, my love," said Josit, smiling once more, "as you once told me: find another avenue."

* * *

Iyone returned home in a temper, sent away Elysa and all her attendants, and began to throw together clothes and money for a madcap trip to Terinea. Then rage gave way to resentment, and she unpacked everything again.

She did not doubt that Josit was Marguerit's sister. Such facts were easily verifiable. The child, on the other hand... If it was stillborn, why the incredible secrecy? Why, twenty-three years later, was Josit still afraid that someone might find out? If Iyone visited the convent, she could ask a few questions for herself. But Josit's threats had been plain enough. If she went away, there was no telling what might befall Shandei in her absence. She had made a promise to Hiraen. And her father had put his affairs in order, and was ready to march out with his small army any day now.

These days, Iyone's mind was a whirlwind of disparate ideas that kept her tossing all night. They coalesced now, like ingredients in a diviner's cauldron, into a near-coherent plan. Her father would pass through Terinea. She could not ask him for help—he had all the subtlety of an ill-tempered mule, heavens preserve him—but with him would go four hundred soldiers and an assortment of servants, cooks, and camp-followers. One more would not be noticed.

Her father and mother were bickering in the parlour. The guards were preparing for the march to Medrai, and Elysa was out. No one was paying Iyone any attention. She crept down the hall to the spare room that more or less belonged to Savonn, borrowed a few choice pieces of clothing, and slipped out of the house.

Hiraen had been a frequent guest at the Second Captain's home, but Iyone herself had never visited. The walk across the city was long and, after the events of the previous night, vaguely nerve-wracking in the dark. The white-roofed house that now belonged to Shandei was quiet, the windows unlit; but as Iyone stood listening in the shadows on the street, a curious, regular beat of thuds and twangs drifted to her from the backyard.

She went round the house, past the fragrant hedges and herb beds, and found Shandei shooting arrows into a straw man.

They had met but twice, both times under harried circumstances. She had never noticed how lively Shandei's eyes were, how she moved from the hip and balanced her weight on the balls of her feet like a cheetah about to spring. Her bow was a recurve, like Hiraen's. The pull of her arm was straight and strong, and every arrow struck home in the straw man's chest.

Without turning around, Shandei said, "I could teach you if you wanted."

In her muddled memories, the Thorn's voice was a gruff rasp. Shandei's, sweet and clear, was incongruent enough to break Iyone out of her reverie. "Hiraen tried," she said. "I'm afraid he gave up after I shot him in his hat-pin."

"Accidentally?"

"That's what I told him."

Shandei lowered the bow and came, half smiling, across the yard. Her roving eyes took in the oversized work-shirt and patched trousers Iyone was wearing, and her gaze settled somewhere over Iyone's left shoulder, as if in a deliberate effort not to stare. Her voice was not as steady as her hands on the bow—on

Iyone's neck—had been. "I'm sorry. It was the only thing I could think to do, when I heard you were in trouble with the Efrens. I— I didn't hurt you?"

This would be complicated. In a fair world Iyone would have met Shandei at a ball, or a play, or in passing at the bazaar, and Hiraen and Savonn would have had nothing to do with it. Perhaps they would have found themselves eyeing the same brooch; and Iyone, in a fit of star-struck generosity, would have bought it for Shandei and pinned it on her cloak to make her blush. It could have been so simple. But she had stopped believing in fairness a long time ago.

"Not in the least," she said. "In fact, it was the most fun I've had since Savonn left town." Distantly, she remembered what she had come for. "I promised to call on you after Midsummer. How rude of me to be tardy."

"You were being followed," said Shandei. Her eyes flitted up to capture Iyone's, then darted away again. "Hence the disguise."

"Yes," said Iyone. "Surely you've worked out by now that Josit is the Thorn?"

She saw she was mistaken. The look on Shandei's face transitioned from wrong-footed surprise to wide-eyed hurt to thin-lipped indignation, a fine-grained triptych under sterling moonlight. "But—she was kind to me. She even came to my father's funeral. Why would she..."

Justice is not kindness, Iyone remembered. Particularly if the justice was not meant for you. "Is that a rhetorical question?"

"No," said Shandei. "Yes. No."

"Quite simply," said Iyone, "she was stalling the Efrens."

In the perfumed hush of the garden, she found it was easy to be patient. "Willon has been too distracted to make another bid for power. His supporters have all been scared off. If Savonn waltzed back home tonight, he would find himself declared Governor of Cassarah *and* High Commander of the army before he could so much as pull out one of his wigs. The only problem, really, is that the poor fellow has no interest in power except as a private joke."

"I see," said Shandei slowly, in the voice of one who didn't see at all.

"What, doesn't it make sense?"

"It makes perfect sense," said Shandei. "That's the problem." She looked down at the bow in her hands. "I thought..."

"We all thought many things about Josit," said Iyone. She could have gone on, but it occurred to her that she had been talking a lot, at volume, and rather breathlessly. That was the trouble with her. She knew too much, and wasn't subtle enough. It came of being friends with Savonn. Bad chess, Josit would say.

"I thought," said Shandei, "she fancied herself an avenging spirit. But she just needed a scapegoat, didn't she? She's put all her arrows in Lord Silvertongue's quiver, and now she has to make him fire them one way or another."

Once more she met Iyone's gaze, and this time held it. "If you ask me, she looked the wrong way. You would make a much better ruler than Savonn."

"Most people would," said Iyone dryly. Eager not to be sidetracked, she added, "You should also know that my father is leading a host into the Farfallens. The Council thinks there will be war."

Shandei took a step forward. "Oh, gods."

Instinctively, Iyone reached out a hand to reassure her. Then she withdrew it with a jerk, disconcerted, when it brushed against Shandei's own, outstretched in the same palliative gesture. The look on Shandei's face, which she had assumed to be fear, transpired instead to be concern. Off-balance again, Iyone realised what she had forgotten: that Shandei, a soldier's daughter, knew exactly what it was to fear for her kin; that her own brother, so much younger than Hiraen and Savonn, was deep in the Farfallens himself, in far more danger than Lord Lucien was likely to see.

Iyone said, "It doesn't matter. I came here to say—"

"Of course it matters, don't be—"

"To say," said Iyone firmly, "that this development suits everyone. My father is concerned about Hiraen. Josit is concerned about Savonn. Willon is concerned about himself, and anyone who might impede his precious ambitions. It will please him only too well to see my father off to the Farfallens. So our brothers will get the help they need, and..."

"And you?" asked Shandei.

"And I," said Iyone, "get to smuggle you away, out of Josit's reach."

A cricket was screaming. With Josit, one played chess. With Savonn, it was poker. With Shandei, whose idea of helping people consisted of stalking them down and strangling them half to death, Iyone was at a loss, feeling her way from toehold to toehold up a sheer rock face. Shandei said, "And if I don't want to be smuggled away?"

"It would be annoying," said Iyone, "to be thwarted on all fronts. I'm sure I'll think of something else. I just thought, since yours was the life she was risking, you might like to help me strike a blow against her." She paused. "Find some leverage, so to speak."

Shandei frowned. "What leverage?"

Using as few words as possible, Iyone explained the situation with Josit. When Shandei stared, eyes alight with curiosity, she knew she had won. "Marguerit's *sister*! Surely not!"

In spite of herself, Iyone was smiling. "If I'd known you liked gossip, I would have led with this," she said. "I wonder which alarms you more: the prospect of Willon as Governor, or Josit as Queen of Sarei?"

"Both," said Shandei flatly. She kicked off her shoes and sat down on the porch stoop, the bow laid across her lap like an infant. After a moment, Iyone joined her. The moonlight peered through the foliage to cast diaphanous shadow-webs at their feet, and overhead, a night bird hooted. "You want me to visit this convent. To dig out this child of hers."

"That's an indelicate verb."

"But this is an indelicate job," said Shandei. "Do you really think she'll stop if we find the child? What if she was telling the truth, and it *was* stillborn? What if she doesn't care either way?"

"She does," said Iyone. The crash of the harpsichord still resounded at the back of her mind. "I've never seen her so angry before."

"That's because you're poking your nose into her personal affairs," said Shandei, with the air of a schoolmistress haranguing a slow student. "It's a dead child, not some riddle for you to solve. We're being terribly rude."

"So we are."

Shandei scrubbed the back of her hand across her face. "It's just," she said, "do we need to get in her way? She's tormenting the Efrens. They're hardly innocent."

Looking down at her booted feet next to Shandei's bare ones, Iyone realised where she was going wrong. Shandei's objection had very little to do with Josit, and everything to do with her blood feud. She did not want to leave Cassarah because, as far as she was concerned, she had to kill Willon. And it was beyond Iyone to explain that she didn't have to, because it was not, in fact, Willon who had slain the Second Captain.

"She's using you," she said.

"*I'm* not innocent," said Shandei. She drew her big toe in a vicious arc across the grass, and one or two blades went flying. "Vesmer died because of me. Josit did that too, didn't she? I thought I saw someone on the Rose Bridge that night. If I hadn't gone up there—"

"For heaven's sake," said Iyone. Shandei was beginning to remind her of Hiraen. "You can't take the world's ills on your shoulders. Josit does whatever she pleases. Sooner or later he would have died some other way."

"Maybe," said Shandei. "But I thought—"

She stared down at her hands. "I thought maybe the Ceriyes killed him for me. It all felt very righteous, even if it was horrible. But now I know it was just Josit, there's nothing righteous about it at all. He's just one more dead man."

It took Iyone a moment to remember that—for many people—the gods were real, and existed outside of books and temples. So much about Shandei was unexpected. "No one's innocent," said Iyone. "Neither am I. So I don't factor such things into my decisions."

"Then why are you doing this?"

Gods, if Shandei only knew. "It's just like you said. I'm trying to solve a riddle. Besides, I grow enamoured of girls who knock me down in dark alleys and give me roses."

Shandei struggled to keep a straight face, the curves of her mouth tightening. Then she gave in, and grinned, and dropped her face into her upturned palms. "That's unfair. You're no better than Josit."

"Of course not," said Iyone. There was a strange feeling in her stomach, akin to the sensation one felt when missing a step on the stairs. "I would be overjoyed to possess a thimble-cup of her brilliance. Will you help me or not?"

Shandei tore a hand through her hair, pulling some of it loose from its knot. "Fine," she said, sitting up again. "I'll visit your convent. I'll find this child. And then it will be *your* turn to give me roses."

Victory: ever elusive, and sweet enough to always be worth the chasing. "My dear," said Iyone, giddy with triumph, "right now, I could be persuaded to give you an entire rose hedge and all the thorns in it."

CHAPTER 17

Deep in the Farfallens, summer was feeble and quick to flee, and autumn was unheard of. The yard at Onaressi underwent an overnight transformation from muddy and malodorous to slick and frosty, and by the time the garrison woke in the morning to find the crenellations of the ramparts gilded with fresh coats of glittering ice, Anyas already regretted agreeing to stay behind. The Captain must have reached Astorre by now, and no doubt *he* was safe and warm, and attending a different fancy ball every night.

"Or dead," said Poldam, his lieutenant, who was so dour it actually cheered one up to talk to him. They were warming their hands at a brazier on the ringwall, eyeing the ballooning clouds above the postern. It was just before dawn, and the stars were faint pinpricks against a violet sky. "It's hard work, it is, being dead. All them pleas and prayers to answer, and the odd haunting, and there ain't no pay for that."

Anyas did not like to think of Savonn being dead. Sure, things had been easier under the old Captain—one always knew where one stood with Merrott, even if he was blunt and irritable at the best of times—but Savonn had proven a frighteningly competent leader under the theatre-boy gilding, and it was hard not to admire him. "Huh," he said, distracted. It was too cold for speech. The sentries he had posted along the wall were walking fast to stay warm, breath puffing around their blue faces in waiflike clouds.

"And," said Poldam, gathering steam for a good rant, "if the Captain doesn't come back before the snow sets in, he won't get through again till spring. We best hope them Astorrians are feeling hospitable. Else they'll be living off their boot leather by then."

"No one eats boot leather," piped up young Cerris. "That's only in stories. They'd eat each other first."

"No one'd eat *you*," said Poldam gloomily. "You've got no meat on you to speak of."

Just then Anyas froze; or at least, the parts of him that were not already frozen did. He thought he had heard something. "Shut up for a moment."

Trained to a fault despite their grousing, they fell silent at once. The coals sizzled in the brazier, and the wind, ever-present, moaned its dirge between the white-veiled mountains. The more imaginative men sometimes said they could still hear the voices of the Saraians they had killed on Midsummer, a sacred night, their death-cries trapped to echo up and down the Pass for all eternity. Perhaps Anyas, too, was growing superstitious. But then he heard it again—a broken call, faint on the wind—and all doubt fled.

They exchanged looks. Anyas fetched a lantern and leaned out over the ringwall. "Who's there?"

Illuminated and exposed on the wall, he knew he made a fine target for archers lying in wait. But the lantern-light revealed nothing besides the scrubby grass, pockmarked with patches of frost. Then the shadows stirred, and a hand came into view near the door, stretched towards the light in entreaty. "Help," cried a reedy voice, nearly lost in the howling wind. "Help me!"

A fist pounded on the postern. Then it stopped, as if the supplicant had run out of strength. Anyas shoved the lantern into Poldam's hands and headed to the stairs. "Open the door!"

The two sentries at the postern were already sliding back the bolts, their spears couched, when Anyas reached ground level with Poldam and Cerris. The door creaked half an inch ajar, then screamed all the way open as the wind caught it in its grasp. Anyas swore. The gale sunk its claws into his face, coaxing tears from his eyes. It was a moment before he could make out the figure crouched on hands and knees, cowering like a beaten cur under the spears. Between full-bodied shivers, a man's voice sobbed. "Help me... milords..."

"Mother Above," said Anyas. At his gesture, the sentries lowered their spears. The stranger was barefoot, his hose ripped, his tunic slathered with dirt. He had no weapon, not even a swordbelt. "What is your name, sir? What befell you?"

He knelt beside the wounded man and reached for his arm, meaning to see where he was hurt, but the fellow made a keening noise and recoiled. He reeked of earth and sweat, and beneath that, something more primal, like blood. His muddy hair tumbled into his eyes, lending his face a strange feral cast. "Sir," said Anyas, "try to answer. What befell you?"

Without needing orders, Poldam and the others had fanned out to surround them, holding up torches so Anyas could see. The man lay sobbing in their midst, curled in on himself with his arms wrapped around his chest. Injuries aside, he must have been half frozen. "Bandits... just out of Astorre..."

He spoke decent Falwynian. A merchant, Anyas guessed, travelling on business from Astorre. He would have been ripe picking for the bandits, both in and out of Marguerit's pay. "You are among friends," Anyas said. "Where are you hurt? Let us help you."

Delirious, the man did not seem to understand. He wailed when Anyas tried to lift the bloody tunic, and twitched away from

218

Poldam and Cerris when they made to hoist him, scratching his hands and wrists on the brambles. At length someone had the wits to fetch him a thick woollen cloak, and in the renewed warmth, he came back to himself. Interrupted by frequent tremors, he told them his tale. His party of eight had been set upon near Astorre and robbed of all they had. Only he and his brother had lived, and come on foot through Forech's Pass to Onaressi, which they had heard was garrisoned by the Silvertongue's men these days. The brother was too weak to climb the winding track to the fort, so he was waiting below for help. All they had with them was a wagon of wine, which the bandits had left untouched.

By now, a crowd had gathered at the postern. The men murmured among themselves, peering into the darkness. The prospects were grim. In this weather, it was unlikely that the brother would survive. But their wine ration was running low. Anyas snapped his fingers at Poldam. "Take your patrol down to the Pass and see what you can do. We'll bring this fellow inside."

Poldam and his men departed at once, their cressets bobbing like disembodied eyes down the mountainside. "All right," said Anyas to their supplicant. "Now you."

The man did not want to be carried. He staggered to his feet, hobbled a few laborious steps, and fell down again on the threshold of the postern. Anyas was beginning to lose his patience. "Fetch a stretcher," he said. "And the doctor."

Cerris was gaping. "He won't live through the night."

"We have to try."

But before he could move, one of the others seized Anyas's arm, pointing. "Look!"

Anyas turned. One or two of the cressets weaving down the track had gone out, as if their bearers had dropped their torches. The remaining lights swayed at erratic angles. Then came a shout, and the hiss of swords scraping from their scabbards; and the clamour, unmistakeable after all these years on the battlefield, of steel crashing on steel. "It's Poldam, sir!" Cerris cried, his own sword already in hand. "He's been attacked!"

Anyas swore again. The injured man screamed and flung his arms around his head, gibbering a mottled stream of prayers and pleas and oaths. "Gods," said Anyas. "Cerris, take *your* patrol and go see what's happened. Don't go far. There can't be many of them. Where's the bloody stretcher?"

Cerris ran off, shouting. Someone else went to find the doctor. Alone once more with the postern sentries, Anyas bent and, ignoring the man's protesting screeches, seized him under the arms to haul him back to standing. "You have to come in, sir. We need to close the gate. You'll be safe inside. Now, if you please…"

They tottered through the gate. Adrenaline seemed to have lent the man strength: he did not stumble again, and barely leaned on Anyas at all. "Sit down," said Anyas, once they had cleared the ringwall. There was another brazier by the postern, which would stave off the worst of the cold. "I must go to my lieutenant. The doctor will be here any moment."

"You are kind," said the man. "In the next life you will have your reward."

His voice had altered. It was languid now, and smoky, the last blaze of a funeral pyre. Anyas looked up. The man was standing without help, meeting his gaze full on in the light of the brazier. His face was young and shapely, with deep golden skin that clung tight to the prominent curve of his high cheekbones. Beneath his auburn hair, his eyes were perfectly lucid, and shining with mischief. "Not in *this* life, I fear."

In times like these, fear fled, to be replaced by a decade's worth of hard-won battle instinct. Responding before he was aware of any conscious thought, Anyas lurched back, snatching up a spear. "To arms!" he shouted. "It's a trick! *To arms!*"

The sentries scrambled to bolt the postern. But quicker than one would have thought possible, the redhead was already moving. A pair of throwing knives materialised in his hands, as if he

220

had conjured them out of thought. Then his wrists flicked. Anyas looked away from the man for a moment, long enough to see both sentries on the ground, slender silver hilts glimmering in their throats.

A moment too long. The redhead was smiling at him, hands hovering over the brass brazier. The noise of battle had grown louder, and closer. "Do you recognise the knives?"

Anyas did. He also recognised the throw. "Savonn," he said. "What have you done with him?"

No answer. His spear-tip met thin air. The man moved; the brazier winked; and then all Anyas knew were falling coals, and the bite of fire, and the high, thin sound of his own screams.

CHAPTER 18

Freshly exiled, Emaris and the men of Betronett took three forts along Ilsa's Pass on their way back to Medrai.

The first, Nikas showed them, had a wall with a crumbling section. Daine lit a dozen cookfires in front of the fort to make it look as if they were settling down for a long siege; then Savonn and Hiraen led them over the weak spot in the wall, and took it within the hour. The second fort did not hold out much longer, though the defenders fought admirably, hurling rocks from the ramparts and shooting at them through arrow slits. Given the dubious honour of leading the van, Emaris and his patrol grappled their way over the palisade to open a postern for the others, and were feted like kings when the day was won. All the same, he was relieved when the garrison of the third fort—having heard of their predecessors' defeat—abandoned their posts in the night and melted into the new snow.

This one was a tiny holdfast labelled Kimmet on their maps, the last inhabitable fort on Ilsa's Pass. "Send out scouts to track the garrison," Savonn told Emaris, as they concluded their tour of the kitchens—not meanly provisioned—and the empty stables, still smelling of horse. "They can't have gone far in this weather."

The road was slushy with sleet, the first sign that autumn was about to sink its teeth into the Farfallens and spit them out into the paralysing cold of winter. They had come nearly full circle from where they had begun. Another two days or so, and they would see the towers of Medrai rising through the mists. "And after that?" Emaris asked as they stopped in the hallway outside Savonn's quarters. He was not hopeful. The shape of home was tiny and faraway in his mind, like a jewel viewed from the wrong end of a looking-glass. "Back to the Bitten Hill? Cassarah?"

Between the two extremes of trivialities and matters of life and death, they had had little to say to each other since Astorre. Savonn seldom slept, and never seemed to be looking properly at anyone. "That depends on Hiraen, when he decides to start talking to me again," he said. "He may want to regroup at Medrai. Or take you lot home and give the Council a few choicely worded instructions on what to do with their heads and their bungholes."

The use of the second person pronoun was alarming. "Us? What about you?"

"I thought," said Savonn, "I made it quite clear that I had a personal feud to attend to. Since my adversary appears to frighten you all so much, I shall deal with him myself."

He was already listing towards the open door of his chamber. He no longer roomed with Hiraen, a development on which only Nikas had been blithe enough to comment. Emaris planted himself in Savonn's path, scowling. He had not abandoned his sister and his dead father only to be turned off in the middle of a campaign. "Wherever you go, I shall follow you."

"Presently," said Savonn, with his most malefic smile, "I am not going anywhere except to bed. If you insist on coming along, I shall charge admission."

Emaris glowered, turned his back, and beat a dignified retreat.

* * *

223

It felt like his head had barely hit the pillow when a hand touched his shoulder, shaking him awake. He groaned and swatted it away, still submerged in fragmented dreams of snowstorms and rockfalls and the gleam of lamplight on auburn hair. Then a voice spoke into his ear. "Emaris!"

It was Nikas, hunkering low to whisper. "The scouts found the runaway garrison. Not many, maybe thirty. They're about fifteen miles off, fleeing southward down the Pass."

Emaris pushed himself up on an elbow, rubbing bleary eyes. The sky had faded to a watery blue-grey, the moon a pale wafer wallowing in its shallows. A foot away, Lomas was snoring. "How fast are they going?"

"Slow. We'll catch up by noon if we leave now." Nikas hesitated, his hair a fuzzy halo around his face. "Should I wake the Captain?"

These days, any message for Savonn usually passed through Emaris first, since no one else wanted to risk incurring his ire. He sighed. "I better do it."

He stepped over the sleeping forms of his patrol and padded out into the hall. Savonn's door did not lock, but a tripwire had been rigged across the bottom of the doorway, with the effect that Emaris nearly entered the room head first. He found the Captain asleep for once, curled up like a nestling bird in a shaft of twilight with his head under a pillow. Remembering the last time he had touched Savonn, Emaris decided against laying hands on his person, and tugged at the blanket instead. "Savonn?"

With Savonn, the transition between sleeping and waking was a quick and abrupt one, unmarked by any external sign save a tensing of the muscles and a shift in his breathing. Crouched by the bunk, Emaris relayed the news to him. "I'll wake my patrol. We'll be ready at once."

Savonn pushed the pillow away. His gaze went straight through Emaris to the ceiling. "Who brought the news?"

"Nikas."

A missed beat. Then Savonn sat up, still fully dressed. "Let your boys rest. Wake Hiraen's patrol, I'll take them instead."

Emaris did so, and came back to the room with a chunk of bread and a flask of water. Despite the muffled chink of cuirass and sword and the murmur of the arming men, most of the doors were still shut, the rooms quiet. "Go back to bed, gazelle," said Savonn, stepping out into the hall with the food Emaris had brought. "I won't be long."

But all thoughts of sleep had fled. Emaris ran after him to the stairwell landing, the stone floor chilling his bare feet with the savage cold unique to early mornings. "You're not taking me with you?"

"There's no need. Your place is with your patrol."

"I'm your *squire*!"

Savonn smiled. There was something different about it this morning, something soft-edged and sad. "I promoted you."

He disappeared down the stairs. Emaris turned away, seething. He swung a kick at the baluster, quite forgetting that he was unshod, and all but crushed his toes. He was hopping on one foot, yelling, when someone peered down from the attic landing. "What's all the noise about?"

It was Hiraen. A fresh surge of outrage bordering on absurdity loomed over Emaris, and crashed over his head. Savonn had not even woken Hiraen, his deputy, to tell him where he was going—with Hiraen's own patrol at that. "He's gone. He took your men and went after the bandits."

Shirtless and tousled from sleep, Hiraen's response was still sharp. "Who brought word?"

It was the same question Savonn had asked. "Nikas."

Hiraen swore, invoking the Mother Above and at least four minor deities. He vanished for a moment and reappeared with a crumpled shirt on, holding his bow and quiver. "Get your things," he said. "Leave your patrol, there isn't time."

Emaris started to limp towards his room. "You think he'll let us come?"

Hiraen shrugged. His face was a thunderclap made flesh. "He won't know we're there until it's too late."

* * *

Under the impression that their patrol leader was playing a trick on their commander, Hiraen's men did not comment on the stowaways trailing the column. Savonn remained unaware of their presence for a good two hours, until they halted for a meal and he came to mingle with the men. As usual, he revealed no surprise when he spotted them among the ranks, but his shoulders tightened and his lips came together in a narrow line, and he concluded his conversation at once to go over to them. Under his breath, he said, "What are you doing?"

"I could ask you the same," said Hiraen. "It's my patrol."

"We're hunting Saraians," said Savonn shortly. "I thought to let you sleep."

"You *thought*—" Hiraen threw up his hands. "Gods, how much of an idiot do you take me for? Whatever game you're playing with your friend from the wrong side of the border, you'd best leave my men out of it."

Emaris edged away, wishing he were out of earshot. He had very little idea what they were fighting about, and thought it might be best to stay ignorant. Savonn was rigid and pale, his fingers furled tight at his sides. "This is the road the scouts said the garrison took. Ask *him*." He jerked his head in Emaris's direction. "Or don't. I may have corrupted him into lying for me, after all. I have such a way of doing that."

He flung off to the front of the column, and soon they were moving again.

They were more than a mile away before Emaris dared to break the icy silence. "He's right, you know." It was easier to address his feet than look at Hiraen. "Nikas said they went this way."

"I know," said Hiraen. He sighed, blowing some hair out of his face. "I'm an ass."

Emaris said nothing. He hated quarrelling.

"It's not you he's angry with," Hiraen added. "Never you." He grimaced. Unlike Savonn, trained to a hair-splitting fault in the great theatre of Cassarah, he did not often trouble to school his face. "We grew up together. That's a long time to accumulate grudges."

"That night in Astorre—"

"Yes." Hiraen fidgeted with a strap on his cuirass. "You must have questions."

The buckles on the strap clinked against each other, an agitated, discordant noise. Emaris worried at his bottom lip with his teeth. "They were lovers," said Hiraen abruptly. "Years ago, before he became Captain. You've probably guessed."

"I—"

Hiraen spoke over him with a sort of vicious desperation. "Being Savonn, he chose the most lethal of Astorre's beautiful men to toy with. The Saraian consul. He didn't even try to pretend he didn't know. The danger was half the attraction." He pulled the strap loose altogether, stared blankly at it, and let his hand fall. "When we get back, I'll make him explain. You deserve to know. About this and—other things."

Something in his voice struck a chord of dread deep in Emaris's memory. *He killed for me*, Savonn had said. "Does it have anything to do with—"

The words caught in his throat. He swallowed. "Rendell?" Hiraen suggested, his eyes dark with loathing. "Your father knew about the whole business, no doubt. One can only imagine what he made of it."

Emaris fought down a wave of dizziness. More than ever, he missed his sister. Shandei could always make palatable what was hard to swallow, and what she could not put right, she would beat up. "The problem with Savonn," said Hiraen, the words coming low and quick, "no, the problem with *everything*, is that I owe him too much." He said it as if in answer to a question, though Emaris had not spoken. "It was my fault, him coming to serve under Merrott at all. He never wanted to leave the theatre."

"His father made him," said Emaris, baffled. Everyone knew that.

"Yes. But it was about me. Gods, this isn't the time. I'll—"

He broke off. Emaris said, "What's wrong?"

Hiraen had stopped walking, his head cocked to one side. When Emaris started to speak again, he shushed him. "Pursuit."

"*What?*"

Hiraen crouched down, swept aside a patch of old snow with his gloved hands, and put his ear to the ground. Emaris imitated him. They were still at the back of the column, and no one took notice. After a moment the sound came to Emaris too, a messy rhythm of dull clips and clops on the cold packed earth. A sizeable host on horseback, by the sounds of it. "But we can't have passed the garrison yet," he said. "Not if they're mounted."

"It's not the garrison. If they're mounted, they probably came straight from Astorre. A fortnight. Celisse must have let them go early." Emaris was still unravelling this thread of thought when Hiraen leapt up and sprinted to the front of the column. "Savonn! It's a trick! They're behind us!"

A man of Betronett needed no orders. Almost in unison, the patrol stopped and drew their swords, or began stringing their bows. Emaris scrambled after Hiraen, checking his quiver as he went. "At least fifty," Hiraen was saying. "A quarter-mile off. They'll be on us in no time."

Savonn looked from him to Emaris and back. His eyes were the same colour as the blade of the shortsword gleaming in his hand. If he felt anything beyond mild irritation, it did not show. "You shouldn't have come."

Hiraen ignored him. "We're outnumbered two to one. If you pull that disappearing trick of yours, you and Emaris might be able to slip back to Kimmet and get help. We'll try to hold them off—"

"Martyrdom doesn't suit you," said Savonn. "Stop talking and nock your bow."

He took in the terrain, gaze alighting on rock and tree and tract of hoarfrost. There were several large boulders on either side of the road, which might provide some cover and encumber a horse. Apart from that, the terrain was utterly unhelpful. "We haven't got spears, so there's no sense trying to repel a charge. Split up and get behind those rocks. We'll shoot as soon as they come into range, throw them into disorder before they close in. I hope," he added, off-handed, as if the thought had only just occurred to him, "that none of you are afraid to die?"

The men chorused their vehement assent. Hiraen's patrol was much older and hardier than Emaris's new-formed one. These were soldiers who had been serving for decades, who had fought under Merrott at the Battle of the Morivant and then, rich as merchant-princes with plunder, simply went back to the Bitten Hill and kept fighting. Death, faced down and defeated a dozen times, had lost its power to frighten. But Emaris was not like them. He wanted to live.

He exhaled, and fumbled for an arrow. Everyone wanted to live.

"I'll take the right side of the road," Savonn was saying, as the patrol divided itself up and got down in the ungenerous cover of the rocks. "You two can take the left."

"I'll stay with you," said Emaris at once.

Savonn's stare was glacially impersonal, as if Emaris were no more than an obstacle in the road to be levelled. "No."

Hiraen's hand found Emaris's shoulder, drawing him off to the opposite side of the road. He went unresisting. There was no time for an argument, or even for hurt. Already the hoofbeats were plain to them all, and soon their attackers would be among them.

Scarcely after they had concealed themselves, the first riders came round the bend in the road. They bore no standard, but their horses' trappings fluttered white and grey in the wind of their speed. Emaris squinted. The sun played on the scarred seams of frost, drawing the eye in confusing patterns. Spears, swords, a few bows. No Empath, but the big figure in the lead had to be the Marshal. Isemain was shouting, hand lifted in a signal. He had seen the rocks.

"Hold," Hiraen whispered.

Emaris's fingers perspired in their gloves, tense on the bow-string. Shoot in the calm between breaths, or so a long string of teachers had exhorted him, his sister and his father and Daine and Hiraen and Savonn. But he was breathing so fast that it was impossible. The Saraians had slowed, swords bared like shining teeth. Their armour shone as they approached, not the patchwork of mismatched plate and mail like that of the brigands they had routed from the forts, but the costly finery of Marguerit's army, flashing bold and brazen in the noonday sun. "Hold," Hiraen muttered again. "A bit more..."

Just then Savonn's head and shoulders broke the rockline on the far side of the road, and his clear, ringing voice called, "Fancy seeing you here, ugly!"

Isemain brought his arm down. The horsemen swerved, cantering towards Savonn in a sudden burst of speed. A hail of arrows peppered the rocks. Hiraen swore. "Loose!"

Hiraen had already marked the Marshal, so Emaris aimed at the man behind Isemain and released his arrow with a thrum. He thought he saw the fellow fall. Hiraen's orange arrow sunk into the flank of the Marshal's horse, and it reared up on its hind legs, yowling like a cat in labour. Isemain let go of the reins and bailed neatly, landing on his feet. The host, now in disarray, continued to advance. The front ranks were dismounting, the better to get among the rocks. Emaris got off two more shots and ducked down behind his boulder as an arrow hissed over his head. Then the Saraians were on them.

He jettisoned his bow and drew his sword. The soldier who leapt over the boulder to engage him was a woman, or at least he thought it was; he could see very little besides her shiny bell-shaped helm and big bronze shield, both of which kept reflecting the sun into his eyes. Half blind, he rained futile blows on the shield, dancing away from the Saraian's sword and spewing a constant stream of curses. Then good sense kicked in, or perhaps the bruise-laden memory of the long afternoons he had spent getting battered by Shandei. He dropped to a crouch, and slashed at the soldier's leg above the greave. Blood frothed. She staggered, shouting. Emaris seized the chance to steal round her flank and hew at her shield-arm, and then her neck. She collapsed at his feet, still burbling.

Thereafter, it was chaos. The Saraians overran the rock outcropping, and Emaris's world narrowed to the slash and parry of blades and the burn of fatigue spreading up his tired arms. He lost his sword in someone's collarbone and found an axe instead. Then he misplaced that too, and acquired a dagger. Hiraen was at his side, a blur of limbs and steel, fighting off several assailants at once. And yet, for every soldier that fell, another sprang up fresh to fill the gap in the line. The Saraians were a solid wall around them, impenetrable in their mail, and the dead littered the ground like puppets with their strings cut.

Emaris was done. His breath came in harsh, ragged sobs, the air rattling in his chest on each inhale, and pain lanced down his back every time he lifted his arm. If he was going to die, it seemed better to go sooner rather than later. But Hiraen was there, fighting back to back with him, and he could not very well collapse like a craven when his friend needed him—

Hiraen yelled and darted forward, making for the road.

He must have seen something that Emaris had not. A pair of Saraians advanced, but Hiraen dodged around them without bothering to engage. Moving on reflex alone, Emaris followed him. He had forgotten that theirs was only half the skirmish. Across the road, the rest of their patrol had nearly been overwhelmed, and he could not see Savonn. The Marshal had found another horse and was swinging one foot into a stirrup, calling orders over the clamour. Hiraen was shouting, too. He caught up a spear from the ground, and hurled it at Isemain.

The Marshal ducked at the last moment. The spear struck him in the left shoulder, piercing the gap between rondel and breastplate. He bellowed, yanked it out in a brusque motion, and turned on Hiraen.

Emaris ran to help. He was not sure what, exactly, he was going to do. All his strength was gone, and he could barely lift even his dagger. But if Savonn was dead already, and Hiraen about to join him, then he could by no means hang back. Shandei would have been ashamed. And loyalty was the highest of all virtues, or so his father had always said—even if it got one killed—

He was still thinking along these lines when something moved on the periphery of his vision, and there was a sharp whistling in his ear.

He felt only curiosity, and a dim, nebulous urgency that told him he probably ought to move aside. Before he could make up his mind, the moving thing connected with the back of his skull with a crack like the snap of a branch. Even the pain was slow and half-hearted. His vision clung to a crisp final image: Hiraen and Isemain exchanging a flurry of blows, while in the distance a great many riders receded. Then blackness enveloped him, and that, too, was gone.

CHAPTER 19

Under the command of Lucien Safin, who was not a general, the Council of Cassarah marched its army into the highlands. And unbeknownst to them, Shandei, who was not a soldier, marched in their midst.

She had a good time on the road. She fit quite well into Emaris's old cuirass once the straps were adjusted, and with a helm over her face she made a passable adolescent squire. The Betronett bow drew too much attention, so she left it at home and took her father's sword instead, with the ivory dagger in her belt. She would have liked to follow the army into the Farfallens once she concluded her own mission, and kill a Saraian or two at Emaris's side. But there was too much of a risk that one of Lord Lucien's lieutenants would recognise her. There were three: Bonner Efren, Willon's middle son, newly summoned from the country estate to command his father's forces; Daron Sydell, Oriane's nephew; and a Saraian-born freedman called Zarin, the leader of Josit's squadron. All they ever did was argue, and Shandei was almost pleased to slip away at Terinea to run Iyone's errand.

The township of the Cayns was an ancient settlement, older than Cassarah and nearly as sprawling. It was arrayed in a series of concentric circles, radiating out from the thirty-foot brick tower from which Lord Jehan governed his people. Coming in through the gate, one encountered first the district of the commoners, shops and houses crammed ten or twelve to a street, the air rank with the mingling smells of sweat and horseflesh and wet market goods. In the next circle were the public buildings, granaries and archives and libraries and barracks. Then came the manors of the rich, each with its own garden and complement of outbuildings; and finally, in the shadow of Jehan's tower, were the temples and convents. In one of these, a long time ago, the errant Danei Cayn had taken up residence, accompanied by her Saraian slave and confidante. Josit.

Here, Shandei trod carefully. The soldiers were encamped beyond the walls, but Lord Lucien and his lieutenants had gone to pay their respects to the Cayns, and the officers had been given leave to explore the town that night. Taking care not to cross paths with any of them, she ducked into a barn to strip off her armour and change into the modest grey dress she had packed for this purpose. Then she set out in search of Danei's convent.

It was not difficult to find. There were three convents of Mother Alakyne in town, but only one looked fit to have played host to Jehan's daughter during her turbulent pregnancy: a rambling three-storey building with whitewashed walls vined with ivy, all its windows lit up against the darkening sky. Shandei was greeted at the door by an acolyte, who took her to a priestess, who, at her insistent request, brought her to the solar of the Governess of the Convent.

This was a brown-haired, brown-robed woman who introduced herself as Persis. At first glance it was obvious that she was far too young to have been in charge here during Danei's stay. She was only about thirty, and the harried way she glanced at Shandei over the ledgers on her desk made it clear that she had better things to do than gossip about the past. "Got yourself into a spot of trouble, girl?"

234

On the way here, Shandei had planned and rehearsed an elaborate subterfuge. *My mother's name is Serenisa*, she would say, gazing beseechingly into the kindly eyes of an elderly priestess. *She gave birth to me twenty-three years ago, right here in this convent.* If she put up her hair, she could look a couple years older than she was. *I thought perhaps—if there was some record of her—I might be able to find her and take her to the grave of my father, who has been m-murdered.*

At this point her eyes would well up, and after stuffing a handkerchief into her palm, the priestess would hurry to the archival vault. *I'm terribly sorry, my dear, but there were only two women who gave birth here that month, and they were...*

But Governess Persis was not the sort of person one could cry to. Shandei scowled. "I'm not pregnant."

"What a pleasant change," said Persis, shuffling her papers into a thick stack. "On the run, then? Stole something? Killed someone? Oh, don't look so scandalised. All we ever do is take in girls in trouble. Yours must be dire indeed, if you've come all the way here for help. You're from the city?"

Her accent must have given her away. Her plan fled, and in its wake her mind was stubbornly blank. When she opened her mouth, what limped forth was the truth, warts and welts and all. "Yes. My name is Shandei. I'm looking for a child that was born here the summer of 1512."

Already losing interest, Persis turned away, rummaging through a drawer with the stack of ledgers in her free hand. "If you haven't noticed," she said, "there's a war brewing. I barely have time to pray for the children born *this* summer, let alone—"

"It was Josit Ansa's," said Shandei. "The councillor."

Persis paused.

"She was still a slave at the time," said Shandei. Her palms were damp. "So she hid the child. But now she wants to find it again."

Persis frowned, turning back to the desk. "She sent you? Why now, after so long?"

Shandei drew a short breath. Iyone had protected her, even lifted the burden of Vesmer's death from her shoulders. She was not, as it turned out, a murderer; the relief had brought her to tears at least twice since that strange evening in her backyard. After all that, it seemed shameful to invoke Iyone's name out of fear. Pressed hard, the truth transmogrified and acquired a disguise. "It was—it was Lord Kedris's dying wish. He thought the child might have been his. Lady Josit wanted to honour his request."

The frown deepened. "That was a long time ago. If there *was* a child, it would be grown by now, and impossible to find." Persis got up. "Look, if you'll excuse me, I really have to—"

"Of course," said Shandei, rising as well. "I'm sure she will understand." She pulled out the pouch of gold Iyone had given her and laid it with a loud *clink* on the desk. "Thirty drochii for your trouble, Governess. Her ladyship was willing to pay a good deal more for news of the child itself, but well, even a rich woman's life comes with its fair share of disappointments."

Persis hesitated, her fingers going still on the sheaf of ledgers. It was hard to tell what sort of priestess she was, whether she was at all susceptible to bribery, but no one could easily turn down that much money. In a convent like this, there were always stray mouths to feed. "How much more?"

"Sixty drochii," said Shandei. Unabating silence. She said, "Ninety."

"I can't make any promises," said Persis. "That was long before my time. I don't know if the last Governess bothered to keep any records—"

"A hundred."

"—but," said Persis, "I could send an acolyte to look, if it will be of any help."

"It will," said Shandei quickly. She was perspiring. The prospect of failing Iyone had been unbearable. "Thank you, milady."

* * *

A girl was summoned, given instructions, and dismissed again. Another led Shandei to an antechamber and offered her mulled wine, which she declined, and buttered scones, which she devoured. Her heart was still palpitating. She had not even invented a false identity. If Josit ever found out—

Two hours passed before she was summoned back to the Governess's solar. It was fully dark now, and a fire had been lit. Persis was standing by the hearth, frowning over a heavy leather-bound book. The paper was yellowing, and the ink had begun to fade. Curious, Shandei went over and peered over her shoulder. "Is that the record?"

"It ought to be," said Persis. "July 1512. But..."

"But?"

"There was only one guest that summer," said Persis, tracing the spidery script with a forefinger. "And only one recorded birth. Lady Josit's name is not mentioned."

Shandei leaned closer to read the writing. *Danei Cayn, eldest daughter of Lord Jehan, with child by Kedris Andalle of Cassarah. Sought sanctuary because of disagreements with her family. In poor health and spirits throughout her stay. Refused doctors and midwives; attended only by handmaids of her own household.*

Shandei hesitated. "It makes sense, Governess. Josit would have been a slave in Danei's entourage. There was no reason for her name to be recorded."

"True enough," said Persis. "But if she had given birth, it would certainly have been noted. Our laws mandate it."

Shandei took a deep breath. "Even if the child was stillborn?"

"Even if," said Persis. "Every new life, slave or free, is beloved by Mother Alakyne, and would never have gone unmarked. Even

237

those that end before they begin." A thin smile crossed her face. "Even the abortions. The elders used to perform a fair few each year for slaves who didn't want to bring forth a child into bondage."

Shandei glanced at the final line of Danei's entry. *Son delivered in good health 21 July. Named Savonn Andalle.* Nothing more.

"All right," she said. A premature resolution to the mystery, or perhaps another clue. Only Iyone would know which. "Thank you, Governess. I will tell her ladyship so."

CHAPTER 20

Against all his wishes, Savonn was awake.

He had been stabbed with a blowdart, or hit on the head, or both. Memory was uncooperative on that point. Then he had been carried a long way on the back of a horse, jouncing up and down like a shot deer. Several times he had woken, found oblivion more welcoming, and induced his captors through various means to knock him back out. But now awareness was returning with vengeful finality, and he was becoming conscious of one thing at a time, as if squinting at the world through a pinprick in a worn tapestry.

He was sitting more or less upright, strapped into some sort of device with his hands tied behind his back. His shoulders were sore, his blood pulsing in an insistent staccato throb at his temples. All his knives were gone. Voices were conversing in Saraian, none of them familiar. "—report no disturbances in the night," one said. A nice soprano. "But another host is coming up the highway to Medrai, four hundred strong. If we don't stop them, they'll be here within the week."

"I've sent for another detachment of cavalry," said another voice. Male. Baritone. Grating. "Otherwise we're not getting back home, with or without this bastard. The passes are crawling with Betronett men."

The voices made echoes unique to small, round rooms. The stillness of the air meant few open windows. There was probably a wall behind him. His mouth felt lined with sawdust, his lips barnacle-crusted. If he moved his head he might pass out again. It was an appealing idea.

Having arrived at this conclusion, Savonn Silvertongue opened his eyes and sat up straight, tossing back his curls with a flick of his head. "Friends," he said in stubborn Falwynian, favouring the room at large with a benign smile. "How lovely to meet you. And in my own fort, too."

Disappointingly, he did not faint. His swimming vision gave him what his equally wobbly mind had guessed. Bare room. Panelled walls, swarming with mildew. One bright window, high and narrow, covered with a lattice. A tower cell. Onaressi. Unsurprising. It was the largest holdfast, and the only one fit for the Marshal of Sarei. For there he sat, the owner of the baritone, frowning at Savonn with his armpit swathed in linen wrappings. There were four others with him. Two men, two women. Swords, daggers, muddy boots, mail. A great many bandages. No other prisoners. He wanted to laugh.

"Lord Silvertongue," said the Marshal. He was still using Saraian. "We have never been formally introduced. I am Isemain of Daliss, Marshal of Sarei."

Savonn took another moment to establish his own position. What he had taken for a torture device was, in fact, an ordinary chair. With his wrists bound fast, he could not feel his fingers. He was not confident he still had any. "I'm afraid, my lord," he said, "that we may need an interpreter."

Incomprehension greeted him, accompanied by a flurry of uncertain looks. His intuition had not failed him. The man was helplessly monolingual. What befell next depended on how much the Empath had told him.

The Empath, who knew Savonn in all the myriad uses of the word.

"We were informed," said Isemain at last, "that you understood Saraian."

He spoke slowly and clearly, as if he thought that might help. Savonn arranged his face into a look of baffled concern. "Oh, well," he said. "Your attentions are very flattering. I would blush if I had any blood left..."

The soprano stepped forward and clouted him with a gauntleted fist. As it transpired, he did have blood left. It trickled from his split lip down his chin and onto his shirt, already ripped and stained in several other places. The world tipped perilously on its side. He heard Isemain say, "You can stop pretending. Unlike your friend the Empath, I don't play games."

His mind clung to consciousness, the same mulish instinct that kept him awake most nights. Perhaps a few more blows would do the trick. "Oh, *really*," he said, peering at the Marshal. "I would've thought so great a general would have better manners."

The woman hit him again. "I thought," he said, through a flitting haze of white stars and black blobs, "I thought we were going to talk"—*wham*—"like civilised people. I thought you would offer me"— *wham*—"tea, maybe a castle somewhere in Sarei, while you awaited my exorbitant ransom." *Wham.* "My friends the Safins are very rich, you know."

He could have been talking, or just making slurred sounds with his mouth. It probably sounded funny. With certain people, there was a vinegary satisfaction in making them hit you where the bruises would show. Later they would find it discomfiting. It demeaned them, the physical evidence of their brutishness. Kedris always fired the servants who left obvious marks on his son. People might talk, after all. He doubted the Marshal had the same scruples.

"Enough," said Isemain sharply. "I said enough. You'll kill him."

So they wanted him alive. The blows ceased. His assailant receded from view. "Oh, don't go!" he wailed, spraying blood with each word. "It was just getting fun!"

"He's pretending, milord," said the person attached to the fist, somewhere to his left. "That's what the Empath said he would do. Pretend."

"Fetch him, then," Isemain snapped. "*He* speaks every language I've ever heard of. If Lord Silvertongue wants him, he can damned well have him."

The door opened and shut. His eyes were still uncooperative, the room teetering at an angle not altogether congruent with the laws of nature. He warred with the twin urges to blow a bloody raspberry at the Marshal and to throw up, long and hard, all over himself. He wondered if the streambed under the ringwall was still passable. Then he remembered, to his annoyance, that he had personally instructed Anyas to board it up.

Anyas. What had happened to him?

The door opened again. Gods above, which one was it this time? The leering guardsman? He was the worst. The fusty old stablemaster with the horse-whip wasn't too bad. He had a weak arm, and was far too easily riled... Savonn struggled to recall what misdemeanor he was being punished for. Then it came back to him that his father was long gone, and who had killed him. "The king is dead," he murmured, an aside to no one. "Long live the king."

He pulled his head up with a grand effort and looked. Auburn hair. Clear hazel eyes. That, at least, had not changed. Maybe the hair still smelled like honey and woodsmoke. Face: symmetrical, frowning. Cloak: red on the inside, black on the outside. In his semi-conscious state this struck Savonn as an extraordinarily amusing detail, and his aching face manufactured a grin.

Concentrating hard, he said, "Hello. How awkward to meet again like this."

Frown: gone. Smile: violent, and genuine as steel. A long time ago, Savonn had spent a gratifying summer inventing new ways to coax out that smile. "Did you like me as Ismil?" asked the Empath, taking the chair opposite him. "I hope so. It was a pain, the crowd."

That old, unforgettable tenor, versatile as a lute. Someone else said, "He claims not to understand Saraian. I can't get an intelligible word out of him."

The Marshal. Savonn had forgotten he was there. The rest of the world returned with vicious clarity—the faces milling above him, the obnoxious sunlight slanting in through the window, the furious throb of his head. "So you turned him red and purple," said the Empath. "Your resourcefulness continues to impress. What did you want me to do, tune him like a lyre?"

Isemain's scowl deepened. He got up, shoving his chair back with a scrape that sent nails pounding through Savonn's cranium. "Make him the offer. Break a few bones for all I care. Just try not to kill him."

He stalked out. The Empath looked at the others, standing around like furniture. "Well? Why are you still here?"

They scuttled out in single file, heads hung, not a mutter to be heard. In Astorre the Saraians had prostrated themselves before the Empath as if to a god. They were scared stiff of him. The bandit chief Mordel had told Savonn as much, and it appeared to be true. The strangest thing about this man was how all the rumours about him were true.

He stood watching Savonn now, the long unbound hair stirring with each breath. Then he said, "You look unwell."

He was speaking Falwynian. After all these years abroad, he could surely have shed his Dalissan accent—so deceptively charming—with a little effort. But to him it would have felt like making a concession, and that went against his very nature. He

243

never made concessions. "I would imagine so," said Savonn, in his sweetest, most sinuous tones. "Given the blood caked in my shirt, the impressive knots in this rope, and the fact that I can no longer feel my extremities. Your company shames you, Dervain Teraille."

The heavy-lashed eyes, which had wandered down to take in said bloodstains, flicked back to Savonn's face. It was a look of appraisal, of comparison, recording the things that had changed and the things that had not. It was three years since the end of their idyll, when they had known each other only as Marguerit's consul and Merrott's errand-boy. Three years was a lifetime for a spy.

"I should have warned you," said Dervain, "that Isemain will give you the back of his fist any time you ask for it. Gods bless him, he has nothing else to give."

"And you?" asked Savonn. The old pattern of banter, so easy to fall back into. "What do you have?"

Dervain's hand disappeared into his cloak, and Savonn's disordered faculties warned him of an incoming flash of silver.

It was impossible to stop his flinch. He ducked with such force that the chair rocked onto its front legs and slammed back down with a stomach-churning thud. Every muscle in his body screamed. *Breathe. Breathe. Breathe.* After four or five breaths, it dawned on him that the pain came not from having been impaled on a sharp object, but rather moving all his bruised limbs at once. As for the knife, it had embedded itself in the wall above his head with quite a bit of damage to the wood panelling, but none to his person.

He sat up slowly. Dervain was watching him with bland interest. He remembered the stories, and quashed his sharp flare of rage to a smouldering ember. The Empath. A fairytale. One could never be too sure. He worked his arms over his head, ignoring the strenuous objections of his back and shoulders, and found the knife-hilt with his fingers. Briskly, he jerked his bound wrists

244

back and forth along the serrated blade, slicing his hands open on the sharp edge, until at last the rope gave way and he pulled his arms free. Blood flooded back into his fingers. His eyes watered. The knife, he saw without surprise, was his own.

"I am hearing," said Dervain, "that you took this place from poor Mordel with five men?"

Savonn flung the rope-ends away. "I shan't brag. You did, after all, provide me with one of them."

Dervain grinned. "Yes. In any case, I have outdone you. Your friend Anyas is still alive, more or less, and will never again open the door to a bleeding stranger. Isemain thinks the remains of your garrison will make him a fortune on the auction block when we get home."

"And my patrol?"

Hiraen's patrol. Not his. Dervain gazed at him, his absurd lashes casting long shadows over the fine-lined geometry of cheek and nose. "Slaughtered to a man."

He was not aware of having stood up. The room veered off centre, and the floor heaved beneath his feet like the deck of Ismil's ship. Against all odds, the knife was still in his hand. Hiraen, beloved nuisance, start and finish of all things, in whose home he had first known kindness. Emaris, who would never see eighteen. *O gazelle...*

"Predictable," he said. "They had to die, or they might have worked out that it was Nikas who walked them into the ambush. How much are you paying him? He must have had hundreds of chances to kill me... but no, you want to do that yourself."

Was he still on his feet? He could not tell. A chair scraped, and Dervain's hand curled around his wrist—the slightest of touches, just firm enough to immobilise the knife. Iyone had dared him, as a child, to pass his fingers through a candle-flame; he had done so, and jerked his hand back feeling the same as he did now: deer-startled, not by any grievous hurt but by its absence, and so wide awake it was as if he had been comatose

245

before. "To my grief," said Dervain, "no one is about to kill you. Sit down, son of Kedris."

The anger was harder to put away this time. *Master your face*, Josit had taught him when he was small. Josit, who had protected him as best she could from the whips and the cudgels and the scorn. He had seldom had to master his heart. "Do not touch me again."

Instantly, the steadying restraint was gone. Dervain was six feet away, the knife in his palm. Savonn did not recall having relinquished it. "Nikas, snake and snake-charmer both," said Dervain. "I was thinking you might like him. When did you guess?"

Savonn was seeing quadruple. He sat back down. If Hiraen was dead, nothing carried any more weight than a dream. "The moment I first saw him. When else?"

"And you feigned ignorance, knowing he would lead you to your father's killer," said Dervain. "See, I was right. You have a mind for games. But did you not guess whose spy he was?"

After the talk at Onaressi, he had begun to suspect. *The Red Death.* One could not easily forget that hair. But at the time he had dismissed, or tried to dismiss, the thought as mere fancy. "How could I? You never told me you belonged to the Sanctuary."

"And you never told me your true name," said Dervain. "I suppose you were loath that I should find out whose son you were? Just as I did not want you to know I was... what I was." His lips twitched. "The inevitable symmetry. What poets we are."

And so Marguerit's consul had turned out to be the Sanctuary's slave, just as Merrott's errand-boy was Kedris's. Half-truths and white lies, the unspoken foundations on which their affair was built. But now the Empath called himself what he was, even though Kedris's son did not.

Talking hurt slightly less than thinking. Savonn said, "You also failed to mention your blood feud."

Dervain laughed. It was a dangerous laugh, the hiss of a sword from a sheath. "It is a surprise to you? Half of Sarei has a blood feud with Kedris Andalle. His forces massacred my village when I was small."

Savonn made the obvious guess. "The Battle of the Morivant."

"Yes," said Dervain. "Eighteen years ago. They all died. My parents, my sisters, my brother... I survived because I was hiding in the temple, under the altar. I used to go there when the world was noisy. For me the world is always noisy."

His brow was lightly furrowed, as if he were considering a mathematical problem on paper. "The slavers came two, maybe three days later. I was past the age the Sanctuary usually prefers, but they bought me all the same because of my gift." The word was gnarled with irony. "It is an investment they have never regretted, though I often give them cause to regret it."

"And Nikas?"

"He has been telling you he escaped, yes? He, too, is a liar, though not as good as you. No one escapes." He looked rueful. "Slave children have no families, and so no compunctions. We are bought young and moulded into killers from earliest childhood. We own nothing, and need nothing, and fail at nothing. Kings and queens beggar themselves to hire our services. The High Priest receives the gold and gives us our assignments, and we go without question. Everybody wishes to run away at some point. But no one runs once they hear what happens to those who do."

"Nikas seemed to believe otherwise," said Savonn. "He kept lamenting about his mother."

It was an invitation to elaborate, but Dervain was too shrewd to take it. "He has his own work. I borrowed him for mine. He kept sending me portraits of you... It was very vexing."

Breathe. Breathe. Perhaps, if he tried hard enough, it was possible to feel nothing. "Kedris used to free slaves. It was Lady Josit's idea. Surely you appreciate the irony."

"Josit? The queen who should have been?" Again, the lethal laugh. The knife spun between Dervain's fingers. "Oh, I see you know about that. If Kedris Andalle was a sword, she was the hand on the hilt. Be free, she preaches, all the while her chains rattle round our necks. How unlucky for her that this one ended up not in a brothel or a bath-house, but consecrated to the god of death himself."

Symmetry and inevitability, thought Savonn. The pillars of stagecraft. "And you want me dead," he said. "Because I am my father's blood? Because it rankles your pride that you never guessed? Or because I left you?"

Dervain took a step forward. The air had closed ranks around them, and each breath was painful. "Do we call it that?" he asked. "You leaving me? I thought it was that I killed a man for you and you, having got what you wanted, abandoned your tools and ran back home to your father without so much as a farewell."

This time it was not possible to will himself into numbness. "So it is that, then."

"It is all the things you mentioned," said Dervain. His smile seemed to reach into Savonn's chest and do something savage to his insides. He had thought he was past this. "The proportions change from one day to the next. Alas, I have no orders to kill you, a fact which is causing me great torment. But you must not be overly surprised. Our brief dalliance was, you see, extremely profitable to the Queen."

"I gave her nothing," said Savonn. As falsehoods went, it was a hollow one. He had bankrupted himself in several ways over this man.

"She disagrees," said Dervain. "Shall I tell you why you are here? Because, in light of—what shall we call them?—past favours received, she has a number of rewards lined up for you. And possibly some new tasks."

Abruptly, Savonn got up and went to the window. There was no glass pane, only the lattice of slender wooden slats. The crisp air was bracing, and his head was cruelly clear. He said, "*I gave you nothing.*"

Dervain sighed. "My dear," he said. "This, even now?"

The twilit upper room of the consulate. The maps he had stolen from Merrott's solar. The tickle of long red hair on his bare arm as they studied them together, and then the press of warm chapped lips against his own, a silent promise. *You will be safe. Your friend will be safe.* And then Merrott had died.

Savonn's knuckles were white around the slats. "I have no need of a reward. My loyalties are where they have always lain, with myself and my friends. If Marguerit wants payment for what you did for me, I have only my life to give."

Having no preternatural powers of his own, he could not read the complex series of expressions that scudded across Dervain's face. Surprise, perhaps. Or disappointment. Or respect. Dervain was as skilled an actor as he was. Maybe better. "Believe me," said Dervain, "I have told her countless times. Every day since I found out who you were, I have begged her for the privilege of bringing her your head. But she still thinks she can find a use for you. So my blood feud will have to wait."

What sort of use? A spy like Dervain, perhaps, if not quite of his calibre. A soldier. A court jester. Savonn laughed. "Kill me now, and say I took a blade to myself. No one would know."

Dervain met his eye. Then he lifted the knife and threw.

Savonn did not flinch again. This time, with Dervain's forewarning, he did not misread the movement. The knife flew a clean trajectory away from them both, thudding hilt-deep into the door. From the other side came a startled squawk. Footsteps receded at a run. Dervain spread his hands in a helpless gesture. "You see, you are not the only one plagued by eavesdropping squires."

On any other day Savonn would have shared the joke. But not now, when he would have given anything for Emaris and Hiraen to have stayed at Kimmet, far away from him and Dervain and all the chaos that attended them.

"The point is," said Dervain, turning to go, "Marguerit needs me enough that I may kill anyone I please in this fort, with two exceptions. You, and our poor, damnable Marshal Isemain." He frowned. "No. Perhaps even Isemain. I may try it next time he takes a fist to you. But when I kill you I want to do it in the open, on my own terms. You deserve to die as you lived, with an audience, and fireworks, and streamers, and perhaps a little accompaniment on the lute.

"For," he said, as he wrenched the knife from the door and flung it open, "I was very fond of you, my songbird. You were very entertaining. You still are."

CHAPTER 21

"Emaris."

He had not thought being dead would hurt so much. His neck was sore, his head a morass of screeching nerves, and his ribcage appeared to be on fire. Was it supposed to be this drawn out? The pain was so relentless and all-encompassing that it no longer felt like something applied to him by an external force, but a state of being.

"Emaris!"

Perhaps he had not died. But that was unlikely, when he could not feel the rest of his body. He was certainly dead. His sister was going to be very annoyed. Perhaps those were her urgent hands on him, turning him over to lie on his—front? back?—and fluttering at his throat to check for a pulse. "*Emaris!*"

It was not Shandei's voice, the only one he wished to hear. Nor was it their father's, which would have made more sense if Emaris really were dead. He thought of himself as a man of reasonable virtue, and therefore it was odd that his afterlife should consist of so much pain, not to mention persons of unmannerly persistence. Perhaps he *was* still alive. He ought to check, just in case.

Slowly, as the person continued to slap his cheeks and call his name, he forced his eyelids open.

He was lying on his back. The sun was still up, glaring into his protesting eyes, and at first all he could make out was a head and a pair of shoulders. The air was thick with the acrid stench of smoke and burning... meat? He was hungry. Then he blinked, and took in the rumpled brown hair above him, and the anxious green eyes. Familiar relics from a life that did not seem to have ended after all.

"Get up," said Hiraen Safin. "They're gone."

This seemed a preposterous order. Emaris rolled first onto one elbow, every vein in his head pounding fit to burst. Then, with Hiraen's help, he pulled himself to a sitting position. It was coming back to him: the skirmish, the Marshal, the retreating horses. Everything hurt, especially the back of his head and the contusion blooming over his lowest rib. He did not remember sustaining either injury. "Where is everyone?"

"Dead," said Hiraen shortly. "The Marshal gave orders to leave no one alive. If I hadn't lain on top of you and held my breath, they would have run you through."

Emaris looked around. Two great pyres stood smouldering, one on either side of the road. That explained the smell. All hunger having fled, he turned his head away, retched, and threw up most of his breakfast.

"They left two men to take care of the dead," Hiraen went on, his voice devoid of inflection. "I stabbed them when they tried to drag me to the pyre. They're burning now, same as all the others. So now we have their horses. One for me, one for you."

It was a long time before Emaris stopped throwing up. One thing at a time. One grief at a time. Hiraen was alive. "Savonn?"

"They took him. By force or otherwise, I have no idea." Hiraen pushed a waterskin into Emaris's hands. "Drink. We have a lot to do. You *do* know we were sold out?"

In his aching delirium, none of it made sense. But then, none of it ever had. He remembered Nikas at Onaressi, showing them how to breach the ringwall. Standing before Celisse, the picture of contrition after the fight he had started. Crouching over Emaris's pillow to whisper the piece of false news that would lead them into the ambush. It had all been part of the plan, drafted and executed with the care of a master jewel-smith, to lure Savonn into the trap the Saraians had sprung for him.

And Savonn...

Who brought the news? he had asked. And then, having been told, he had gone.

"He knew," said Emaris. He was too exhausted to feel anything beyond dull disbelief. "Savonn knew Nikas was a mole from the start. He tried to stop us coming along—drew their attention when they attacked—"

He picked up the waterskin, held it to his lips, and set it back down before he started heaving again. "Why didn't he..."

"Because," said Hiraen, with a jerkiness that suggested he was speaking through a clenched jaw, "he knew Nikas had been planted to lead him to his father's killer."

"Daine," said Emaris in a sudden panic. "We left him at Kimmet with Nikas. Vion and Lomas..."

He had to go. He had to warn them. He was already on his feet and preparing to rise when Hiraen stopped him with a hand on his arm. "Nikas won't blow his cover yet. There may still be a thing or two the Empath wants him to do. Daine will be all right for now." He glanced down the road, in the direction the Saraians had gone. "At a guess, the Marshal's brought Savonn to Onaressi. They may have retaken it. I'll have to go after them."

"But we can't storm Onaressi alone," said Emaris. "And Daine hasn't got enough men to force the ringwall again. We'll need help."

"From Medrai," said Hiraen. He had assembled a motley sheaf of undamaged arrows, and was cramming them into his quiver:

the orange ones he always used, and the cream ones of his patrol, and the heavy black ones the Saraians had been shooting at them. "It's a long ride. Can you manage it?"

"Of course," said Emaris, more from pride than conviction. He lifted the waterskin and managed to swallow a few drops before his stomach churned again. "You're not coming with me? You can't save Savonn alone."

Hiraen bit his lip, clutching a handful of arrows. For a moment he seemed very young. "It doesn't matter. I have to try. He— he protected me once." He clipped the quiver on his belt. It took him a few tries. "Like I said. I owe him a debt. There isn't a single thing in this world I wouldn't do for him."

"I understand."

"I wish you didn't," said Hiraen. He turned away, as if he could no longer bear to look at Emaris. "Go with haste, but be careful. Get to cover if you hear pursuit. Shoot anyone who sees you. And..."

He looked back. "Emaris?"

"Yes?"

His smile was sad. "I'm sorry," he said. "About everything."

* * *

Lucien Safin had reached Medrai, the last place in the world he wanted to be.

He was too old for this. As a rule, he left the adventuring to Hiraen, his pride and joy, and that demon-begotten child Savonn. Or even his thrice-damned daughter Iyone, too smart for her own good and incapable of resisting a challenge. But she was safe at home, busy with whatever nefarious hobby she got up to in her spare time; and the boys had disappeared into the Farfallens, leaving him here to walk the ramparts with his pestilential compatriots.

As the only councillor who had troubled to come in person, he had the command. Already he had quarrelled thrice with that stonehead Bonner Efren, ginger-haired and lantern-jawed, who started every sentence with *My father would*, and seemed to be planning nothing more than a mass evacuation of the town. When Lucien dissented, Daron—the spitting image of his aunt, except more polite—pointed out that they had no idea where the Betronett company was, and would it not be better to wait for news?

Zarin, the freedman, was ready to march to Onaressi and see if Savonn was still there, but no one paid him any attention. It was improper, Lucien felt, and more than a little cruel, sending a soldier to face his own countrymen in battle.

What they did know was disheartening. They had arrived on a gusty evening to find the town half empty, the people streaming out with overflowing wagons and heavy-laden oxen, leading their children on ponies. Every other house stood deserted, windows boarded up, lawns unkempt and overgrown. Only a few stubborn peasants remained to bring in the harvest. They were received in the mansion belonging to the Lord of Medrai by an extremely pregnant young woman called Rozane Cassus, the niece of his lordship, who had long fled to the lowlands with all his household. "And you have no wish to flee?" asked Daron, as she brought them to her parlour. "Surely there are carriages that could take you?"

Rozane, reclining in an armchair packed with cushions, waved a fleshy wrist in a snippy gesture. "And go into labour in some stinking fleabed inn? No, thank you. If you have help, we could use it. If not, I suppose you chose a good time to come sightseeing. All the finest houses are empty."

"The Council received a strange letter from your uncle," said Bonner. "He said that the Marshal of Sarei had shown up with a few hundred men and—a sorcerer?"

They had heard as much from the fleeing peasants they interviewed on the road. No two of them had agreed on the nature of this fellow's powers, or even whether he was man or beast or hellish entity, but all confirmed he was red-haired and red-cloaked and red-handed, like Death itself made flesh. "I don't know anything about a sorcerer, but the Marshal's probably at Onaressi," said Rozane. Misinterpreting their confused looks, she gestured at the map of the Farfallens on the wall behind her. "Big fort in the mountains, a few days from here. At the intersection of—"

"We know," said Lucien. He was pacing, too anxious to sit. "We thought the Silvertongue was occupying it."

"Oh," said Rozane. "He took it on Midsummer, but the Saraians wrested it back a week ago. We had the news from a raggle of Betronett boys who got away from the battle. Died of their wounds before you arrived. The rest of the garrison's been taken."

"Dear gods," said Lucien involuntarily.

"And Lord Silvertongue?" asked Zarin. He had said nothing till then, standing motionless by the window. "No news of him?"

"Who knows? Pissed off somewhere, no doubt." Rozane shrugged. "Pardon my language. But it's hard to get news out of the Farfallens at the best of times. He left garrisons up and down Forech's Pass, and then fell off the edge of the world. Last we heard, he'd got himself thrown out of Astorre for brawling."

Lucien sighed, rubbing the bridge of his nose. Bonner said, "That sounds just like him."

"I suppose," said Zarin, changing the subject with admirable deftness, "we shall have to retake Onaressi?"

Rozane shook her head. "You don't have enough men to force the gate or breach the ringwall. It's fallen twice by trickery now; that won't happen again. If you ask me, you'd do better to blockade the passes and starve them out. They won't last through the winter."

"And neither will we," said Bonner dryly.

They took their leave of Rozane with nothing decided; and later that night, walking the ramparts together, they received more unpleasant news. A returning scout announced that another

Saraian host had arrived at Onaressi. Worse, there was smoke in the mountains, near the southern end of Ilsa's Pass. Like a signalling beacon, or a pyre.

Zarin glanced at Lucien. The others had gone to question the scout themselves, leaving them alone on the wall. "The Saraians burn their dead, my lord," he said. "And those of their enemies."

Lucien said nothing. From here he could see the narrow road twisting its way into the Farfallens, weaving between stands of trees in their fiery autumn raiments and the terraced cornfields golden with the harvest. The sight brought back memories, disjointed and painful, of the last time he had passed this way with Kedris. The rattle of pebbles before the rockfall. The hiss of a bowstring, a sound Lucien had hitherto associated only with his son, laughing and flamboyant in the training yard. Kedris's last words—*Draw the spear...*

Lucien liked to think he had been friends with the Lord Governor. Everyone did. Kedris was an easy man to like, after all, dashing and handsome and full of charm. Hiraen, just thirteen, had joined the Betronett company at his suggestion. Even Iyone had admired him in that aloof kittenish way of hers, always eager to ply him with questions, or show him some book she was reading. Savonn's animosity towards Kedris had been inexplicable. He either hated his father, or longed to *be* him; Lucien had never worked out which.

Zarin was still talking. "The smoke means there must have been a recent battle," he said. "If we hurry, there may still be tracks we could follow."

Lucien was not paying attention. A lone horseman was winding his way down the road towards the town gate. So had he come the day after Kedris died, bringing the news to the people of Medrai. "Perhaps."

"There may be other ways to take Onaressi," said Zarin, more insistently now. "If Lord Silvertongue infiltrated it before—"

"Lord Silvertongue," said Lucien, in no mood to speak of war, "is no longer there. Neither is my son. They may be dead, or captured, or..."

He lost his thought. A guard was questioning the rider through one of the arrow slits in the wall. "The gate is not to be opened after nightfall. What is your business here?"

The newcomer cursed faintly. He was listing sideways in the saddle, as if wounded or very drunk. "They will not open it," said Zarin. "Lady Rozane said Onaressi fell to a trick just like this."

Someone called, summoning the lieutenant of the watch. A window opened in the guardhouse, flooding the road with yellow light. The rider flung up an arm to shield his eyes, but not before Lucien glimpsed his face.

He caught his breath. He knew those pretty features. He had last seen them in his own house months ago, the night before Hiraen and Savonn left home. The dishevelled blond boy on the horse was thin and wan and considerably older now, his rags streaked with grime and blood, but the face was unmistakeable. The youth banged hard on the gate with the hilt of his sword. "There's no time! Open in the name of Betronett!"

"Let him in!" Lucien yelled. His stomach broiled with fear. "That's Savonn Silvertongue's squire!"

Pandemonium erupted. The guards stared up at Lucien, then put their heads together to confer. It seemed an eternity before the lieutenant barked a sharp order, and the gate began to crank open. Lucien found the nearest stairwell and hurried down, taking the steps three at a time with Zarin on his heels. The boy had ridden through the gate onto the grassy lawn, surrounded by guards, the flanks of his decrepit horse steaming in the brisk night. He swung one leg over and sat side-saddle on its bony back for a moment, gazing at the spectators in confusion. "I'm not his squire," he said. "Not anymore."

Then he loosened his other foot from the stirrup, and fell off.

258

Lucien caught him before he hit the ground. The boy sat down on the grass, rubbing his eyes with a peevish, set-upon scowl. "Are they coming?" asked the lieutenant. "Should we warn the missus? Stand to arms?"

"Stand *back*," said Lucien. "Let him breathe."

The boy—Emaris, that was his name—stared at him. He must have been on the road for days. His face was windburnt, his lips grey with cold, his jaw furred to the ears with dirty golden stubble. "They took him," he said. "They ambushed us and killed the whole patrol and they took him."

"Who, Hiraen?"

"He's gone too." Emaris's eyes had a fixed, glazy cast to them. "He lay on me so they wouldn't kill me. Then he went after him alone."

"Went after *whom*?"

"Savonn, who else?" demanded the boy. Then his eyes widened, as if recognition had only just dawned on him. "Gods. Milord Lucien. Beg pardon, I didn't…"

He collected himself. "Hiraen's all right. He crossed swords with the Marshal, but he's not hurt. Not badly, anyway. He set out for Onaressi"—he glanced at the dark sky—"nearly two days ago. He thinks they took Savonn there. Sir, you must send help."

"We can't," snapped Bonner, who had come up with Daron. "Rozane said we didn't have the men to retake it. We'd get ourselves killed."

"Don't be a moron," said Emaris. "We took it with five men last summer. Hole in the wall. Over the streambed. Fetch me a fresh horse and I'll show you."

He staggered to his feet, as if ready to gallop back into the night that very moment. Bonner's mouth, Lucien saw with faint satisfaction, was hanging open. "I'll need a new sword too," Emaris was saying. "I keep losing mine. Savonn'll laugh. And some food for the journey. And," he added, slurring slightly, as Lucien hurried to steady him, "maybe something for the pain."

He slumped into Lucien's arms, and was still.

Lucien raised his brows at Bonner. "I think," he said, "that settles it."

* * *

The boy was not badly hurt. The guards carried him into Rozane's house, where her physician diagnosed him with exhaustion, concussion, and a minor rib fracture, and put him to bed. Soon after, Lucien and his forces were ready to march.

His colleagues had dissented valiantly. "What are we going to do when we get there?" Bonner demanded. "Storm the fort? Offer a ransom? What if they kill him as soon as they see us coming?"

It was not the worst of the scenarios that had flitted through Lucien's head. "I don't know," he said. He was already armed and mounted, wearing the same cuirass he had worn the day Kedris died. "But my son is there. I have to go. And," he added, struck by vicious inspiration, "if you don't come, and I survive, I shall tell your father you were too craven to go into battle." He rounded on Daron. "*And* your aunt."

Bonner looked incensed, Daron mortified. Zarin, who had given Lucien no trouble from beginning to end, was already waiting on his own horse. He had his orders from Josit, and Josit was a queen to her freedmen, respected unto death, her orders accepted without question.

"Goodbye," said Lucien, and kicked his horse into a trot.

He did not have to look back to know that they were following. They issued without fanfare out of Medrai and into the Farfallens, four hundred cavalry with their banners fluttering grey in the starlight: the sunburst of Safin, the eagle of Efren, the porpoise of Sydell. The Council of Cassarah, in reluctant agreement for once, going into battle side by side to rescue Savonn Silvertongue. It was a thought as hilarious as it was hair-raising.

CHAPTER 22

By mid-morning Emaris was out of bed, dressed, and determined to fight his way out of Medrai if he had to.

"But you have a fractured rib," his doctor kept pointing out, along with everybody else he encountered from the time he opened his eyes to find Lucien Safin gone without him. "You shouldn't be out of bed. You shouldn't even—where do you think you're going?"

It took him an hour to find his belongings and procure a horse, since the servants were inclined to hinder rather than help him. At length he lost his temper and demanded an audience with the Lady of the house, who was also being fussed over by several physicians, and informed her that he had to go back to his patrol. "Mistress," he said, "there is a traitor in my company. My commander has been abducted. My friend Hiraen has gone after him alone, with no plan other than to try his damndest to rescue him. If I sat here with my feet up while my betters risk their lives, I ought to be ashamed to show my face again."

Lady Rozane, who had been pacing up and down the length of her room with one hand around her belly and the other knuckling the small of her back, stopped mid-step to frown at him. "Not your betters, but surely your equals by now," she said. "How old are you?"

He was impatient to be gone. He knew where the armoury was. He could break in and steal a bow, if nobody gave him one. "Eighteen next week, milady—no." He counted again. "Tomorrow, in fact."

"Oh?" Rozane sounded surprised. If he had not been in such a hurry, he might have asked how old she'd thought he was. "I'm afraid I can't spare you as big an escort as you deserve, but will you at least allow me to send a couple of guards with you? And the most repugnant of my doctors."

She snapped her fingers at the man at her side, who was trying to make her drink some kind of potion. "They'll slow me down," said Emaris. "I'll go alone. But thank you."

He was ready to leave almost at once. The stewards gave him a change of clothes and a bulging satchel of food, as well as his pick of the armoury: a bow and quiver, and a couple of throwing-spears to sling from his saddle. The household's whispers followed him all the way to the gate. They thought he was terribly brave. They did not know that he was only doing this because Savonn seemed determined to leave him behind, and Emaris had no choice but to go by force where he was not allowed to follow.

After the ambush, he had ridden almost two days straight in increasing pain. The journey to Kimmet in reverse seemed twice as long, perhaps because he was no longer delirious, and therefore excruciatingly aware of the delay. He passed the banners and cookfires of Lucien's army the first evening, and was invited by an outrider to travel with the Council's army, but declined. A lone rider could traverse winding trails that a host of hundreds could not. Otherwise he met no one on the road, though at least once an hour he thought he heard hoofbeats on the wind and had to dismount to press his ear to the ground.

The pyres were still smoking when he passed them.

It was the middle of the second night when the crumbling wall of Kimmet rose into view beyond the bare crags and lonely cliffs of Ilsa's Pass. By then he had dismounted to rest his exhausted stallion, moving his leaden feet as if by clockwork, ignoring the persistent throb of his rib only through brute willpower. He was thinking of the day, nearly four years ago, when Savonn requested him as squire. His tremulous joy had been mingled liberally with horror. "Why me?" he asked. Savonn had, after all, already dismissed a number of other candidates, older and smarter and from wealthier families, and his fastidious tastes were becoming a matter of legend.

"Why you?" Savonn parroted. "Because arbitrary choices are a despot's signature, and you, my sunflower, are my arbitrary choice. You do not mind doing work of a non-decorative nature?"

Emaris bristled. "I have killed twelve men in battle, sir." The count was a little inflated, but Savonn would never know.

"Dear me," said Savonn. There was devilry in every smiling line of his face. "I'd thought it was twenty-something. Well, I shall have to make do. You have no objection to following me to the ends of the earth, where—depending on which author you prefer—a starless void, a bottomless chasm, or the beginnings of all things await?"

It took some time to parse this. "Follow you?" Emaris asked, imitating the mockingbird inflections syllable for syllable. "I would go there myself, sir, and pull you along in a wagon."

But there had been no wagon-pulling in all his years as Savonn's squire; and now, by the looks of it, there would be considerably less following, too.

Lost in thought, Emaris had come within twelve feet of the indistinct figure pacing the road before he saw it: a man in mail, with a longbow in his hand and a quiver on his back, no doubt one of the sentries Daine had posted along the approaches to Kimmet. He raised his voice to hail the fellow. "Go and fetch Daine. I have important news."

As luck would have mandated, it was Nikas. "Emaris!" he cried. "We thought you were dead!"

Speech abandoned him for a moment. The sight of Nikas—big, broad-shouldered, smiling—filled him with shock, shock that segued seamlessly into a single-minded, exultant rage. Good men were dead because of him. Savonn was gone, and Hiraen too. And Emaris, having travelled five days almost nonstop, forgot the ache in his head and shoulders, the smoulder of his fractured rib, the blisters where his thighs had been chafed raw against the horse. He had been brought up to despise treachery. Shandei, if she were here, would have struck down this man on the spot. And his father...

Sense returned. He could not outfight Nikas. He had turned down Rozane's offer of an escort; they were alone with no witnesses. Nikas, assassin-priest that he was, could very well contrive a sudden and permanent disappearance for him, and Daine would never even find out. This was no time for self-indulgence.

"I thought *I* was dead," said Emaris. His voice sounded so much like Savonn's that it startled him, derision slathered with layers of caustic courtesy. "The Marshal ambushed us on the Pass. You must have seen the smoke from the pyres."

Nikas's consternation was almost convincing. Savonn would have done better. "We feared something like that might have happened. Where are the others? The Captain?"

"Killed," said Emaris shortly. "Didn't you look?"

He watched, unimpressed, as worry transformed into dismay. "*Killed*? All of them?" When he did not respond, Nikas seemed to remember his question. "We did, of course. Daine sent out search parties for miles around—"

"I didn't meet any."

"Didn't you?" asked Nikas in surprise. "But that was a couple days ago. The last one got in this morning, and Daine didn't want to risk any more." Now, horror entered the ring. "You haven't

264

been wandering around the Pass for—what—five days, have you? Where did the horse come from?"

"It was one of the Marshal's," said Emaris. The sigils of Medrai were traced all along the stallion's bridle, but it was too dark for Nikas to make them out, or so he hoped. "I tried to follow them, but I lost the trail."

"You're worn out," said Nikas. He reached for Emaris's arm. "Come with me. You need something warm to eat, and then a long nap. Give me the horse."

Emaris's fingers tightened on the reins. If only he had time to mount, he might just be able to ride Nikas down and escape to the fort. But Nikas had a bow, and was still gripping his wrist. "Come on."

"I can't walk any farther," said Emaris. "Give me a leg up into the saddle."

Nikas gazed at him. What either of them would have done next, he had no idea. A shout splintered the frosty air, making them both jump. Nikas spun around. A large figure and a small one had appeared at the bend of the road. "Emaris, you bastard!" roared a voice, all too familiar. Vion. "What was the afterlife like?"

Nikas made a grab for the reins, but they slithered through his fingers. Torn between hysteria and relief, Emaris threw himself astride the horse. "Cold and boring," he called, unslinging one of his throwing-spears. "So I came back. Do you mind yelling a little louder?"

Where making noise was concerned, Lomas never minded. "*Wake up!*" he bellowed, every word resounding sevenfold from road and crag and barren clifftop. "Sound the horns! Wind the trumpets! Bray the donkeys! The dead arise!"

It was a shout to start avalanches. Nikas's hand strayed to his bow, but Emaris moved first. He launched his spear in an overhand throw, and at such close range it was only Nikas's quick reflexes that got him aside in time. Vion added his voice to the din.

Two swords—his and Lomas's—scraped out of their sheaths in unison. No, more than two. The rest of the patrol must be on their way.

"Even for the Empath's lapdog, these look like lousy odds," Emaris remarked, hoisting his second spear. In the same breath, Nikas drew his bow. "Are you going to shoot me, or just stand there till your bowstring snaps?"

Lithe-footed, Nikas moved towards the thick underbrush by the side of the road. "Oh, you brave gazelle," he said. "Lord Silvertongue would be so proud. Unless, of course, he really is dead."

Emaris pushed his heels into the flanks of his stallion, speartip turning with him. Vion and the others, still shouting, were too far off to be any help if Nikas decided to release his arrow. "You don't believe me?"

"Don't take it personally," said Nikas. He was smiling. "I just happen to have it on good authority that Queen Marguerit wants Savonn alive. He was, after all, her Empath's favourite plaything. And one of her most useful double agents—why, even more useful than poor little me..."

Emaris hurled his spear. Nikas saw it coming. He stepped aside, and once more it thudded harmlessly away. Emaris had no others. "Go on," he said. His voice sounded hollow to his own ears. *He made a mistake there once*, Hiraen had said of Savonn. "Tell me more."

"Ask him yourself," said Nikas, and dove into the underbrush.

Emaris seized his own bow, ripped an arrow from his quiver, and shot. A fern quivered. He nocked and released again. Again. And yet again. There was no sound from the foliage. Nikas had gone.

He was still sitting frozen on his horse, his bowstring taut under his fingers, when Vion reached him. "What was that? Did he try to kill you? He betrayed us, didn't he?"

Lomas was hot on his heels, still hollering, the rest of the patrol swarming behind him. It was almost funny. Distantly, Emaris wondered if any of them had overheard what Nikas said. Perhaps it did not matter. Even if they had, none of them would believe it. From a man like Nikas, words were only misdirection, and could be rinsed off like so much stale sweat.

The trouble was that much the same could be said of Savonn—a fact of which Emaris had long been aware, and usually tried to forget.

There was no time to worry. When they rescued Savonn, Emaris could confront him face to face, and he would laugh off the allegations and all would be well again. Emaris forced his fingers to unbend, to lower the bow and put it away. Solicitous hands reached for his reins. He had never been so grateful for Lomas's rock-steady grip.

"Take me to Daine," he said. "We have to go to Onaressi. The Empath is there. He's got Savonn."

CHAPTER 23

When Hiraen reached Onaressi, it was the same as he had found it on Midsummer's Eve, with two differences: it was no longer undermanned and culpably led, and the channel under the ringwall had been boarded up with a thin wooden grille, as a deterrent against future invaders. In a situation like this, one could either despair (which was what he longed to do); or get down on his knees in the stream, cursing Anyas for his efficiency, and set about unbarring the way (which was what he did).

The one mercy: steel was hard to come by in the wilderness, so Anyas had had to resort to wood, and the grille was already beginning to rot in the muddy water. Hiraen worked fast with his dagger. He had to be quiet. The ringwall was lit every ten yards with a watchfire, and white and grey banners flew from the ramparts. Guards stumped overhead now and then, greeting each other with a mutter. Hiraen had as yet given no thought to how he was going to get past them to wherever the Empath was keeping Savonn, and was only trusting to his own instinctive courage, the god-inspired madness of the tragedian who had forgotten his lines.

The grille cost him a quarter of an hour, and on the far side of the channel his head came up against another one. By the time he had done away with that, too, he was frozen stiff from the neck down, and the voices drifting from the keep had grown much louder. A stomach-rumbling aroma of roasting meat wafted to him from the yard, where the soldiers must have been turning something on a spit. A matter of violent irritation—he had eaten nothing since the ambush but a handful of nuts and berries. The conversation was in Saraian, and therefore mostly incomprehensible. Still, he understood the subdued quality of the murmuring just fine. He had led men half his life, and would be dismayed to hear his patrol like this. These were uneasy soldiers, cut off behind enemy lines in inclement weather, and they did not want to be here any more than he did.

He stuck the dagger between his teeth and began to inch out of the stream on elbows and knees, careful to keep his bow out of the water. After the close rankness of the channel, the fresh air was sweet and dizzying. He untangled his bow from his shoulders and dropped it in a clump of reeds by the stream. His quiver followed. He had half risen from the water on limbs he could not quite feel, dripping copiously, when something scuffed in the grass close by and a shadow flitted across his line of sight. Someone roared, "*El kapis!*"

Thought was a luxury he could not afford. His body moved of its own accord, as it so often did on the field. He drew a side-splitting breath and splashed back into the stream, water crashing over his head. He glimpsed a scattering of small round pebbles in the mud between his hands, gleaming green with spots of phosphorescence. A shoal of guppies, startled by his movement, flashed past his face. The shadows shifted on the stream-bed as the guard leaned over the channel to see where he had gone. Closer. Closer. Now.

Hiraen sprang back up, slashing blindly with his dagger. Water sluiced down his face and burned in his nose and throat.

His blade hit something hard. A man grunted. He withdrew the dagger and stabbed again. This time the blade sank into flesh. The man shouted, and tottered forward into him.

Death was a noisy and protracted affair. He shoved his assailant aside and stumbled out of the stream, snatching up his bow and quiver. Someone shrilled an order from the ringwall. Another guard was sprinting after him. A spear hissed past his head and into the stream, sending up a spray of water. He grabbed an arrow from his quiver, nocked, and loosed without looking at his hands. The second guard fell.

By the sounds of it, three or four others were on their way. So much for stealth. He glanced around the courtyard, made a rapid decision, and ran for the outbuildings.

There was a disused stable behind the main keep, the roof of which had fallen in years ago. He flung himself into a musty stall to catch his breath, clutching a stitch in his side. He seemed to have roused half the fort. Guards were running back and forth across the yard, shouting, their torches turning the ground into a frenzied theatre of shadow-puppets. Soon they would find the dead men and the broken grilles. Then the Marshal would order a manhunt, and it was only a matter of time before the Empath sniffed him out.

The yelling had grown angry, as if a dispute had broken out among his pursuers. He leaned against the side of the stall and shut his eyes, trying to catch his breath. *Think, Hiraen, think.* There was no question of success or failure, of chance and improbability, only *how* and *when*. There was the main keep and two smaller wings. The dungeons were under the easternmost building, not far from the stable. Savonn might be there. Anyas and his garrison too, if they were still alive. Hiraen would have to slip in somehow and free them, then fight a way back out of the fort. Or perhaps die trying, at the age of twenty-four.

He thought of Emaris, and buried his face in his hands. It would not even be the worst thing he and Savonn had done for each other.

* * *

Isemain Dalissos had a headache, a frequent affliction among those who had dealings with the Empath.

To begin with, his scouting party had returned with a full complement of bad news. "Four hundred cavalry," said their leader, who was sixteen, terrified, and trying without much success to conceal both facts. They were in the solar that had once belonged to that fool Mordel, with maps strewn over the desk and pinned across the walls. "I swear it, sir. I counted them myself. They set out from Medrai last night, the Safins and the Efrens and the Sydells all together."

In a predicament less dire, this would have been worth a chuckle. "And the woman? Was she there?"

"No, milord," said the scout. "But she sent a force with them."

Isemain paced to the window and back. His left shoulder was still throbbing where that fiend of an archer had speared him at the ambush. Damn the man. "What about the company at Kimmet?"

"No news, sir. Nikas ought to be delaying them."

"Nikas," Isemain repeated, not troubling to hide his distaste. He mistrusted men like these, who built their careers on schemes and trickery. The idea that Marguerit was about to acquire another made him ill. "To hell with Nikas. Betronett doesn't trouble me. They're nothing without the Silvertongue and that Safin fellow. What concerns me is the Council's—"

The door crashed open, chasing the words from the tip of his tongue.

The scout jumped. Isemain's headache intensified. Without having to turn around, he knew who it was. Only one person would have dared barge in on him like this. Sure enough, Dervain Teraille was framed in the doorway like a tailor's mannequin, eyes bright with mockery. He moved aside, and two servants stepped in behind him.

They were carrying a dead man: one of Dervain's, with a scraggly black arrow in his throat. They laid him out on the floor and retreated again. No one spoke. Isemain stared at the corpse, then its harbinger. The air felt heavy and wrong somehow, as if a storm were coming.

He gestured at the scout without taking his eyes from Dervain. "Out."

The wretch fled. The door shut, stranding Isemain alone with the killer slave. "Let me see," said Dervain. "A steady bubbling of irritation. Your shoulder must be troubling you. Did the scout bring bad news? And, like Celisse of Astorre, you do not appreciate unsolicited gifts of corpses."

"Most people don't," said Isemain. "Get out of my head."

Dervain stepped over the unexplained body and sank with obscene grace into a chair at the desk. "I wish I could. People so rarely feel nice things, my lord Marshal."

A pause, during which Isemain continued to stare him down. Dervain sighed. "Do you require everything to be spelled out for you? My man, your arrow. Did you not hear the shouting?"

Ignoring him, Isemain bent over the dead man. The arrow was, indeed, one of those his bowmen used. "How did this happen?"

"A fight broke out at the stream," said Dervain. "One man knifed, another shot. Nobody has owned up."

He leaned forward with his chin propped on interlocked fingers, watching Isemain with unblinking eyes. He was, of course, in an even worse mood than usual because Isemain had had his lover beaten, but this was more than that. He did not look well. On closer inspection, his fine bronze skin was ashen with

272

greyish undertones, his eyes swollen with sleeplessness. Apprehension tingled down Isemain's back. This boded ill.

He stood up. "Arrows are hardly difficult to come by. The armoury is not under guard. Has it occurred to you that one of your men might have shot this arrow to put the blame on one of mine?"

"It has," said Dervain. He was terrifying like this, unflappable and smooth as ice. Sanctuary property. God's property. Isemain preferred it when he lost his temper. "But try telling them that. They were uneasy to begin with. Now they're mutinous. If you still mean to present the Queen with our hostage, we'd best set off soon."

That would explain the illness. Always sensitive, the Empath's faculties swelled up like a sail whenever there was unrest afoot. "You don't approve," said Isemain.

With satisfaction, he watched the lines ripple across Dervain's forehead. It was only this past summer that he had learnt of the history between Savonn Silvertongue and the Empath, who in the telling transpired to be human after all, and stricken as they all were by human frailties. "I don't," said Dervain curtly. "There are attack dogs and there are vipers. It baffles me that Her Magnificence cannot tell the difference."

What he needed was a good slap. But Isemain was a decent, god-fearing man, and knew that if he raised a hand to the High Priest's protégé, it would not be long before he was relieved of said hands. The Sanctuary protected its own. "It's not your place to decide for her."

Dervain stretched out his legs and got up. His eyes were narrowed in concentration. Isemain wondered what he was looking for: the bright flashing lights of alarm, perhaps, or dull festering resentment, or the acrid stench of anger. "I see," he said slowly. "You know why she wants him. And you will not tell me."

It was the one advantage Isemain had. He was confidant to the Queen, and the father of her oldest and finest child, who would one day inherit her kingdom. For all his striking looks, Dervain was far too young and volatile for her. He was nothing but murderous chattel. "The Queen has a few questions for your pet magpie. I have no idea what they concern. Nor should you. After that, she may find a use for him, or let you dispose of him as you see fit."

The muscles tightened in Dervain's jaw. "We have a blood feud. It is my god-given right to kill him in a fair fight. Or to be killed by him, if events fall out that way."

He made death sound terribly quotidian, like chipping a tooth or tripping down the stairs. "I don't disagree," said Isemain. In fact, he would have liked nothing more than to arrange such a fight. Either way it was bound to rid him of at least one thorn in his side. "But the Queen's will is our bond. So you might like to make yourself useful in other ways."

"Such as?"

"There are four hundred Cassarans marching on us as we speak," said Isemain. "Ostensibly led by Lucien Safin, but you and I know who has been behind the sword and shield of Cassarah for years now. If she gets her way, neither you nor Marguerit will get yours."

Locking eyes with the Empath was always a bloodcurdling experience. Isemain bore it as stalwartly as he could. "And," said Dervain, his fine features growing rigid, "you are dispatching me to deal with it? You want me to leave the hostage here, with you, and go?"

"I want you to fall into a pit of hell and never come back," said Isemain, "but yes, failing that, removing our opposition would be helpful. A rabble of cowards who hate one another. Easy pickings."

"Thus removing the threat of mutiny, and dealing with this new army in one fell stroke," said Dervain. "And in all the excitement, you intend to steal away with the prisoner and see that he reaches the Queen alive. Well done, my lord Marshal.

274

Your usual lack of intellect makes this little triumph all the more precious."

Isemain refused the bait. Full of hearty cheer, he said, "Aren't you leaving?"

Dervain moved to the door, stepping over the corpse again. Judging by the look on his face, Isemain was going to have to double the guard on his bedchamber and sleep in armour for the rest of his life. It was worth it. "I will go now," said Dervain. "But I shouldn't feel too pleased with myself if I were you, my lord. Your prisoner has worn so many masks he has forgotten the look of his own face. Question him if you like, and let him fill you up with falsehoods. You will find nothing real about him."

He executed a flawless bow, and was gone.

* * *

In the furthest recesses of Savonn's mind, a lyre was laughing.

He was half asleep, his thoughts not quite dreams, only images from memory with the associations between them loosened. He was with his patrol in the tavern called the Merman, watching the genesis of a drunken brawl. Some of the more reckless boys had taken a dislike to the band of Saraians at the next table, with predictable results. Insults were exchanged, escalating first into threats and then the brandishing of steak knives: a sight that made him laugh, because he was only eighteen, and wild, and—had he only known it—at the starting post of the best year of his life. Rendell was trying to break it up, but of course, with their abysmal luck, someone from the city guard arrived just as one of his brothers-in-arms started grappling with a Saraian. The newcomer, irritation writ large all over his face, was the man who would later introduce himself as Gelmir. "What the hell are you lot doing?"

It occurred to Savonn mid-laugh that both they and the Saraians were about to be thrown out of Astorre, and he had not even visited the theatres yet. An unconscionable waste. Propelled by this impetus, he rose and interposed himself at Gelmir's side. "Dancing, or trying our damndest to," he said. "You must pardon the excess of left feet."

It was an unconvincing lie, at least without a sizeable bribe to back it up. But the surprise made the staggering men break apart; and then, in the far corner of the room, one of the Saraians caught up a lyre and launched into a lively tune.

He was beautiful: a half-seen shadow by the wall, red and gold and black, lyrestrings pliant under his clever fingers. Put Dervain in the same room as a musical instrument, and the two would always gravitate together. Someone would push a harp into his hands, or roll a flute over and beg a song; or, to escape a tedious conversation, he would flee to the spinet and start playing. And then, as now, the room would fall silent. One would forget what one had been doing. One would simply go still and listen, like the magpie at the minstrel's song.

Eventually, the brawlers caught on. They produced a few valiant twirls for Gelmir's benefit, the Merman resounding with laughter around them. A giggling barmaid grabbed a merchant's wife and started a waltz between the tables. A chair toppled. The Saraians began to clap to the rhythm, and Savonn's patrol filled in the words, mostly rude ones. Rendell did not even try to keep a straight face, and was howling into his ale-glass. One missed him. Gods, how one missed him.

Gelmir rolled his eyes to high heaven, and retreated.

The music died away to applause so thunderous that a portrait fell off the wall. Amid a chorus of hoots and whistles, the two brawlers—scarlet with indignation—withdrew to their respective tables to be thumped on the back by their friends. The bartender, still cackling, poured them fresh drinks on the house. Every stray sound, every odour and texture and flicker of light had taken on a fresh, blossoming lustre, like the world after a rainstorm:

washed clean and made new and exciting all over again, a rebirth in a heartbeat.

As if in a dream, Savonn wandered to the counter and bought a fresh tankard of ale. He judged his moment and, with a magician's timing, sent the drink sliding down the counter to the lyre-player with a flick of his wrist.

He stood there, empty-handed and without expectations, wanting nothing, needing nothing, exulting only in the uncomplicated joy of what they had orchestrated together. Even in peacetime, there could be no discourse between Saraian and Falwynian. The man could not come over and pull up a stool beside Savonn, as any other interested party might. What he could do was what he had, in fact, done: accepted the drink, and studied Savonn across the rim of the tankard, his warm eyes thoughtful and curious and above all, entertained.

Looking at him, one felt like a steeple catching fire from heaven. One would not have noticed, or cared, if anybody else was watching—not even Rendell, who would keep the secret for many years.

The scrape of the lock was a foreign sound that did not belong in the dream-memory. Savonn roused at once and sat up on his pallet, his fine-honed senses springing to alertness.

Unsurprisingly, it was Dervain. In the early days, when they used to prowl the streets near the Merman in the hopes of running into each other, the very thought of him often seemed to conjure a flash of auburn among the passing heads glimpsed from a window, or a secret smile across a market-stall. Tonight he was in full armour: cuirass, jerkin, greaves and boots. The planes of his face always looked more severe when his hair was knotted back. His cloak hung red and black from his shoulders, and for some reason, his lute was in his hand.

Coming to adulthood in the house of Kedris and Danei, one learned to sense quickly from stance and expression when something was amiss. A palpable thundercloud followed Dervain into the room. The guards out in the hall sensed it, too; they shifted and fidgeted as the cell door swung shut. Dervain caught his eye and held it, their customary greeting whenever time and place permitted them nothing else. Then he set his lute on the stool, and went to the barred window.

"I was thinking," he said, "that surely you would have engineered an escape by now. I always overestimate you."

Savonn's wounds had ceased to trouble him, and could not be used as an excuse. The window, he had found, overlooked a second-floor balcony which he thought led to an unused parlour. In the last two nights, a piecemeal plan had begun to come together in his mind, riddled with ifs and maybes. If he wrenched the flimsy lattice away from the window, he might be able to swing down to the balcony. If the parlour door was unlocked, he could get inside, steal some clothes and knives, hide his face in a helm, and pass himself off as one of the Saraians. Then he might devise some way to slip out through the postern.

It was a decent plan, if tentative. There was no reason why he should not have given it a shot. The fact was that only three things were salient to his exhausted mind: Hiraen was dead; they had both failed to protect Emaris; and now all that remained to him was a blood feud and a man he had loved, the two inextricably intertwined.

He could not decide between a flippant response and a cold one. "You really do."

He stood up, so Dervain would not loom over him. That he was not tall had been a cause of some grief in his adolescence. But with Dervain, it did not seem to matter. It felt quite natural to join him at the window, to study him out of the corner of one's eye. Still they kept several inches of empty space between them, careful not to touch. "You are cold?" asked Dervain. "I asked them to bring up more firewood."

Savonn looked down. His arms were goosebumped, but not from cold. For a wild moment he imagined pressing himself into the heat of Dervain's body, pulling them both onto the pallet and ceasing to exist for a while. But he needed his wits about him to play this game. "You can bring it yourself later," he said, "after you finish whatever you are about to do."

"That will be quite a while," said Dervain.

No elaboration was forthcoming. Savonn considered his moves. "I heard shouting in the yard."

"Yes."

They were both adroit at elusion and misinformation. It had been one of their favourite pastimes, wheedling accidental crumbs of truth out of each other. "And now you're going to battle?"

Dervain was an expert at smiling without moving his lips. His eyes took on a different cast: the lines around them shifted and reformed, every plane and angle shot through with obscure amusement. "The Council of Cassarah has sent an army," he said. "It appears they are trying to rescue you."

The laugh that slipped from Savonn was startled, and therefore genuine. It seemed to surprise Dervain. He looked over sharply, as if his eye had been caught by a burst of light, and for a fleeting instant the smile lines deepened on his face. "Too many players on the board, *etruska*," he said. "Isemain. Marguerit. The Council. I confess, when I set out to kill you, I envisioned a game for two."

More ifs and maybes: if he did not escape, the Council might rescue him. If Dervain stopped them first, he would be taken to Daliss. Then, if he did not wish to die, he would make himself useful to Marguerit. He was good at making himself useful. Everyone learned that sooner or later. Even Merrott. Even Kedris. It was funny to think that, after all these years, he and Dervain could soon be on the same side.

But it was impossible. One might as well try to square a circle. Dervain wanted to kill him. And Savonn, too, had a debt he owed to the dead.

"Do you remember," said Dervain presently, "the time I received that urgent dispatch from Marguerit? The courier had barely even set it down when I was called away, and you broke in to steal it."

Savonn grinned. It was hard not to. "You caught me."

"And you flung it unopened in the fire, and to this day we do not know what the Queen wanted." Dervain's voice was soft, his gaze fond. "It was then that I knew—or thought I knew—what manner of man I was dealing with."

They had laughed about it after, lying on the floor of the consulate among bits of kindling and scraps of blackened vellum. Savonn had traded Merrott's patrol maps for the next dispatch. A good price—Dervain would have needed them in any case, to do what he had promised Savonn. Lord Kedris, far away in Cassarah, would get what he wanted, and remain none the wiser about how his wastrel son had contrived it. One could not have *everything*.

It was no wonder Hiraen despised him.

Savonn opened his mouth to say something pithy. What came out instead was, "It was not my choice to leave you."

Dervain went still, but did not speak. He had not expected this. Savonn pressed his advantage. "My father wanted Betronett at any cost. Hiraen wouldn't kill Merrott for him. That's why I had to take care of it. I thought, after it was done—"

He had fancied himself free of his obligations to Kedris, free to take his lover and go where he pleased. A pretty dream. In the end he had come back to do his father's bidding where Hiraen, brave stubborn idiot, had balked. To obey, to command Betronett like a puppet on a string, to serve as weregild for Hiraen's life. In his father's anger, no one was safe. "My—feelings—were not of a transient nature," he said. "If you are truly an empath, you know this."

"I know," said Dervain. His lashes dipped, and rose again. "Neither are mine. That changes nothing."

They stood for a moment before the dark panels of the window-lattice. Savonn listened to the tell-tale pulse pattering in the spaces between his brains and his ears, and wondered what a pounding heart felt like to Dervain at second hand. Dervain was right, of course. They spoke of choice, but one of them was a slave, the other his father's son. Savonn knew better than most that feelings were irrelevant. He had felt, and he had left.

He let out a long breath and rallied his defences. "I just wanted to establish the rules," he said. "It seems important if we are to keep playing. The stakes are higher now. But if you know me, you know nothing will keep me from the game. Here, or in Daliss, or anywhere else you might take me."

Any less would be cowardice, unworthy of his adversary. "Maybe," said Dervain. "But there is something I have neglected to mention, either to you or Isemain. Someone has stolen in under the ringwall and murdered two of my men. It seems you suffer no lack of rescuers."

For a moment, Savonn forgot to inhale. His first thought was *Hiraen, late as usual.* His second thought was *I told you to go back to sleep, gazelle.* His third—*They are dead, both of them, because of us.*

"But if you escaped," Dervain went on, "where would we resume our game? We can hardly duel to the death in Astorre, under Celisse's eye."

"I said nothing of escaping," said Savonn.

"Perhaps," said Dervain, paying him no heed, "we can meet only as cursed creatures do: in secret, shrouded by night. On the edge of the crescent moon, in the unholy light of evenfall." He smiled, this time with his mouth. "If you abide there for me, I shall come to you. Just like old times."

Speech, now, would reveal too much. Savonn stood by the window, forcing away thought and emotion, both of which would make him easy prey. Dervain gave him a last, heavy look and departed, locking the door behind him.

It was not until Savonn saw the lute on the table that he understood.

The way to freedom stood open. More than that, it had been waved in his face. Dervain did not want the Marshal to take him to Marguerit, under whose eaves he could not be killed. If Savonn fled, they could meet elsewhere, alone and undisturbed, and make an end one way or another. *Evenfall.* The ruin of Ederen Andalle's ancient palace, on its haunted isle in the Morivant. Dervain never did anything by chance.

He examined the lute, its supple strings well-tended and in perfect tune. The bass strings were made of several strands of sheepgut woven together, thick and resonant and sturdy. It was the hardest thing he had ever done to unfasten them from the soundboard and bridge, and to tie them each one to the next, so they formed a cord of some five or six feet in length. Then he looped one end around a strut of the window-lattice and weighed the other down with his foot.

It took some negotiation, but in a moment the frame sprang loose almost noiselessly. Soon Dervain would leave with his men to meet the Council's force. The holdfast would be half empty. In the confusion Savonn could climb out and meet with one or all of his rescuers, if he so pleased, or find his way alone to his rendezvous.

Being human, one had to admire the elegance of the plan. Being human, one also had to take into consideration what was going to happen at Evenfall: he would have to fight Dervain Teraille to the death, an encounter he was unlikely to relish; or, ultimately, to survive.

One had to admit going over to Marguerit made a much more appealing alternative.

CHAPTER 24

Close to midnight, a trumpet sounded.

The quality of the shouting had changed again. Lying in the stable, Hiraen heard the orders relayed across the yard. Men were forming up in their ranks: three or four hundred, almost half of that mounted, with the Empath at their head. A cloak, sable and scarlet, billowed from his shoulders as he cantered through the gate on his black destrier, the others flowing after him in four neat files. Hiraen gazed at the back of his brilliant head with hatred. It took an age for the last of the soldiers to vanish down the mountainside. Then the gate was shut once more, and only the thunder of the horses was left, receding down the Pass.

One of two things must have happened, both of them good omens. Either Daine had found them, or Emaris had reached Medrai and raised an army out of thin air. The former seemed more plausible, but given Emaris's occasional bouts of brick-splitting obstinacy, the latter would hardly be surprising. So the Saraians had divided their forces: the Empath to deal with this new threat, the Marshal to hold the fort and the prisoners. And by some stroke of luck, no one seemed to be searching for the intruder in their midst.

There was no better time to move.

His clothes were almost dry, though still reeking of fish. He covered his bow under his cloak and, as though he were passing through the tents of a Betronett encampment, sauntered out of the stable into the open.

The yard was quiet now, the grass trampled where many feet and hooves had recently marched. Onaressi felt vast and echoing without the Empath. Hiraen passed a pair of squires sharing a wineskin by the spring, and nodded amiably when they glanced at him. A servant hurried past with a horseshoe. If he avoided the light of the cookfires, and did not move too quickly, no one could tell he was a stranger. He made his way to the east wing where the dungeons were, and proffered a winsome smile to the two sentries at the entrance.

The prisoners were not heavily guarded. The Empath had taken as many soldiers as the Marshal could spare, and probably a few more besides. The sentries looked him up and down. One of them wrinkled her nose. The other said, "*Ja i semoy?*"

His meaning was not difficult to guess. Nodding, Hiraen gestured towards the entrance and mimed walking his fingers down a flight of imaginary stairs, then handing over a scrap of paper. A message for the dungeon guards. The sentries looked at each other. The woman laughed. "*Gera*," she said, which—if Hiraen did not miss his guess—meant *mute*.

They waved him through, yawning. He had been here not long ago, supervising a tally of the inventory with Anyas before they left for Astorre. The armoury was on the ground floor, behind a pair of double doors—locked, but not guarded. More good news. Nearby was the granary, and upstairs an archive of dusty scrolls, into which only Savonn had cared to venture. The dungeons were in the basement, far under the building. No one else was around. Hiraen crept to the stair and went down.

It was warmer here, the air musty. A lamp flickered on the half-landing, almost out of oil. Two more guards were dicing at

284

the foot of the stairs. They glanced up at his footfall, and one of them barked a question.

He did not answer immediately. His attention had been drawn to what was behind them: a long hallway, smoky and dim, running between steel-barred cells that put him in mind of bestiary cages. The lamplight laddered the floor with shadowy rungs. And from the other side, the garrison was peering back. One or two men he recognised were sitting near the bars, looking with dim, crusty eyes for the source of the disturbance. Others were lying on dirty pallets, asleep, or perhaps dead. Many sported bandages. If they had seen him, they were either too smart to call out, or too far gone.

The roaring pulse in Hiraen's ears was not fear, but something more lethal. His fingers tingled for his bowstring. The guard was repeating his question, more impatiently now. Hiraen looked at him and his companion. Mail shirt, bare head, no gorget. Sword-belts dangling from a rack on the wall: not far away, but not near enough. Easy.

Clearly, Hiraen said, "*Ja i semoy.*"

The guard was still asking him what his errand was when he pulled an arrow from his quiver and plunged it tip down into the man's eye socket.

One down. A sonorous clatter. The second guard knocked over the table in a wild grab for his sword. Hiraen fitted another arrow to his bow, cracking his elbow on the wall as he drew, and shot him from three inches away. Two down. Someone shouted a question from above. The sentries at the entrance must have heard the noise. One of the prisoners yelled, "Keys on his belt!"

Hiraen grabbed the brass ring of heavy steel keys on the second guard's belt and ran to the cells. "They've got Savonn," said the prisoner who had called to him, a youngish man, as Hiraen unlocked the first door. There were blood-soaked bandages around most of his puffy face, and patches of his scalp showed pink and raw through his uneven brown mane, as if the

285

rest of his hair had recently been burned away. His eyes had the unfocused glossiness one associated with delirious fevers, but somehow he was on his feet. "He's in the main keep, on the third floor. We heard the guards say so."

The voice was familiar. Hiraen said, "*Anyas?*"

Someone was coming down the stairs, grumbling. Hiraen tossed the keyring through the bars of the next cell and nocked his bow again. "What happened to you?"

Anyas said, "The Empath."

The guard had reached the half-landing. It was the woman from before, who had called him mute. He drew his bow, watching her shadow flow down the steps before her like a silent herald. He had about the span of a breath to make a kill shot before she raised the alarm. Timing was everything.

As soon as the guard appeared round the bend in the stair, he released the bowstring. He did not miss. He never missed: the culmination of twenty years of hard training, and the need to prove that he could do something Savonn and Iyone could not. At point-blank range, the arrow punched through armour and found its mark in the guard's heart. A thump, a steely whisper of mail. Three down.

With characteristic efficiency, all the cell doors had been opened, the prisoners gathering around him. There were about sixty. He did not ask what had happened to the others. "Listen," said Hiraen, as Anyas pulled one of the swords from the rack and handed the other to his lieutenant. "The Empath is gone. Isemain only has a skeleton force left. Break into the armoury and steal whatever you need, then rush the postern. You should be able to overwhelm the guards. Stay together and march to Medrai."

Anyas frowned, handing him a couple of daggers from the dead guards' sword-belts. He was swaying on his feet. "What about you?"

It dawned on Hiraen that they did not know he had come alone. This did not bear explaining. They would lose their nerve, and so would he. "I have to get Savonn," he said. He made it sound very simple, like stopping by a tavern to fetch him out of a rousing party. "I'll join you after. Gods go with you."

He pelted back up the stairs before they could ask any more questions. The last guard met him on the ground floor, just inside the door, talking very fast. His frown made clear what he was asking: had Hiraen delivered his message? Why had he made so much noise? And where was the other sentry, who had gone down to check on him?

"Let me show you," said Hiraen. He dispatched the man with a dagger to the throat, and set off at a purposeful walk for the main keep. Four down. He stopped counting.

* * *

Tongues of fire were rising from the east wing, streaking the sky with shades of red and gold. Judging by the noise, Savonn's fellow prisoners had escaped.

That complicated matters.

There was now no question of staying put. If he did not join the garrison in a minute or two, they were likely to get themselves killed trying to find him. That, or the Marshal's men would bundle him into some jolting cart and haul him off to Sarei, effectively dousing all hopes of making it to his rendezvous. If he did not make a move now, he never would.

He considered, then slung the lute over his shoulder and swung a leg across the windowsill.

It was a tight fit, impossible for a bigger man. The night chill stung his face, the wind carding ungentle fingers through his hair. The second-floor balcony was just below. Beyond that, a wedgehead of men in mismatched armour and dirty bandages was forcing its way across the yard, waving torches and swords. Arrows flew from every direction. Without difficulty, he found finger- and toe-holds between the crumbling bricks, and was just beginning his descent when the door of his cell flew open. Out of sight, someone bellowed, "He's gone!"

Savonn weighed his options: a longer fall than he would have liked, versus the indignity of being swatted on the wall like a lizard. The guards had barely taken three steps into his cell when he made up his mind and let go.

He struck the balcony feet first, rolled, and came up staggering. The door that led indoors was locked, and footsteps were approaching from the other side. The lute was still in his hand. Other than that, he had nothing else on him but the shirt, boots, and ripped hose he had been wearing the day of his capture, not even a brooch or a sharp ring. With remote irritation, he wondered if Dervain had even considered the possibility that he would not survive his escape.

There was nothing for it. Almost as soon as he ducked into the shadows behind the door, it flew open to disgorge two men, their swords bared. "Where is he?" *"He's not here—"*

Savonn stepped behind one of them and cracked him on the back of the head with the lute. The man fell over, shouting, until Savonn shut him up with a good kick. The second guard whipped round, his sword already flashing down.

"Don't be rude," Savonn admonished, sidling away from the blade. He could not sidle forever. "I have an appointment to keep."

As if in response, the man choked, round-eyed. His windpipe sprouted an arrow. As he went down, breath whistling in his throat, Savonn saw that the fletching was bright orange.

Sound and action came to a standstill. His conscious mind informed him that the dull ache in his fingers came of clutching the lute too hard. It was also trying to tell him that both men had knives on their belts he could pilfer. That he should pilfer them, now, and move before anyone else arrived. But his limbs would not obey.

Someone stepped through the balcony door, someone with Hiraen Safin's messy chestnut hair and Hiraen Safin's goldenwood bow. That someone looked at Savonn, took in his bloodstained shirt and his impressive array of injuries, and produced Hiraen Safin's annoyed grimace. It was the sort of thing that happened in hallucinations, or dreams, or plays.

Through the swelling in his throat, Savonn said, "What a coincidence."

"I know," said Hiraen. His eyes passed, incredulous, over the lute. "Lutenists everywhere. It's a bloody infestation. Pick up the damned knives and get behind me."

Once in a very long while, Savonn could take orders. He did so now. The parlour was a wreckage of overturned chairs, a cold draught gusting through the room. A guard showed her face in the doorway, and received an arrow through the eye. Another managed a few steps into the room before Savonn's knife, flung over Hiraen's shoulder, took him in the chest. "They told me you were dead," said Savonn.

"I don't blame them," said Hiraen. "I was very convincing."

He led the way across the parlour. "There's going to be a battle," said Savonn, following him. "Dervain said the Council's marching a force up the pass."

He expected laughter. In the exhilaration of the rescue he had forgotten, however briefly, that the Hiraen he now knew was not the Hiraen of his boyhood. "Who the hell is Dervain? Back on first-name terms now, are you?"

It seemed like more trouble than it was worth to quarrel. They were in the hallway, jogging to the stairs; then they were out in the open air, crossing the yard while servants pelted to and fro with buckets of water from the spring. The fire had spread to the outbuildings, and Isemain's guards were streaming towards the postern in pursuit of Anyas and his garrison. In the dizzying chiaroscuro of firelight and shadow, no one took notice of them.

"But that would explain it," Hiraen was saying. "I sent Emaris to Medrai for help. He must have brought the Council."

A ghostly hush fell. "Emaris?"

Hiraen stopped in his tracks. For the first time, his face softened. "What on earth did they tell you? He's alive. Would I have let anything happen to him?"

But I did, thought Savonn. "You—"

"No, wait, someone's coming."

One of the guards had seen them. He blundered over, his jerkin charred, his spear raised in a vaguely threatening manner. Hiraen dodged, and Savonn tripped the man up in passing. "The stables," said Hiraen. "There'll be horses."

They set off at a sprint. The fire was already devouring the stable with the collapsed roof. The other two still stood, just barely. Hiraen started flinging open stall doors one by one, and Savonn joined him, following the agitated neighing. His thoughts were catching up with his body. Emaris was alive. Anyas was free. The Council was here. And somewhere along Forech's Pass, a man called Dervain Teraille was on a collision course with them, a fox among hens.

There would be time enough to worry about that later. Hiraen was leading out one of the horses by its bridle. Savonn had just opened the last stall to free its occupant when a javelin flew past him, lifting the hair on his head, and thudded into the stall door between two of his fingers.

He turned. Isemain Dalissos, Marshal of Sarei, was standing in front of the stable, another javelin poised in his hand. In full armour, he could have been half giant. "Lord Safin," he said, as Hiraen moved to stand between him and Savonn. His voice was hollow and brassy in his helmet. "I neglected to kill you properly. Let me rectify the error."

Hiraen looked nonplussed. Knife in hand, Savonn found himself overcome by inopportune hilarity. "Shall I translate?"

They both looked at him with distaste. Before Hiraen could string his bow, the second javelin struck the ground just beyond them. Hiraen snatched it up, throwing the reins of the horse to Savonn, and danced away just as Isemain brought his sword down in a great arc. He parried twice, yielding ground. "Go! Find Anyas and get out!"

"All right," said Savonn, who had no intention of doing so. He caught the horse's bridle and swung himself up bareback. The fight was too close to risk throwing a knife, so he resorted to his second favourite weapon. "It seems a little rude to leave without saying goodbye, though. My lord Marshal, I'm escaping!"

Isemain glanced up, distracted. It was only a moment's respite, but it was enough. Hiraen's bow was nocked and drawn in the span of a heartbeat, arrow-tip trained on Isemain's eye, the only exposed part of him. At such close quarters, even a lesser archer could not have missed. Savonn felt a grin crack his face. Seeing his chance, he switched to the most disgustingly idiomatic Saraian he could muster. "He hits eleven targets out of ten, my lord. You'd better let us go. After all, it's bad enough you burned my fort down—"

"Lord Isemain," said another voice. A figure had stepped out from the shadow of the stable. "There's no time. You have to go."

I have conjured him again, Savonn thought. But the head of the speaker was jet black, not auburn. Hiraen stepped forward, his face a mask of quiet fury. "It's you."

Savonn said, "Don't—"

The bowstring hissed. The arrow struck Nikas in the right shoulder and sunk deep, the tip protruding out again through his back near the breastbone. Isemain started towards him. "Don't kill him?" Hiraen suggested. "Coming from *you*?"

Nikas glanced down at the wound with no sign of pain. "The men of Betronett are coming, Marshal. My cover is blown. I escaped to warn you."

Savonn shouted, "Hiraen!"

They moved together seamlessly, a left hand and its right. Savonn kicked the horse, yanking at the reins, and Hiraen sprang to meet him. Isemain's sword cut the air. Hiraen seized Savonn's outstretched hand and swung up into the saddle behind him, and then they were galloping towards the ringwall, between buildings lit up like candles and stragglers scurrying to get out of their way. Hiraen shot one, and they rode another down. They were at the postern. They were through. They were cantering along the winding track beneath the wall, torches bobbing in the Pass below, swords singing, horns blaring. They were out of Onaressi. They were free.

After a moment Hiraen said, "You're going the wrong way."

Downward to the battle in the Pass, to Medrai, to Anyas and Daine and Emaris and the Council. Or upward into the meandering trails above Onaressi, where one could descend by circuitous paths and lonely moors into the lowlands, towards an isle in the Morivant, and whatever awaited there. It was not a choice.

"I'm not," he said. "I'm going to Evenfall."

* * *

It was dawn by the time Hiraen managed to get a sensible word out of Savonn.

After the sounds of battle died away behind them, they stopped for a rest by a quiet pool in the trackless wastes above Onaressi. The trees, bristling fiery orange, peered down at their mirrored doubles in the marmoreal surface of the pool. It was too cold to bathe, but the water was clean and soothing in Hiraen's parched throat. In the company of anyone else, it would have been like a holiday. "There's just been a battle," he said, when they had wiped themselves down and drunk their fill. "We don't even know who won."

Savonn was sitting at the foot of a larch, examining the damaged lute he had brought out of Onaressi. The Empath's lute. "So turn back."

Hiraen had never been patient. He was neither Rendell nor Emaris, and would not suffer to be led by the nose through Savonn's vast mazes of circumlocution. "You're going to meet him. What did he want?"

"I believe," said Savonn, "Marguerit wished to remove me from the board with bribes and promises before she opened the war. Dervain felt this was a bad idea."

A chill was seeping through Hiraen's insides, a chill that had nothing to do with the water he had just drunk. "Did you accept?"

Savonn traced a finger along the soundboard of the lute. Louder, Hiraen said, "*Did you accept?*"

Once, there would have been no need to ask. Once, he and Savonn had known each other like their own souls. Before the Empath. Before Merrott. Before Kedris. But the blank-eyed stare that greeted him now was the face of a stranger, one of thousands of dispensable masks taken off as easily as they were put on. "Did I, indeed," said Savonn. He wore his mockery like a shirt of mail, bright and cold and imperturbable. "Alas, your well-timed rescue deprived you of the chance to find out."

The black rage returned. Savonn had turned traitor for him once before. And Hiraen had done the same for him, in his way. It made him sick. With effort, he kept his fists at his sides. "A few days ago, my patrol was massacred because of you. Yesterday, I risked my life to rescue you from a captivity you seem to have very much enjoyed. And quite soon, I am about to *lose my temper and punch you in the jaw.*"

Savonn put the lute aside and stood up. Beneath the violet bruises on his face, his olive skin had taken on a waxy undertone, the sort you saw in corpses on slabs. "Not being prone to martyrdom," he said, enunciating every syllable with violent clarity, "I considered that if word got out about my past activities, I would be much safer in Marguerit's hands than the Council's. However, she is unlikely to sit back and let me kill her favourite spy. So I escaped. Is the logic sound? Do you still wish to punch me?"

Hiraen did. "Was that all you thought about?" he demanded. A sparrow that had alighted on a branch by his head took fright and flurried away. "Only yourself, and this vendetta of yours? What about the rest of us?"

"I thought you were dead," said Savonn. "What did it matter, then?"

Hiraen started to answer, then stopped. Savonn shrugged, a delicate, economical dip of his head towards one shoulder. Lately it had become fashionable among the younger boys to imitate the way their Captain moved: the acrobatic walk, the plumbline posture, the slant of his head when he was concentrating. Even Emaris did it sometimes, when he thought no one was looking. Gods, Emaris. "I did all of it to protect you from my father," said Savonn. "Betronett. Merrott. Dervain was the only part of it I kept for myself. If you were dead, then—it was over."

He pushed a stray curl out of his face, a brief, impatient movement. When he spoke again his voice was dry and dispassionate, as though he were reading from a treatise. "*Home is not a place. Not walls of stone or roofs of brick, nor a name on any map...* No, you wouldn't know the quote."

Iyone might. Iyone always knew what Savonn was reading. Thick as twins, so close they used to answer to each other's names when they were small. "Did you think," said Hiraen, almost unable to speak, "did you think even for a moment that—Daine and Emaris and the rest—that they wouldn't care if you disappeared?"

"You were dead," said Savonn again. "My capacity for rational thought was circumscribed."

Hiraen's sinuses ached. He reached for Savonn, saw in time his habitual flinch, and lowered his hand without touching him. The lute was still lying at their feet, a silent witness. "But now I'm alive," said Hiraen. "So if you want to go to Evenfall, you'll have to take me along."

Savonn turned away, businesslike again. "I am going there to kill my lover. I doubt you'll enjoy the spectacle. Go and find Emaris and tell him I died at Onaressi. It would be kinder."

Another lie. Another secret. Hiraen was up to his neck in them. Kedris. Merrott. Rendell. How did Savonn keep them straight in his head? "I," he said, with so much force his teeth clicked together, "am done lying for you. Do it yourself."

"It would be kinder from you," said Savonn again. His face was still averted. "To him, and to me as well, if it makes a difference."

Something twisted in Hiraen's heart. They could never stay angry with each other. "Savonn," he said helplessly. How long had it been since they last curled around each other behind a closed door and listened to the adults rowing below? "Don't do this to yourself. Don't go to Evenfall. I'll fight him for you."

"No." With Savonn's head in profile, Hiraen could only guess at his expression. "He is mine to kill."

"But could you?" asked Hiraen, before he could think better of it. "Could you do it? Could you take a blade to his throat with your own hand and watch the light in his eyes go out?"

Savonn had bent to pick up the lute. He stopped. Then he straightened, empty-handed, and turned to meet Hiraen's gaze full on. His smile stung like a brand, but whether it was directed at himself or Hiraen, no one could have known.

"I suppose," he said, "we are going to find out."

CHAPTER 25

By the time Emaris reached Onaressi with Daine and the rest of their forces, the battle was over.

It had left its mark on the mountain. The trail at the bottom of Forech's Pass was littered with souvenirs: dead men and dead horses, a dinted helm here, a broken spear there. Most of the outbuildings had burned to the ground, leaving only charred, smoking skeletons where walls and roofs had once been. But the main keep still stood, and from the soot-blackened ringwall flew the proud standard of House Safin, its conqueror, the orange sunburst bright beneath an unimpressed grey sky.

Emaris burst into the front hall, half expecting to be greeted by Hiraen himself, with Savonn in tow. Instead, it was a man with a bandaged face who met him at the foot of the main stair, swaths of fresh linen criss-crossing his cheeks and nose and jaw. "Anyas?" asked Emaris, alarmed. "Is it you?"

"It's quite funny," said Anyas's familiar voice, "having to reintroduce myself to everyone I meet. I don't even know what I look like under these bandages anymore." He took Emaris's elbow. "The Saraians are gone. They saw you lot coming and clattered back to Astorre to hide behind Celisse's skirts. We won."

"And the Empath?"

Anyas grimaced, or at least Emaris thought he did. It was hard to tell. "Disappeared. Evaporated like dew, so far as anyone can tell. The Marshal at least was worth his salt. Wrangled an orderly retreat, so we didn't get to kill many of them, but..."

Emaris shouldered past him, starting up the stairs. "I have to go see Hiraen. There's something he promised me."

Anyas pulled him back. "You don't want to go in there. Lord Safin's quarrelling with his lieutenants in the parlour. One of them is an Efren."

"Lord Safin?" asked Emaris, disoriented. Then his heart sank. "Oh. You mean Lucien. Where's Hiraen?"

"That's what they're fighting about," said Anyas. "They haven't found Hiraen or Savonn. Not in the dungeon, nor in the keep—" He saw Emaris's expression change. "Not among the corpses, either. They checked. There aren't many, and they're mostly Saraians. Look, Emaris, I *saw* him. Hiraen, that is. He killed the dungeon guards and set us loose and said he was going to find Savonn. I told him exactly where they were keeping him. I can't understand it."

It was a lot to take in. Emaris rubbed the back of his head, which had begun to ache again. "Maybe they went down into the Pass? To Medrai?"

"Or," said Anyas, "the Saraians took them when they fled." His voice was raspier than usual, but it could have been the bandages. "Lord Lucien's just about ready to ride into Astorre after them. Efren and Sydell are talking him down. Him over there—" He pointed to a stranger sitting on the window-sill across the hall, whom Emaris had not noticed before. The man caught his eye and nodded. "That's Zarin, Lady Josit's man. He got bored of the bickering and left."

Emaris took in perhaps one word in three. He said, stupidly, "But Hiraen said he would find Savonn. He said he would try. He said—"

He stopped short. All that was between him and Hiraen. "Ni-kas," he said, changing the subject. "He sold us out. He was the Empath's spy all this time. I tried to kill him at Kimmet, but he ran off."

"We haven't seen him either," said Anyas. "Dead or fled, then. Good riddance, if you ask me."

The freedman called Zarin stepped forward. He was in his forties, Emaris guessed, with grey eyes so pale they were almost lilac. "Did you say the traitor is called Nikas?"

"Yes," said Emaris. "Have you heard of him?"

"The name is known to us," said Zarin. "He is a source of some amusement to Josit her ladyship. They have been in touch from time to time. Suffice it to say that this man Nikas fancies himself a lost scion of the royal house of Sarei, and wishes for his status to be... acknowledged."

"*What*?" said Anyas.

Zarin shrugged. "We keep tabs on him, not altogether successfully. So, we are told, does Marguerit."

Emaris could not have cared less about Josit and Marguerit and Nikas. He said, "Savonn disappears all the time. He always turns up sooner or later, with Hiraen and—and a choir and fireworks and a goddamned dragon if he feels like it. They're not dead."

"No one is saying they're dead," said Anyas, with unbearable gentleness. He squeezed Emaris's elbow. "Emaris. Are you listening? Lord Lucien won't give up the search. The men are so drunk on victory, they'll march on Daliss tonight if that's what it takes to get them back."

"Yes," said Emaris automatically. It seemed like too much effort to detach himself, so he only stared at his arm until Anyas let go. "Of course."

He believed Anyas. He believed Lucien. Most of all, he believed Hiraen, who had never once let him down. Hiraen was a man of his word. If he was alive, he would find his way back somehow. But Savonn—

Emaris might never get to ask his questions now, and he had no answers but the equivocal ones Nikas had given him. Already they were percolating into his mind, seeping into the cracks and fissures left by past hurts. Savonn's voice, drifting out through a succession of closed doors. Savonn's face that first evening in Astorre, the mountain glowing scarlet behind him. Savonn dancing with the Empath, the magpie and the nightingale. Emaris stood again in the hallway of Daine's house, light spilling from the back room to puddle at his feet; but this time, when he looked to Savonn, seeking comfort, he found he could barely picture his face.

CHAPTER 26

Lissein was a little backwater village on the east bank of the Morivant, notable only in one aspect: it lay just two miles south of the Singing Ford, where Kedris Andalle had routed the Saraians eighteen years ago. The villagers never forgot this, and now that Marguerit had suffered another blow, it was all anyone could talk about. Lucien Safin had driven the Marshal of Sarei and his pet sorcerer out of the mountains, and his lordship's son Hiraen had pulled off a heroic rescue of their prisoners in the same night. Surely a cause for celebration, even if Hiraen *had* vanished from the battlefield right afterwards, along with that rascal Savonn Silvertongue. Probably dead; such a pity, and so young, too, but could there be any better way to go?

The deceased, listening from the back of a tavern, had to be physically restrained from launching himself to his feet. It was their last stop before Evenfall, which brooded on its isle in the Morivant not far north of the Ford. At Savonn's insistence, they had lived off the land all the way from Onaressi, shunning even the shepherds' lonely cottages to sleep under the stars, and concealing themselves by the wayside on the few occasions they heard another traveller on the road. Hiraen did not learn of his purported death until days after the fact, by which time it was too late to prevent the news from reaching Cassarah.

"But we can't let them grieve," he hissed, from beneath the broad-brimmed hat that Savonn had forbidden him to remove under pain of death. "My mother—she isn't young anymore, and Iyone—don't you *care*?"

Savonn yawned, stretching his arms out above his head. He had made no attempt to alter his appearance. It did not matter. When the Silvertongue wished to disappear, he was unrecognisable. "Iyone," he said, "would survive the apocalypse and complain it was boring."

His arms, still outstretched, socked a passing merchant in the stomach. The man squawked, and Savonn, wearing the lazy smile he had put on for the day, allowed himself to be smacked in the head. To Hiraen he said, "You can turn back if you like. I, on the other hand, must be in Evenfall tomorrow night."

Hiraen eyed the space between Savonn and the retreating merchant. "Why?"

"It's the last day of the crescent moon," said Savonn. It was just one of the many incomprehensible things he had said over the course of their long and nerve-wracking friendship. He placed his cupped palms on the table and opened them, a conjurer revealing a secret. Inside was a pouch Hiraen had never seen in his life, full to the brim with gold drochii. "This should be enough for everything we need, shouldn't it? Oh, at least pretend to be impressed. You're a terrible audience."

He disappeared soon after to buy, of all things, lutestrings. The merchant remained none the wiser about the theft of his pouch. Hiraen took advantage of Savonn's absence to write two brief, carefully worded letters, one addressed to Emaris, the other to Iyone. Then he realised there was no one to whom he could entrust the letters, and threw them in the fireplace.

They set out the next day on fresh horses, their saddlebags laden with food. They passed the Singing Ford at a judicious distance—it was guarded more heavily than usual, with a phalanx of pikemen and a catapult—and made their way north to Evenfall, keeping close to the riverbank. It was not far to where the Morivant parted to flow around the little island rising in midstream. They saw the cypresses of Evenfall first, bristling red and gold above the water like a contingent of watchful guardians. Then the isle itself came into view.

Hiraen knew all the stories. Evenfall had lain desolate for a thousand years, passing like a counterfeit coin from owner to owner. No trace of Ederen Andalle's palace now remained save a few sinister standing stones, and anyone who tried to live there went mad sooner or later. Even Kedris, with his penchant for making everything his own, had not cared to go near the isle. "We are in time," said Savonn.

Hiraen followed his gaze to the dusky sky. The moon had been waning all through their journey from Onaressi. It was in its death throes now, a sliver of a crescent snared between the distant mountain peaks. Tomorrow it would be gone.

He decided not to ask. Above the rumble of the rushing torrent, he called, "Has it occurred to you that this might be a trap?"

"Many times," said Savonn.

Riding up and down the bank, he had found a shallow place where the channel could be forded. With a brief backwards glance at Hiraen, he urged his horse down the gentle bank and began to splash across. Hiraen followed. The water was cold and the current inexorable, and it took every ounce of his considerable horsemanship to guide his mare across, nose-deep in the river. "He won't come alone," he said.

"No," Savonn agreed. "He will bring a witness, like I did. It will probably be Nikas, unless you have killed him."

They reached the sandy shore of the isle without event. The thicket was already dark, the wind sighing in the eaves like a human voice, and at the treeline Hiraen's mare balked. He dismounted to lead her on foot, keeping a hand on his bow. There was no sign of the Empath, nor of any other living creature, human or animal—no birdsong, not even the flutter of wings or the scurry of rodent feet. The soil was as pristine as if no one had trodden here since Ederen's day. "No tracks," Hiraen remarked.

Even against the thunder of the Morivant, every word and movement seemed sacrilegiously loud in the stillness of the wood. Savonn slid out of the saddle. He had found himself a sword in Lissein, and wore it openly on his hip, as he so seldom did. "Then we have beaten him here. He should turn up in a few hours."

"Will he?"

Savonn did not answer. They walked on in silence, until the trees began to thin and the thicket gave way to a grassy clearing, about as big as the stage in the House of Charissos. One side gave onto a sheltered shell-shaped cove, which fed in turn into the river. Scattered through the clearing were the remains of what had once been a colonnade: here a chipped stone column, taller than Hiraen; there the base of a collapsed obelisk, its strange markings worn almost smooth by the centuries. Farther inland, he could see the indistinct hulks of more crumbling walls and pillars. There was nothing else. Anything of worth had long been looted by intrepid explorers.

Without speaking, they gathered brushwood and lit a fire by the cove. Striking inland after dark was out of the question. "I'll take first watch," said Savonn. "Unless, of course, you don't trust me."

From long experience, Hiraen ignored the goad. "It's an odd place for a rendezvous, is all."

"Don't let it surprise you," said Savonn. They had spread their saddle-blankets close to the fire. He was propped against one of the fallen columns, facing away from the flames. His left hand lay curled on the grass, slender and childlike; his right hand was concealed in the folds of his cloak, no doubt holding a knife. "He takes his poetry to extremes. My family—which he despises—is inextricably linked to Ederen. And then there is the temple they tried to build here, until the priests lost their minds and killed each other and they had to abandon it... You know the tale?"

Beyond the trees, the moon lurked like a creature lying in wait. "I know. A temple to the god of death. The guardian of the Sanctuary."

In Cassarah they worshipped Mother Alakyne, who had sung the world into being, and her dread daughters Aebria and Casteia. But there were others. Flamboyant Charissos, lord of the stage, who might have been Savonn's patron god if he had had a different upbringing. Amitei, love and beauty embodied. And the Father, Alakyne's nameless consort, herald of death and the end of the world, who was sought only in desolate places like these—in the night and the fog and the deep cold of winter, when things perished and returned to the earth. There were no hymns for him. He was worshipped only in silence, as the Mother was with music.

"It was two hundred years ago," said Savonn. "The High Priest said he had received a vision from on high, that the world was coming to an end, and the only way to stop it was for his devout servants to deliver each other to the Father as sacrifices. Brother against sister, parent against child, lover against lover. So they did. An acolyte found them the next morning, forty grisly bodies strewn around the altar."

He trailed off, as if imagining the scene. "My father used to say that the gods do nothing but addle people's minds."

"Scepticism keeps your mind clear," said Hiraen. His eyes were slipping shut. "But it also makes you terminally stupid about other things."

"I know," said Savonn.

* * *

Hiraen dozed, and woke, and dozed again.

Trumpets blared. Heavy feet tramped past their fire with the brisk, fevered regularity of a battle march. Low voices chanted a paean, now and then interrupted by a far-off shriek. Once he opened his eyes and saw banners, white and gold and red and silver, unfurling on the wind between the whispering cypresses. Moonlight glinted on helmeted heads. The obelisks moaned. The fire was burning low, and in the darkness he lay suspended in a nightmarish hellscape, the trees—living pillars of a house of horrors—casting freakish shadows over the clearing. He tried to call to Savonn, but his voice choked in his throat as if he were underwater, and then the shades were gone.

All but one. Kedris Andalle stood over him, an imposing figure in plate and mail, his naked longsword shining in his hand. Under his visor there was no face, only two brilliant eyes that blazed blue like starfire. "Get up," he said. A spear blossomed out of his heart, blood spreading from the tip like crimson petals. "I am offering you an honour beyond anything you deserve. You need only do as I say, and one day you will be Captain of Betronett."

Hiraen still could not speak. Instead he heard in his head the answer he had given as a boy of seventeen. *It is no honour. What you ask is murder.*

He stood in Merrott's sickroom on the Bitten Hill, the air close and cloying with the reek of opiates. Another spear, another scarlet flower, blooming and putrefying in the old man's chest. Across the deathbed Savonn would not meet his eye. "I would have put Betronett in your hands, but you would not kill for me," said Kedris, every word solemn and hollow with avuncular grief. "I have loved you like a father, but it seems I have no luck with my sons..."

I have *killed*, Hiraen tried to say. *For Savonn, not for you.* But even as he formed the thought, Kedris's clear brown skin withered away like paper over an open flame, and he vanished in a cloud of ash. Then it began to rain, and Hiraen stood on the wet

305

cobbles of the street in Cassarah he had seen a hundred times in his dreams. His hands were red with sticky blood all the way to his wrists. *I killed to keep his secrets, and he must never know.*

He awoke, drenched in sweat. It was still dark. The ground was dry and unmarked as ever, and the moon sailed on its last voyage through the sky, glimmering at him like a satyr's smile. Savonn was building up the fire. "I had a strange dream," said Hiraen.

The silence spread itself thin and untenable between them. Dimly, he wondered if he had cried out in his sleep.

"I read a book about this," said Savonn. His face was a dissimulation of light and shadow, deep vales and sharp peaks thrown into violent contrast. "It said that the ruins of Evenfall are surrounded by minute fissures in the ground, cracks that run deep into the earth and release gases from some underground chamber. The gases are odourless, but they bring visions and hallucinations that can turn a person mad."

After a moment, Hiraen identified this as an attempt to offer comfort. "Gases or ghouls, it makes no difference," he said. "This place is haunted."

"Don't be superstitious," said Savonn. "Shut up and go back to sleep."

Hiraen meant to stay awake, to keep watch for the Empath, but his eyelids grew heavy and drooped and shut altogether. Isemain Dalissos faced him with a sword in his hand, narrow-set eyes alight with the joy of the fight. Parry. Twist. Duck. The sky was aflame, searing the ground to ivory beneath their feet, and at the back of his mind was the dull roar of a crowd. Emaris looked on, wide gazelle eyes filled with tears. Someone picked out a slow, mournful chord on a lute. He tried to open his eyes. The Empath was here. The fight was beginning. He had to—

"But don't you see?" asked Kedris, so earnest, so sincere, a voice to start wars and topple mountains. "Betronett is far too important to lie fallow in the hands of that old codger. Merrott is a lost cause. But a man like you, whose bow is guided by the very hands of Casteia—a commander like you on the frontier of the Farfallens—the fame, the glory, the songs that would be sung!"

His younger self answered. *I am not a killer.* It had been true then. *Neither is Savonn. Find someone else.*

A chiming laugh, or perhaps that was the lute. "Savonn is whatever he wishes to be on any given day. A useful child. If you cannot rise to the challenge, surely he will."

"*Don't touch him,*" said Hiraen aloud, and lurched bolt upright.

The moon was past its zenith, a long-horned fragment behind bulbous clouds. Savonn was playing his lute, watching him across the fire with catlike eyes. "Gases and ghouls," he said softly.

Hiraen staggered first to his knees, and then his feet. He felt weak all over, as if his tendons and sinews had been undone one by one by the god of the Sanctuary. There was cold sweat on his face and neck. "If I stay here a moment longer," he said, "even a *moment*, I am going to lose my mind."

Savonn's fingers went still on the lutestrings. "Then go away. I'm staying."

Hiraen flung up his hands. "What for? We've waited all night. He's not going to show. He sent us here on a wild goose chase because that sort of joke appeals to people like him—people like you—"

"There's still some time before moonset," said Savonn. "Play the lute and stay awake, if that helps. I shall take a nap."

He pushed the instrument into Hiraen's hands and settled himself on his cloak, between the fire and his sword. Hiraen stared at the lute, helpless. It had been a long time since he'd played. He had had lessons in his childhood, a few from his mother, a few from Josit, but mostly from an impatient school-master who liked to tell him that his head was so full of earth, there was no room left over in it for music or philosophy. But that could not be true, because he was friends with Savonn. Anybody else, if they had even a smidge of sense, would have run for their lives.

He fumbled through the three or four songs he still knew, too distracted to listen to himself, his eyes and ears pricked for movement in the thicket. If anyone approached, the music would betray their location at once. Minutes passed, or perhaps an hour. The moon was thin as a fingernail. The moon had drifted beneath the treetops. The moon was skimming the Morivant, silvering the water with faint luminescence. He drifted in a soporific haze, fingers seguing from chord to aimless chord. Fingers that had held a bow, a sword, a dagger. Feet that had moved, soft with stealth and urgent with fear, down the cobbles of a back alley. Rendell's voice asked, "What are you doing here?" and his own answered, "Keeping a secret."

The moon was drowning itself in the river. Across the fire, Savonn murmured something indistinct and rolled over.

To fall asleep was madness. Hiraen saw that now. He edged over on stiff knees and clammy palms, keeping his face towards the fire. As a child he had often stayed up all night with Savonn and Iyone, swapping scary stories on the roof of the manor until none of them dared shut their eyes. But they were children no longer. "Savonn," he said.

Savonn tensed like a coiled spring at the touch of his hand, and then relaxed again, still half asleep. "*Etruska?*"

"No," said Hiraen. "Just me."

He came awake at once, a knife glinting in his closed palm. The back of his shirt was soaked through. Distantly, Hiraen wondered what he had been dreaming about. "Look," he said. "Your crescent moon. It's set. He's not coming."

Venus had risen in the east, blinking in and out behind a wisp of cloud. Otherwise their solitude was complete. Tomorrow night was the new moon. "He may have been delayed," said Hiraen. "Or captured, or wounded. He might not even have survived the battle."

308

He thought perhaps he sounded too hopeful. Then he realised Savonn was not listening at all. His cheeks were flushed, the twin upsweeps of his lashes heavy with beaded moisture, the bright pinprick of Venus reflected twice in his glassy eyes. Hiraen had seen him like this before, unmasked at the masquerade, and again in the House of Charissos after the play. Apprehension thrummed in his chest, a misplaced chord in a minor key.

As if to himself, Savonn said, "He never meant to come."

Hiraen rubbed his eyes. "That's what I've been trying to tell you."

"No," said Savonn. His voice was muted, deadly. "*On the edge of the crescent moon, in the unholy light of evenfall.* He was stalling us. It's been nine days."

"What?"

"Nine days since he said that to me. Nine days between the battle and the last night of the crescent moon. Nine days," said Savonn, louder now, every consonant sharpened with suppressed hysteria, "is just enough time to get from Onaressi to Cassarah."

Hiraen drew a sharp breath. "With his army? No, that's insane. Alone."

"Alone," Savonn echoed. He looked like a candle burning at both ends, though with what fuel, Hiraen could not tell. Hatred and wonder and anger and love were all mirror images in that bizarre magpie mind. "With the most powerful weapon he has. Secrets. It's our game. *Just like old times...*"

"Stop it," said Hiraen. His hands found Savonn's shoulders. "Stop talking in riddles. What did he mean? What's he going to do?"

He knew the answer even as he asked. "Expose me to the Council, of course," said Savonn. His eyes were unnaturally bright, and his lips were straining into a smile, gruesome and hideous. "So all the world will know me for what I've done. I can hear him even now. Spy. Traitor. Murderer... No, sit down," he said, as Hiraen reared to his feet. "He'll have arrived by now. It's

309

too late. There is nothing we can do except watch the curtain rise, and marvel at the genius of it all."

His fingers closed around Hiraen's wrist, his grip brutal, his face glimmering wet. "They have him." There was a strange new note in his voice, brittle and aching. It was grief. "Hiraen, *they have him.*"

CHAPTER 27

"I won't believe it," said Iyone, "until I see their bodies."

She had called on Josit at the Street of Canaries, half expecting to be turned away at the door, but desperate for a reprieve from the well-meaning friends who kept foisting their condolences on her. Her brothers were not dead. Savonn was merely hard to find, that was all, and Hiraen was with him. If this was as much an exercise in denial as in logic, then so be it. Gods help her, she had enough to worry about as it was.

"We should prepare for the worst," said Josit. There was no sign that she remembered Iyone's threats about the child, or had marked Shandei's abrupt disappearance. She was paler than Iyone had ever seen her, the skin of her face blanched and fragile as eggshells, her fingers taut around the stem of her goblet. "Zarin is on his way back. His last letter told of a traitor in the Betronett camp, one who sold them out to the Marshal. It seems likely that Savonn and Hiraen were killed, or at least taken to Sarei."

In spite of herself, Iyone pictured her brothers as prisoners, hauled before Marguerit in chains. Savonn would make the best of it, of course. Given a week, he would be chorusing dirty songs with the fiercest of his gaolers; in another, he would be an honoured guest at Marguerit's court, clothed in silks and jewels and spewing absinthe-fuelled poetry. He loved life a little too much for *death before dishonour*. Hiraen, though, was another matter. She imagined him on the rack, spitting curses at his tormentors, refusing to forswear his allegiance even as his bones popped and his sinews tore—

She pulled herself out of it. Savonn and Hiraen were only one of her problems. Josit still sat across the table from her, bold as day, new schemes probably taking shape in every recess of her mind as they spoke. And there was the letter from Terinea, distracting and infuriating. *There was no stillborn child, Iyone,* Shandei had written. *The convent's records show that there was only one infant delivered there in July 1512: your gnatlike friend Savonn. Either someone is misleading you, or there has been a mistake. I don't know what to make of it, but I'm sure you do.*

The letter had not ended there. Iyone had been surprised to discover that, given pen and paper, Shandei could be dramatically verbose. *Thus far I have scandalised three acolytes with bedroom tales, and showed another how to kill a man with a sewing-needle. (Have I mentioned I am doing a lot of sewing? Heavens help me.) The blessed Governess Persis is about to fling me out of her convent. No, that is unlikely—she is too pious for that, but I am bored out of my mind, and desperately tempted to test her patience. How, I wonder, can any hot-blooded woman take a priestess's vows?*

I have thought about following your father's army to Medrai and beyond, to look for my brother and join him in arms against the Saraians. But then I remember the thing I have to do in Cassarah... and I remember you, Iyone. I know you would prefer I stayed in Terinea until you finished pruning the Thorn, but every day I am away from home is a little death I die. It is my city as well as yours, and there is so much talk of war. Soon, you may be glad of a warrior.

What I mean to say is that I have packed my bags and am on my way to you. You will probably be angry. You will just have to put up with me. I look forward to seeing you again.

It was exasperating. After all her work to put Shandei out of harm's way, the girl was simply coming back. She might kill Willon Efren, or he might arrest her, or—a non-negligible possibility—Josit might do both.

"Let's not worry about things we can't help," said Iyone bracingly, as much for her own benefit as Josit's. "The mountains will soon be impassable. When Marguerit attacks, she will have to come by the west, over the Morivant. The blow will fall on Cassarah. Let us drink another cup, and then convene the Council." She leaned across the table to ring the handbell at Josit's elbow. "More mulled wine, please."

Josit frowned. She seemed to have aged several years in the span of hours: her cheeks had thinned, and a green webbing of veins showed through the fine translucent skin at her temple. One could see the marks of a difficult life led with pride and honour and no small success. "I prefer to be sober when dealing with you."

"That," said Iyone, "is the highest compliment I have ever received. Let us speak of sober things, then. Why do you think Savonn was taken?"

"I can guess," said Josit. "He has a knack of making himself intolerable. Not just to his friends, but also his enemies. Marguerit may have grown alarmed."

The solar door slid open to admit a servant with a fresh jug of wine. Smoothly, Josit changed the subject to a safer one. "Speaking of the Council," she said, "you should have heard Willon today. I suggested twelve different ways in which the city could be fortified, and he barely listened. He's gotten worse since Lucien left."

Perhaps it was time they removed him. But that was a matter for when they were alone. "He dislikes being proven wrong," said Iyone, reaching for her refilled cup. The wine smelled of cloves and cinnamon. "A common failing of old men. We must win over Oriane, or nothing can be done."

The servant had retreated to the back of the room with his hands clasped behind his back. Iyone raised an eyebrow at him. "We don't need anything else. You can leave."

"Wait," said Josit. "I don't know your name."

Iyone wondered where Josit's usual maid had gone. The man must be new—she was sure she would have remembered the long red hair falling in a fat braid across one shoulder. His eyes were demure and downcast. "Why, ladyship? I am nothing."

"I know the names of all my servants," said Josit. "It's a habit of mine."

Something in the tenor of her voice arrested Iyone in mid-sip. She put the cup down without drinking. The servant looked politely surprised. "A name is only a word, ladyship. You may call me what you please."

Josit said, "You are not one of my household."

Iyone began to rise. But before she could call out, the man straightened his shoulders and stepped away from the wall. It was a simple movement, but one that set off a complex sequence of chain reactions. The servility fell away from him like a doffed hat. He stood taller, his chin firmer, and all trace of reverence fled his eyes. It was a transformation of a familiar sort, one she had witnessed before. "No, I suppose not," he said. "But I am your countryman, after all. They say in Daliss that you are shrewder than Marguerit. I thought such a thing was impossible."

Iyone had known fear like this only once before, by the Marigold Bridge, in the instant before the Thorn's hood had fallen away to show her Shandei's face. "*Who are you?*"

The man smiled. "My name is Dervain Teraille, though you may have heard me called the Empath. We have a mutual friend."

Iyone saw only a flurry of skirts and sleeves. With astonishing speed, Josit knocked her chair over and kicked it between them and the false servant. One slim hand shoved Iyone behind her. The other caught up the flask of scalding wine and flung it full

314

into the man's face. He dodged, but not fast enough; some of it splattered on his face and shirt.

"Gods!" he exclaimed. His glee, undeniably genuine, reminded Iyone of Savonn. "Look at you. No wonder Her Magnificence fears you more than anyone living."

"She should," said Josit. A long dagger had materialised in her hand. Iyone glanced at the handbell, wondering if she could reach it fast enough, but Josit shook her head. "If you move, he'll throw a knife at you." She looked back at the Empath. "What have you done with Savonn?"

Iyone stared at her. She had never seen Josit like this before. And yet, parallel to that thread of thought ran another that said, *I have seen her like this every day.* Josit, familiar old Josit, vivid as a viper coiled round an ankle. So slight, so fearless, with the black curls spilling loose down her back. Iyone knew someone else with curls like that. Iyone knew someone else who stood like that, with the same arrogant grace, steady hand grasping a blade like a dancer's baton—

Only one child. The final puzzle-piece clicked into place. Brilliant, Iyone thought. The genius of the deception lay in its simplicity, its utter audacity, so brazen it had been under her nose the whole time. Savonn. Of course. Of course.

"Something amuses you?" the Empath asked. He was looking at Iyone, and at length she remembered that she was in imminent danger of death. She had said nothing, nor—she was quite sure—had her expression altered. "I understand. I feel the same when I think of Savonn. He will be here in a few days. He is detouring to Evenfall, you see, to commune with his ancestral ghosts. I thought I should pay you a courtesy call while he was away."

So he was alive. Alive and free. But what about Hiraen? "Oh," said Josit. She gave the dagger a few thoughtful spins and lowered it to her side. "You're one of his conquests. Let me try to remember which one. Not his first, and by no means his last, but certainly among the most exotic. How is he?"

The smile slipped a little, then regained its footing. "Afraid, I think," said Dervain Teraille. "With good reason. After all, he will soon be a wanted man."

Surely he must have been able to hear the timbre of Iyone's thoughts. He looked round at them, drawing out the suspense like a master showman. "What, has he not bragged to you of his escapades? We used to pass each other information in exchange for certain favours. The death of his old commander, for instance. What was he called? Merrott?"

It was a name Hiraen had brought up before, in passing. "And in return, he told me so much about these forts in the Farfallens," Dervain went on. "It came in handy when I needed someplace to keep all the Marshal's bandits. I expect Savonn was delighted when it got his father killed. He hated the man, did you know?"

Iyone fought down a wave of nausea. Savonn, her brother in mischief if not in blood. "Of course I know," Josit was saying. "Your story fails to entertain me. On the other hand, it will almost certainly interest a man called Willon Efren. If you wished to blacken Savonn's name, you should have gone to him instead."

"Have no fear," said the Empath. "I have already sent him a tip. Can you imagine what he will think when he learns that his colleague is meeting a Saraian spy? His men ought to be here any moment. He will—oh, forsooth!"

Josit hurled the dagger at his face. It struck the wall, knocked over a porcelain vase, and sent it crashing to the floor. Iyone saw her chance. She ducked round Josit, flung the door open, and flew into the hallway. "Guards! *Guards!*"

Most of Josit's retainers had gone to Medrai with Zarin, but a few remained. Someone called, "Mistress?"

"Intruder!" she shouted. "Up here! Hurry!"

Something shattered in the solar. Iyone ran back inside, her heart in her teeth. "Josit?"

The Empath was gone. The room was a wreckage of glass shards, tendrils of mist drifting in through the broken window.

Josit was peering down into the garden, wind gusting through her ringlets. "He jumped out."

A guard poked his head into the room. "Mistress." He took in the carnage, the whites of his eyes showing. "There are men here to see you. Lord Efren's men."

Someone else shouldered him aside. Iyone, her sense of the ludicrous so far suspended it threatened to lift off into space, saw that it was Cahal. His sword was already drawn. "Where's the spy?"

Sense returned, along with the first vestiges of a counter-deception. "He jumped out the window," said Iyone. Her voice shivered with adrenaline, but that was fine. It made her sound angry. "What took you so long? We sent word to Lord Willon ages ago."

Cahal opened his mouth. Then he shut it again. Gaining steam, Iyone trundled on. "Why so shocked? Of course Josit sent the tip herself. Why else lure this fellow here? Are you planning to arrest him or not?"

Cahal stared at her. Without another word, he pushed back into the hallway and shouted an order. In a moment they saw him sprint across the yard, a dozen Efren men pouring after him.

Josit turned away from the broken window, moving her head as if with a great effort. Her gaze seemed to go right through Iyone. "That was quick thinking. But I think, my dear, we have been outplayed."

"No," said Iyone. Her shoes crunched on broken glass and porcelain with a series of furious snaps. "Willon won't believe him. I'll make him see sense myself."

"You amateur," said Josit. "What have I said? Sentiment makes you slow and stupid. Have you worked out his plan, or must I break it down for you like baby's food?" She did not wait for an answer. "The Empath will let himself be caught and interrogated. Willon will be ecstatic, of course, to have captured one of the generals who slipped through your father's fingers. All the more if the man gives him an excuse to get rid of me."

"Even Willon can't—"

"The Empath," said Josit, speaking over her, "will keep his silence, feigning loyalty to me. Then Willon will give him to the torturers, and he will tell them everything he wants them to believe. About Savonn. About me. And they will eat it all from his hand. There are no liars on the rack, after all."

Out of the fog, the alarum-bells were tolling. Once, twice, thrice. *To arms. To arms.* Between shallow breaths, Iyone said, "Was it true? What he said about Savonn?"

The pause lasted just a beat too long. With her musician's sensibilities, Josit ought to have known better. "Don't believe everything you hear," she said. "Savonn is, for the most part, a harmless romantic who watches too many plays. I thought you knew him."

"So harmless he got his father killed?"

Josit gave her a sharp look. "He did not, though Kedris gave him every reason to. As fathers go, our Lord Governor was particularly unkind. You wouldn't have guessed it, watching him smile and throw coins in public. The Empath is right. Savonn loathed him."

"Merrott—"

Josit picked up a malachite jar from the sideboard, turning it over and over in her hands. "Savonn had no choice in the matter. Kedris forced his hand. And he has been trying to make amends ever since. Have *you* never erred?"

"Often," said Iyone, with a calm she did not feel. "But as a rule, I don't make my mother cover up for me."

A trembling hush. Very slowly, Josit turned around. "What did you say?"

On a better day, Iyone would have bided her time, keeping her revelation to herself until the perfect moment arrived. Now she unleashed it with the basest of motives, the need to hurt. "Only one child was born in Danei's convent that month," she said. She had burned Shandei's letter, though not before she learnt it by

318

heart. "Savonn. But he was born to you, not Danei. She must have miscarried, and you passed off your son as hers. Otherwise he would have been raised in slavery. Does he know? Did Kedris?"

Deliberately, Josit opened her hand. The jar joined the rest of the debris with a crash. "Wily girl," she said. Her voice was a rasp of steel. "So clever you would dissect even a tomb. Savonn doesn't know, but of course Kedris did. Danei was never even pregnant."

Thrills tingled down Iyone's spine, the thrills of resolution. That explained everything. A pillow in one's girdle could give the appearance of an advanced pregnancy, but the trick would not stand up to closer examination. Hence the secrecy. The seclusion from her own family. "She couldn't?"

Josit laughed. "Who knows? She didn't try very hard, and I didn't encourage her. She and Kedris despised each other."

"So you bore Kedris's child instead."

"Yes," said Josit. "It was an arrangement that suited us all. He got himself a brilliant if occasionally treasonous son. Danei did not have to risk her fragile health to carry a child she did not want. My heir was brought up in a noble household, safe from Marguerit's long arm. I had always longed for children." Her lip curled. "I got my freedom out of the bargain, too. So we were all happy. If only the Andalles had found it in their strange hearts to love one another, we could have stayed that way."

"But Marguerit must have suspected," said Iyone. "That's why she had Savonn abducted."

Josit gazed unseeingly at the mess on the floor. "It took her a long time. Do you know why?"

"Tell me."

"There were three likely children born at the time of my confinement," said Josit. "One is Savonn. An actor of frivolous repute for most of his life, and therefore of little interest to my sister till recently. Another is a Saraian named Nikas, who was born to Terinean slaves and believes himself to be my son, though his undistinguished parentage has long been proven beyond doubt.

319

Marguerit finds him useful from time to time. And the last, my dear—"

"—is me," said Iyone. It was just possible, if she tried hard enough, to feign indifference. "But I was born in Cassarah."

Josit's smile was bitter. "Do you know," she said, "I have often wished you were my daughter. You have more of me in you than Savonn ever will. But now—"

"Now Marguerit is after him, and the Empath is going to turn the Council against you." Iyone was thinking hard. The puzzle was so neat, so expertly designed, it seemed impossible that she could have anything to add. But of course she did. She, Iyone, almost a queen's heiress. "Well, I can't do anything about the latter. You'll have to flee. It serves you right, after all you did to Shandei and the Efrens. But the former..."

"You have a solution?"

The question was not a rhetorical one. For once, Iyone was a step ahead of Josit. "Birth registries can be forged," she said. "Mothers can be induced to lie. The child could just as easily be me. Why, the idea must have crossed Marguerit's mind by now."

Josit said, "*What is your solution?*"

She could kill Iyone here and now and blame it on the Empath, or the Thorn, and no one would ever know. Ecstatic with victory, Iyone could not have cared less. "I will keep your secret," she said. "I will tell Marguerit, if I have to, that I am her niece. I imagine she would find the idea quite terrifying."

"And the price?" asked Josit.

Unlike her other plans, Iyone had given none of this any prior thought. She knew what she was risking. But for this, perhaps, it was worth it. "That you write and sign an affidavit to the Council. Confess to the Rose Killings, and clear Shandei of all blame. I will help you escape."

Josit laughed. Her eyes were dark and wild with rage. "And if Savonn lives? What will you tell him?"

"Whatever I please." Savonn was the last person in the world to deserve truth from her. "Do you want him to know?"

Josit's shoulders rose and fell. "No."

"I may tell him. Or I may not. It depends."

Josit gazed around the room: the books, the harpsichord, the delicate long-legged chairs. Iyone saw what she was thinking. If she went on the run, all this must be left behind. These, and the home she had built, and the gardens she had tended with her own hands. Even Kedris's grave.

She was a graceful loser. Iyone had expected no less from her. "Clever daughter," said Josit at last. "You have won only by chance, but all the same, I have enjoyed our game... I will do one more thing for you before I go, though you have not asked."

Iyone knew what it was. Still, she said, "Yes?"

"I shall clear the way for you," said Josit. "I shall kill Willon Efren."

CHAPTER 28

As the Morivant swallowed the plunging sun, belching forth in its place a gauzy river fog that settled over the walls and house-tops of the city, Shandei rode back into Cassarah.

Making good on her threat, she had abandoned the convent, swindled a hapless ostler out of a horse, and galloped home. On the way she had taken pains to ask for news of Emaris, and learnt with mingled pride and alarm that not only was he alive and well, he had also become something of a hero. The disappearance of Savonn Silvertongue and his friend did not interest her as much. The Captain was an eccentricity; this was hardly the strangest thing he had done. She was just glad it was Hiraen he had taken with him, and not her brother.

Bundled up to the nose in coats and furs, she got through the Salt Gate without being recognised. Carts jostled past her at the entrance, and the familiar reek of home—the mire of horse and human, fish and river, fruit and musk—rose to assault her senses. She stabled her stolen mare and set off on foot at once for the Safin residence. She wanted to call on Iyone. After so long away, she needed to see a friendly face.

She was passing a row of blue-walled houses on the Street of Hyacinths when shouting erupted at the junction ahead, accompanied by the unmistakeable chink of mail. Armed men, coming her way. That was never a good sign. She looked around, searching for the source of the disturbance, but save for a few freedmen pushing a wagon, she was quite alone. A chill took root in her stomach. The Efrens were onto her. Somehow or other, they knew she had returned, and now at last they would catch her.

Common sense resurfaced. No one knew she was coming back except Iyone, and in any case the city guard could not have mobilised so quickly. All the same, she ducked for the nearest house and swung over the low fence into its yard. The windows were dark; the residents must be asleep. She scanned the terrain. The clamour was coming closer. There was a bush she could crawl under, but it would give only meagre shelter. Then her eye fell on the sturdy apple tree next to it, and she made up her mind.

She shed her outermost cloak and scrambled up the branches. From there, it was an easy slither onto the housetop. Almost as soon as she threw herself flat on the roof, hands searching desperately for purchase among the bricks, the front door flew open and light streamed onto the lawn. "Ama! Apa!" cried a child's high voice. "Look! The Saraians are coming!"

A woman answered in rebuke. Then the door slammed shut again. Shandei stilled. The prospect of an invasion, bandied about in every tavern from Terinea to Cassarah, seemed distant and surreal now that she was behind the city's high walls. It was impossible. Marguerit could not be marching so soon. Besides—

From her vantage point, she could see guards fanning out to barricade the end of the street. She glimpsed their livery—cream and bronze—and the bare steel in their hands. Efren men, not Saraians. Then a figure broke loose from between two houses farther up the row, and pelted down the street towards her.

His auburn hair shivered like living flame. She had met him but once, at a funeral months ago. Even now she could have picked him out of a crowd in a heartbeat. Relief dizzied her, and left her vision smudged with tears. She was not the quarry of the hunt after all. The man had halted just beneath her, in the shadow of the apple tree. As soon as the guards came closer, they would see him.

It would have been easy to stay where she was until the Efrens caught him and left. Instead, she pushed herself onto her elbows and leaned out from the roof. "Hey!"

At first there was no answer. The man's silhouette had joined the mass of shadows pooled under the fence. She swung back to the tree, squinting down with her face pressed against an upper branch. A foot scraped on the cobbles. Then the darkness parted, and out of its midst came her redheaded diviner.

He stood in the lane just beyond the house, out of sight of the windows, a ruffled figure in a plain brown servant's tunic. Perspiration glistened on his forehead, but he was not panting. "Daughter of Rendell."

He remembered her. She had not expected that. "They're coming this way," she whispered. "You'd better get up here."

He glanced at the house behind her. The child and its parents were still inside, tucked away from the commotion behind their shuttered windows. "That would not be wise."

"Why not?" asked Shandei. "What did you do? Why are they chasing you?"

"Because we are playing a game," said the diviner. He smiled. "But you can't play with us. Run home, sunflower. You don't want to be caught with me."

"If you come up here you won't get caught."

He did not move. She made a small sound of irritation and slid down the tree, landing light-footed across the picket fence from him. "What's wrong with you? Are you hurt?"

"No," said the man. The Efren contingent was splitting up, flowing down the street and into the spaces between the houses. "I have only had the worst summer of my life, and now I am about

324

to have the worst autumn... but that is not important. You have less than a minute to get back on that roof and lie very still. They won't see you."

"But why—"

"Anything," he said, "for my sweet, lying lover."

He grabbed her elbow in a practised grip and flung her back. She stumbled into the tree and lost her breath. In the next moment he had bounded away from the fence and into the middle of the street, shouting. "*Mi indror!* Here I am!"

He had spoken in Saraian. The child had been right, after all.

Terror lent her speed. She scrambled back up the tree and tumbled onto the roof, breathless, just as the Efrens came pounding down the street. The man drew a silver blade from his sleeve and flung it at the foremost of his pursuers. The guard went down, neat as a domino. Then the others were on him.

She rolled and hit the ground on the far side of the house. Even before she started to run, she heard him call, laughing. "These knives come with love from Savonn Silvertongue."

END OF BOOK ONE

Keep reading for a special preview of *Swansong*, the second and final installment of the *Magpie Ballads.*

CHAPTER 1

"Again," said Emaris. "Aim lower. And keep your eyes on the target."

Archery practice with his patrol was a chore if one was participating, a joke if one was spectating, and a tragedy if one was trying, as Emaris was, to make a rabble of uncoordinated boys shoot straight. "I can't," said Lomas plaintively, staring at the stubby grass at the edge of the practice yard where his first two arrows had disappeared. They were at the foot of the Bitten Hill, the home base of the Betronett company, so named for the distinctive shape of its twin peaks. Legend had it that the ice giant Forech had taken a bite out of the hill a hundred thousand years ago, but it tasted so bad he spat it out again, making little bluffs and knolls from the crumbs. "Look at the target. He's grinning at me. Any minute now he'll open his fat cloth mouth and say something smart."

The dummy was sixty yards away—an easy shot as far as Emaris was concerned, though if anyone had asked him, its woollen hair was more vermilion than auburn. "You made that straw man, Lomas, you can damn well live with it."

"He can't, really," said Vion. He was sitting cross-legged on the grass, hugging an armful of arrows they had retrieved from trees, shrubs, and—in one memorable instance—a passing sentry's shield. "His father was a farmer and his father's father before him and his father's father's father before *him*. Can't hammer a ploughshare into a bow."

The other boys made morose noises of agreement. "I'm from the choir," said Klemene, sprawled belly-up beside Vion with his face swaddled in three scarves and a snotty handkerchief. Winter had furred every rock and tree with dirty frost, and the wind kept them up all night, howling like a bagful of mad zephyrs against the little keep on the hill. "I'm a countertenor, not an archer. Eh, Rougen?"

Rougen bobbed his head up and down. He never spoke. No one even knew if he could, but it was common knowledge that if a sparrow so much as beat its wings at the far end of a field, he would hear it. "Well, you're all we've got," said Emaris. "So you could at least try to survive the war."

After Onaressi, that seemed a lot to ask. They just stared at him, huddled close like a dozen wet-nosed pups. "Emaris," said Lomas, with the awkwardness of one trying to carry a larger handful of tact than he could manage. "Wasn't there another dispatch from Medrai yesterday?"

"Yes," said Klemene eagerly. Through his blocked nose, he sounded rather less like a countertenor than a sick parrot. "Did they find Savonn? Or Hiraen?"

Emaris ground his molars together. They had been waiting for a full fortnight. The speculation was unbearable, and every day the temptation to desert his post and join Lord Lucien's search parties grew. "You know they haven't. They're dead or captured or don't want to be found. Savonn's good at disappearing."

"And reappearing," said Vion. "That's why you don't believe he's dead, not really."

Sometimes Emaris forgot that his patrol had been hand-picked by Savonn himself, and only pretended to be obtuse to annoy him. He wished he could confide in them. It was one thing for Savonn to be dead, quite another for him to be in hiding because he had done something horrible—something to do with the Empath, or his late father, or worse, *Emaris's* late father. His mind had become an echo-chamber where Nikas's accusations resounded without cease. *Marguerit's double agent. The Empath's favourite plaything.*

But such thoughts were poison, and best kept to himself.

"Look," he said. "Either they'll turn up or they won't. And if they do, they'll die laughing at the way you shoot. Vion, your turn."

Lomas's shoulders sagged with relief. With all the enthusiasm of a silver miner descending into a shaft, Vion uncurled in a scatter of arrows and took the bow. "Maybe," he said, "we need our patrol leader to demonstrate? How to stand and how to adjust for the wind and all?"

"Oh, yes," said Klemene. Rougen bobbed his head some more, and another boy, Corl, gave a cheer. "Go on, Emaris. You're the best shot in Betronett now that—ow!"

Lomas kicked him in the shin. Emaris ignored them. "Vion first. Three shots. Now."

Vion was the bravest of the lot, and the least unaware of where his limbs were at any given moment. His first arrow struck the dummy square in the chest. Lomas and Klemene whooped. Unfortunately, so did Vion, with the effect that his second shot flew twelve feet wide. "Lower," said Emaris, as Vion sighted again with his tongue between his teeth. "That'll go into the trees."

"I can't find his head for all that hair," said Vion, scowling down the arrow-shaft. "Why don't we leave the shooting to you when the Saraians invade? I'll carry your quiver and Lomas can hand you arrows."

"He'd probably stab me by accident," said Emaris gloomily. "No, that's too low now—for Casteia's sake, you're doing this on purpose—"

"Emaris?" said Lomas.

"What?"

But Lomas was looking at Rougen. The boy had gone still as a deer, gazing past the dummy into the grey daylight. He squinted. Then he dropped flat to the grass and pressed his ear to the ground. Vion lowered the bow. "Should we be running?"

"Quiet," said Emaris. "Let him listen."

Klemene sprang to his feet, scarves flying. "There! There! I see it!"

And so did Emaris. A lone rider was coming up the dirt track that passed for a highway in these parts, connecting the Bitten Hill to the villages in the shadow of the Farfallens. He bore no standard, but the grey stallion trotting beneath him was young and plainly expensive. Possibilities scuttled through Emaris's head, each grimmer than the last. A Saraian herald, with a proclamation of war. Orders from some new commander sent to replace Savonn. News from Medrai, only a day's ride away, that Lucien Safin had found the remains of his son and his protégé. Emaris was just becoming convinced of this last option when the rider adjusted his seat and unslung his bow.

It was like waking from a dream. Emaris yanked his own bow from Vion's hands and snatched up a fistful of arrows. "Move."

The patrol scattered for cover. The grey stallion broke into a gallop, hooves clip-clip-clopping down the track. Freeing his hands from the reins, the rider nocked and sighted. "Emaris," called Vion.

Emaris hated shooting horses, but the stallion was a bigger target than its rider. Going this fast, a fall would kill the man as handily as a shot through the heart. He took aim. "Emaris!" Vion yelled. "Look, damn you!"

Emaris glanced up. Then at last, he realised that the rider was not aiming at them, but the straw redhead. And his bow, golden-wood and ebony, was one they all knew.

He stopped breathing. The rider released his arrow without slowing, his bow tilted to compensate for the wind. There was a streak of brilliant orange. The arrow pierced the target where its heart would have been, if either the dummy or the devil on whom it was modelled had had one. Klemene squawked.

But the rider was not done. He hurtled past the target, turning in the saddle with the sureness of a highbred cavalryman trained from earliest childhood to ride without reins. His arm was a straight line, his back an elegant arc. Another bright whistling flight. The second arrow struck the dummy from behind, quivering a half-inch from the first. Then the man reined up, vaulted from the saddle, landed on his feet, and shot again.

The third arrow sprouted through the target's neck. This was no more than a hand's width across, an impossible shot. The dummy rocked reproachfully on its pole. "Mother Above!" yelled Lomas.

Emaris's eyes watered, though the wind had died down. His own bow was still drawn. He drew a lungful of chilly air, picked a spot for his arrow to land, and loosed.

Vion shouted. So did the rider. The arrow flew into the grass four feet to the man's left. Emaris loosed another, this one lodging point-down an inch from the man's foot. The great stallion startled and tried to bolt. The man dropped his bow and seized its bridle, swearing at the top of his lungs. Emaris shot again. The last arrow flew over the heads of horse and rider both, ruffling mane and hair; and finally Vion yanked the bow out of his hands.

Straining with the horse, Hiraen Safin yelled, "What the hell d'you think you're doing?"

A strange hush fell over the patrol. The boys gathered round, wide-eyed, as Emaris started across the field to the newcomer. His fingers were tingling, his palms clammy. This, at the end of two long weeks. "Teaching archery," he said. "You shoot like a madman."

"So do you," said Hiraen. "You've grown."

He was alive. More than alive—his green eyes were bright, his cheeks flushed, his dark hair tumbled like that of an errant schoolboy just out of bed. The echo-chamber in Emaris's head had fallen silent. "I turned eighteen," he said, "while you were dead."

Last summer, weeping for his father on the threshold of a lamplit room, he had thought death a close acquaintance. What he had not known then was that grief came in many flavours, each as unpalatable as the last. He had shed no tears over Savonn and Hiraen—he was too old to cry, or so he told himself, and his patrol looked up to him an example—but he *had* nearly fractured a knuckle punching a wall, and several doors in Onaressi were going to hang askew on their hinges for a long time.

He meant to reveal none of this. But an intimation of it must have crossed his face, because Hiraen came closer and flung an arm around him. "I'm sorry," he said. Then, softer—"I'm sorry. I'm sorry. I'm sorry."

Used to Savonn's stand-offishness, Emaris did not see it coming. The embrace was a relief, like a cold drink after a long hot march, one he had not even known he needed. He pressed his face into the collar of Hiraen's shirt and screwed his eyes shut. Even blind, it was impossible to mistake him for Savonn. "You could have sent word."

"I know," said Hiraen. "I'm sorry."

"Where were you?"

"Took a detour. I'll tell you later. Your patrol's coming. Can you keep a secret?"

Emaris scowled. "Depends what it is."

Hiraen lowered his voice to a whisper. "I got Savonn out. He's gone to Cassarah. I couldn't stop him. But he's fine, and you have to remember that, no matter what happens. He said to tell you so."

Emaris's heart stuttered. He wriggled one arm free. "What'd he go there for?"

"The Empath. The Council has him."

"*What?*"

But the others were upon them, and Hiraen's attention was called away. Now that the showboating was over, Emaris saw how ragged and worn he looked. He was smiling, but it did not hide the grim shadows circling his eyes, even as he slapped Klemene's back and reached up the requisite five inches to tousle Lomas's hair. "I swear, Lomas, you're turning into a lightning hazard. Where's Vion? Oh, there you are." A punch on the shoulder, almost natural. "The second-best archer in this little pack, so long as no one makes you laugh. Someone fetch Daine. We're going back to the city."

"Now?" Klemene's handkerchief had fallen off, and his nose was redder than ever. "What about Savonn?"

He might as well have uttered a magic word. The shouting gave way to a sudden, expectant quiet. Vion glanced at Emaris. Emaris did not look back.

"Nothing to be done," said Hiraen. He had stopped trying to smile. "The search is over. The real work's in Cassarah now. You see," he said, jostled shoulder to shoulder against Emaris in the crowd, "Savonn is dead."

SWANSONG

Everyone has a secret to keep.

Alone, disgraced, his unsavoury past on the brink
of exposure, Savonn Silvertongue returns to
Cassarah to face his nemesis on the eve of open
war. Dervain Teraille—once his lover and
confidant—is in the hands of the Council, and will
not scruple to reveal all he knows. If Savonn does
not defeat him, he faces his own utter destruction.

Meanwhile, Hiraen and Iyone Safin struggle to
defend their city from Queen Marguerit of Sarei.
But they, too, are caught up in Savonn's spiderweb
of intrigue, and it is only a matter of time before
their own secrets are dragged into the light.

**Now available in ebook and paperback
from all the usual places.**

ABOUT THE AUTHOR

Vale Aida lives in Singapore, with a stuffed whale and fewer cats than is optimal. She wrote most of this book from—among other places— a haunted psychology lab, the back of a boring lecture, an examining table (the curtain was drawn), and a thumbnail-sized window on the office computer. She likes coffee, podcasts, arch-nemeses, and not sweating to death in the sun.

Get the latest updates from Vale at http://valeaida.tumblr.com.

CPSIA information can be obtained
at www.ICGtesting.com
Printed in the USA
FSHW011458070921
84593FS